THE SNAKE THAT BITES ITS TAIL

THE
SNAKE
THAT
BITES
ITS TAIL

Bob Farrand

Copyright © 2022 Bob Farrand

The moral right of the author has been asserted.

Apart from any fair dealing for the purposes of research or private study, or criticism or review, as permitted under the Copyright, Designs and Patents Act 1988, this publication may only be reproduced, stored or transmitted, in any form or by any means, with the prior permission in writing of the publishers, or in the case of reprographic reproduction in accordance with the terms of licences issued by the Copyright Licensing Agency. Enquiries concerning reproduction outside those terms should be sent to the publishers.

This is largely a work of fiction although some episodes are based on real events. Names, characters and businesses are either the product of the author's imagination or used in a fictitious manner. Any resemblance to actual persons, living or dead is purely coincidental.

Matador
Unit E2 Airfield Business Park,
Harrison Road, Market Harborough,
Leicestershire. LE16 7UL
Tel: 0116 2792299
Email: books@troubador.co.uk
Web: www.troubador.co.uk/matador
Twitter: @matadorbooks

ISBN 978 1803130 675

British Library Cataloguing in Publication Data.
A catalogue record for this book is available from the British Library.

Printed and bound in Great Britain by 4edge Limited
Typeset in 11pt Minion Pro by Troubador Publishing Ltd, Leicester, UK

Matador is an imprint of Troubador Publishing Ltd

For Linda
None of what we achieved together
could have happened without you.

And for Jim
No better brother ever walked this earth.

ACKNOWLEDGEMENT

Grateful thanks to Glynn Christian, a true friend whose patient encouragement, hours of tutelage and extraordinary good humour throughout the writing of this novel have been a blessing.

'I neither affirm nor deny the immortality of man. I see no reason for believing it, but, on the other hand, I have no means of disproving it. I have no *a priori* objections to the doctrine. No man who has to deal daily and hourly with nature can trouble himself about *a priori* difficulties. Give me such evidence as would justify me in believing in anything else, and I will believe that. Why should I not?'

Thomas Henry Huxley

PART ONE

ONE

21ˢᵀ OCTOBER 1965

There can be few thoughts more disheartening for a nineteen-year-old than the prospect of a life of tedium and financial penury wasted as an insurance clerk. A year ago, a fate this cheerless hung over Robin Farnham like a Stygian cloud, yet today, it is a face brimming with youthful optimism that stares back at him from the mirror on the wardrobe door.

He painstakingly threads a white leather belt through the loops of his dark blue Sta-Prest Levi's, slips a matching denim jacket on over a black roll neck and quickly buffs his black Cuban heels on the backs of his legs. Happy with what he sees, he grabs a bulging green canvas overnight bag from the foot of his unmade bed and hurries out through the front door of his flat on Lonsdale Road, close to the Thames in south-west London.

Picking his way over uneven paving stones on the path leading to the front gate, he pauses for a moment to admire the shiny dark green 1200cc Ford Cortina parked on the roadside.

Casually tossing the bag into the back of the car, he slides his short, stocky frame into the driver's seat and fires up the engine. Engaging first gear, he checks the rear-view mirror before seamlessly merging into the stream of rush-hour traffic crawling north towards Hammersmith Bridge on a Thursday evening. He is looking forward to the drive west out of London and the prospect of a long weekend at his parents' house in Dorset.

Polished paintwork flashes at each passing streetlamp as he cruises past Heathrow Airport into suburban Surrey, its wide, tree-lined roads and high hedgerows shielding elegant homes of the comfortably well-off. The sort Robin is certain he will own, one day.

As the evening light fades, a familiar sadness fills his mind. His pain over the love he lost little more than a year ago, burns more fiercely at the end of each day.

With the darkness comes the emptiness of longing, the aching hollowness of her absence and plaintive hope she may occasionally think of him as she's making love.

In the blackness of the night, it is her face dominating his every thought, and in the hours before sleep brings paltry relief, his silent plea for the pain to ease by morning will go unheeded. This weekend, he plans to settle the matter once and for all.

His melancholy lingers until the familiar outline of Stonehenge rises above the undulating curves of Salisbury Plain, black-rock solid against the silvery blue remnants of daylight now sinking beneath the western skyline. His journey is nearing its end and angst gives way to the anticipation of a few days in the town he still thinks of as home and showing off his shiny new car to parents and siblings.

Shortly after the rambling village of Chicklade, he swings left onto the A350 and allows the Cortina to gain speed down the incline past Willoughby Hedge. After navigating the narrow bends through the village of East Knoyle, he accelerates along the dark open road towards the foot of Semley Hollow, the twisting, steep hill that marks the final leg of his journey.

From nowhere, a blinding light looms large in his rear-view mirror. A car at speed and with headlights switched to full beam draws close behind, making no attempt to overtake.

Tense hands tighten around the Bakelite steering wheel and he squeezes the throttle to the floor, eager to build space between the two cars. The first of the tight bends on the hill emerges from the darkness and he brakes gently, fearful the car behind is too close. With only inches between them, they corner at speed, and, in the moment he gains speed up a straight stretch leading to the next bend, his headlights pick out a lone figure in the middle of the road.

Later, it surprised him how much detail he absorbed in what seemed like a fraction of a second. The face that flicked up to meet his headlights was ragged and weary, eyes little more than dark incisions over sunken cheeks, brown blotched skin speckled with blood and capped with tangled grey hair.

The man is stooped low, perhaps retrieving something from the road.

The Cortina's front wheels lock as it judders to a halt and Robin's body instinctively braces for a violent blow to his spine as the car behind slams into his.

He feels no pain, hears no tortured screech of compressing metal. The only sound breaking the night silence is a persistent clicking as the car's engine cools.

Fumbling in the darkness, he locates the glove compartment and grabs his torch. Gingerly, he opens the car door, wary of what he is about to see.

Barely daring to breathe, he approaches the front of the vehicle and directs the torch underneath. No old man lies crushed beneath the wheels.

Moving to the rear, he swings the torch to check for damage. He sees nothing, no car crumpled into the Cortina's boot. No driver, dead or alive.

Leaning against the cold metal of the car for support, he bites his bottom lip to control a trembling jaw. He can make no sense of what happened. Assuming anything did happen.

As he returns to the driver's door, the thin beam of light from the torch glints off something lying in the road. He bends and picks up a bracelet; it feels heavy and looks as if it might be gold. There is an inscription etched on the inside which in the half-light, he cannot read.

The bracelet feels warm – as if in this moment it has fallen from the wearer's wrist. The warmth seeps into Robin's hands and upwards through his arms and shoulders.

He is about to pass out and gently lowers himself onto cold tarmac. In a second, the darkness swallows him.

TWO

7TH MAY 1981

As the clock in the living room downstairs chimes seven, Jane Foster hears the ominous click as her bedroom door opens. It is the sound she has dreaded each Thursday this past three years.

Trembling like a puppy in deep snow, she fights the urge to retch at the all-too-familiar stench of her father's body as it lurches towards her. Leering down at her through half-closed, watery eyes, he unzips his soiled work trousers.

Jane will comply, exactly as she'd been forced to comply since the night she rebelled, and he took his belt to her. She was never sure if the beating was the lesser or greater of the two evils.

An hour earlier, she had cast her eyes around her bedroom for what she knew would be the last time. In sixteen years, no pop-star poster nor photograph of family or friends had ever lifted the drab bareness of the walls.

It occurred to her she should feel a trace of emotion. The room had served as her special place for thirteen years, her sanctuary, from parents incapable of giving love, and an outside world too consumed with its own problems to understand how a sweet child could so abruptly degenerate into a disruptive, angry teenager.

What no one outside these walls could possibly know was that one evening three years ago, at the age of thirteen, Jane and her sanctuary were defiled in the most appalling way.

On that evening, her childhood was stripped of its innocence in the most brutal way, her self-respect crushed to non-existence. Every Thursday since, the chimes of the clock and click of her bedroom door signalled the same terror and the only escape from the awfulness of life was to bury her emotions so deep, nothing could prick them.

From as far back as she could recall, she knew she was adopted. Too often her parents would remind her, 'Your real mother didn't want you, didn't love you.' But neither did her adoptive parents; God alone knows why they adopted her in the first place.

She was the child who was never taken on holiday, nor given a birthday party, whose friends were never invited home. In the wake of increasingly disruptive behaviour at school, there wasn't a mother in the district eager for their daughter to mix with her.

It was around this time the violence at home started. The beatings, with belt or plastic curtain rail or anything else her mother approvingly handed her father.

And then, at the age of thirteen, one further ghastly layer of torment was added to her miserable existence. Every Thursday evening at 7pm, her father would put her through an unimaginable ordeal. Almost defying belief, her mother would, from time to time, sit on the bed and watch. Try getting your head around that one and stay normal.

Earlier this evening, on the eve of her sixteenth birthday, she packed her meagre selection of clothing and toiletries into a canvas bag lifted from Woolworth's at the weekend and, with money saved from her Saturday job cleaning ovens in the local baker's, she was set to leave Bristol for good. To make her way to London.

Muscular arms still moist with grime and sweat from a day's toil reach out and hands ingrained with dirt grasp freshly washed hair, forcing the skinny teenager to her knees. On this last evening, even as she trembles, she carefully positions her right foot flat on the floor with the knee bent at a right angle and the toes and ball of her left foot poised to propel upward movement.

Mercifully, her mother has chosen not to watch tonight. She'd gone out and wouldn't return until after closing time. Jane squeezes her eyes shut in the hope of blanking it out. It never does and she wonders, as she wonders every Thursday evening, if knowing what is about to happen is worse than not knowing.

Sensing the filthy sod is on the verge of his grunting climax, she gently removes her right hand from the instrument of her torture while sustaining the necessary degree of pressure with her left. Her free hand slips beneath the thin blanket on her bed and grasps the shaft of solid iron found on a stretch of waste ground while walking home from school.

The next five seconds play out as a slow-motion movie, four precise movements, each rehearsed a hundred times and more these past three years and each perfectly executed.

Through half-closed eyes, she watches for the moment his eyelids flicker in perverted anticipation. Sharp young teeth then close with savage ferocity and his fingers instantly loosen their grip, as he shrieks like a shagging fox. In a split second, Jane's left foot thrusts her body upwards and as her father's hands instinctively reach to his groin, her right arm swings the iron bar smack onto the sweating pervert's temple.

His head jerks sideways with the impact and a deep red indentation oozes blood towards his eyes. Doubled up in pain, he attempts to raise his arms to ward off further blows but is too slow.

Now gripping the bar with both hands and driven by the potency of her loathing, Jane slams it onto his skull a second and a third time. Silently, he drops to the floor, his flabby white body twitching hideously as a stream of blood lends fresh colour to a tired beige carpet.

Still trembling and close to hyperventilating, she stares down at her tormentor and sees he is still breathing. She resists the urge to finish him off; it makes no sense. Not this time, anyway.

She throws up as always before rinsing her soiled mouth under the tap in the bathroom, then grabs her bag and coat and hurries downstairs. Once out through the front door, she leaps into the back of the black cab waiting to drive her the short distance to Temple Meads station and the 8.20pm to Paddington, London.

As the car turns the corner at the end of her road, she sinks back into cold leather and allows herself the luxury of a thin smile. Her pretty features relax for the first time that day, perhaps in that lifetime.

She doubts her father will report the attack, nor that she is missing, for fear the abuse might be revealed. Neither he nor her appalling mother would, for a single moment regret Jane leaving home. Neither would Jane.

THREE
20TH OCTOBER 2020

Lucy Farnham leaves her husband on his own for little more than a couple of hours. Tuesday evenings are her Italian classes, and the company of fellow students is eagerly anticipated. Time away from home is becoming increasingly difficult since Robin's diagnosis and she needs to stimulate her brain, set herself fresh challenges. The isolation during the Covid-19 pandemic and resulting difficulties with the family business seem to have accelerated his decline.

The carers from the local dementia home visit twice a day now. Being so tiny, she finds it difficult helping Robin wash and dress on his bad days, particularly now, with her arthritis and dodgy hip. The early evening carer assured her leaving him for a couple of hours would be fine, as long as outside doors were locked and keys safely hidden.

She returns as normal around 9.30pm, parks her car in the carport and catches sight of him through the living-room window as she approaches the front door. He is sound asleep in his favourite chair, the one she bought him for his seventieth birthday.

Arthritic fingers struggle with the key to the front door; she keeps meaning to call the local locksmith to fit something more user-friendly but can never quite find the time. On hanging her coat in the cloakroom cupboard, she makes her way to the kitchen and puts the kettle on for a bedtime drink. Robin won't want one, as she had caught sight of the empty wine decanter and glass on the small table beside his chair.

She walks into the living room and looks kindly at her husband. He is slowly disappearing into the darkness they both knew would consume him but still has good days, days his memory can sustain an afternoon of fireside reminiscences. The balmy comfort of nostalgia preceding the bitterness of separation.

Today had been that sort of day. With the easing of lockdown, they had taken a trip to the local farm shop and later, enjoyed a quiet lunch at home. Fresh bread, his three favourite cheeses and a glass each of fine Bordeaux. It looks as if he's polished off what was left while she was out.

She settles in the chair alongside his and leans in close. His breathing sounds weak, barely audible. She glances at the small table to his right, and an icy chill rips through her at the sight of several empty foil strips of paracetamol. She then notices a half-empty bottle of Armagnac lying flat on the carpet beside his chair.

An envelope propped against the round porcelain base of a table lamp is addressed in her husband's large but still quite ordered handwriting to *'My darling Lucy'*.

The ambulance is reassuringly quick reaching the village, its flashing lights casting iridescent blue across Robin's alabaster complexion as it pulls up outside the window.

The paramedics are lightning fast. Lucy watches through hot tears as they check her husband's airway, place him in the recovery position, attach an oxygen mask over his tranquil face and raise a shirtsleeve to insert a hypodermic needle into papery skin. He is breathing, albeit faintly, and she hears one of them report over the radio that his pulse is below thirty. She thinks that might be serious.

She gives the paramedics a brief rundown of her husband's medical history, including the Alzheimer's, and they reassure her that a combination of paracetamol and alcohol is rarely fatal and as soon as he is out of danger, he will likely be transferred from Yeovil Hospital to Barton Hall, a local dementia care home.

Once the ambulance has left with Robin, Lucy sits in a living room desolate with silence. She wanted to accompany her husband to the hospital, but the medics advised against it; the A&E department at Yeovil is no place for a little old lady on her own at this time of night.

She always thought herself a strong woman, able to make the best of any situation. Habitually, she looks forward, rarely back. The future is where we need to focus, she constantly told herself, and others.

Optimism seems more difficult now.

She knows Robin will spend the rest of his days in Barton Hall. He'll be comfortable, of that she is certain, but the aggressiveness of his disease appears to have beaten the experimental drug his doctors prescribed. Any significant improvement seems unlikely now. The staff at the care home are better equipped to handle his deteriorating condition, although any sense of relief as the burden of care lifts from her shoulders fills her with shame.

Every couple lives in the almost certain knowledge that one of them will face their final years alone. Her time has come. But why did it have to be like this? After thirty-six years of love and partnership, her last memory of Robin in this house will be his attempt to end his life.

Not knowing what questions now to ask and anyway, dreading the answers, she takes a sleeping tablet and makes ready for bed, alone.

PART TWO

ONE

A pitch-black, dreamless sleep fades to pink as sunlight bleeds into Robin Farnham's eyelids. He blinks to clear the sticky drowsiness before gingerly lifting his head an inch or so from a punishingly firm pillow. 'Oh, fuck,' he growls weakly, his dehydrated tongue sticking to the roof of his mouth. 'I'm still alive.'

A dull ache pounding the inside of his skull forces him back down, where he lies motionless for several minutes. Tentatively, he turns onto his left side and the tell-tale crackle of a plastic mattress-sheet suggests this is not his bed. He must be in hospital. Every muscle in his age-weary body complains as he slowly raises himself to a sitting position.

His eyes focus on four walls painted a cheerless shade of magnolia and an off-white door with an observation window at head height. A blue-and-white cotton dressing gown hangs from a hook on a second door which he thinks may open to a bathroom. That's not his dressing gown.

A threadbare rug that might once have been beige lies shabby on pale grey tiles beneath him. He wonders if the shuffling feet of a thousand visitors crushed its pile to lifelessness, each counting the minutes until they could respectably take their leave.

Assuming visitors are allowed.

'Where the hell's Lucy?' he yells at the wall. 'Why's she not here with me? Jesus Christ, why couldn't they just let me die in peace?'

His stomach aches as if a horse kicked him while he slept; maybe the medics pumped the tablets and booze out of him. He was so certain he'd mixed the perfect cocktail for a peaceful exit.

He'd first noticed the odd lapses in memory maybe three years back although at the time, they seemed sufficiently vague and infrequent to be ignored. Next came periods of confusion, lasting little more than minutes at the beginning but over a period of months, extending to hours and then days. That was when he finally acknowledged something was wrong, by which time, of course, it was too late.

In the months following the diagnosis, his daughter Katie's anxiety worsened and her doctor prescribed Temazepam. It was simple enough for him to squirrel away the odd tablet or two from her bedside table each time he and Lucy visited the grandchildren.

A dull opiate of Temazepam, three strips of paracetamol, a bottle and a half of Chateau Pavie Grand Cru '96 and two large measures of Armagnac don't appear to have done the trick.

The '96 was a stunning vintage… although, wasn't that the year his mother died? No, no, that was twenty years earlier in '76. He needs to stay on top of his dates. Dropped dead from a heart attack while on the loo. Just like Elvis would a year later. The stress of an alcoholic husband, five children and a twenty-a-day Woodbine habit did for her at fifty-six.

Over the course of two years, the disease reduced him from a confident seventy-two-year-old, contented in his old-aged awareness, to a hollowed-out shell whose memories of life as a magazine publisher, husband, father and grandfather were fast disappearing.

But today he is like his old self, BA Robin – Before Alzheimer's.

Yesterday was a good day too. Lucy had driven him to the farm shop beyond the racecourse to buy meat and cheese; all masked up, of course. It makes him sad he can no longer drive. Faceless civil servants at the DVLA cancelled his licence, assessed him unfit to drive. Thought he might end up killing someone. Never crossed their minds that someone might be himself.

He'd agonised long and hard over sharing his intentions with Lucy but knew she'd try to stop him. Persuade him the time was not yet right.

He saw no reason to drag out the coming months, maybe even years. The inevitable decline into those awful debilitating months of open-mouthed, wide-eyed gawping as some gentle soul fed him soup through a straw and wiped his bum.

He'd enjoyed a great life, a wonderful life and was grateful for his seventy-four years on planet earth. It is possible he could have cared for himself a little better during his later years, less wine, less cheese and rich food and more exercise, but in the prophetic words of Kingsley Amis: *'No pleasure is worth giving up for the sake of two more years in a geriatric home in Weston-super-Mare.'*

'Now look at me,' he growls at the wall. 'I fucked up. It didn't work and in their infinite wisdom, a bunch of ethical bloody doctors decided my life's worth saving. It beggars belief, it really does.'

Following his diagnosis, some nameless consultant prescribed a drug still on clinical trial. The first time the pharmacist handed Robin the packet of pills, he half-jokingly suggested he was now officially a guinea pig. Robin commented wryly it was a pity guinea pigs enjoyed such short lives.

A sharp rap on the white door disturbs his train of thought and as it swings open, a tall man in a dark suit and polished black shoes marches in, followed by two male nurses in blue, short-sleeved scrubs. One of them, an older thick-set man with a three-day stubble the colour of cardboard on his chin and a spider tattooed to his neck, positions himself legs apart, blocking the doorway.

'Mr Farnham, good afternoon,' bids the man in the suit, in a loud voice. 'I'm delighted to see you're back with us. I'm Peter Lakmaker, consultant psychiatrist here at Barton Hall.'

He moves closer to Robin but avoids shaking hands, a social nicety that fell into disuse earlier in the year. 'How're you feeling? Not too sore in the tummy, I hope?'

Robin stares at him through narrow eyes. He looks like a doctor; over six feet tall, tight black hair trimmed short, slim build, early to mid-fifties with a trace of Middle Eastern features and skin tone. The voice is cultured, confident, with no hint of an accent. He exudes the imperious air Robin associates with senior medical consultants.

The suit is expensive, well-tailored in fine wool. Midnight blue with hand-stitched lapels and worn over a cream cotton shirt and heavy silk tie of blue and red diagonal stripes. Robin's need for fine tailoring declined following his retirement. A lightweight sandstone two-piece does for the odd wedding and a second in heavy charcoal grey wool for the all-too-frequent funerals.

He knows Barton Hall. It's a home for dementia sufferers some seven miles from home. He and Lucy looked around the place a couple of months back. He feels he might have met this doctor at the time.

'Since you ask, Doctor, I'm bloody angry,' he barks. 'Why the hell couldn't you allow me to die in peace like I wanted?'

Conscious he, too, is speaking loudly he lowers the volume while struggling to contain his rising anger. 'I presume you're aware I've Alzheimer's, with little prospect of any quality of life from now on. Couldn't you have shown a little compassion?'

The doctor nods. 'I'm a doctor. My concern is for saving lives not hastening death although, even assuming I'd been minded to allow you to die, I was persuaded to do everything within my power to save your life.'

'Not by my wife, surely?'

'No,' he answered pointedly. 'By the police.'

'What? Suicide isn't a crime, is it?'

'No, it isn't, but the police are eager to question you as they have reason to believe you may be able to help them with their inquiries into an unsolved crime.'

'What sort of crime?' Robin's eyes narrow again.

'According to Detective Chief Superintendent Davidson, it involves a murder dating back to 1994. You recall you were questioned by the police at the time in connection with the death of a man in Suffolk.'

He groans loudly. Okay, so they've dug up that old chestnut again. Couldn't pin it on him at the time but still clinging to the belief he was guilty.

'Yes, of course I remember,' he snaps. 'He was someone I'd fallen out with over a business matter, but I was miles away at the time he was killed. I couldn't possibly have had anything to do with it. If that's what they want to question me about, they're wasting your time and theirs.'

'Apparently, they need to talk to you about some new forensic evidence they've uncovered.'

Robin gulps a slow, deep breath to feed oxygen into tired old lungs and his head slumps forward, chin resting on his chest.

The doctor nods to the younger, clean-shaven nurse who gently eases Robin back into a lying position where he stares blankly at flaking white paint clinging to the ceiling above his head. The large nurse moves from the doorway and attaches a pulse oximeter to the end of Robin's middle finger and a blood pressure monitor, which tightens like a tourniquet around his upper arm. The only sound breaking the silence is the soft hum from the monitor and an electronic bleeping as green lines dance across a black screen on the wall above his head.

'There's no need to concern yourself with the police, I've refused them permission to question you. Right now, you're not strong enough and I'm unsure how long it might be before you are.'

Strange are the concerns that trouble an old man's mind at critical moments.

A year ago, he was diagnosed with a diseased brain that sooner rather than later would cease functioning and kill him. Yesterday, he screwed up a meticulously planned suicide attempt and today, he awakes to find the police want to question him about a murder. A murder he didn't commit. In theory, he shouldn't give a toss. He'd sooner be dead.

Lakmaker studies the readings on the screen. 'I think you're strong enough for us to move you into the private suite adjoining my consulting room. You'll be more comfortable there. Do you feel up to walking or shall I call for a wheelchair?'

'I'm not that decrepit,' Robin barks.

The younger nurse removes the monitors and gently, but firmly, eases Robin up to a standing position. His tattooed colleague takes the dressing gown from its hook and places it over Robin's pyjamas. A pair of slippers is retrieved from under the bed; they're not his but fit perfectly.

He stumbles as he moves to walk. Both legs seem to have forgotten how to function. Maybe a wheelchair is a good idea but before he can say anything, the nurses grab an elbow each and taking most of his weight, follow the doctor out through the door.

Harsh fluorescent lighting pierces Robin's eyes and the pungency of disinfectant and old-age incontinence prick his nostrils. The group swings left along a seemingly endless corridor, striding at a pace an unaided Robin would never have matched. Apart from their footsteps, the place is eerily quiet.

After a dozen or so steps, they steer sharp right into a second corridor leading to a dark, wooden door, which the tattooed nurse unlocks using a key from a bunch hanging on a chain attached to his belt.

Two women, smart in white uniforms, perch on stools behind a gently curving reception desk that overlooks a waiting area fronted by floor-to-ceiling glass entrance doors. They acknowledge the doctor with a nod and smile kindly at Robin.

The group crosses the reception area into a second, more softly lit corridor with sage-green walls and matching carpet. After about ten metres, the doctor stops abruptly, turns to his right and unlocks a polished walnut door bearing a brass plate engraved with his name.

He leads them into a spacious consulting room painted the same soft green as the corridor. Robin recalls reading that the Victorians thought this quiet shade relaxing.

A rosewood desk and chestnut-brown leather chair front a wide window with half-open vent and fringed by quarter-drawn vertical blinds. A slim black computer screen sits on the left side of the desk with a keyboard beyond. Two shabby leather armchairs to the right are separated by a modern circular glass-topped, chrome-framed coffee table.

A floor-to-ceiling bookcase packed with what appears at first glance to be thick, leather-bound reference books fills one wall, with two silver-framed photographs facing outwards from a lower shelf.

One is of Lakmaker, alongside an attractive blonde in her late forties and three teenage children, two boys and a girl. The second is a group shot of golfers raising a silver cup, suggesting how the doctor enjoys his down-time away from the consulting room.

'May I offer you tea, Robin?' Lakmaker asks as he gestures him to sit in one of the armchairs.

'Thank you,' he replies, and settles in the chair facing the window. 'I'd be grateful for a couple of paracetamol as well, if you've got some. I've a thumping headache.'

The doctor asks the nurses for two teas and nods in the direction of the door. They leave. He lifts a buff-coloured file from a desk drawer along with a pack of painkillers and sets them on the coffee table before settling into the armchair opposite Robin.

He opens the file, which is fat with typewritten sheets, and removes a slim, gold fountain pen from the inside pocket of his jacket. Robin once owned an identical pen, a Caran d'Ache, which he thinks was stolen from his jacket pocket the day he was diagnosed with Alzheimer's. It had been a wedding present.

There is a knock on the door and as it swings open, one of the women from reception enters, carrying a tray which she places on the table. Tea is served in a china teapot with cups, saucers, and a strainer rather than mugs and tea bags.

As Lakmaker pours, he asks if Robin wants milk and adds a little to both cups. Robin swallows two paracetamol tablets along with a mouthful of piping-hot tea before slumping back into the soft leather.

'Would you be comfortable with me recording our conversations?'

'Is that necessary?' Robin asks sharply.

'It'll help me monitor the effectiveness of the new drug you're taking.'

Robin nods, grudgingly.

The doctor takes a black mobile phone from his jacket pocket, lays it flat on the coffee table and his index finger taps and traces across the screen.

'It would be helpful if you could confirm a few details about yourself and your immediate family for the purposes of identification and to establish the state of your memory today.'

'My name is Robin Giles Farnham and I was born on the 28th February 1946. My mother was Margaret Joan, and she was born in 1920 and died aged fifty-six in 1976. My father was John Dennis, born in 1917 and he died in '84. I've a grown-up son and daughter and four grandchildren. Will that do?'

Lakmaker checks the top sheet of paper in the open file while Robin looks him over. He is of slim build, some might say thin, and he wears a strained gauntness to his features. His eyelids droop more than might be thought typical for a man his age, as do the corners of his mouth.

'I'd like you to give me a few short sentences of background; where you've lived, when you were married, that sort of thing.'

'I grew up in Shaftesbury in Dorset, left home at eighteen and worked in and around London for over thirty years, mostly in magazine publishing. I married my first wife, Penny, in '68 and we were divorced in '84. I met Lucy the same year and we finally married in 1993. In '95, we moved our home and business to Dorset, close to where I grew up. I retired at sixty-nine, handing the business over to my son, Giles, although I remain as chairman.'

'Hmm! That's encouraging. In spite of what you put yourself through yesterday, your memory appears in good shape.' Lakmaker pauses briefly, perhaps deciding how to phrase his next question.

'How *are* you feeling today?'

'What, apart from bloody annoyed you prevented me from dying?'

The doctor smiles wanly. 'Yes, apart from that.'

'Well, as you say, the old brain seems in good order, which it has been for the past three days. For a couple of weeks prior to that, it was dreadful, which is why I decided I'd be better off dead.'

'Can you describe your symptoms during that period?'

Robin sighs. 'Utter bloody confusion, no idea what was going on around me. It was like... like fragments of memory replaying over and over inside my head, movie clips from the past and the present, the two indiscernible, all jumbled together. My first wife, Penny, and colleagues I worked with donkey's years ago, arguing with my son and daughter and friends from my village and lying about... me... and about stuff that wasn't true and had nothing to do with me or them.'

Robin squeezes his eyes shut, his lined brow furrowing deeper as he moves his head from side to side. 'When I finally surfaced into some sort of normality a few days back and... and could hold my sense of being for longer than a few hours, I realised I'd reached that fine line between sanity and insanity.' He opens his eyes and looks straight at the doctor. 'There seemed absolutely no point in putting off the inevitable.'

Lakmaker presses his lips together and nods matter-of-factly in that sentient way doctors have of assuring patients they are familiar with the symptoms described yet can offer no cure. He stares at Robin, waiting for him to continue.

'I… I just sort of knew, at that moment… I needed to die, for my sake and for the sake of those closest to me.'

More nodding from the doctor. 'Thinking back over your life, would you describe it as being largely pleasurable?'

Robin's eyes narrow in bemusement at the question, but he is resigned to answering. 'There were times when I struggled financially, the break-up of my first marriage wasn't great, neither were my business problems in the early '90s and more recently with the pandemic. But I wouldn't want to give anyone the idea I've had a tough life because I haven't. I've been blessed, with my family, with the way the business grew and the success we enjoyed. It's been pretty wonderful.'

'A shame to end it by suicide.'

Robin glares at the doctor and leans in towards him. 'That's cheap! I wanted nothing more than to protect my family from the misery of watching my decline and anyway, what's the point of old age if all the memories you enjoy looking back on are disappearing?'

'You have to appreciate my views on suicide differ from yours.'

'I don't give a shit what you think. This country doesn't have the medics, the facilities, the infrastructure, or the money to care for the number of old people suffering dementia. Too many of my generation face a miserable end to their lives. I wanted to die on my terms, with my dignity intact.'

'You have no fear of death?'

Robin casts his mind back to his state of mind immediately after swallowing the tablets and sipping the last glass of Armagnac. There had been no fear, no anxiety, more a feeling of relaxed euphoria, a sense of relief he had finally made his decision and completed the task. The soporific state of his mind owed much to the alcohol of course, but even now, stone-cold sober as he was, he doubts he would baulk at doing the same again. Only better.

'Nope, it's the slow process of dying that scares me. Once we're dead, it's reasonable to presume we return to whatever state we were in before we were born which as far as I can recall, gave me no trouble at all.'

'That's an interesting viewpoint.'

'Yeah, well, I'll probably have forgotten it by tomorrow,' Robin replies, with a wry grin.

Lakmaker ignores the attempt at humour. 'That's why, Robin, we need to record your past now, while you still remember it. Tomorrow might be too late.'

Robin lapses into silence before venting a deep groan as he raises himself from the chair and shuffles over to the window. As he walks, shafts of late afternoon sun suddenly bathe the room in a warm honeyed glow. He aches to see the last of the daylight, breathe a little of the fresh air spilling through the open vent.

The sun is sitting low beneath a thin line of crimson-tipped white clouds, casting deep shadows across a freshly mown lawn. Shafts of dappled sunlight filter through the branches of a nearby beech tree, burning its leaves golden-brown before their time.

His muscles ease as his senses fill with the sweet scent of cut grass, and boxwood flute of a solitary blackbird. Leaning with both hands against the windowsill for support, he is mesmerised by leaves floating on a soft breeze, pirouetting like mating butterflies, crafting the illusion each is dancing to the tempo of birdsong. Do blackbirds sing in September?

He wipes a single tear from each eye as Lakmaker interrupts his train of thought by asking him what he's thinking.

'Just how much I love this time of day and if you guys hadn't treated me as you did, I wouldn't have…' His voice tails into silence.

'That's why you should never give up, Robin. Life is too precious. It's all we know, and this new drug is showing encouraging results. It might offer you a decent period of remission, time with your family, maybe even a couple more holidays.'

'Your recording of this conversation,' Robin asks bluntly, 'is it to do with the clinical trial or for the police?'

'Including you, Robin, we've five Alzheimer sufferers here at Barton Hall taking part in the trial. The recordings are enabling us to monitor how the drug is managing each patient's condition on a daily basis. As far as the police are concerned, they're aware of your condition but all they're interested in is what you recall from the two-year period leading up to 1994.'

'They still believe I killed that man, don't they?'

Ignoring the question, Lakmaker continues, 'It makes perfect sense to give them the information they need so that they can eliminate you from their inquiries.'

'How do you suggest I do that?'

'Each patient on the trial is writing daily records of their life experiences, particularly stressful periods, even those they may have gone through as teenagers.'

'What relevance could something that happened in our teenage years have now?'

'You'd be surprised, Robin. The origin of much old-age depression stems from our early years. I've treated D-Day veterans whose ordeal didn't manifest until they were well into their seventies.

'Trauma, rather than happier times, buries itself deeper into the subconscious, so what you remembered yesterday but can't today monitors the drug's effectiveness.'

'Sounds reasonable, I suppose,' Robin replies as he returns to his chair, not entirely convinced. The doctor moves to the desk and lifts an Apple laptop from a drawer. He opens it on the coffee table, and it springs into life.

'You know how to use one of these?' he asks.

Robin grasps the mouse with his left hand, moves the screen to face him and shifts the cursor to the drop-down menu. Without a moment's thought, he opens a new Microsoft Word document and saves it to the desktop as Memo No. 1.

He is strangely calm, silently admitting the challenge might be interesting. At least there'll be no one in the room while he is digging into the dark corners of his resistant and forgetful mind. He thinks more clearly on his own, always has done.

'So you suggest I start with my schooldays?'

'If you experienced any sort of trauma during that period, then yes. Begin at the beginning.'

TWO

From: Robin Farnham
To: Dr Lakmaker, Barton Hall
Ref. No: 1

My teenage years left me with few fond memories although, during my late forties, I rediscovered a lasting affection for the region in which I grew up.

In the 1960s, small country towns like Shaftesbury fashioned a state education rarely matched in urban areas. Schools were smaller and more personal by today's standards, a mere 240 pupils in the grammar school I attended. Teachers knew us all by name and most youngsters in the town were on nodding terms with others their own age, regardless of which school they attended.

I knew Jo, of course. We'd bumped into each other at the swimming pool and occasionally chatted, about nothing much in particular. She always struck me as immature for her age, a little ungainly with round, fleshy features, and chubby knock-knees.

One of the few social gatherings I attempted as a sixteen-year-old was the weekly country-dancing club in the gymnasium of the local secondary modern school. The husband and wife instructors would arrange us in pairs at the start of each evening, which happily removed the need for me to pluck up courage to ask someone of the opposite sex to dance with me.

One evening in the October of '62, I was a few minutes late and hung around the edge of the room, unsure what to do. The only female I could see without a partner was Jo, which didn't best please me.

'Looks like you're stuck with me, Robin,' she giggled as she walked up, grabbed both my wrists, and dragged me onto the dance floor. Our eyes met and stayed locked for a good half minute. Her face had lengthened and grown more angular, gracing her with high cheekbones and a wide, sensual mouth. Chestnut-brown eyes stared back at me and I couldn't help noticing her body had changed too, making her less of a flabby juvenile, more a curvy and appealing young woman.

Her easy manner fascinated me, as did the ease with which her face broke into the prettiest of smiles. Her warm eyes locked on to mine as we moved around the room to the music and, as the third dance was ending, it was she who suggested we step outside into the chilled autumn air.

We leaned side by side, our backs against the wall of the school gymnasium, staring straight ahead.

'You don't seem very happy, Robin. What's up? Is it 'cos you've been paired with me?'

'Course not.'

'You grumpy or something?'

'No.'

'You wanna to go back inside, then?'

'Nope, I'm okay here.'

'Could have fooled me.'

'Look, I'm not in a good place right now,' I mumbled, staring down at my feet, the toe of my left shoe tracing circles on the playground tarmac.

'Wanna talk about it?' she asked in a whisper, maybe worried someone might overhear.

'About what?'

'Why you're not in a good place, stupid.'

'Not really.'

'You got trouble at school?'

'For Christ's sake, Jo,' I flew at her angrily. 'The whole bloody world knows I messed up my GCEs. Don't pretend you didn't.'

I saw she was upset. 'Sorry. P'raps it's best we go back inside.'

'No, it's my fault, Robin.' Her voice grew softer. 'I didn't mean to pry but I'm having problems at school too. I just thought you might be able to… well, you know, give me some advice.'

She explained quietly how she failed her 11-plus exam but was moved from the secondary modern school up to the girls' high school a year later after it became clear she was brighter than others in her year. She was a year older than her classmates at the new school and struggling with the challenge of her GCEs next June.

'Some of the others in my class make fun of me 'cos I failed my 11-plus. They say I'm thick.'

She went on to tell me about her father's explosive

temper and how fearful she was of what he might do to her if she failed her exams. I found her openness intriguing but at the same time, it was scary how her anxieties seemed to mirror mine.

Could I bring myself to risk sharing my own sense of failure? She turned to face me and gripped my hands tightly. Somehow, her warmth helped me summon the courage to speak.

I told her of my despair at failing five of the nine GCE subjects I had sat and the raw sense of botching pretty much every part of life, with the possible exception of cricket and rugby.

I explained how my mother had tried to ease the misery and school encouraged me to re-sit the failed subjects, but nothing lifted the black cloud. There was just too much shit going on.

The longer Jo and I talked, the more that cloud seemed to lift. Digging deep, I even admitted contemplating suicide but my 'gutless inability' to go through with it was yet another failure. She somehow encouraged me to reveal things that had only ever been thoughts.

'You don't need me around you, Jo,' I bemoaned. 'I'm too bloody miserable and can't talk about... you know, personal stuff.'

'But you've just told me how you feel,' she answered quietly. She leaned into me, gently coaxing the collar of my shirt towards her as her left hand pressed on my cheek, forcing me to look into her eyes. She kissed me full on the lips and as her tongue explored the inside of my mouth, I instinctively pulled back.

'What's the matter, Robin, don't you like French kissing?'

she whispered. I'd heard older boys joke about it, but until that moment, had little idea of what it involved.

'That's the best kiss I've ever had,' I answered, smiling for the first time that evening.

We never did go back inside the dance hall, and the ten-minute walk to the end of Jo's road took a good half hour, as we shared our adolescent anxieties. She spoke of her family, her bossy elder sister and aggravating younger brother, and a mother dominated by a violent father.

My father dominated our household too, but in a different fashion. He was ruled by his dependency on alcohol, which led to unpredictable mood swings and pitched our family into needless poverty.

Standing close to Jo beneath the shadowy glow of the solitary lamp at the end of her road, I grew conscious of a growing sense of freedom from inferiority. For a further half hour, we talked without ever coming close to exhausting the things we needed to say.

Before parting, I buried my face in the soft skin of her neck; warm, fragrantly scented and teenage-smooth. Our touching grew more intimate as we explored emotions which I sensed we were both experiencing for the first time.

Was this the first moment in my life that I was genuinely comfortable in the company of another human being?

'Jo, I… I've had a great time this evening. You make me feel sort of different, not so… well, on my own.' I was grateful the half-light was more than likely hiding my burning cheeks. 'Talking to you has been well… Jo, what I'm trying to say is… can we meet again?'

'Robin Farnham, are you asking me for a date?' Her

mouth parted into an impish grin. I nodded and her smile was enough of an answer.

On my walk home, I skipped down the unlit narrow lane like a five-year-old. I had met someone like me. A misfit who showed me how joyful life might be, and at the time, I could even have been in love. No, thinking back, I *was* in love, and it felt as good as it was supposed to.

After that first night, we met as often as inquisitive parents and school timetables allowed and talked endlessly of how our inadequacies singled us out as different from others. We created a fantasy of escape, fleeing to some remote island where Jo would be free of her father's violence and the unbearable pressure of an education designed to make her fit a mould she would rather not be forced into.

In our world, there would be no shame in failing exams or not fulfilling the expectations of others. Neither of us would need friends, as we had each other, and we were both learning to trust the first real happiness of our lives.

There was another aspect of my life I eventually revealed to Jo, and which was the real cause of my being cast as an outsider.

School was difficult, not merely because of my inability to pass exams but owing to a contradiction of ideas that did little to lighten my teenage angst. The paradox between the words of hymns we were made to sing each morning in assembly and the training given in the art of warfare each Tuesday and Thursday was fast pitching me into even deeper adolescent confusion.

Joining the school's Combined Cadet Force was compulsory, save for those whose parents objected on grounds of religion or pacifism. Far from objecting, my father was all for it, convinced a war with Soviet Russia was inevitable.

'We've bugger-all chance of winning the next war if youngsters don't get two years of discipline in the armed forces to knock 'em into shape,' he would thunder through a miasma of beer and whisky.

Conscription had ended a few years earlier and training boy soldiers at school was thought the next best thing. It was also considered a privilege. At one time, only the upper classes at private schools were given military training, preparing the next generation of officers, regardless of intellectual ability.

Cadet Force parades kicked off with the full brigade called to attention in the school quadrangle, each boy-soldier bedecked in regulation, cardboard-stiff, sandpaper-rough khaki.

For thirty minutes, we were marched up and down to the bellicose commands of an acned, sixth-form bully. Every minute was purgatory, further distancing me from my peers who revelled in the ritual of playing at being soldiers.

Once a year, a rusting bucket of a coach spewed toxic fumes as it spluttered out of Shaftesbury up Zip-Zag Hill to Melbury, where forty uniformed cadets were issued with Lee Enfield rifles and several rounds of blank ammunition before being deployed in the middle of the rolling Dorset countryside.

We were in the midst of a make-believe war zone and ordered to belly-crawl through rain-sodden grass pitted with cow shit and stinging nettles to hunt down an unseen foe. Our enemy was neither German nor Russian but a second group of cadets, deposited earlier behind bushes, up trees and in ditches.

I loathed the cow shit and stinging nettles as much as the thought of aiming a rifle at another human being and pulling the trigger.

In church and school, vicars and schoolmasters assured me God was real and cared for us all but every Tuesday and Thursday, I'd be ordered to ignore the love-thy-neighbour bit and murder my enemy.

Over a period of months, I read every relevant book I could lay my hands on from the school library, desperate for conclusive evidence that our or anyone else's God was real. The evidence appeared flimsy. From what I could see, the Bible was little more than a collection of questionable stories heavily reliant on hearsay, written by people whose very existence was unproven and, if they had existed, it was doubtful any of them could write.

On the other hand, the brutality of war was undeniable; vividly reported in TV news bulletins and underpinned by my father's torrents of abuse directed at Germans, who he blamed for two World Wars and the deaths of millions.

So, at the age of sixteen, I experienced an epiphany. I was suddenly conscious that Christianity, Hinduism, Judaism and every other of the world's religious doctrines seemed not to stand up to scrutiny. All the evidence suggested each to be a massive confidence trick against humanity, designed to lock the meek and the poor into lifelong servitude with its promise of better things to come in the next life.

I saw it for what it was and arrived at the only logical conclusion.

MEMO ENDS rf

THREE

Lakmaker looks up from reading Robin's printed memo. 'So, the outcome of this teenage trauma was that you became an atheist?'

Robin nods. 'Yeah, and a pacifist too, I guess.'

'You were eventually discharged from the Cadet Force, weren't you?'

The old man turns his head to one side, his jaw tightly clenched. Why couldn't he just read what was written and let it rest? No, he wants more, to dig deeper. How does he know that anyway?

'You've admitted you're a pacifist, why not expand on it?' Lakmaker's tone is quiet, almost reassuring, although to Robin, it feels intrusive.

Without doubt, he had a wretched time as a teenager, but what good would it do now, scratching at wounds that healed sixty years ago? It could hold no significance to the clinical trial. An adolescent angst conquered in his own way and without the need to diminish himself by sharing it with others.

His chest goes into spasm. If talking does help, was this why people talk about getting something off their chest? Mildly amused by the connection, he gives in to Lakmaker.

'I loathed that awful bloody uniform, the mindless, unquestioning obedience and shooting, so I invented excuses for missing parades. My absences were starting to get noticed, and the matter came to a head during some kind of military proficiency test.'

'What happened, Robin?'

'Some bigwig from Sandhurst was putting me through a sort of initiative test and told me to imagine I was in the first-floor room of a house guarding a crossroads in a war zone as two enemy soldiers approached. He asked me where in the room I would stand so as not to be visible when shooting at them.'

'Your answer?'

'I told him I had no intention of ever shooting anyone.'

'That would have surprised him.'

'Oh, it caused massive ructions, and the master in charge of the Cadet Force visited home to sort out what was best with my parents.'

'And?'

'I was discharged from the Force, which was a mixed blessing. Everyone knew the reason and I was called a coward, a draft dodger… and worse.'

Robin holds Lakmaker's gaze, unsure if he should relate an experience that has stayed with him into old age, as vivid today as it was all those years ago.

'There was one incident which still… it still makes me shiver each time I think about it.'

'Do you want to share it with me?' Lakmaker leans forward, clearly interested.

'One Thursday lunchtime, we were being shown how to clean an old machine gun, a Bren I think it was. The officer in charge asked if anyone was prepared to try and strip it down in readiness for cleaning. For a reason I never fathomed, I volunteered and stunned myself, the officer, and the platoon by deftly dismantling the firearm and laying its component parts neatly on the ground. On being told it must have been a lucky fluke, I just as quickly put it all back together again.'

'Impressive. Where had you learnt to do that?'

'That's the weirdest part. I'd never seen a machine gun before, only in films. I'd certainly never touched one.'

'Have you ever come up with any sort of explanation?'

'Well, that's the thing. The only one I came up with is a bit bizarre, but…'

'I'd still like to hear it.'

In that moment, it occurs to Robin that he has never shared this with anyone, and he is anxious it would open a door he might find impossible to close. He struggles to look the doctor in the eye and speaks quickly, the words tumbling from his lips.

'I was conceived at the close of the Second World War and I sort of convinced myself I might be a continuation of the spirit of a gunner killed during the last few days of fighting. I sometimes wonder if he too may have been a pacifist forced to join the battle.'

'Reincarnation is a source of comfort for many, Robin. Do *you* believe in life after death?'

'Not really. Without any religion, it's logical to presume death is the end and nothing comes afterwards.'

'We can never be certain, Robin. In life or death.' The doctor shifts uncomfortably in his seat. 'Do you think it possible you could have worked harder at building relationships with others at school, help them understand your point of view?'

'That's a bit harsh,' Robin snaps, but then recognises the doctor is not making a judgment, merely asking him to explain, give his side of it.

'In the end, I just got used to the idea that I was different, never part of a group. I didn't relate to those around me and had little in common with them. In conversation, I'd quickly exhaust everything I had to say, so I avoided situations where I'd get involved.'

'Did you think of yourself as a loner?'

'I didn't think of myself as anything.'

Robin exhales audibly. He sees little point in expanding further on his relationships with his fellow pupils. It was all too long ago. During his final years at school, little else mattered so long as Jo was by his side.

*

From: Robin Farnham
To: Dr Lakmaker
Ref. No: 2

Standing at the end of her road, my weight shifted from one foot to the other and back again as I glanced at my watch for the third time in three minutes.

'Meet me at three,' she had said when we last parted, and it was already ten-past. Sunday lunch must have finished, dishes washed and dried and her tyrant of a father sunk in an armchair snoring loudly.

The previous week had dragged by; every lesson dreary and Saturday's First XI cricket match, normally a highlight of my week, flat and unexciting.

It was Jo's suggestion; she was the one who assured me we had loved each other long enough. And now, Sunday afternoon had arrived with a heady mix of excitement and trepidation. Or was it perhaps anxiety whipped up by my parents' Victorian morality?

The relaxed morals of the twenty-first century make it difficult to fathom the buttoned-up standards of early 1960s small-town England. Constant fear of out-of-wedlock pregnancy and its ghastly consequences plagued every teenage romance.

My mother, who by the way was quite possibly pregnant with me at the time she married my father, had unwittingly, or perhaps deliberately, deepened the anxiety. 'You'll lose respect for any girl who allows you to have sex with her before you're married,' she opined. 'And if you make her pregnant, it'll ruin both your lives. You'll be forced to leave school without qualifications, and you'll never find a decent job.'

A year or so earlier, she had made me cross the road as we were walking into town one afternoon because a young lady approaching had, as she explained through tight lips and a rigid jaw, 'recently left town to give birth to a bastard.'

The young lady in question was a pretty young thing in her high heels, short skirt, flared petticoats and shocking pink lipstick. She can't have been much more than a couple of years older than me. It was hard to believe she should be shunned as an outcast. Maybe my mother feared I might catch something if we passed by too closely.

Jo and I met after school as often as my sports timetable and her dictatorial father permitted. King Alfred's Kitchen was the favoured hangout for Shaftesbury's teenagers eager for private conversations over long-drawn-out coffees.

On Sunday afternoons, we would escape for a few hours and stroll hand in hand the length of Wincombe Lane. This private road on the edge of town was lined with several large houses before narrowing into a little-used, unmade track leading through farmland to open countryside.

On the second of our walks, we came across a field where spring grass stood tall in readiness for silage making. Once settled on flattened grass and well-hidden from prying eyes, we idly talked away the afternoon, relishing the time and the space to ourselves.

The following Sunday, emboldened with our new-found independence, we lay side by side, stretched out beneath the spring sunshine, lazily chatting as skylarks twisted and turned in courtship dances above. I envied their lack of inhibition as I fumbled nervously with the buttons on Jo's blouse.

She was less restrained as she guided my hand inside her blouse. The moment the mysteries of unclasping a bra were mastered, the first sight of her breasts exhilarated me. Porcelain white mounds, firm to the eye yet so soft to touch and stirring sensations I barely understood.

The moment I kissed her firm, upright nipples, she responded. Her muscles tightened as my fingertips traced down the taut skin of her tummy.

'Why don't you touch me further down?' she whispered.

'I… I wasn't sure you'd want me to.'

She giggled, answering in a sort of sing-song voice, 'It's up to boys to try and girls to deny. I'm not denying, Robin.'

The moment my hand slipped between the warm silkiness of her inner thighs, the last remnants of self-control abandoned me, and I silently came in my pants.

'You okay, Robin?' she asked in a voice barely audible, my face clearly betraying my embarrassment. I was moved to confess.

'Robin, we've been going out now for over eight months and… well, we do love each other, don't we?'

I nodded, a little too eagerly, perhaps.

'Then it's the right time for us to… well… you know, to make love.' As she spoke, her hands cupped the burning cheeks of my face. Her words stunned me to silence.

'Say something, you bugger.'

'You mean, you'd be okay with… with us doing it?' My voice faltered even as the errant piece in my pants showed signs of renewed interest.

'Robin, I do love you and I want… I want you to be the first… well, you know, I want it to be the first time for us both… together. It *will* be the first time for you too, won't it?'

At that moment, more eager nodding was as much as I could manage as I fought to contain the mounting excitement.

She hadn't finished. 'We're old enough and if we're sensible, we'll be safe as long as we take precautions, won't we?'

In an age before the contraceptive pill, every journey into manhood involved a visit to the local chemist or barber's shop for a packet of what were universally known as 'johnnies'. In parochial Shaftesbury, the barber or pharmacist would almost certainly know our parents, raising the risk and trepidation associated with such a purchase.

As it turned out, my trip to the chemist later that week was stress-free. A new assistant, little more than a year older than me, smiled knowingly as she handed me my precious packet of three.

After what had seemed the wait of a lifetime, Jo finally appeared at the far end of her road, heading towards me, radiant in a flowered summer skirt loosely tracing her gently swaying hips, its hem dancing above her knees with each eagerly taken step. The white cotton blouse close cut to her waist and buttoned tightly across her breasts was clearly chosen to accentuate her figure. As she approached, she cocked her head to one side, grinning impishly. 'Nervous?'

We had never walked a more furious pace to the far end of Wincombe Lane and into our special field than on that warm Sunday afternoon.

It was a disaster. Not the preamble, although that was more frenzied than I later discovered it should be. The sight and feel of slipping down her white knickers, each touch of her naked skin on mine, the soft brush of hair and dampness of expectation brought me ominously closer to an unwanted climax. Several fumbling attempts at attaching the necessary precaution told me I should have practised the art of donning a 'johnny' beforehand in the privacy of my bedroom.

Thirty seconds into my first real sexual experience, my first real climax hit me with the force of an express train. Jo's face showed disappointment.

'I'm so sorry, Jo, but I… I lost control.' My cheeks were on fire and shame burned my insides. I struggled to hold eye contact.

Thinking back, she was clearly more sexually aware than I, even though we were of a similar age and she, like me, a virgin.

'It's our first time. We'll do it better soon, Robin,' she whispered encouragingly. 'I know we will.'

Muscles as tight as watch springs unwound slowly as we lay together, lazy in the warm sunshine, wanting nothing other than more time in each other's company.

Five minutes drifted to twenty before her right hand slowly reached inside my still-unbuttoned pants and began teasing me, four fingertips delicately tracing circles, close but never directly touching my limp dick.

Anticipation grew as my muscles tensed, and the moment it dawned on me I might be capable of performing a second time, my fingertips began to tease her in similar fashion.

The events of that afternoon have barely crossed my mind in over half a century, but it was clear then as it is now, Jo set the pace, gently encouraging me to work to her rhythm. We climaxed almost simultaneously, an explosion of sensations and emotions so extraordinary, to this day I find it impossible to put into words.

Ten minutes of easy silence passed before she turned onto her side, edged closer and smiled. 'That was good, wasn't it, Robin?' My self-satisfied grin said more than words.

Her eyes widened as she raised herself onto one elbow, idly sucking a long piece of grass, and asked softly, 'You won't lose respect for me now, will you?' I'd forgotten telling her of my mother's warning of the consequence of out-of-wedlock sex.

'I respect you *more* because of what you've allowed me to share with you.' Salt from a single tear touched my lips as I kissed her cheek.

'But do you *really* love me?' she asked in mock seriousness as she rested her head back on the grass, staring upwards.

My eyes followed hers as two skylarks danced high above us. My stomach froze with anxiety and for a full minute, I was unable to utter a word.

Finally, I found my voice. 'I'm… I'm sort of frightened to answer you.'

She raised herself back onto her elbow, the palm of her right hand supporting her head as she studied me though narrow eyes. 'What d'you mean?'

'I'm frightened if I say the words, it'll make me even more scared.'

'Scared of what?'

'Of losing you.'

'Of losing me? I love you too much to lose you.'

Her soft eyes and gentle easy smile seemed to lift my anxiety to a fresh level. 'That's the problem. I'm petrified of losing the best feeling I've ever had in my life.'

'And that stops you saying you love me?' she asked quizzically.

'S'pose so.'

'You're scared of telling me what really goes on inside that head of yours, Robin Farnham, that's your trouble. You're my buttoned-up lover boy, aren't you?'

'I do love you.' The words spilled out far too quickly.

'No, tell me properly,' she ordered in mock anger.

I traced the index finger of my right hand around her lips. 'I love you every waking hour and in my sleep. I love you even though one day, we'll be parted. Maybe it'll be next month or next year. Or perhaps not until we're so old we cry at the thought of being parted in death. But one day, Jo Brighouse, you'll leave me and that's what makes me so frightened.'

She sat up, leaned over me and, cupping my face in both her hands, squeezed my cheeks. 'That's so lovely, Robin, but I promise I'll never, ever leave you.'

Each Sunday throughout that blissful summer of '63, we learned new ways to excite and anticipate each other's climax. Our happiness knew few boundaries until the afternoon I stupidly ran out of contraceptives. Despite my assurances it would be easy to withdraw before climaxing, neither of us was certain I made it in time.

Panic escalated over the coming weeks as Jo's period failed to make an appearance. Four weeks became six and anxiety became fear.

'Mum asked me yesterday if I'd had my period as she hadn't seen… well, you know.' Jo's face was drawn, and I sensed her fear. 'My dad will kill you, Robin, and God knows what he'll do to me,' she warned, tears welling in her eyes.

I rested both my arms on her shoulders, my hands cupping her cheeks. 'Jo, you know how much I love you. If you're pregnant, nothing would make me happier than for us to get married. I'll leave school and find a job.'

Tom Croxon, the local accountant and captain of the town cricket team, had already sounded me out as a trainee.

'I'll study accountancy, which should bring in enough for us to rent a flat. You can finish your GCEs after the baby is born. You'd be happy marrying me, wouldn't you, Jo?' How much she believed my thin veil of confidence was unclear.

'You've no idea what my father's like. He's ferocious when he loses his temper and if he finds out I'm pregnant, he'll stop me ever seeing you. He'll never let me get married and he'd make me have the baby adopted.'

The thought of losing Jo revived every adolescent anxiety I'd happily jettisoned since learning to love her.

I needn't have worried.

Seven weeks after that fateful Sunday, her period finally arrived and the relief was enormous. Normality returned as winter approached and, with it, the looming fear of her exams, the continual challenge of escaping overbearing parents and the need for more care during stolen hours together.

Loving Jo gave me purpose and freedom from teenage angst. We shared everything and there was little doubt in my mind we would continue to do so for the rest of our lives. With her alongside me, all of what once seemed impossibly challenging ceased to bother me because we faced it together.

It was with great relief that I left school in July of 1964 and shared Jo's elation on learning she had passed all her GCEs. A few weeks later, our joy was tempered when it was confirmed I would be leaving Shaftesbury for London.

For a year or so, my parents had been dropping hints about me moving away, as much because sleepy Shaftesbury promised few career prospects as their need for one less mouth to feed.

From time to time, Jo and I talked about the possibility of my leaving, although it wasn't until the letter of appointment from the Legal and General Assurance Society arrived on the doormat that reality hit us.

She was tearful, as was I, but we agreed to write each week, speak regularly by telephone and I would return for weekends as often as finances allowed. The first two weeks in September were tense.

On the third Friday, nine days before I was due to leave and almost two years after we met, everything changed.

We were walking home from a friend's party we'd left early because her father had ordered her back by 9.30pm. It was good to be on our own, but she had seemed uncommonly distant all evening. Thinking my impending move might be playing on her mind, I accepted her monosyllabic responses to mundane questions.

We were due to meet again on Sunday and I would show her how much I was going to miss her as we lay together in the dry autumn grass of our special field.

On reaching the end of her road, I moved to put my arms around her, but she immediately froze and pulled away. 'I am sorry, Robin,' she said, her voice faltering. 'I… I don't know how to tell you this but… well, I think we shouldn't see each other anymore.'

'Why?' was the only word I could choke out.

She looked down at her fingers, which were twisting the strap on her handbag. 'Two weekends ago I met… I met someone. I didn't mean it to happen, I promise you I didn't, but…'

She hesitated. Normally I would have encouraged her to go on. Not this time. It seemed the air had been stolen from my lungs and I set my face rigid so she couldn't see any reaction, sense any emotion.

'We were on a family visit to friends of my parents, people we haven't seen for ages and, well, their eldest son was home from university. We've sort of known each other since we were kids and... well...'

My mind was empty, Jo's words rendered me speechless, but she had to go on, of course, trying to help me understand, I suppose. 'He looks a bit like you, only taller. He's... he's more grown up than, well, than our age group. He's three years older than us, even drives his own car.' Tears burst from both her eyes and tracked down her cheeks, shiny in the soft glow of the streetlamp.

When I finally managed to speak, it was little more than a croak. 'But... but, Jo, I love you. You can't turn me off like a tap. You're my world. Please don't... What have I done to upset you?'

'Nothing, Robin, you've done nothing, I promise.'

She fumbled inside her handbag and took a small handkerchief to her eyes. She was sobbing as she spoke. 'Robin, I'm so sorry but we can't meet again... ever. I... I have to go.'

With that, she turned in the direction of her house and disappeared into the darkness, the click of her heels on the pavement the only sound breaking the night silence.

Numb but desperate to follow, to make her tell me there had been some awful mistake and we could still be together, I could do no more than drop to my knees on the cold tarmac and sob.

When I eventually stumbled along the pitch-black lane towards home, I could feel the shutters slamming shut. By the time I was in bed, every one of my old anxieties had miserably returned.

A self-pitying despondency plunged me into despair, nurturing a fantasy of committing suicide clutching a final tear-stained letter addressed to my beloved Jo.

It was his fault, not hers. The man from university who stole her. The tall bugger with his own car and, very possibly, loaded with all the confidence I lacked.

On our final Sunday afternoon together, just five days before she dumped me, we had bumped into a school friend as we were leaving our special field. She took a photograph of Jo and me sitting on the five-bar gate, happy, smiling, so much in love. Or so I thought.

For half a century the photograph remained in my wallet, a happy remembrance of a first love or, perhaps, a warning against lowering my defences, inviting others into my world.

The past plays fast and loose with our feelings, often exaggerating the emotions once stirred by barely remembered events. In old age, I now see my angst and self-loathing for what they were, little more than a rite of passage. In the moment, of course, it was harrowing.

MEMO ENDS rf

FOUR

Lakmaker is busy arranging the printed pages of Robin's latest memo, meticulously lining up the corners of each sheet before stapling them together.

'What fascinates me reading both your memos, Robin, is the fine detail you recollect from events that took place over half a century ago.'

'It's what old people do. We struggle to remember last week but the driftwood of our youth remains with us for ever. I recently came to the conclusion that old age dissolves the past into the present, which is the reason this bloody disease is so cruel; it robs sufferers of any sense of being. You'll maybe understand better when you reach my age.'

The doctor manages a weary half-smile and the sudden expression of disillusionment on his face surprises Robin. Has he somehow fallen short of his life ambitions? Is he perhaps disappointed ending his medical career monitoring a clinical trial in a small West Country care home?

Lakmaker clears his throat. 'Are the emotions experienced at the time as vivid and painful reliving them?'

'In the moment of writing...' Robin pauses as he mulls over how he felt when probing his teenage years. 'Yeah, maybe they are, but the moment a memory is committed to page, the emotion is spent. The beauty of cathartic writing, I guess.'

'You appeared to have suffered a feeling of insecurity during your relationship with Jo. Why were you so convinced you'd be parted?'

Robin loses himself in thought for a minute. 'I guess that for the first time in my life, and thankfully not the last, I'd found a soulmate, someone I truly felt comfortable with.'

'That was clear but why the premonition it wouldn't last?'

'The fear of losing someone close has always plagued me. The brutal irony is we're all parted in the end.'

'Yes, that's one of life's crueller jokes,' Lakmaker comments wistfully. 'Did you have any contact with Jo after she ended the relationship?'

'Nope.' He clips the word; the catharsis is complete. Only it isn't.

Lakmaker takes a sheet of paper from the buff folder and studies it. After a minute of unhopeful silence, he looks up and speaks slowly, purposefully.

'Is there any possibility, Robin, you might recall where you were on the evening of Friday 22nd October 1965?'

The old man rolls his eyes like a stroppy teenager bemused by a stupid question from a prying parent but then snorts a derisory laugh. 'Strangely enough, I do remember that period of my life quite well. I'd recently moved into a flat south of Hammersmith and passed my driving test. I'd bought my first car around that time and was feeling pretty damned pleased with myself.'

The doctor's eyes fall back to the sheet of paper, double-checking a detail, perhaps. 'You weren't by any chance in Dorset on the evening of the 22nd, staying with your parents, perhaps?'

'I might have been. Why?'

The earnest expression on the doctor's face suggests Robin is not going to like what he is about to hear. 'Did you ever know a man by the name of John Warner?'

'Not that I recall, but my memory for names or faces was never good. Who is he?'

'He was the young man Jo left you for.'

'What about him?'

'He was killed in a car crash at around 6.30pm that evening while driving along a stretch of the main A30, two miles east of Shaftesbury. At first, the police thought he may have hit a patch of black ice or oil and skidded head-on into a tree. He died instantly. He was on his way to see Jo.'

'I vaguely remember my mother telling me something about a fatal accident around that time but had no idea it was him. Poor Jo, she must have been devastated.'

Lakmaker continues. 'According to the coroner's report, ice and oil were eliminated as the cause of the accident. The brakes and tyres were in good order, but the car's windscreen had shattered. A subsequent examination suggested it may have smashed prior to the crash, most probably as a result of an impact from a stone or other solid object.'

'A stone thrown up by a car in front, I'd imagine.' Robin was still thinking how distraught Jo must have been.

'Following extensive investigation, the police identified only one vehicle using that stretch of the A30 around the time of the accident. A farm tractor passed the site some five minutes before. The police and the coroner speculated a missile may have been deliberately directed at the car.'

'What, kids chucking stones at cars? Happens all the time.'

'Or by someone who wanted to get even with the driver for some reason.'

Silence cloaks the room like a shroud. The blackbird in the beech tree beyond the window no longer sings; maybe it too senses the tension. Bile oozes from the pit of Robin's stomach, slithers upwards through a taut oesophagus into the back of his throat. Lakmaker is motionless, his features pinched.

'You're not seriously suggesting I had anything to do with that man's death, are you?'

The doctor reads on, the pitch of his voice as flat as a stationmaster's announcement. 'It appears there was a dance in Shaftesbury town hall on that Friday evening and around 10pm, two local youths forced their way in, somewhat the worse for drink, and within minutes started an affray.

'Several chairs and tables were damaged, as were two guitars belonging to the band, but more significantly, two members of the public suffered severe cuts and bruising. The police arrived and arrested the troublemakers, who subsequently appeared at Dorchester Assize Court, and records confirm a Robin Farnham appeared as a witness for the prosecution. You were at the dance that evening, Robin. You were in Shaftesbury the day John Warner was killed.'

A look of astonishment fills Robin's face. 'I, er... I don't understand. I have no recollection of that weekend or of any court appearance.'

He is hunched up as he broods over what he has heard, his features screwed tightly in his confusion. He then erupts. 'This is all bollocks, Lakmaker. You... and the police for that matter, must be living in some kind of fantasy world if you honestly believe someone could plan and commit a murder in that way. It doesn't stack up, it's... it's utterly improbable.'

'Robin, the police think differently. They are of the opinion you may be connected in some way with this man's death.'

Robin rises to his feet, visibly rattled, and moves aggressively closer to Lakmaker. 'You're messing with my head and d'you know what, I'm not even sure you're a doctor. Why does a care home need a psychiatrist anyway? You're a bloody copper, aren't you, an undercover cop trying to convince me I'm something I'm not?'

'I *am* a psychiatrist, Robin. I'm head consultant here at Barton Hall attached to the clinical investigation team monitoring the trial of the new drug you're taking.'

'You're lying, you're a fucking copper, and as for the insane suggestion I could somehow manage to throw a stone at a car driven by Jo's boyfriend, when I hadn't the foggiest idea who he was or what he looked like, no idea what car he drove, on what bloody road he might be driving or at what time, you're out of your mind, Lakmaker, or whatever your name is. I demand to be discharged and if the police want to question me then so be it because I'M NOT A MURDERER.'

The door swings open and the large, tattooed nurse rushes in. Lakmaker looks up and, seemingly unperturbed, gives two gentle shakes of his head. The nurse leaves almost as quickly as he arrived.

'If that's what you want, I'll discharge you, but the police will arrest you the moment you leave; they're convinced they have sufficient evidence to charge you with the hit-and-run killing in Suffolk. Is that what you want?'

Robin slumps back into the chair and buries his face in both hands. 'I just want to die!' Tears leak through tightly closed eyelids, hot, stinging tears. Old man's tears that flow more freely as the years shorten. His heart is beating like a blacksmith's hammer and a clammy sweat clings to his skin like paint to a woollen blanket.

'Please, I need some water and… and something to calm me down.' His hands fall to his lap as he looks up at the doctor, eyes pleading for comfort, sympathy even. The face staring back shows no compassion.

Lakmaker moves to his desk, presses a button on a telephone and asks for water. He unlocks the top right-hand desk drawer and squeezes two small tablets from a foil strip.

In a matter of seconds, the nurse returns with a bottle of mineral water and two glasses. Lakmaker fills one and hands Robin the tablets, which he swallows. He concentrates on his breathing, deliberately slowing it to a steady rhythm; in through the nose, hold for a couple of seconds and then gently exhale through the mouth. His pulse gradually calms.

Instinctively, he looks to his wrist to check the time. His watch is gone. Surely he was wearing it when he attempted suicide? Maybe Lucy removed it before the paramedics carted him off to hospital. He scans the room: not a single clock. A steady tick might soften the awful silence. He has no idea of the time.

Lakmaker slowly and deliberately replaces the gold pen inside his jacket pocket, closes the file and looks up.

'Robin, your medical notes suggest your Alzheimer's was diagnosed at a late stage because you were reluctant to seek help for symptoms you'd been experiencing for several years. Is it true you've suffered periods of memory loss throughout your life?'

'I always thought there must be periods in all lives when little happens for weeks on end. I was blessed with a memory incapable of storing trivia but able to recall important events with pinpoint accuracy.'

The doctor does that waiting thing again, the penetrating gaze, lips moving slowly but without speaking, all the time compelling Robin to continue. 'Are you suggesting I suffered periods of amnesia?'

'I'm not sure, Robin. I think it likely your subconscious buries unwanted or unpleasant memories. We need to establish if that's what's happening.'

'I'm not sure I want to. It frightens me there'll be more gaps. Even worse is the thought I might be a killer.'

The doctor stands and tucks the file under his arm as he makes ready to leave. 'I have a suspicion, Robin, that the more you write, the more your subconscious will reveal.'

Robin reaches for the thin comfort of the water and sips slowly. How much better were it a glass of Burgundy.

'Yeah, but what happens when the police find out… well, that I have no memory of that weekend when Jo's boyfriend died?'

'Don't bother yourself about the police, I just need you to keep writing.'

'I'd like my wife to be allowed to visit me. It'll make me less anxious and might even help me remember stuff.'

'No, I'm afraid that's not possible.'

'Why the hell not? I'm not in police custody, am I?'

'Technically, no, but they're refusing you visitors until you give them the information they need. Anyway, I get the impression you enjoy writing about yourself.'

'Bloody sight easier than talking to you, that's for sure!'

'I'm at a conference for a couple of days so you'll have the time to write without interruption. Use this room during the day and sleep in the suite next door which you'll find through there. Your washbag and clothes have already been brought down for you.'

Robin glances across the room at a door adjacent to the bookcase then turns back to Lakmaker, who has clearly read his thoughts.

'The hospital is secure, Robin, all doors and windows are alarmed, so please don't get any ideas about leaving. If you try, the police will take you into custody and I don't think either of us want that.'

The idea of sitting alone, digging into seventy-four years of living, has some appeal. Not so alluring is the thought of discovering he's not the person he always thought himself to be.

Has he ever intentionally harmed anyone? No, not him, not the shy pacifist, the short man in the shadows shunning confrontation; much happier writing, always has been, but he is increasingly wary of what is buried in his subconscious and might reveal itself through his fingers.

*

From: Robin Farnham
To: Dr Lakmaker
Ref. No: 3

At eighteen years of age, riddled with anxiety, empty of confidence, and depressed over a broken romance, my enthusiasm for leaving home was wafer-thin. The only crumb of comfort was my mother's encouragement.

She had jettisoned, sacrificed might be a more accurate word, any hope for her own life, having married in haste at the close of the Second World War and given birth to me less than nine months later.

Five children and years of relentless poverty resigned her to a pitiful existence sharing a bed with a lazy, selfish, alcoholic husband. By day, he repaired television sets for a local electrical retailer and each evening he would piss away a sizeable portion of his earnings in the Old Two Brewers, the Half Moon, the Ship or the Mitre in the company of like-minded wasters who long ago exchanged ambition for hours propped against a bar putting the world to rights. Men who knew everything save how to care for their families and put in a decent day's work.

My mother was forced to supplement the household income by working evenings at the local telephone exchange.

Somehow, she kept an inner spark alive, never losing touch with what better things she might have done with her life. By now her ambitions rested only in her children and, being the eldest, it was me she first encouraged to flee the suffocating limitations of small-town Dorset.

She wanted so much more for me than a mind-numbing office job, early marriage, five kids in a three-bed council house and saloon-bar evenings shared with others too spineless to break out.

She was determined Shaftesbury would not condemn me to the life into which she had been compelled to settle. The family purse was juggled to provide my first grey business suit and two non-iron white shirts, all ordered from a catalogue, all paid for on the never-never.

After a deal of patient encouragement away from inquisitive ears, she helped me pack my few possessions into a tired leather suitcase unearthed at a local jumble sale and, on the last Sunday in September 1964, I left Shaftesbury and hitched a ride to London, slumped in the back of a neighbour's car.

In truth, there cannot have been a time when I felt more desperate, more lost and alone, and less optimistic. Leaving Dorset should have helped me forget Jo but if anything, those first few months served only to deepen the loss.

The contrast between life in sleepy Shaftesbury and that of an insurance clerk in 1960s London was stark. Wedged inside a mass of jostling bodies crammed into a suffocatingly stuffy Underground carriage for half an hour each morning and evening was poor exchange for a five-minute bicycle ride to school.

On arriving at Holborn station, I would race up the left-hand side of the escalator, silently praying the ticket collector wouldn't spot mine was out of date, before hurrying the length of Kingsway, a wide, leafy thoroughfare teeming with more offices, shops and restaurants than in the whole of sleepy Dorset.

The roar of buses, lorries and cars crawling bumper to bumper like ants scurrying to and from a rotting carcass deafened ears more at ease with birdsong and cattle lowing in distant fields.

At school, we were taught it polite to move to the outside of the pavement as women approached. London, it seemed, moved to a different etiquette. Commuters with heads lowered walked straight, each defending their path, regardless of who or what was approaching.

Several times during my first week, this solid stream of humanity shunted me into the gutter. Two close encounters with the nearside wheels of London buses convinced me to trade Dorset manners for London's barely concealed aggression.

The end of Kingsway merged into Aldwych, a crescent linking Fleet Street to the Strand and Waterloo Bridge, where I turned left towards Aldwych House, the offices of the Central London Branch of the Legal and General Assurance Company. Designed in the grand Edwardian style of architecture, the once handsome cool-grey stone facade was tarnished grimy black by smoke from a million coal fires and several thousand Nazi bombs.

L & G's offices engendered an air of Dickensian misery. An open-plan layout of fifty or more desks precisely spaced in ordered lines condemned each hapless worker to a lifetime staring at the back of the poor soul in front. I was appointed to Fire Claims and within days, maybe hours, had resigned myself to a life of terminal tedium. Apart, that is, from a vision of extraordinary loveliness.

Sometime, during the afternoon of my third or fourth day, Penny appeared. Her pulse-quickening entrance was made through a door leading from the typing pool to my right, in the far corner of the office.

In an instant, I was captivated by her long upward-curling eyelashes brushed thickly with deep-blue mascara and a widish snub nose resting attractively above shimmering pink lips. Her clear blue eyes danced around the room and my heart missed uncounted beats the moment she picked me out as the new kid in the office. She met my gaze with what my father would later crudely describe as 'come-to-bed eyes'.

As she drifted self-consciously across the floor to deliver a batch of typed letters, the unblinking eyes of every man below the age of forty followed her progress.

In less than a week, I was dictating my own letters into a Dictaphone, which necessitated a trip to the typing pool to deposit a workbag full of files and a completed tape into a work-pending tray.

The room was narrow and rectangular, with dark-brown wooden desks arranged in a line facing outwards from one long wall. With fingers poised over IBM typewriters, eight young typists filled the room with the staccato clatter of clicking keys and constant chatter, which somehow seemed to rise above the dictation playing through their earphones.

Penny's desk was on the left at the far end and occasionally I would venture half a smile and blush awkwardly if it was returned. Over the weeks, the smiles developed into short chats, mainly about corrections needed to a letter. She was friendly enough but offered no encouragement. In fact, she'd eagerly remind me, and anyone else listening, that she was entrenched in a long-term relationship with a tall, good-looking young man working in Accounts. In any case, it was clear I was way out of her league.

At the time, home was a dreary hostel in Colville Terrace, a charmless street adjoining Portobello Road, where the Saturday antique and flea market ends and a long, noisy row of daily fruit and vegetable stalls begins, whatever the weather.

It took time for me to feel remotely comfortable in this rundown part of Notting Hill. The pockmarked stonework and flaking paintwork of neglected Victorian terraces towering over sunless streets stood in brutal contrast to the semi-manicured tranquillity of the Blackmore Vale back in Dorset, its hedgerows, fields and elegant trees painted a thousand shades of green.

Some might claim west London's streets are manicured too, although to a different template. It intrigued me to think that each of these once-proud five-storeyed buildings squeezed into long terraces was at one time the gracious home of a nineteenth-century family, with their fine manners and finer clothes and servants eking out their lives on the margins of slavery in a damp basement, ever-hungry for daylight.

By the time it became home to me, a more transient population crammed each room on every floor, less well-heeled and coarser mannered, but more travelled. My new neighbours acquainted me with the lilt of Caribbean music and the gentle rhythm of Irish tongues telling tall stories at the bar of the Baroque-fronted Windsor Castle on the corner of Colville Terrace and Ledbury Road.

The optimism of people who had abandoned poverty and sunshine for grey west-London skies and mindless intolerance of neighbours eager to make them feel unwelcome astonished me. Around Notting Hill, clumsy handwritten signs taped to ground-floor windows offered flats or bedsits to rent, adding 'no blacks, no Irish, no dogs'.

For £19 a month, I shared a basement bedroom in a hostel in the company of a disagreeable young man from Suffolk who I thought best to avoid owing to his interminable dullness. He very possibly felt the same about me.

From Monday to Friday, a rosy-cheeked housekeeper, stout of stature and odious of body, served cooked breakfasts and evening meals to a dozen or more lodgers in a communal dining room foetid with cigarette smoke and rancid cooking oil.

My finances were shaky. Monthly board and lodging left me barely £23 to cover Underground fares, lunches, food at weekends and £2 per month to Montague Burton for clothing.

Surviving the weekend before pay day was tricky. From Saturday breakfast until Monday morning, my diet comprised a family-size tin of baked beans and half a loaf of bread. There was no bargain hunting in Portobello Road's junk arcades and no fresh fruit or vegetables from its stalls, either.

After three months of this impoverished existence, I was seriously considering a return to the more familiar poverty of Dorset. My mother came to the rescue, again.

During one of our infrequent telephone conversations, she mentioned that she had spoken with my father's cousin, my Aunt Kathleen, who kindly suggested I meet with her eldest son, Robert, a CID detective in the Metropolitan Police. He lived and worked but a stone's throw from my lodgings.

Robert was five years older than me, and we had not met in a decade or more. We agreed to meet in the Windsor Castle pub, which left me feeling uneasy. I barely had enough money for fares to work, let alone a round of drinks.

Cousin Robert was tall and stocky and looked older than his twenty-three years. His close-cropped hair, thin, pronounced nose and under-bite that pushed his jaw forward gave him an air of determination and strength of character.

He wasn't dressed in the old raincoat and squashy hat I half-expected a detective to wear. His jeans, black roll-neck sweater and denim bomber jacket were smart, casual and relaxed, matching a personality I found easy-going and friendly. He was also generous. No sooner had I plucked up the courage to explain my lack of funds than he reached into a trouser pocket and handed me a couple of pound notes.

'I can't possibly take that,' I pleaded. 'I'm not sure when I'll ever be able to pay you back.'

'Shut up and buy me a drink,' he said with a breezy detachment. 'You'll return it soon enough,' he laughed. 'I'll see to that.'

DC Robert Partridge was based at Paddington Green police station, and it soon became clear that Met life had imparted wisdom and experience beyond his years.

His father was a staid, old-school Church of England vicar, eking out his later years in the fens of Cambridgeshire, and it was soon clear that Robert was no chip off the old block. He had carved himself a lifestyle in stark contrast to the church-dominated rural parochialism of his boyhood.

He had matured into a likeable, old-style metropolitan copper alive to the benefits of his position. I later learnt he also had the capacity and confidence to deal out a measure of rough but fair justice when needed.

The chat was easy, mostly about drinking, rugby, and women, all of which had been beyond my resources since moving to London. I explained how tough I was finding life. 'You need to get out and see more,' Robert said. 'London's great if you know where to look.'

The following week, he drove me in his multi-scarred but serviceable pale-blue Mini into London's West End, to a district I later learned was Soho. He parked up halfway down Dean Street on a double yellow line.

Steps away, he knocked at an anonymous, flaky wooden door fronting a dilapidated four-storey tenement building sandwiched between an Italian deli and a seedy Chinese restaurant. A wooden panel at head height slid sideways to reveal a face that hadn't seen a razor in days, with an unlit cigarette dangling languidly from the corner of its mouth. 'Ev'nin', Mr Partridge,' the disembodied head muttered. 'Come in, Guv.'

Robert beckoned me to follow him down a flight of poorly lit and uneven stone steps into an equally dim, long, narrow smoke-filled room. The walls were a grimy ochre and thin strands of abandoned spiders' webs hung lazily from dusty nicotine-stained light shades.

At the far end was a small, flat-fronted bar swathed in chipped woodgrain laminate. Scattered throughout was an assortment of wooden tables, each with two or three upright chairs. The place rumbled with competitive male conversation and as Robert made his way towards the bar, a couple of drinkers acknowledged him with nothing more than a cursory nod.

A tall, middle-aged barman wearing a paunch threatening to escape a shiny off-white nylon shirt greeted us without enthusiasm. Two pints of Watney's Red Barrel were ordered, poured and slapped on the damp, sticky bar.

'What is this place?' I asked once we'd found a free table.

'A private drinking club. It's open fifteen or more hours a day.'

'You a member?'

'No, but I help with security,' he replied, with a wry grin. 'The club's not entirely legal; no fire safety certificate and it doesn't have a licence to sell alcohol.'

What he was telling me made no sense. 'So how come you spend time here?'

'There are a lot more unpleasant people in London than those running illegal drinking clubs. Nasty bastards who demand payment in return for protection and threaten owners who won't pay. Their clubs get burnt down or they mysteriously fall down steps. One finished up buried in a cement column holding up the Hammersmith Flyover. I and a few of my colleagues do our level best to make sure these things don't happen, and, in return, the owners feed us snippets of information when it's needed.'

'Oh, I see,' although I didn't. Still confused, I asked, 'So, who are all these people?'

He surveyed the room full of men in suits or smart casual with hair cut regulation short. The flowing locks of 1960s rock groups had yet to grace Soho's illicit drinkers.

'My guess is they're mostly journalists and businessmen entertaining clients. There's a copper over there I know but there may be others I don't recognise 'cos they're undercover.' Robert took another deep draught of beer.

'Why would they be undercover?'

'There's a growing drug problem in London; gangs fighting for control of territory. Dealers use clubs like this, and our boys go undercover posing as addicts.'

My God, I was learning so much so quickly and felt uncomfortably out of my depth. We chatted easily for an hour or so and after polishing off our third pint, Robert stood, bid goodnight to the barman and ushered me to the exit.

'We didn't pay for our drinks,' I pointed out quietly.

'We don't,' was the barely audible reply.

Shortly afterwards, as we hurtled back along the Bayswater Road at a steady 60mph, the ominous sight and sound of a police patrol car pulled alongside. Robert reduced speed and wound down his window as a black-capped officer yelled at him, 'Partridge, you piss-head. For fuck's sake, take it easy.'

The patrol car slid off and Robert stayed inside the limit for thirty seconds before accelerating again.

I found myself smiling. All night we had been breaking rules and getting away with it and I was enjoying every minute.

The following week, Robert took me greyhound racing at the White City. He cheerfully paid for the entrance tickets and warned me not to place any bets. The caution was unnecessary as my pockets barely held sufficient to see me through the month.

As we ambled along the rails, Robert chatted to on-course bookmakers and a few other characters before ushering me into the main saloon. Two pints of Watney's were ordered at the crowded bar and paid for. *Oh*, I thought, *this is different and above board.* No, it wasn't.

We stood chatting, tepid beer in hand as we watched the first two races. I was beginning to worry how my limited funds might stretch to buying Robert a drink when five minutes before the third race, a man in his late thirties, smartly turned out in a thick Harris Tweed jacket, brown trousers, Trilby hat and polished brogues, ambled up to Robert. He cupped a hand over his mouth and spoke directly into his ear before disappearing into the crowd.

'Right,' said Robert, cheerfully rubbing his hands together as we moved from the bar. He reached into his trouser pocket. 'Here's a fiver. See that bookie over there, "Starmaker", get over and place it on the six-dog. It's gotta be that bookie and it must be the six-dog to win. And don't lose the betting slip. Goddit?'

I did his bidding and the six-dog romped home a comfortable distance in front of the other five, none of which showed the slightest interest in catching the hare.

It took a moment to appreciate what had happened and my entire body was shaking as I collected the winnings. At six to one, it was more than half my monthly earnings. 'Now, give me back my stake money, the cost of your entrance ticket and the two quid you owe me from last week and the rest is yours.'

His words and his generosity rendered me speechless. In a matter of minutes, he had transformed me from a penniless country bumpkin into a city boy with bulging pockets. It all seemed so wrong and yet it didn't appear we were guilty of any sort of crime.

The following week found us in south London at Catford dog track. What remained from the previous week's winnings was reinvested on a greyhound recommended by a different, but similarly dressed, contact. My stake was a little larger, the odds much the same, my pockets fuller.

I was at a loss to understand how this weird system worked but figured it probably wasn't legal. Perhaps I should have questioned my cousin more deeply about it but, well… it seemed ungrateful to do so. This inside intelligence was only passed once at each meeting and it was easier to say nothing, increase the size of my wager each time and fill my pockets.

Robert's care for me translated into a goodly stash, and being able to eat at weekends and afford a few luxuries was a major improvement in the quality of life. Jo's memory lingered on, but the more comfortable lifestyle was lifting a little of the melancholy.

Robert and I were chatting over a beer in one of his regular haunts when he asked if I played poker.

'Nah! Played a bit of bridge and three-card brag but not poker. Why?'

Without answering, he rose from the table and walked to the bar for a brief conversation with the owner before leading me through the door into the gents' lavatory. At the far end, beyond a single stained and cracked urinal, was a scruffy wooden door that might have opened into a cupboard storing cleaning materials, except there was precious little evidence of their use.

Robert knocked and the door opened to reveal a heavy-set man in his sixties, almost fitting a double-breasted black-and-grey-striped suit pockmarked with cigarette ash.

He stood aside to reveal a low-ceilinged, windowless, smoke-filled cellar no larger than 150ft square and dominated by a circular, green baize-topped table around which were sat four men.

They looked up but barely acknowledged Robert, who made his way to the only vacant chair at the table and suggested I sit against the wall behind him. The game, I learned later, was five-card draw poker and the stakes were not massive, mostly pots between £40 and £60. Even with fuller pockets, I was not ready for gambling at this level.

Five intensely focused but disparate characters around the table exchanged few words apart from 'raise', 'fold', 'check', and 'call'. I was fascinated and transfixed in equal measure.

For three weeks, the idiosyncrasies of all players, including Robert, enthralled me. Each commanded aptitudes of memory, intuition and deception far better suited to more edifying vocations than that of a professional gambler. For all I knew, they may well have been lawyers, bankers, or doctors.

A paperback entitled *Poker: Game of Skill*, unearthed on the shelves of W.H. Smith's at the bottom end of Kingsway, rendered my twenty-minute tube ride to and from work shorter and more illuminating as I immersed myself in an exciting new world.

After reading it cover to cover three times, the impudence of youth convinced me I had mastered the levels of passivity and aggression essential for successful bluffing. I was ready to risk my winnings at the dog track and join a session.

Robert was considerate enough to sit out for a few weeks and after three sessions I was marginally in profit, mainly through a level of cautiousness ensuring I neither won nor lost to excess.

Caution was jettisoned during the fourth session and my winnings were close to £200, nearly four times my monthly net pay. On the journey back to Notting Hill, Robert was fulsome in his praise for my skill out-bluffing older and more seasoned players.

Little point in revealing that whatever else I lacked, years of hiding my true thoughts from others was perfect training for the poker table.

Gambling was also a welcome distraction from the loss of Jo. The intensity of the game consumed every fibre of my being in the company of strangers who, if they judged me at all, conducted it in disinterested silence. I'd found a corner of the world in which I could comfortably exist. I was not expected to talk with anyone, and no one showed the slightest concern over my reluctance to engage in any alpha-male banter.

This may also explain the extraordinary exhilaration I enjoyed facing down a player during the final stages of a game. The excitement and uneasiness of ambiguity. Is he bluffing? Have I pushed him far enough? Should I check or risk a further raise?

The sensation during those moments was without doubt erotic; a singularly different form of sexual climax, weirdly addictive and, as I would later discover, brutally compelling.

Driving home in the early hours after one late-night session, Robert unexpectedly turned sharp right off the Bayswater Road.

'There's a police road block near Queensway. Don't need the aggravation at this time of night.'

As the Mini cruised up tree-lined Westbourne Terrace, a uniformed soldier stepped from the pavement into the road, waving frantically.

Robert pulled into the curb and told me to sit tight. He walked over to the soldier who was probably in his mid-twenties, although his close-cropped ginger hair standing to attention like an upturned scrubbing brush made it tricky to be sure. He pointed to the badge of the Royal Anglian Regiment on his shoulders and cap as he told Robert he had returned from a tour of duty in Aden that morning. He explained he needed money because he'd been beaten up and robbed.

Robert flashed his Metropolitan Police warrant card to the soldier who, on realising he wasn't being nicked, continued his story.

After several hours drinking in clubs in the West End with fellow soldiers, he'd picked up a prostitute. He'd paid the taxi fare to Westbourne Terrace and the woman led him up three flights of stairs to a bedsitting room, closed the door and demanded money upfront.

'How much?' Robert asked.

'A tenner,' he spat, 'but I never 'ad no chance to do nuffin' as straight away, these two blokes come rushin' fru' the door and frows me on the bed. They punches me in the guts, which doubles me up then nicks all me money and scarper wiv the prossie.'

'Did you go after them?'

'I tried to, but I was winded, weren' I, an' they was gone in a flash anyway.'

'How much did they take from you?'

'Hundred quid an' more, I reckon.'

'Could you take me to the bedsitter?'

'Yeah, it's over there,' the soldier said as he pointed towards a once-elegant early Victorian, six-storey terraced house, one of dozens along Westbourne Terrace.

'Do you want to stay in the car or come with us?' Robert called out to me.

Safety in numbers seemed a better bet. No one was bluffing here. We made our way up to the third floor where one of three doors on the landing was ajar.

'That's it,' the soldier announced.

I followed the other two into a large bedsitting room, complete with double bed, dressing table and sink. No cooking or toilet facilities were visible.

'Did she tell you her name?'

'She said it was Denise but… well… who knows?'

Robert switched to copper mode. He deftly opened each of the drawers in the dressing table but found them all empty. He pulled it away from the wall but again found nothing. He dropped to his hands and knees, searched under the bed and then surfaced holding a small piece of thick blue paper.

'What ya got?' asked the soldier.

'A name,' Robert said. 'A name I know. Paddington Green is my nick so I'm familiar with most of the local pros and pimps. It's a dry-cleaning slip with the name Butler written across it. There's a tart living no more than three houses up from here called Dorothy Butler, who often uses the name Denise when she's working. Bit careless leaving this around. This woman that rolled you, what did she look like?'

'She was 'bout five foot six with red hair and a birfmark on 'er neck.'

'That's her all right.'

'Feevin' bitch. Will ya take me there, guv?'

'Happy to.'

Really? This sounded far too dangerous, and I was beginning to wish I had stayed in the car. Five minutes later we were at the front door of Flat 6 on the third floor of a slightly better-preserved building. I was shaking.

Robert thumped the door several times before suggesting the soldier used his shoulder to break it open. The flat was in darkness and Robert called out before switching on the hall light. A quick search confirmed no one was at home.

He moved directly to the main bedroom, which was the first door off to the right. 'I need to check this is the right flat, I'm pretty sure it is but… well… better be hundred per cent.'

He sifted expertly through the contents of the dressing table and then the wardrobe, sparse with a few dresses, blouses, and skirts but each on its own hanger and all seemingly well cared for. He removed a thin felt cover from a garment.

'Aha! Gotcha.' He ripped a blue dry-cleaning tag from the dress, identical to the one found in the bedsitter. 'And look at that – it belongs to a certain Miss Butler.'

The soldier looked as if he was about to explode. 'Can you arrest the bitch?'

'In due course maybe, but she has a record as long as your arm and she'll not grass on the thugs who rolled you. They're the ones we rarely catch. We could charge her with aiding and abetting a felon, but you could put your last fiver on her having a cast-iron alibi for this evening, even if you picked her out in a line-up.

'Her brief would claim you were pissed, which you likely were, so she won't get done for robbing you and there's no way you'll get your money back.' Robert's face showed sympathy, although it was clear he was unable to give the soldier the comfort he needed.

'Fuck,' was his only response.

'If it'll make you feel any better, we'll wait outside while you search for anything you feel is worth your hundred quid. It might even ease your temper if one or two items accidentally get broken or some clothing was somehow ripped.'

Robert and I walked back onto the landing and closed the door. We waited in silence as an assortment of muffled bumps and crashes sounded from within.

The soldier eventually emerged clutching two bulging bags and wearing a broad smile. 'Found some dosh and—'

Robert stopped him. 'I don't wanna know. Just be on your way and I hope you've learned your lesson.'

An almost cheery 'Fanks, Officer' drifted back up as he hurried down the stairs.

'Is this how it works in London?' I queried tentatively once we were safely back in Robert's car.

'It's a weird kind of justice, Robin, but I've yet to discover a better way of dealing with this sort of situation. The law lets people down, mainly because bent defence lawyers intimidate prosecution witnesses, by implying they're unreliable, lying, or hold some sort of grudge against the accused.

'Time after time the guilty walk free and the injured party is the one suffering. When you're faced with that kind of justice, you end up bending the evidence to nail the real bastards, and occasionally, those guilty of lesser offences get away with it in return for a few favours. No one pretends it's ethical or even honest, but I don't see any time soon when it's likely to get any better.'

He dropped me back at the hostel in Colville Terrace, assuring me he'd pick me up next week for dog racing at the White City.

In the cool darkness of the night as I sat on the cold steps leading up to the front door, one last cigarette seemed a good idea even though the stale dryness in my mouth suggested I'd already smoked too many. The gentle lilt of a calypso floated from an open third-floor window opposite, accompanied by occasional bursts of contented laughter.

These past weeks with Robert had been astonishing, the most exciting of my life, especially tonight. If I stayed in London and continued gambling, there'd be occasions when I'd be ripped off, cheated or on the receiving end of injustice. But the excitement on offer seemed worth the risk.

The moral codes learned at school and at home now appeared hopelessly outmoded. I tried to remember them: never tell on your classmates, play the game with a straight bat, and walk if you've nicked a catch to the keeper. Own up when asked who's guilty and hand that 10-shilling note found on the pavement in at the police station.

Those were the life lessons Shaftesbury had taught me. Now the opposite seemed more likely to work in the real world. Even if you played a decent game, you'd be dealing with people who didn't. Why should the crooked buggers always be the ones who win?

Robert was a good copper and he showed me an alternative code for living, one that promised a better life than his parents or mine ever enjoyed. It was edgy, yes, and not altogether safe or legal, but it was a code as old as time itself.

Childhood failed miserably to prepare either of us for the adult world. Not in London anyway. We both needed to learn real life had little in common with the soft moral codes we were given at school or by his God-fearing vicar of a father.

This rougher, tougher world encouraged risk to achieve success. If you fail, you're fucked, but the risk is worth the gamble. And God has nothing to do with any of it.

I could choose to walk away, take a different direction. My cousin's world and its confused interpretation of right and wrong would continue with or without me, making its own perfect sense, profitable for those happy to play the game.

Why turn my back on life's opportunities?

Whatever else was happening, I was learning something useful at last and thoughts of a return to Shaftesbury disappeared.

MEMO ENDS rf

FIVE

From: Robin Farnham
To: Dr Lakmaker
Ref. No: 4

In every life, there must be pivotal moments, occasions that in hindsight we later come to recognise as life-changing. Looking back, I now see the 1965 office Christmas party at the Legal and General as a… and I'm searching for something that isn't a cliché but failing miserably. Unquestionably, it was a turning point, a crossroads, a Pauline moment, a… well, you choose.

In the fifteen months since leaving Dorset, what little female company I chanced upon had amounted to little more than one-off loveless and largely unsatisfactory sexual encounters. Jo's memory still dominated my thoughts but as December approached, I found myself thinking more about the gorgeous Penny.

Not that she had offered me any encouragement. The tall man she was 'almost engaged to' was still very much in evidence but there was something in her eagerness to pass time chatting with me that suggested I might be in with a chance. Call it instinct if you like but I sensed something.

By the autumn, the mind-numbing monotony of my job had all but persuaded me the seductive life of a professional gambler promised a great deal more, even if it meant never seeing Penny again. On the day I planned to hand in my notice, the office was buzzing with the news that Penny's accountant boyfriend had resigned to take up a new position elsewhere.

Penny would be on her own at the Christmas party, the perfect opportunity to make a play for her affections. Firstly though, I needed to smarten up my act.

Gambling was funding a lifestyle that a year ago seemed impossible. My move into a smart flat in Barnes, south of the river, was a comfortable step up from the shabby hostel in Notting Hill and I had taken delivery of a brand-new Ford Cortina. I was eating in good restaurants and enjoying fine wines but now needed to spruce up my appearance with two trendy made-to-measure suits.

I took a couple of hours off one morning to shop at the Kingsway branch of Austin Reed, the tailors. The time had come to stop envying other business types in their shiny mohair suits and have some made for me. Proper Savile Row tailoring would have to wait a little longer.

Two fabrics took my eye, one rich and bright, almost a royal blue, the other a more discreet midnight blue.

'These fabrics may be a little out of sir's price range,' the assistant warned, staring at me through dull eyes. His thin lips parted into a mean-spirited half-smile revealing ugly, nicotine-stained teeth tilting like tombstones in an abandoned graveyard.

A few months back I might have agreed or been cowed. Or worse, been rude back to him. Instead, I reached inside my right-hand trouser pocket, pulled out a large roll of banknotes, laid it on the counter and smiled sweetly at the condescending shit.

'Oh, and the lapels must be hand-stitched.'

Two fittings later, and I was confident I was dressed with more style and elegance than most nineteen-year-olds in London at the time. The country boy was going up in the world.

The office Christmas party took place in the upstairs room of a decaying Fleet Street pub adjacent to the Law Courts. The central area of a dark wood-panelled room was cleared of tables and chairs for dancing and for the entire evening, a sweating mass of writhing bodies packed the floor.

A clapped-out fuzzy loudspeaker banged out a succession of popular songs, all the while losing the battle against the boisterous yelling and whooping of typists and insurance clerks making the most of the festivities. No one appeared to partner anyone; the 1960s fashioned its own social etiquette. Dancing had become a collective activity, communally celebrated in large circles.

My reluctance to join any crowd left me happier alone at the bar, drinking while focusing on my objective for the evening. Penny looked stunning in a tight-fitting red skirt cut just above the knee and a white cotton blouse finished with a pale-blue lace collar. Light-brown hair, back-combed high and falling to her shoulders, framed high cheekbones, mascara-laden eyelashes, and moist, pale-pink lips.

She was rarely off the floor, moving in and out of each circle, gyrating around young and old alike. With the security of new clothes, a pocket full of cash and two large whiskies, I made what, for me, was the boldest of moves and joined the group on the floor.

Self-consciously twisting and turning, I manoeuvred close enough to Penny for her to just about hear me above an off-key communal singalong to the latest Beatles hit. 'Wanna another drink?' I yelled.

'Yeah, great,' she shouted back, and to my delight, accompanied me to the bar. Hers was a Bacardi and Coke and mine a third large whisky. As we sipped our drinks, conversation was all but impossible against the blast of the music, but she heard me all right as I moved my mouth to within an inch of her left ear and told her, 'You look absolutely gorgeous, Penny.'

She flushed and smiled broadly but before long was back on the dance floor, eager for more fun. I hoped my opening move had been successful. I remained at the bar, watching her intently, so much so, that her closest friend from the typing pool sidled up to me and remarked I seemed unusually interested in Penny.

'I find her very attractive,' I answered honestly, and to my delight, she revealed Penny had confided in her she thought I was good-looking. That was the encouragement I needed, and later, as the party was drawing to a close, the tempo of the music slowed and I nimbly stepped in to ask her for the last dance.

The soft ballad gave me reason to place my arms around her waist and she responded, linking her hands around the back of my neck. I thought I sensed something, a warmth perhaps, as her thumbs moved gently up and down the nape of my neck. Tentatively, I offered to accompany her on the short walk to Temple Underground station.

Standing close on the platform, we waited twenty minutes for the train I hoped would never come. She talked animatedly of her life in Barking, east London, happily sharing a three-bedroom terraced house with parents, younger brother and older sister.

She listened intently to my reminiscences of growing up in Dorset, my excitement at moving into a new flat and the thrill of driving a new car. I saw no reason to explain how the money to pay for all this had accrued and she didn't care to ask.

Her childish innocence captivated me, as did her uncompromisingly simplistic outlook. Whatever ambitions she nurtured, they appeared to have little to do with building a successful career or earning vast sums of money.

As the carriage doors were about to close, she leaned out and kissed me full on the lips.

Early in January, I summoned the courage to invite Penny for a drink after work and, a week later, for a meal. She accepted without a moment's hesitation on both occasions. At the end of our dinner date, I accompanied her on the forty-five-minute Underground journey from Temple to Barking. Side by side, we chatted and for only the second time in my life, I was at no time short of conversation.

Tucked close into a dark, secluded corner inside the concourse on Barking station, the warmth of the kisses and intimate touching told me all I needed to know about her feelings towards me. There was little doubt I was falling in love again and for most of that late-night tube journey back to my flat, all I saw in the blackness of the carriage window opposite was the reflection of my stupid, love-struck grin.

Over a period of weeks, we enjoyed a somewhat furtive relationship owing to the continued presence of the accountant. 'We're almost engaged to be married, you know,' she would tediously remind me and yet her casual infidelity seemed not to trouble her in the slightest.

With Jo's memory fading like ship's smoke on a distant horizon, I needed commitment, one way or another. I started putting pressure on her, gently at first, and mostly by way of cheesy tokens of my love designed to persuade her to settle for me rather than the accountant.

Over a period of months, she changed her mind with frightening regularity. Should she stick with her original suitor to whom she was 'almost engaged' or choose the shorter, better-spoken young man from the West Country? Her indecisiveness ought to have rung alarm bells.

Eventually, the accountant made the decision for her. Somehow, he learned a third person had breached the relationship and ended the 'almost' engagement without the slightest fuss. Something perhaps I should have noted more carefully.

I stole the woman he loved and was only too aware of what he might have been going through. At the time I hardly gave him a second thought.

MEMO ENDS rf

*

From: Robin Farnham
To: Dr Lakmaker
Ref. No: 5

My last-ever poker game was in the spring of '66 and might well qualify as the sort of trauma you urged me to focus on, Doctor.

The same six players, including Robert and me, made up our regular sessions. One of them, a rigidly upright, leonine-featured man in his mid-fifties, who frequently alluded to his years in the army, had adopted a singularly unfriendly attitude towards me.

I guess it was partly my own fault, as everyone apart from me respectfully addressed him as the Brigadier. This clearly annoyed him but his clipped way of speaking through a protruding lower lip drawn tight across manicured teeth reminded me too much of the over-privileged, plum-in-the-mouth authoritarian boarders at school; the rosy-cheeked, pampered sons of military officers whose future career paths were mapped out long before they entered prep school. I didn't like him and, infused with the obstinacy of youth, refused to use his title. He made it clear he disliked me.

He goaded me, called me short-arse or shorty. During tension-filled minutes of the final stages of a poker hand, he would mockingly enquire if I needed to get up early for school in the morning. What began as humorous banter eventually degenerated into thinly disguised contempt as my winnings mounted.

Holding my discipline was crucial: never risk more than £50 during an evening session, avoid personal involvement and rarely speak unless spoken to.

The game preceding my last poker session opened at a gentler pace than was usual. The game was five-card stud with the 'ante' or 'bring-in' set at £1 and the maximum raise a fiver. The Brigadier was agitated, impatient no one appeared to be taking risks.

Following a third hand cut short by us all folding our cards early and leaving him a meagre pot on what, I guessed, was a strong hand, he raised himself to full military bearing and addressed us as if we were a bunch of raw recruits.

'This is too fucking slow,' he thundered, his jaw jutting forward imperiously. 'We should up the ante to a fiver and maximum raise to a tenner.' His clipped words ricocheted around the cellar walls.

'Not for us,' my cousin stabbed back instantly and turned to me. 'Come on, Robin, we're leaving. This'll get heavy.'

I wonder now, as an old man, how often in life I instinctively knew the logical response to a given situation, yet on opening my mouth, somehow contrived to articulate the opposite?

'Come off it, Robert, a couple more hands won't hurt.'

His face flushed the colour of a blood orange as he leaned in towards me with such urgency, I feared he was about to headbutt me. 'He's setting you up,' he whispered, so quietly I could hardly make out what he was saying.

Not quietly enough.

'Go on, Shorty, do as Daddy tells you. Fuck off home, it's way past your bedtime,' he barked, accompanied by a humourless smirk.

It was my turn to flush, as Robert told me again that he was leaving, and I would need to find my own way home if I stayed. As he scooped up his cash from the table, something in his expression troubled me. His encouragement had matured me beyond recognition over the past twelve months yet, at odd moments, my low self-confidence would resurface.

He had transformed an anxious, melancholic schoolboy into a young man better equipped to handle life's harsher moments. Except, I wasn't quite ready to fully loosen the apron strings.

The Brigadier's stare bore right through me as I looked him in the eye. 'Sorry, I've got less than fifty notes on me. Thanks for the game.'

'What about next week? Let's have a proper game.'

'Might be interested. If so, I'll come prepared.'

We made a quick exit and marched in silence to Robert's car. Once inside, he turned on me with a ferocity that put the fear of God in me. 'Listen, you stupid bugger, he's setting you up! At least two of them have been building you up for this for weeks. They wanna teach you a lesson, take you down a peg or two. They'll rob you blind.'

'What? Cheat?'

'Yes, Robin, cheat. Fix the cards. Bend the game. They'll make sure you're dealt a hand so good you'll go all the way on it, only to find one of them is holding something better.'

Chastened and angry, we were halfway down Oxford Street before I broke the silence. 'We can't let them get away with it, Robert. There must be a way to stop them fixing the game.' He laughed a low, sarcastic growl but said nothing more during the drive back to my flat in Barnes.

'Okay for dogs on Friday?' I asked.

'Yeah, see you then.' The car roared away so quickly, I barely had time to close the door. He wasn't a happy cousin.

The following morning, I phoned the Legal and General and spun my boss a yarn about food poisoning and the need to stay close to a lavatory. I took the tube eastbound to Leicester Square and walked north up Charing Cross Road to Foyles Bookshop.

A pretty young assistant showed me a selection of books on conjuring tricks using playing cards and suggested *The Expert at the Card Table* written in 1902 by S.W. Erdnase. She assured me it was one of the most influential works on the art of manipulating playing cards at gaming tables and with a perceptive grin, leaned towards me and whispered, 'It's commonly known as the Cheat's Bible.' Exactly what was needed to give me a scintilla of a chance in a high-stakes game.

Over the following three days, I immersed myself in the subtleties of overhand shuffling and stacking, bottom dealing, Greek and second dealing in the hope it might enable me to spot anyone cheating.

Quite how I would handle such a situation should it arise barely crossed my mind.

Robert picked me up on Friday and was his normal affable self until I told him of my newly acquired skills. 'Robin,' he warned sternly, 'if you want to play for higher stakes, that's your decision. But you're on your own.' His tone made it clear the matter was no longer open for discussion.

A few months earlier, the movie *The Cincinnati Kid*, starring Steve McQueen, had transported me to another world, into the glitzy life of high-stakes gambling. I dreamed of emulating the young upstart's battles against seasoned old pros.

The following Tuesday, alone and a little apprehensive, I

made my way by train to the Soho club, clutching £430, three-quarters of my accumulated winnings from the previous year, the equivalent of eight months' salary at the Legal and General.

The anticipation churning my insides was weirdly similar to that of waiting for Jo, that spring afternoon we made love for the first time. I hoped I had prepared better on this occasion.

On walking into the poker room, the others were already there, and the Brigadier's face broke into a self-satisfied smirk as he thrust his jaw forward.

'Dad let you out, Shorty?'

Pointedly ignoring him, I muttered good evening to no one in particular, and took my normal seat.

It was the regular crowd minus my cousin. On my immediate left was Stan, an emaciated bookmaker, his alabaster complexion and rasping cough suggesting he might not be long for this world. His tweed suit hung loosely from bony shoulders and thin knees pointed sharply from beneath threadbare trousers.

Next to him sat Gordon, a middle-aged porker of a man who rarely smiled and at one time alluded to running a business in the motor trade. He dressed as you might picture a 1960s car salesman; black-and-grey-striped double-breasted suit, red braces lifting trousers high over an expansive belly, cream shirt, large gold cufflinks and a black and red-spotted bow tie. His gravelled voice owed much to the noxious French cigarette permanently suspended from his nicotine-stained lips.

To his left sat the Brigadier and on my immediate right was Phil, a lean, muscular man in his late twenties whose glowing complexion hinted at hours spent in the gym or days working outside in the fresh air. He was articulate when speaking, which was hardly ever, and the most difficult to read.

The game was five-card stud, considered by many the purest form of poker. The dealer changes with each hand, moving to the player on the left. In the version we played, two cards were dealt to each player, the first face down, the 'hole' or hidden card, and the second face up. After each player discreetly inspects his 'hole' card, a round of betting follows.

The third and fourth cards were dealt face up, each followed by a round of betting. The final card was dealt face down, giving each player the luxury of two secret cards.

There was nothing as sophisticated as gaming chips in gambling dens closeted behind gents' lavatories in 1960s drinking clubs. Our stakes were real money, crumpled and often ragged 10 shilling, £1 and £5 notes along with the occasional £10 note.

'Are we agreed on a £5 ante and a £10 maximum raise?' the Brigadier barked as he looked directly at me, adding, 'You bring enough pocket money, Shorty?'

The aggressiveness of my reply surprised both him and me. 'Just fucking get on with it.'

The Brigadier dealt and I focused on his hand movements as he distributed the cards. It looked straight. For the first half hour, the cards fell evenly for all players, nothing more than a pair of sevens coming my way, although a bold bluff on an ace high scooped me a half-decent pot.

As Stan shuffled before dealing the fifth hand, I thought I spotted him holding cards in place at the base of the pack. As he dealt the first two, those he gave the

Brigadier and me were almost certainly flipped from the base of the pack.

My 'hole' card was an ace and a second ace stared at me face up from the table. If it was a set-up, it wasn't subtle.

It was me to bet first and I laid £10. All except Phil followed before Stan dealt our third cards face up. The eight of diamonds was no help to me but the Brigadier was now sitting on a pair of jacks. He threw £10 into the middle, which I matched before the other two stacked.

That left the Brigadier and me. It was difficult to spot if the fourth cards were dealt from the base of the pack, but I picked up an eight of spades, giving me two pairs, aces and eights. The Brigadier was showing the ten of diamonds to his pair of jacks. It was him to bet first.

He held my gaze as he moved ten £5 notes into the pot and declared, 'I'll raise you fifty.'

'Aren't we playing a maximum tenner raise?' I enquired.

'Got a problem, Shorty? Losing your nerve?'

It looked likely that Stan had dealt several cards from the base of the pack, so I held my face rigid, ensuring no twitch of eyelid or cheek muscle, no bead of sweat on my brow. I gave nothing away while running through my options.

If this deal is crooked, he'll know I'm sitting on two pairs, aces and eights and he will also know what his and my final cards will be. On the other hand, if the deal is straight, it is likely he is bluffing.

I found the tension exhilarating.

Was a £50 bet worth a crooked deal? Was he setting me up? Don't be a prick, of course he is. Robert said he would.

I lowered my eyes, bowed to common sense, and lifted

the single card from the table before laying my two pairs face down into the middle.

His gloating smile hurt. 'You're playing with the big boys now, Shorty. You sure you got the spunk for it?'

Little happened for an hour. A couple of moderate pots came my way and one was lost, leaving me neither up nor down. It was well after midnight when the best hand of the evening was dealt. And it was on my deal.

I dealt the first cards face down before dealing Stan the six of spades, Gordon the ace of clubs, the Brigadier the jack of clubs and Phil the king of hearts. The queen of diamonds landed face up in front of me and my hidden card was the queen of spades. A promising start but there were other high-value cards on the table.

Gordon opened the betting at £10 on the strength of his ace which we all matched.

Stan's third card was the six of clubs, giving him a pair, Gordon the seven of hearts. The Brigadier drew the nine of clubs, Phil the eight of clubs and I showed the ten of diamonds.

Stan bet first on the strength of his pair of sixes. I covered the £10 and raised him £20. The others matched.

I dealt the ace of spades as Stan's fourth card, Gordon drew the king of diamonds, the Brigadier the king of clubs and Phil the eight of spades, giving him a pair. The queen of clubs joined my queen of diamonds, and my heart rate grew faster. My hand was a possible game-clinching three queens.

The highest hand showing on the table was my pair of queens and I raised the bet to £50. Gordon growled as he threw in his hand, but Stan matched me as the Brigadier sat deep in thought.

It was possible he wasn't holding much but feared loss of face if he pulled out early in the betting. Particularly against me. He pushed £50 into the centre of the table and Phil hesitated for a second before adding his £50.

The final cards were dealt face down and I drew the eight of hearts, no improvement on three queens. It was still me to bet so I pushed a further £50 into the pot.

Stan took time making up his mind. 'Come on, we haven't got all night,' fumed the Brigadier, who seemed strangely agitated, a good sign perhaps. Stan moved £50 to the centre of the table, looked up at no one in particular and smiled feebly. The Brigadier blinked and took a moment or two before he too matched the bet, followed by Phil.

By this time, I was grappling with the odds against the other three holding better cards than me.

Stan's three cards lying face-up on the table were showing an ace and a pair of sixes. The odds favoured him holding another ace, which would give him two pairs – aces and sixes or an additional six, giving three of them. My three queens would beat either of those hands. He could, of course, be sitting on a third ace which would kill me.

The Brigadier's king, jack and nine was an unpromising combination and his aggressive betting suggested he might be bluffing. However, his two hidden cards could be a second jack and a nine to give him two pairs, which I would beat. On the other hand, he might just be holding two more kings, which would give him three kings to beat my three queens.

I dug deeply into lessons learnt from the handbook. Remembering every card dealt helps calculate the odds for or against each opponent holding a particular card.

Both Gordon and Phil had been dealt kings so there was

no chance of the Brigadier holding three of them. There was, however, an outside chance he was holding a ten and a queen, which would give him a straight run of nine, ten, jack, queen, king. That would beat me. I held three of the four available queens so the odds of him drawing the fourth were slim, although possible.

Phil was showing a king and two eights. He couldn't be holding a third king as all four had been dealt but if he'd drawn a third eight for three of a kind, my hand would beat his. He might just have pulled another eight to give him four, which would be painful.

But the cards were straight. I was the dealer.

I raised another £50. 'Too heavy for me,' Stan mumbled as he threw his cards into the middle face down, leaving me, Phil and the Brigadier, who stared at me, eyes unblinking. 'I'll match your fifty and raise another fifty.'

His expression was as cold as dry ice. I stared at his pencil-straight nose between cheeks blotched crimson by broken veins and perched arrogantly above a patrician chin. The epitome of everything I loathed about rank and privilege.

The skin of Phil's cheek twitched beneath his left eye. His hand was almost certainly good, but the game was moving to a different league. He shifted uneasily on his chair as he pushed a further £100 into the middle.

Jesus Christ, the game had become very heavy. I had never been remotely close to risking this much money. I'd never even seen this much cash in one place. The Brigadier smiled, or was it a smirk? I pushed my fifty into the middle to match the bet and deliberately allowed my right hand to hover above my dwindling pile of notes.

My insides knotted tighter than a metal worker's vice and yet, my every sense, my very being was consumed by the most exhilarating sensation. My head floated over the green baize, hovering above the flaccid nicotine haze and fusty odour of edgy men at day's end. The adrenalin surging through my veins was teasing every single nerve end.

My hands were rock steady, no more than a hint of dampness across the palms. Here was where I belonged.

Normally, once each player has matched the betting on the final deal, a show of cards follows. I wanted more, I had to pummel them into grovelling submission, particularly the Brigadier. He'd never call me Shorty again.

Slowly, my left hand pushed a further £100 into the middle as my eyes again fixed his stare.

For a split second, it seemed he hesitated, but no. In came his £100 followed by another. 'It'll cost you another ton to see me, Shorty.'

Phil matched the bet and for the first time, a flicker of doubt flashed into my mind.

No, they had to be bluffing. They wanted to teach me a lesson I didn't want to be taught.

On counting what was left in my pile of cash, it was £100 plus a few pennies. I slid all the notes into the middle, leaving me little choice other than to call.

'Okay, let's see what you've got.'

The Brigadier remained impassive, staring straight at me.

Slowly and very deliberately, he turned over his two closed cards, first the ten of spades and then, the queen of hearts. For half a minute, I'm certain to this day, my heart stopped beating.

Against the odds, he had pulled the ten and queen to match his jack, king, nine giving him a straight run. My three queens were beaten.

A gut-wrenching nausea boiled inside as I stared in disbelief at the table, hoping against hope it was an illusion. Phil mumbled something inaudible under his breath and threw his cards face up on the table, showing he had been holding two pairs, jacks and eights. He too was beaten.

A gloating smirk filled the Brigadier's face as his bucket hands gathered up a pot which I later calculated to be £1525. Over twenty grand in today's values. My loss was £445, every single penny I had on me.

'Tough shit, Shorty, now fuck off home.'

Everything hurt. I was the Cincinnati Kid.

After leaving the club, I trudged through Soho to Leicester Square Tube station only to find the last train to Hammersmith had long gone. With no money for a cab, the seven-mile walk to my flat south of Hammersmith gave ample time for reflection.

How had they pulled it off, or had lady luck simply deserted me? Phil and the Brigadier could have been working together, maybe the others, too. Yet that last hand was on my deal, so it was straight. The odds of him pulling that ten and the fourth queen were ridiculously long and yet, he had.

What was so incongruous, so ridiculously paradoxical, was the other-worldly sensation I had experienced as the game drew to its climax, more intense, more sensual than any previous session.

Trudging wearily across Hammersmith Bridge some two hours later, I finally recognised something I had half-suspected for some while. In gambling, the intensity of the thrill is directly proportionate to the degree of risk taken.

The trigger is the amount of money at stake. Only by risking more money than I could comfortably afford to lose is the climax at its most powerful. If losing has little or no financial impact, there is correspondingly less excitement.

In a single evening, two-thirds of my accumulated winnings were gone and yet that awful game had stimulated me more than any previous experience in my life. Lying in bed later, I revised my assessment. Making love to Jo remained with me as an achingly beautiful memory although the lure of gambling had become frighteningly more compulsive.

Sleep came fitfully for what was left of the night.

Later that morning, while chewing a slice of dry toast, it dawned on me that in addition to being a good deal poorer, I could easily have lost more; even ended up in debt. All for the sake of a few moments of ecstasy. Gambling is as addictive as any drug and in that moment, I realised I'd been hooked.

Robert dragged the sorry tale out of me in the bar at the White City two days later and I humbly admitted I should have heeded his warning.

'What really pisses me off, Robert, is that I spotted them dealing from the bottom of the pack earlier in the evening, but it was on my deal they took me to the cleaners. How the hell did they manage it?'

'It's likely a couple of them would have been working in tandem, dropping the odd card in their lap on their deal and passing it on as and when it was needed. You were well and truly hung out to dry.' The tone of voice and look on his face were sympathetic.

Hunger for revenge was eating at my insides although I knew the gambling had to stop before it jeopardised any future I might have with Penny. If she hadn't been in my life at the time, I might well have wasted years and, possibly, a much shorter life in the sordid basements of London's West End.

'That's it, Rob, no more poker,' I assured my cousin. 'I can't be doing with the cheating.'

'We're all cheats, Robin, don't kid yourself. The inside knowledge we're given here at the dog track is as much cheating as that card game. We're all party to it, all guilty, one way or another. The trick is to spot the signs of something bigger and back off before you get burnt.

'And while we're on the subject of backing off, maybe you'll take a little advice from me about Penny?' Something in his tone suggested I wasn't going to like what he was about to tell me.

'You're besotted with her, Robin, but take it from me, you'll get bored. She's a beautiful girl, the physical attraction is obvious, but intellectually… in the end, you'll find you need more from a woman than she'll ever be capable of giving.'

This hacked me off big time. It wasn't what I wanted to hear and what was left of the evening passed with little conversation. Two days later, I called him and explained I was planning to drive down to Dorset for a long weekend and would call him on my return. I never did.

My dreams of life as a full-time gambler were shelved although the continuing tedium and dearth of prospects at the Legal and General convinced me that a change was essential. In June 1966, I answered an advertisement in the

Daily Telegraph for a position selling classified advertising on a trade magazine and, following a short interview, was offered a month's trial.

Goodness knows what made me think I would be suited to a career as a salesman. Few would have described me as the typical hail-fellow-well-met, glib-tongued sort of chap normally associated with those involved in sales. Perhaps the gambler inside was still alive.

My first day in magazine publishing was the Monday after England won the football World Cup in 1966 and it took me a week to sell my first advertisement. A fortnight later, the feel of the freshly printed magazine, complete with the advertisements I personally sold, utterly enthralled me. The sensations were curiously close to those enjoyed during my time at the poker table.

Who knew?

Over time, my love of publishing matured into a different type of addiction, not as profitable as gambling in the short term, but one I felt comfortable pursuing over the longer game. It was challenging and fun and more respectable than poker; a career I was happy discussing with Penny and her family.

Within a year, the company promoted me to selling display advertising and gave me a company car, which enabled me to sell mine. My salary leapt to £1,000 a year, a four-figure milestone at that time.

Penny was a remarkably beautiful woman, blessed with an extraordinarily happy, fun-loving personality. Only occasionally would she offer glimpses of the anxieties that would blight her later years. As a nineteen-year-old, her outlook on life had been moulded by the narrow confines of her close-knit family and she yearned for nothing more than a secure home life, filled with fun and laughter, a happy husband and two children, preferably a boy followed by a girl.

I was her opposite; more serious, less inclined to laughter, absorbed with building a career and ever more prepared to take risks. It's hard to say how I failed to sense the danger in a relationship forged between two such dissimilar personalities.

It's conceivable she embodied the personality I always wanted. Maybe I convinced myself we'd make a good, balanced match, not the same marriage of minds I enjoyed with Jo but a marriage appropriate for us both, in good ways.

On my twenty-first birthday in February 1967, I asked Penny's father for his daughter's hand, and we were married in August the following year.

MEMO ENDS rf

SIX

Robin lifts his fingers from the keyboard as the consulting room door swings open. Lakmaker strides in, wearing an expression Robin has come to recognise as troubling.

'I've ordered a sandwich and a pot of tea, you must be hungry,' he comments matter-of-factly. 'You've been writing solidly all day, haven't you?'

Robin nods, as it dawns on him that he has no idea when he last ate. It must have been breakfast. Did he even eat breakfast?

Lakmaker lays Robin's bulky file of medical notes on the coffee table and drops into his usual chair.

'So, you managed to kick your gambling addiction around the time you asked Penny to marry you?'

'I did,' answers Robin with a look of surprise. 'How come you know about my engagement to Penny and my gambling when I've only this second finished writing about it?' His expression grows more quizzical as he adds a further question. 'Is this laptop connected to another computer?'

Before the doctor can answer, a soft knock on the door announces the arrival of a nurse. She deposits a tray of tea and what appears to be a white bread tuna and sweetcorn sandwich on the table and leaves. Lakmaker pours the tea in silence.

'You're monitoring what I'm writing as I write, aren't you?'

'Yes, I am,' he replies.

'Who else is reading this stuff?'

'No one, although I'm obliged to pass anything that might be of relevance on to the police. You're my patient and I need to read as you write; it helps me monitor the effectiveness of the drug.'

'How the hell does watching me write help you monitor the drug? That's bollocks.'

'It's to do with the way memories flow through the brain, the speed at which you can recall details from years ago.'

Robin needs to get a few things straight. 'How long have you been the consultant here at this hospital? I was told we met all the medics and staff the day Lucy and I were shown around. I don't recall meeting you.'

The doctor's expression gives little away. 'We didn't meet that day, Robin, but I've been here several years.'

'So how come you weren't here on that day?'

The doctor evades the question. 'Robin, following information given in your last memo, the police insist I ask you what, if anything, you know about a Brigadier Simon Robson.'

'Never heard of him,' growls Robin impatiently, clearly annoyed at the man's evasiveness. 'Where were you the day I was shown around here?'

The doctor's eyelids droop shut for a second before he continues. 'Brigadier Simon Robson died following a mugging while walking through London's Soho during the early hours of 21st April 1966.'

'Jesus fucking Christ, you're going to ask me where I was on 21st April 1966, aren't you? Well, I haven't a clue apart from the fact that at that time of day I was more than likely sound asleep in bed.'

Lakmaker leans forward and reaches inside the folder. The black-and-white A4 photograph he lays flat on the table pierces Robin's eyes like hot needles.

It's the Brigadier, the self-righteous, stuck-up, pompous bastard who cheated him in that final poker game. He never knew his full name. Didn't need to.

'You knew this man, didn't you, Robin?'

Lakmaker sees the look of despair on the old man's face and pauses for a moment before repeating the question, this time raising his voice just enough to force a reply.

A heavy dread is pinning Robin to his seat. 'Yes, yes, I do, and you clearly know from reading my memo when and where I met him. Look, I promise you, I've not set eyes on that man since I left that Soho club, the night I lost all my money. I most certainly did not kill him.'

'The police never identified who murdered the Brigadier and the case remains open to this day. On reading your account of that poker game, you can understand why, in their parlance, you've become a person of interest in connection with the man's death.'

'I'm your patient and you have no right to pass my confidential case notes on to the police.' Robin is shouting and hears panic building in his voice. 'When is all this shit going to end? No, I don't remember robbing him, I don't remember killing him but at the time, had I been anything other than a timid twenty-year-old, I might well have done so. Tell that to the coppers and then tell them to leave me alone. For pity's sake.'

His body shudders violently as he squeezes his right hand into a fist and gently runs the smooth skin on the back over his lips and nostrils. Slowly, back and forward he moves it; it brings him comfort while Lakmaker busies himself making notes. It's a while before he looks up.

'Robin, did you experience any sense of loss ending the friendship with your cousin?'

Confused by the sudden change of subject, Robin hesitates before answering, breathing slowly and precisely.

'None at all,' he mutters.

'You didn't miss him?'

'No.'

'Does that not strike you as strange, considering how he cared for you at a time when you needed help?'

'I guess I didn't need him after I'd met Penny. I honestly can't remember, it's so long ago and to be honest, I don't care.'

Lakmaker goes to speak then seems to change his mind and emits a non-committal 'hmm' as he looks down and scribbles another note.

He finally lays his pen on the notebook and points at Robin's left wrist. 'That's an unusual bracelet you're wearing. Where did it come from?'

With a look of weary resignation, Robin extends his wrist towards the doctor to show him the bracelet. 'I found it one evening driving to Dorset to stay at my parents' house. A few miles outside Shaftesbury, I came round a bend on a hill too quickly and saw this old man standing in the middle of the road.'

Robin closes his eyes as he is speaking.

'I had no way of avoiding him. I braked hard and as soon as the car stopped, got out to see if he was okay. But there was nothing there, no old man, no damage to my car, just this bracelet lying in the road.'

'What did the old man look like?' asks Lakmaker.

'I only glimpsed him for a split second, but he looked in a dreadful state; his face was muddy and scratched as if he'd been dragged through a hedge backwards. He was bending over, and I always thought he must have been picking up the bracelet but if he didn't exist, that can't be any sort of rational explanation, can it?'

'When was this?'

'Oh, I don't know, sometime in the autumn of '65, I think. I'd only recently passed my driving test and taken delivery of my first car. That much I do remember. Why?'

'Could it have been the weekend Jo's lover was killed?'

Robin's muscles stiffen. 'I've no idea,' he answers irritably. 'I remember the evening I found the bracelet but have no memory whatsoever of the rest of the weekend.'

'And you've worn the bracelet ever since?' Lakmaker asks.

Robin thinks for a moment. 'I was never sure what made me decide to wear it. I guess I just liked the look of it. The clasp needed repairing but it's been with me ever since.'

'May I have a look?'

With no little difficulty, Robin unfastens the clasp and hands Lakmaker the bracelet. He walks to his desk and takes a jeweller's magnifying loupe from a drawer and nestles it in his right eye.

'An interesting piece. I think it's gold, although there don't appear to be any date marks. The main links are in the shape of the Meander Greek key symbol – a combination of straight lines and right angles. Even more interesting is the circular clasp.'

'It looks like a snake.'

'That's exactly what it is, Robin, it's the *ouroboros*.'

'Ouro what?'

'You've had the bracelet all this time and never wondered what the clasp is or might mean?'

'No, not really. I just got used to it being a part of me. I don't even think it's itemised on our home insurance.'

'Ouroboros is a serpent biting its own tail forming a circle. It signifies renewal and a hope for eternity, particularly of love.'

Lakmaker taps the keyboard on his computer and, for half a minute, stares at the screen before reading aloud.

'*The ouroboros came to us via Egyptian and then Greek tradition and has been adopted as a symbol representing a number of different but loosely related philosophies, including wisdom, commitment, introspection and eternal return. The ouroboros suggests something constantly re-creating itself.*

'*It was an enduring image in many societies although the twentieth century seems to have forgotten it. Queen Victoria asked Prince Albert for her engagement ring to be of a serpent embellished with her birthstone, an emerald.*'

Robin's eyes widen. As important as that during the 1900s but now just a snake with little resonance and plenty of people who'd think it a horrid thing to have on their hand because popular opinion defines snakes as dangerous.

Lakmaker taps in a new search.

'Meander is *"the symbol of victory and unity, a symbol of infinite and eternal life. According to scholars, it was inspired by the numerous bends in the Meander River in south-west Turkey"*.'

'So they're both sort of concerned with eternal life, the snake and that meander thing?'

The doctor is deep in thought.

'And the Latin inscription on the inside?' Robin asks.

More tapping at the keyboard before he answers. '*Vaticinium ex eventu*. Hmm. It's an expression often used in connection with the writings of the Gospels. The literal translation is *"prophecy from the event"* which generally refers to Gospel writers implying a prophecy was made before the event it describes happened.

'As we now know, the Old and New Testaments were written years after the events they describe took place. Secular scholars claim writers fabricated Biblical prophecies, shaping them as predictions, when in fact they describe events actually known about at the time the Testaments were written.'

Lakmaker looks up from the computer screen. 'Essentially, they manipulated facts, appearing to prophesy an event they already knew had happened.'

'Easy enough to be wise after the event,' Robin comments ruefully. 'Why would anyone inscribe that on a bracelet? More to the point, where could it have come from?'

'It would be interesting to find out. I'll dig around and see what else I can come up with.' He hands the bracelet back to Robin and stands.

'I have other patients to see on my evening round, Robin, I'll leave you in peace.'

'I'll get no peace until you stop passing my memos over to the police. Do it once more and I'll stop writing. Do I make myself clear?'

Lakmaker pulls up short at the door and turns back to face his patient. 'I'll do what I can.'

Robin breathes a little easier as the door closes. He stares at the laptop but is too confused to write. Three people he had connections with died violently. Was it coincidence or did some deep-rooted hatred drive him to murder and then wipe the memory clean out of his head? He certainly blamed John Warner for stealing Jo, but he never knew the man, so how could he hate him? The Brigadier was a smug, cheating bastard who got his comeuppance, but no one deserves to die over a game of poker. As for the man killed in Suffolk, he knew for certain he was miles away at the time it happened and in no way could he have had anything to do with it.

Too many questions for an old man who grew comfortable in his skin decades ago. He knew who he was then, his weaknesses, his strengths and achievements. Now he is certain of nothing and the urge to uncover his past eats into him like a caterpillar on a cabbage leaf.

We're happy to accept the misdemeanours of our early years, our guilt often cleansed by time, but if his younger self unknowingly breached the moral codes he always endeavoured to live by, what kind of man does that make him?

He is exhausted and an unsettling hissing sound fills his ears. Suddenly, he feels apprehensive about his surroundings, uncertain of where he is. This is not his sitting room, nor his study; he is alone and hates the solitude.

'Lucy,' he calls, a growing sense of isolation compelling him to raise his voice. 'Are you in the kitchen? Can you come and help me? I need to lie down. I'm not feeling so great.'

She can't hear him. Must be in the greenhouse watering her tomatoes. He calls again, louder. A door opens.

He looks up to see a woman in a nurse's uniform. 'Who are you?' he asks gruffly. She is young and pretty, reminds him a little of Penny, or perhaps he means Jo. So young and with her life stretching endlessly in front of her, so fortunate not to see death looming. What's a nurse doing in his house?

She sets a tray down on the oval table. Robin examines a pale blue china mug filled with a steaming hot milky drink. The nurse hands him two tiny blue pills.

'What are these for?'

'They'll help you sleep, Mr Farnham. Do you need help getting ready for bed?'

'No. I'm not a bloody invalid.'

She frowns and her top teeth bite hard into her bottom lip. She nods and points in the direction of the tray. 'Please take the pills before you sleep, Mr Farnham.' She leaves the room; this room Robin doesn't recognise. He wonders where Lucy could have gone.

He places the pills in his mouth and sips the tepid drink. Thick, dry lumps of undissolved Horlicks powder dry his mouth and throat. He drifts off to sleep still slumped in the armchair.

SEVEN

He awakes with a jolt, startled out of a nightmare and feeling nauseous, as if a snake is slithering upwards from the pit of his stomach. He can taste bile.

Bright sunlight floods the room, bleaching everything out of focus. Is there any focus left in what he sees or in what he writes? The last thing he remembers is dozing off in the chair next door. Now he's in bed dressed in pyjamas.

A drugged sleep streamed scenes from an earlier life, twisting happy memories into nightmares, forcing him to relive long-forgotten conflicts over and over again, like watching some endless grainy black-and-white movie through the peep holes of a slot machine on a seaside pier.

A key turns in a lock. The door to his left swings open, and a male orderly walks in carrying a breakfast tray which he places on the high table alongside the bed. He seems wary, his head bowed as he edges slowly backwards while still facing Robin.

'Are you feeling any better this morning, Mr Farnham?' His voice is hesitant.

'Any better? Unfortunately, my friend, as you can see, I'm still alive, which is not the state I was hoping to find myself in. You don't by any chance have a stash of barbiturates about your person you could let me have? You see, I need to die.' Robin's voice is loud, aggressive.

The orderly backs all the way to the door, his lips moving but he makes no sound. The door closes softly after him and again, the key is turned in the lock. Strange.

Robin eats a little porridge, treacle-thick, sweet and tepid. He drinks a glass of what reminds him of the welfare orange juice he was given as a child and follows it with half a cup of stewed tea. He hates strong tea.

He removes his pyjamas and, standing under a scalding hot shower, scrubs wrinkled skin and wasted muscles, unsure of what he seems eager to wash away.

He dresses in blue denim jeans, a pale-pink Oxford cotton button-down shirt and wrinkled fawn linen jacket before drying thinning grey hair in front of the bathroom mirror. He then settles into his usual chair in the consulting room next door. As he fires up the laptop, another key turns in a lock and he looks up as Lakmaker walks in.

He too is casually dressed; pale-green chinos, open-neck blue shirt, brown loafers, and a beige cotton jacket, which he hangs on a hook on the door. His body movements seem brusque and the expression on his face suggests an edginess. The moment he speaks, it's clear something has happened.

'Are you feeling any better this morning, Robin?' His voice sounds ominous.

'Better than when? Last week, last year?'

'Better than last evening.'

'I feel drowsy, woozy. Did someone give me a strong sedative last night and why, all of a sudden, are the doors locked?'

'We gave you three sedatives last night,' Lakmaker explains. 'The night nurse brought you the first two and I gave you something stronger to knock you out after you attacked her.'

A steel band tightens around Robin's chest as he strains to force air into his lungs.

'I… I attacked a nurse?'

'Unfortunately, you did, Robin, and quite violently too. She came to help settle you for the night, gave you the sedatives and out of the blue, you accused her of kidnapping your wife. You struck her twice, in the chest and shoulder. She fell and was concussed when her head hit the wall.'

'Is she badly hurt?' His head drops and the inside of his mouth feels like a damp woollen blanket.

'We kept her in overnight under observation, and she's bruised and sore but feeling a little better this morning. She'll be discharged later today. That's the reason we took the decision to lock the doors.'

'This is your fault, Lakmaker.' More bile in the back of his throat as he swallows hard. 'You stopped me from dying. This is exactly the reason why I wanted to kill myself before this God-awful bloody disease reduces me to a zombie.'

Robin shakes his head violently from side to side and wraps his arms around his torso.

Lakmaker's eyes narrow. 'You… you don't remember any of it?'

'No. I bloody well don't remember hitting a nurse or seeing you last night.'

Silence falls over the room as Lakmaker writes on the top sheet in Robin's file. On finishing, he looks up and speaks quietly. 'Robin, it seems we may have put you under too much pressure, for which I apologise. Last night, after we sedated you, I met with the police and they're off your case. From now on, I'm the only person reading your memos.'

'Thank you for that but I've decided I have no wish to find out anything more about my life. I just want it to end. This… this existence in this God-awful room is screwing me up, convincing me I'm guilty of crimes completely out of character with the sort of person I always thought myself to be.'

'It's doubtful murder is part of what you can't remember, Robin.' Lakmaker is studying his patient intently as he speaks.

'What makes you so certain?' Robin asks, desperate for any words of comfort.

'To commit cold-blooded murder demands a particular mindset. A second murder suggests some form of personal gratification experienced by the murderer in performing the act. Your personality suggests nothing other than a rejection of the idea of killing another human being, even as an act of revenge.'

A persistent anxiety is gnawing at Robin's insides, and he makes no sound other than an involuntary old-man groan as his knees battle to raise his backside from the armchair. Unsteadily, but slowly and deliberately, he shuffles over to the window behind Lakmaker's desk.

The room is eerily quiet until the doctor breaks the silence. 'Robin, your wife told me about other traumatic periods in your life.'

'Did she? Well, if you already know about them, there'll be no need for me to write about them,' he snaps aggressively and turns away from the window and glares at him.

'Were there difficult times, Robin?'

'My wife's already told you there were,' he shouts, turning back to the window. 'But they were more than dwarfed by the good times. I've been lucky, very lucky, which is why I don't understand these… these accusations that I'm some kind of monster.'

'From what I've been told, these episodes were possibly life-changing, and their impact may yet to have surfaced. Our subconscious can, in certain circumstances, you know, act as a protection device by blocking the memory of trauma. This loss of memory can be short-term, but sometimes the subconscious tricks us into believing a memory has gone forever. The problem is; it hasn't. A deeply upsetting episode that occurred half a lifetime ago remains stored in a part of our brain we're incapable of accessing. That way, we're protected from the associated stress.'

Robin reflects for a couple of minutes before offering his reply. 'All that suggests to me is a justification for letting sleeping dogs lie. If the police are off my back, there's little point in any more writing.'

He gazes across the hospital garden. He imagines how it would feel standing outside, soaking up the stillness of the morning as he runs the palms of both hands up and down the smooth bark of the beech tree.

Beyond the tree, a curved, well-tended flowerbed is teeming with roses still in full bloom, vivid reds, soft apricots, and intense yellows contrasting with the achromatic gloom in the room. No autumn frost to dull their colours.

'For instance,' Lakmaker says, again enunciating each word forcefully and precisely, 'do you feel up to telling me what you remember about that day in May 1975 when you arrived home unexpectedly and surprised your first wife?'

The bent old man grabs the windowsill for support and rests his forehead against the cold windowpane. Why drag that up? What good can it do? Slowly, he turns and is somehow compelled to trudge back to his chair. He pours a glass of water and takes several sips before placing it back on the table. For a reason he cannot quite grasp, he is resigned to telling Lakmaker what he wants to know, yet at the same time, is petrified of what he is about to reveal.

'Why do you want me to keep dragging up all this shit?'

'Because, Robin, you're part of an important drug trial, and your ability to recall these moments tells us which of your memory functions are regenerating. Your progress and that of the others on the trial could well improve the outcome for thousands of sufferers in the future. You're doing well and it would be a shame if you were to give up now.'

'It's fine for you to keep digging into my life but each time I ask you about yours, you clam up, change the subject. You're a closed book, Lakmaker, so come on, you go first. Is that your wife and children in the photograph over there?'

'It is.'

'What's your wife's name?'

'Madelaine.'

'And your kids?'

'Robin, you're the patient here.'

'What's the matter with you? Why don't you talk about yourself?' The doctor sits in silence.

'What are their names?'

It is clear from his expression he has no intention of answering Robin's question.

'We've met before, haven't we?' Robin is determined not to let him off the hook.

'Yes, we have, Robin, and in the fullness of time, I'll explain the circumstances of our meeting, but in the meantime, I must insist we focus on you. What happened on that day in 1975?'

He's been fobbed off again. Old age strips us of resilience, renders us feeble.

Robin goes to speak but is hesitant, uncertain of his words, frightened of their implication and what they might reveal. He is also conscious that what he is about to tell the doctor may sound too much like a clichéd melodrama.

'My daughter was born early that May, the same day I started a new job. I'd been hired to launch a new trade magazine for a start-up business and needed to prove myself quickly.

'I guess during the first couple of weeks after Katie was born, I wasn't at home as much as I should've been. Paternity leave didn't exist then and I thought, as I probably think now, I was doing the right thing, working my arse off to provide for my family.'

He swallows hard, searching for the resolve to tell his story. It takes a while but with huge effort, he retrieves a day he has tried to blot from his memory but never could. Inwardly, he knows he should approach it like he used to evaluate a business project, objectively and without emotion, as if it's someone else he's talking about. But it isn't someone else.

'I left home early that morning, around seven thirty, and drove to Hertfordshire to meet with a potential client I'd hoped would take advertising in the first issue of the new magazine. It was a great meeting and he booked into the first three issues. My spirits were high so, on the spur of the moment, I decided to call in at home to see Penny and the kids on my way back to the offices in Lewisham.'

'A good thing to do?' asks Lakmaker, encouragingly.

'Never quite sure of that. If I hadn't, things might all have been… well, little point thinking about that now.'

A shudder ripples through his body like a mild electric shock. It seems to loosen his memory and his tongue.

'As I walked through the front door, Penny was standing on the small landing halfway up the stairs. She… she looked… sort of strange, almost frightened and as white as a sheet.'

'Did she say anything?'

'No, not a word, but I noticed she was holding something. It looked like the cord from my pyjamas. I started to walk up the stairs and was about to ask what was going on when I saw this thick, deep-red mark around her neck.' Robin squeezes his eyes shut, picturing a scene he really would prefer not to see.

'It was turning blue, like a bruise, and was swollen. I panicked, and remember shouting at her, "What the hell have you done?" Before she could answer, it struck me the house was too quiet. I pushed past her. Where was Giles? Where was our month-old daughter? That's the moment I became frightened rather than angry.

'Penny grabbed my arm. She told me Gladys Smith, a neighbour across the road, was looking after the children. But how did I know that was true?'

Suddenly Robin's mind goes dark, just as it did that day. He has no idea what to say. Lakmaker prompts him. 'Did she often ask a neighbour to look after the children?'

He blinks hard, searching for some order out of the jumble of memories jostling his brain. 'No, I don't think she'd ever done it before. I didn't know whether to run across the road to check the kids were okay or help Penny.

'I just knew something serious and scary was happening. I grabbed her hand and led her downstairs into the living room and that's when she told me she had tried to kill herself. She wanted to die.'

He pauses, breathing deeply, waiting for the heartbeat pummelling his chest to slow down.

'She told me she was depressed and lonely and couldn't cope, and thought she was a useless mother.'

'I have to ask, Robin. How did that make you feel?'

He struggles not to overreact and takes more than a minute to retrieve and then reveal the truth.

'Desperate, helpless, I'm not sure…'

Lakmaker leans forward.

'Was that for you, or for Penny?'

'Bloody hell! What sort of question is that?'

He turns to face the window, unable to look at Lakmaker, not wanting to. He has asked a question Robin is not capable of answering. Can't or doesn't care to?

He sits in silence, patiently waiting until he feels able to look back at his tormentor. 'Can I tell you what happened next?' he asks quietly. Lakmaker nods.

'Two thoughts crossed my mind. Penny needed help and I couldn't risk leaving the kids with her.'

'Did you tell her that?'

'No, not with me, although she assaulted our daughter Katie years later when she was in her teens.'

'And what about you?'

'How do you mean?'

'The irrational trains of thought and persistent delusions associated with the condition often exceed the boundaries of tolerance in those closest to the sufferer.'

Lakmaker's eyes are fixed on Robin, watching for any change of facial expression. 'Did you ever lose your temper with your wife? Did you perhaps... ever strike her... even in a moment of sheer frustration?'

Robin's response is instant. 'No, no, I didn't. I *never* hit Penny.'

Lakmaker continues staring at his patient for a moment longer then casts his eyes back down to the file in front of him.

'I'd like you to think very carefully about that, Robin. You see, this report clearly states that during the doctor's initial physical examination following Penny's admission to hospital, her thighs, back and stomach revealed extensive bruising.

'The consultant added that in his opinion, the injuries could not have been self-inflicted but were almost certainly caused by a series of blows from the hand or fist of another person.'

EIGHT

In the wake of a seemingly endless shift at McDonald's in Praed Street, in west London, Jane Foster struggles with the climb to the fifth-floor bedsitting room in Westbourne Terrace. On her feet since 8am this morning, she worked the best part of a fourteen-hour shift. Almost four months into the job, long hours are a feature of most days but today has been particularly tiring.

She had worked eight straight days without a break but was never going to turn down her manager's plea for extra cover on a busy Saturday. He knew she needed the money. Even so, there was no need for the dirty bugger to be so free with his hands when thanking her at the end of the shift.

Inside the sanctuary of her room, she drops her bag to the floor, strips to her bra and knickers and relishes a much-needed wash down in the sink in the corner by the window. A hot bath would be better, but the lecherous bastard in the bedsit next door would hear her lock the bathroom door and come peering through the keyhole.

She examines the face staring back from the cracked and mottled mirror. Her skin is not good, blemished and dry, and her chestnut eyes are sunk deep into pools of grey. If she wasn't careful, she'd look old way before her time.

Her flatmate, Julian, is away for the weekend with his new boyfriend. She is happy he's met someone but worried they are planning to move in together. She would have to look for somewhere cheaper to live.

She checks out the room. Impeccably tidy, as it always is after one of Julian's cleans, although his brand of orderliness could never mask the griminess of the nicotine-stained Anaglypta wallpaper, and single sash window that hadn't seen a cleaner in a decade. The dark-green linoleum on the floor is worn to flaky brown and two single beds against adjacent walls are neatly draped in off-white candlewick bedspreads. A threadbare brown sofa bed and low laminated plastic table dominate the centre of the room and the only other piece of furniture is a battered Victorian dark-wood wardrobe, its ill-fitting door listlessly hanging open, revealing hers and Julian's meagre collection of clothes.

The bedsit overlooks the noisy junction of Westbourne Terrace and Bishop's Bridge Road, close to Paddington station in west London. The relentless queue of traffic impatiently waiting at the lights below is belching a smog more deadly than the spliff Jane is lighting. It's a dump of a place but better than sleeping rough on Paddington station, dodging the groping hands of drunks, and the transport police.

Her thoughts drift back over the past few months. On leaving her abusive parents in Bristol, she lived on the street for two terrifying weeks, unwashed and perpetually afraid of being robbed or raped by one or more of the local dipsos and dropouts and petrified the police would return her to her parents.

She literally bumped into Julian Philips on her fourteenth afternoon of homelessness as he was hurrying across the Paddington station concourse and, being the sensitive soul she later found him to be, he recognised the fear in her eyes.

He treated her to a coffee and a blueberry muffin in a dimly lit, smoke-filled café crawling with rough sleepers noisily solving the world's problems while eking out tepid dregs from chipped mugs.

'You on the streets?' he asked.

Jane nodded. 'Yeah.'

'How long?'

'Fortnight.'

'Scary, innit?'

'Yeah.'

'You can doss at my place if you want,' he offered. 'It's only a shitty bedsit, but there's two single beds, electric stove and washbasin. The bathroom next door is shared by me and three other tenants.'

Jane was hesitant, for all the right reasons, but Julian explained he'd been forced to leave home after his parents found out he was gay and he, too, had spent several weeks on the streets.

'It was hairy enough for someone like me, but it must be awful for a girl your age. How old *are* you?'

'Sixteen,' she answered, fighting a mouthful of muffin.

'Hmm. Why d'ya leave home?'

'M'dad fucked with me.'

'What'd he do?'

'It don't matter.'

'Okay, no problem, but look, you'll be safer sharing a room with me than out here with this lot.' He nodded in the direction of a couple of winos, ogling her through moist eyes.

'Thanks,' she mumbled, fighting back tears that later, wrapped inside the warmth of sheets and a blanket for the first time in a fortnight, she found impossible to resist.

Julian introduced her to his manager at the McDonald's where he worked, and he offered her a week's trial. A fortnight later, she was working regular shifts and contributing a half-share of the rent.

Over a period of several weeks, she opened up to her roommate. At first, the shame and humiliation of her father's abuse triggered an anger so intense it consumed her like a bushfire. The target for the anger was always the one nearest to her at the time.

But Julian is a sympathetic listener; he identifies with her shame. The moment rage overwhelms her, he calmly walks to the other side of the room, boils the kettle, and soothes her anguish with soft words and a strong brew.

More recently, she has struggled to control her fury on late-evening shifts when drunks and stinking dropouts demand crude extras with their Big Macs. Three weeks ago, Julian sternly suggested they had a talk and he sat her down next to him on the sofa.

She studied her roommate's schoolboy-pink complexion and curly blond hair, tight as an old lady's perm. His slim body wrapped in tight black jeans and waisted pale-blue cotton shirt made him look younger than his years. She relaxed in his company.

'Jane, you gotta get a grip of your temper 'cos the manager told me he'll have to let you go if you cause any more trouble.'

'Yeah, I know. I've let you down.'

'Well, just listen. What my parents did to me was nowhere near as bad as what your father put you through, but it still hurt. I loved them and they loved me until… well, until I told them I was gay. Now, I don't exist and all because of what I am.'

'Parents fuck everything up,' she said, taking a deep drag on the thin spindle of a spliff she had busied herself making while Julian was talking. In the airless room, the soporific blue haze settles around their heads like morning mist over a low-lying vale.

'That's not true, Jane, there're millions of good parents out there, we were just unlucky.'

'Mine certainly fucked me up,' Jane added as she passed the spliff to Julian, who examined it gingerly before putting it to his lips.

He took a deep drag and allowed the smoke to drift out lazily from his lips. 'Look, Jane, the moment I realised my anxiety was controlling me rather than me controlling it, I signed on down the road with a woman doctor who referred me to a psychiatrist. He's a lovely guy. You should see him; he's helped me get my head straight. I've come to terms with my parents' rejection. He made me realise it wasn't my fault they can't handle my sexuality; there's nothin' I can do to change the situation. So there's no bloody point in letting it get to me.'

'So this psychiatrist is a bloke?'

'Yeah, but he's straight, married with kids and all that regular stuff. You should see him.'

'Being married with kids don't mean a thing. I'll think about it.'

Two weeks later, her nightly flashbacks were no less vivid and a further meltdown in front of a lecherous drunk resulted in a final warning from her manager and Jane was persuaded to take the plunge. She signed on with Julian's lady doctor and, following a nerve-shredding thirty-minute consultation, for her and the doctor, she was referred to a psychiatrist at St Mary's Hospital around the corner in Paddington.

She crushes the dying spliff in the ashtray and rolls a second, desperate to ease the apprehension over the day after tomorrow, her first appointment with Dr Peter Lakmaker.

NINE

'Jane Foster.' The shrill voice bounces around the bare walls, shattering the uneasy silence of the half-empty waiting room. Jane is conscious of a dozen or so pairs of eyes staring in her direction as she stands and walks towards the nurse calling her name.

'This way,' the large woman barks as she strides off down a wide corridor. After ten metres, she comes to an abrupt halt and nods in the direction of an open door. Jane hugs a tatty canvas duffle bag, more to stop her body from shaking than from any need to protect her belongings.

'Miss Foster, please take a seat.' The voice is friendly and gentle, but she still clings to the bag.

'Good morning. I'm Dr Peter Lakmaker, consultant psychiatrist here at St Mary's. May I offer you some coffee? It's only instant, I'm afraid, but it'll be wet and warm.' Jane nods and manages a, 'Thanks. White no sugar, please.'

'Two coffees please, nurse,' the doctor calls to the large nurse still blocking the doorway.

'May I call you Jane?' Again, she nods.

'The letter from your GP explains a little of your situation but is scant on detail. This morning, my task is first and foremost to make you feel at ease, assuming that's possible after what you've been through. I have no intention of asking you to talk about anything that might make you anxious or nervous.'

Jane sits bolt upright in the chair, her mouth slightly open, her breathing shallow.

'Now, you consulted your GP about anxiety resulting from abuse at the hands of your adoptive father. Is that correct?' Jane bites her bottom lip and nods.

She scrutinises the man sitting behind the desk opposite her. He is smartly dressed and has an easy smile, nothing like her father or the male teachers at school. His fingernails are clean and cared for, his hands spotless, soft-looking, hairless. She notices a photograph on his desk of him and presumably his wife and children. They look good parents, smiling, arms wrapped around happy kids. Jane can't remember ever having her photograph taken, let alone being cuddled.

'Could you start by giving me a few background details; name, date of birth and so on?'

'I'm Jane Foster and I was born on the 8th of May 1965. I was adopted 'cos my real mother was an eighteen-year-old schoolgirl. S'pose I should be pleased abortion wasn't legal in them days or I wouldn't be here.'

'You were brought up by a couple in Bristol, is that right?'

'Yes.' Jane's voice is barely audible above the clatter of the nurse returning with a tray, on which are two blue china mugs filled with steaming dark-brown liquid.

'You said no sugar?' the nurse asks with little grace.

Jane nods and the cups are placed on the desk between doctor and patient. The nurse leaves.

'And... and you left home how long ago?' asks the doctor.

'In May, the day before my birthday.'

Lakmaker stands and walks to the door, closes it gently, moves to the front of his desk and sits in a second visitor's chair alongside Jane. Instinctively, her upper torso leans further back.

'And where're you living now?'

'In Westbourne Terrace. I share a bedsit with a guy called Julian Philips. You know him. It was 'im who told me I needed to see you.'

'Did he suggest that because you find it difficult talking about what happened to you during your childhood?'

She lowers her head to her chest and stares at the duffle bag. 'It... it makes me... I feel dirty, ashamed, but he said I should see you 'cos of the panic attacks an' me losin' my temper with customers at McDonald's.'

'Jane, whatever you tell me today, or during any other consultation we have, is confidential. Nothing you say will go outside these four walls; I promise you. You have no need to feel shame, I'm your doctor.'

Her resolve is momentarily strengthened by his assurances, and she blurts, 'I wanted to kill 'im,' but immediately wishes she hadn't.

'I doubt, Jane, you really intended to take his life.'

'I did. I hit 'im with an iron bar, three times an' 'e was unconscious when I left. 'E was still breathin' though.'

'Do you feel guilty for attacking him?'

'No.'

'And you really wanted to kill him?'

She nods.

'Because of what he did to you?'

'Yeah.'

'Do you feel able to tell me what it was he did to you?'

She peers at him over the rim of the cup as she sips coffee. It's bitter, worse than McDonald's. Julian assured her she could trust this doctor; he'd taught him how to control his anxiety.

For twenty minutes, the frail teenager spills her heart out, vividly describing her father's abuse and her problems with school and teachers who accused her of being disruptive. She is less inhibited, more animated when describing her attack on her abuser, her escape to London and meeting Julian.

Lakmaker listens attentively, his eyes rarely drifting from her and interrupting only once to clarify her father's condition when she left him. He makes no notes, conscious it might unsettle his patient; she might see it as a breach of confidence. He will write everything up after she leaves.

'I feel dirty an' strange feelings take hold of me. I have to keep washin' myself and all the time I see men who look like 'im. I panic, noises get louder, sort of echo in my ears like I'm hearin' double. I can't breathe an' I just wanna curl up an' disappear… just… just die.'

She squeezes her eyes tight as tears leak out and track down both cheeks. Lakmaker reaches across the desk for a box of tissues and waits in silence as she dries her face.

'Sorry.'

'You've nothing to be sorry about, Jane, but do you often think about killing yourself?'

'When the panic gets to me, life don't seem worth living.'

'Does nothing help with these feelings?'

'Grass.'

'You smoke cannabis?'

She nods.

'How often?'

She shrugs her shoulders. 'Once a day, mostly in the evenin' if I'm not workin'. Stops me thinkin' about bad stuff, helps me sleep without nightmares about… well, you know.'

'Unfortunately, even assuming I wanted to, I can't sanction cannabis as a medication.'

'It works,' she comments.

Lakmaker looks at his patient. She is younger in appearance than her sixteen years, underweight, small in bone structure and, even sitting down, he towers over her. Her legs and arms are thin, her skin pasty white and her face pockmarked with spots. He sees signs of oedema, a slightly distended stomach which is usually a sign of protein malnutrition. He's treated too many children like her, abused, uncared for, starved of a decent diet and of affection.

'I'd prefer you not to smoke cannabis even if it appears to be helping. You're a little under-nourished and I'm going to prescribe a drink that should help build you up to a more normal body weight for your height and age. As far as your anxiety is concerned, the first step is to realise you're in no physical danger at moments when your emotions take control.

'Over the coming weeks, we'll examine the situations that trigger your anxiety. I should be able to teach you ways to relax your muscles and regulate your breathing using special words.

'Going forward, you'll learn how to control those aspects of life that worry you by differentiating between those you're able to manage and those beyond your control.

'I'm going to prescribe you Valium and you should take one tablet three times a day. They'll help ease your anxiety.'

Jane's face is ashen-white. She feels drained and exhausted although strangely liberated. 'Thank you, Doctor, er…'

'Peter, please call me Peter.'

'Thank you, Peter, I'll try an' cut down on the weed.'

'Good. Now, I would like to see you once a week for as long as it takes, which is unlikely to be less than six months. If you see the lady on reception, she'll book a series of weekly consultations at a time to suit us both. I'm conscious of your work commitments.'

He hands her the prescription as she stands and makes ready to leave.

'Give this in at the pharmacy on your way out and please make sure you take the tablets regularly.'

She hesitates a moment before asking one last question. 'You won't tell my parents where I am, will you?' Her eyes widen as she speaks.

'Jane, I promised you everything you tell me will remain within the walls of this consulting room. Legally you're not an adult and your parents ought to be informed of your whereabouts, but I believe your story and as your consultant, I've decided they should not know where you are. Occasionally, rules need to be broken.' He breaks into a reassuring smile.

'But please, only resort to cannabis on those occasions you really feel completely out of control.'

She nods. 'See ya next week then.'

TEN

From: Robin Farnham
To: Dr Lakmaker
Ref. No: 6

That was nasty! No, I have no memory of attacking Penny and I'm sorry I threw up on your carpet. Being called a wife-beater is not easy to take and I'm becoming increasingly concerned over my inability to remember too many incidents from my past.

It feels as if something rooted from way back is trying to force its way into my head. What the hell is it? If I'm capable of hitting the woman I loved, am I also capable of murder?

I don't mind admitting I'm petrified of uncovering the truth, but I don't want to die without knowing what kind of man I really am.

Maybe it will shed light on that period if I explain how Penny's attempted suicide affected me. The situation forced me to take my three-year-old son to Dorset to stay with my parents and my month-old daughter to Penny's parents. I was living alone.

During the weeks she was hospitalised, and before the doctors recommended that she underwent electroconvulsive therapy, the pressure started getting to me. I wasn't making time to eat properly and was drinking too much. After working all day, I would stop off on my way to the hospital for a couple of large whiskies to help me face what I knew was waiting for me there. When I finally made it home after sitting for hours with Penny, the house seemed horribly silent and I would just flop down on the sofa in the living room, turn on the television and drink more, sometimes a lot more.

You see, Doctor, after Jo's rejection, and the tough lessons learned from cousin Robert, I was determined to stand on my own two feet, sort my problems in my own way, but without realising it, I was crumbling.

One evening, I overdid the booze on an empty stomach, fell asleep on the sofa and woke during the night with a God-awful headache. I was shaking uncontrollably and couldn't think straight. I later realised it was a panic attack.

I had never felt so out of control, and it scared me into consulting my GP, who gave me a really hard time over my drinking. He referred me as an urgent case to a psychiatrist in Lewisham Hospital, close to where I was working. You can imagine how that made me feel. Two loonies in the family!

He turned out to be a very good doctor. He encouraged me to express my emotions openly and saw no wrong in a man shedding tears; the complete opposite of my father.

Over a period of months, he taught me how to focus solely on situations within my control. I learned how to accept that if I was unable to change a situation, there was no point worrying or getting anxious over it. There's little doubt he opened my eyes to a new philosophy for life.

I could do nothing about Penny's illness, and I couldn't change the fact that my children were living with their grandparents. But I could get a grip on my performance at work and my drinking.

He prescribed Valium and ordered me to avoid alcohol while taking it. The pills calmed me down, made me less anxious and I stopped drinking for almost a year. His counselling was invaluable although it was complicated by an addiction to Valium, which took me three years and some unpleasant side effects to kick.

Looking back, it's clear I too, was mentally disturbed during that period but the combination of learning a new life philosophy plus coping with a Valium addiction toughened me. I felt more in charge of my life, although it's possible it also made me tougher on those around me. I've struggled since to feel empathy towards those who are incapable of thinking like me, who cannot deal with life's problems the way I do.

But the crucial question is, was I violent towards Penny? Do I even want to know?

MEMO ENDS rf

*

From: Robin Farnham
To: Dr Lakmaker
Ref. No: 7

Of course he smacked her around a bit, she gave him little option, and deserved it; but more of that later. First,

Doc, I need to fill you in on how I dealt with Jo's new boyfriend.

Robin left school in July of '64 and took a summer job with the local accountant before leaving home in late September to live and work in London.

Jo had dumped him the week before he was due to leave and it plunged him into a pathetic, self-pitying melancholy. He couldn't get that bloody girl out of his head.

Her parents' house was at the far end of a no-through road on the edge of town and during those final few days before leaving home, he took to hiding in the field beyond her house, crouching behind a tall hedge, like some kind of weirdo stalker.

Hour after endless bloody hour he hid there, hoping for a glimpse of her. God only knows why. On the final Friday, he spotted the new boyfriend arriving in his fancy blue car. He was weirdly fascinated yet at the same time utterly dejected and an hour later, he watched as they drove off together. Every second tortured him.

For the next two days, the stupid lovesick sod wandered aimlessly around the town, up Wincombe Lane to their 'special' field and to the coffee bar where they used to meet. On the Sunday afternoon, as he was ambling his way home, he spotted the blue car heading east along the A30.

I worked out later the boyfriend must have been staying at Jo's that weekend and this was his route to and from her house.

During those first few weeks in London his depression deepened; no money, dull job, no friends and when he wasn't working, he would sit around all day moping about how much better life would be if he and Jo were still together.

Things improved once he teamed up with Robert and money began flowing, but on the odd occasion he managed to find himself a new woman, no matter how attractive, he was bloody useless. The only one he wanted was Jo.

A week after passing his driving test, he bought his first car and drove to Dorset on that Thursday in October, the evening he found the snake bracelet in the road. He was optimistic he might win her back now he had money in his pocket and drove a smart car.

I was fresh on the scene and had some catching up to do. I watched as he walked the length of the High Street on the Friday afternoon, desperate to see her. As he passed King Alfred's Kitchen, the café where they'd spent so much time together, he spotted her through the steamed-up front window.

She was sitting at what used to be 'their' table with a girlfriend he recognised from her school. He walked into the café and straight to the table. I admired his pluck.

She was surprised to see him and cocked her head to one side as she smiled, the same downward smile she used to give him each time they met. I could feel it shredding him into bits.

'Hiya, Robin, how are you?'

He spoke too quickly. 'I'm fine, Jo, fine, thanks. It's good to see you. How long has it been?' He knew it was exactly thirteen months and three days.

'It must be over a year since you left Dorset. How's life treating you in London?'

'It was… it was difficult to begin with, it's expensive living away from home, specially up there. It took a while to settle.'

'I'm sure it must have but you look as if you're settled now. Love the trendy clothes.'

He thought he sensed warmth in her voice. I sensed something else, an underlying sadness perhaps, but I couldn't put my finger on it.

'Yeah, and I'm home for the weekend and wondered if there was a chance we might have a bite to eat together this evening? You know, for old time's sake. I could pick you up and maybe we could drive to Salisbury?'

Her neck and cheeks flushed crimson, and I could see her struggling for words. 'I'm sorry, Robin, but… I can't, I'm not… I'm already committed. You know how it is. But it's good to see you again and you look like you're doing ever so well.' She smiled that same smile, but now it was somehow different. The warmth was gone and the silence that followed told him everything.

'Yeah, okay. You take care of yourself, Jo. Good seeing you.'

He trudged back to his car and sulked for an hour before it came to me what needed to be done if he was to stand any chance of winning her back.

What he had forgotten but I remembered was the route the boyfriend had taken to Jo's house and there was a better than even chance he would be arriving later that afternoon.

I took over and drove Robin's car back to his parents' house and checked that the old bicycle he used to ride out on his paper round was in the garden shed and still serviceable. The tyres were flat, which was easily sorted, but everything else worked perfectly. I also checked in the saddlebag and found what I was hoping would still be there.

At around 5.30pm, I cycled to the end of Jo's road to see if the blue car was outside her house.

The road was empty, which was what I'd hoped, so I made my way out of town east on the A30 in the direction of Salisbury. After a couple of miles, I dismounted and leaned the bicycle against a hedge at the entrance to a narrow, unmade lane. I reached inside the saddlebag and removed Robin's old wooden-handled catapult from where he'd left it years before.

In the half-light of an autumn dusk, I selected a small round pebble no larger than a child's marble from the gravel on the edge of the lane and eased myself, backside first, into the hedge and crouched down facing the oncoming traffic from the east.

In stark contrast to the snaking streams of traffic choking London's streets, the A30 was like a graveyard that evening. In the ten minutes I squatted in that hedge, one solitary tractor towing a cart dripping with foul-smelling slurry passed by.

It wasn't difficult to spot the pale-blue car through the gloom as it rounded the bend at speed some 150m ahead of me. I gripped the pebble firmly in the leather pouch, raised the catapult and drew the vulcanised rubber back as far as its tension allowed.

The windscreen on a 1960s Austin A40 was frighteningly vulnerable in comparison with those on modern cars. Projected from a distance of some twenty yards, the stone slammed into the glass like a bullet, fracturing the screen into a spider's web of opaque, interlaced cracks.

The driver could have seen nothing as his car veered sharply to the right across the oncoming lane. The front wheels mounted the grass verge and the car lifted off the road. A split second later, it slammed head-on into a large oak tree towering over the small triangle of grass by the roadside.

He would have died the instant the tree trunk rammed the engine block through the dashboard and the steering wheel into his chest. Few people wore seat belts in those days.

The only sound breaking the silence was steam hissing from a broken radiator. I remounted the bicycle and took a leisurely ride through the back lanes to Robin's parents' house.

I'm not convinced I intended to kill the guy. I just wanted him out of the picture, although maybe it had to be that way if Robin was to win Jo back.

What I hadn't accounted for was Robin never learning of the fatal accident, so he didn't call her to offer sympathy or ask her out again.

Now, as I'm in the mood for giving you a few home truths, Doc, I'd better bring you up to speed on what happened with Penny in the days leading up to her attempted suicide.

Robin was working his balls off in his new job, twelve hours a day, and all she did was moan about how difficult her life was.

Bloody hell, only a year before he had agreed to sell their house in the middle of the Kent countryside and move to the suburban jungle of inner Essex so she could be near her parents and siblings. He loathed the bloody place but did it for her, to make her happy. Still she complained about being on her own, and missing the people she used to work with. Day after bloody day.

To my mind, Robin showed the patience of a saint but finally lost it earlier the same week she attempted suicide, although it was a shock to both of us when she tried to kill herself. I was never convinced it was a genuine attempt.

She was an attention seeker who sought to make him feel guilty about working long hours and not spending more time at home.

MEMO ENDS rf

*

Robin slams the laptop shut and rubs tired, scratchy eyes. How long has he been writing this stuff? It seems like days.

A chilling thought flashes through his mind.

What if Lakmaker is doing nothing other than collecting evidence for the police to build a case against him? Wife-beating suggests an aggressive nature, one capable of murder. He never once thought of himself as aggressive. He's never been aggressive.

He worries Lakmaker is screwing up what little remains of his life. He deserves better, to end his days in peace, with Lucy, Giles and Katie. He sinks back into the chair, his hands resting flat on the arms, and sighs deeply.

Should some chapters in our lives stay hidden forever? Are there some corners in all our lives destined to remain forever dark?

His problem is he's now desperate to find out what in his past is hidden from him.

ELEVEN

'So did you also murder the Brigadier?' Lakmaker is in the process of settling himself down opposite Robin and his expression is vaguely aggressive although he is speaking softly, his voice barely audible.

'What d'you mean?' Robin's brow furrows.

'Well, you've admitted assaulting Penny and deliberately causing the accident that killed Jo's lover, so I presume you also took revenge on the man who cheated you at the poker table.'

'What the hell are you talking about? I did nothing of the sort.'

Lakmaker is clearly startled by the abrupt response and hands Robin two typewritten sheets which he reads. Frantically, he fires up the laptop, his hands shaking visibly as he reads the exact same words on the screen as he has this moment seen on paper.

'I didn't write this nonsense. Something's wrong here.'

'What time did you sit up writing until last night?'

'How would I know? My watch is gone and there's no

clock in here. Even the date and time on this computer have been disabled.'

'You were writing well into the small hours of this morning.'

'If you bloody well know what time I sat up until, why ask?' Lakmaker allows the question to hang in the air and sits motionless, staring at his patient.

Robin slumps back in the armchair, squeezes his eyes shut and struggles to retrieve memories of the previous evening. Nothing is clear so he turns back to the computer and flicks the mouse with his index finger to bring the penultimate memo up on screen.

'I certainly wrote the memo before, about my addiction to Valium, but I did not write this last one. You must believe me. Look, it's written in the third person, it's about me, not by me.'

'Yes, it is.'

Old-age confusion is like an amoeba. A minute cell of uncertainty feeding on the fear it generates and, in time, distending to a bloated mass crushing every shred of sanity. Robin shakes his head from side to side like a shaggy dog emerging from the sea.

'Someone must have borrowed this laptop while I was asleep or… or it's been hacked into. I did *not* write this. Oh, shit, have the police read it?'

'I made you a promise, Robin.'

'These are not my words in this memo. I did not assault Penny and I would never cause the death of another human being, no matter how much I disliked them.'

Lakmaker is making notes at pace. Robin wonders why he bothers; his mobile is on the table, the recording light blinking as it marks the passage of both their lives. He must be collecting evidence.

'If you're recording our conversations, I'm bloody certain you must have a CCTV set-up in this room, too.'

The doctor looks up towards the wall behind Robin, who turns to see a tiny camera mounted in the corner, tight up against the ceiling and painted the same pale green as the wall.

'The camera confirms the time you finished writing and the laptop's connection to our main server tells me you retired to bed immediately after finishing that last memo. The one you claim you didn't write.'

'Someone's doctored what I've written, changed it to incriminate me. I'm *not* a killer. I'm *not* a wife-beater.' Robin's fists thump the arms of his chair with such power, clouds of dust drift upwards with each beat.

'Robin, I kept an eye on the CCTV monitor all evening and simultaneously tracked what you were typing on the server. I assure you; you wrote that memo.'

Robin runs the fingers of his right hand through his thin grey hair. His voice lacks any of its old confidence. 'Doctor, I want to go home. I want to enjoy what little time is left to me. I… I don't understand what's happening. If you tell me that you saw me write this memo, I ought to believe you. But the truth is, I don't because I know I didn't write it.'

He stares at Lakmaker, eyes pleading like they've never pleaded before in his lifetime. The doctor nods. 'Robin, I too believe that you believe it wasn't you who wrote the memo. However, it's equally clear from what I saw on CCTV, that you did write it.'

'Maybe I was hallucinating. Perhaps it's all down to this new drug you're giving me?'

Lakmaker moves his lips around in that odd way people sometimes do when weighing up how much they think they need to tell you.

'As you're aware, Robin, it's a common symptom for those in the intermediate stages of Alzheimer's to develop unfounded suspicions that those around them are plotting against them or accusing them of various crimes. Sufferers sometimes hear or see things that aren't there.'

Robin leans forward as he speaks. 'So, could this be a symptom of my Alzheimer's? Could I imagine I committed murder because the police suspect me of it which, in turn, prompts me to write a memo admitting my guilt? What else am I imagining? Are you real? Are the police waiting to charge me with murder real or are they also a figment of my diseased brain?'

'No, Robin, what you see is real, but a second possibility is the experimental drug we're prescribing is causing you to hallucinate.'

'Then take me off the bloody drug.'

'If you're happy about that, it's what we'll do. It'll be a pity though; I believe it's managing your symptoms well.'

Now he has a dilemma. Does he want to prolong useful life taking this drug or throw in the towel and accept his fate?

'No, if there is a possibility the drug is helping me, it makes sense to continue. I can't die without knowing the truth. I have to know.' He slumps back in the chair. 'What happens next?'

'We continue talking, you continue writing and I'll monitor what you write, as you write it. Maybe then we'll get to the bottom of what prompted you to admit to committing murder and assaulting your first wife.'

Robin shuts his eyes and rubs both eyelids with his right thumb and forefinger. Somehow it brings respite. He then moves to speak before Lakmaker has the time to ask yet another question.

'Look, if as you're watching me, you notice me writing in the third person, admitting something you think is out of character, please come in and interrupt me. I need to know what's going on inside my head at that moment.'

'So do I, Robin, which is why I intend to do just that.' Lakmaker pauses a moment and looks down at his notes. Robin is wary; he recognises this as a sign the doctor is about to open a new line of questioning.

'According to my notes, in February '84 you left Penny and your two children and moved into a flat in Surrey.'

'I did,' is the abrupt reply.

'Had you... had you perhaps, met someone else?'

'I most certainly had not,' he retorts sharply, a look of anger on his face.

'So why did you leave?'

'Jesus Christ, why have we got to dig all that up? It can't have any relevance on whether or not I wrote that bloody memo.'

Lakmaker is unmoved by his patient's outburst. 'I need to know what it was that made you leave the family home. It was more trauma, wasn't it?'

Robin's eyelids lower as he emits a long sigh. 'After Penny underwent ECT in '75, she seemed cured. She was again the happy, gregarious woman I'd fallen in love with and for something like seven years, our family life was on an even keel.

'But her condition started to deteriorate early in 1982 and over the course of that year, she just... well, she just slowly disappeared back inside her schizophrenia. It sort of consumed her. She avoided going out, lunches and supper parties at home with friends and siblings stopped, and most days were wasted sitting on the sofa staring aimlessly at a blank wall.'

'Do you have any idea why the illness returned, what might have triggered it?'

Robin swallows hard, aware the answer to this question has haunted him for years. 'I think,' he says softly, before drawing a deep breath, 'it may have been linked to my decision to give up my secure, well-paid job with an established publisher and gamble everything on launching my own business.'

'She would have preferred you not to have gone out on your own?'

He nods, then looks away and makes no further comment. A pause follows, and the silence prompts a further question from the doctor. 'Are you uncomfortable discussing this, Robin?'

He doesn't respond.

'Would you prefer to write about it?'

Still no answer.

'Robin, I need you to write about this period. It's clear you underwent a period of intense trauma and your ability to recall the details will tell us a great deal about how the drug is managing your condition.'

Silence.

'I'll leave you alone to think it over.' The doctor stands and makes his way to the door.

'You know, Robin, we've all gone through tough periods in our lives, times when perhaps we may have got things wrong, made bad decisions. Sometimes writing things down, getting the facts straight in one's head, can ease a deeply rooted guilt that has gnawed at our conscience for years.'

With that, he quietly closes the door behind him.

Robin mouths an obscenity.

TWELVE

'Today, Jane, I would like you to concentrate on what thoughts, if any, were going through your mind during those moments your father was abusing you.' Sitting alongside his patient, Lakmaker is speaking slowly and sensitively. 'Or were you, perhaps, able to blank out what was happening to you?'

'When he hit me or... or the sex thing?'

'The sexual abuse,' Lakmaker confirms, his voice barely louder than a whisper.

It has taken eight consultations for Jane to really trust him. He is a man, and she is uncomfortably familiar with what men are capable of. She now accepts he is different; he listens and is non-judgmental, and during her periods of anxiety, allows her breathing space, time to calm herself.

He in turn is pleased that she now acknowledges there was nothing she could have done to avoid her father's abuse so there is no reason for her to feel shame. He has taught her to focus on relaxing her mind and body during periods of anxiety using deep breathing techniques, and by slowly repeating the word 'calm'.

He then encouraged her to place herself in situations almost certain to arouse anxiety, such as entering a café full of workmen. She was initially reluctant to court such danger but the doctor persevered until, at the close of the fifth consultation, she agreed to confront her demons.

Her attempt ended the moment she hurled a plastic ketchup bottle across the café at a sweaty giant of a man moistening his lips as he eyed her up and down. She left the place screaming abuse and her body burning with shame. Two further sessions with Lakmaker were needed before she could summon the courage for a second attempt.

Uncomfortable feelings bubbled like pools of hot mud the moment she opened the door to Ted's Snack Bar on Praed Street, three streets down from the hospital. A haze of cigarette smoke floated languidly above the raucous alpha-male chat that paused for a second as a dozen or more seemingly malevolent, grimy-handed men looked in her direction.

Her breathing grew shallow and beads of sweat oozed through the pores on her forehead. For a full minute, she was riveted to a spot immediately inside the entrance, before summoning sufficient courage to walk self-consciously towards the counter, silently mouthing the word 'calm.' A fat man in a grease-stained apron asked what he could get her.

'Tea, please,' she whispered, swallowing hard to ease an urge to retch.

'Milk and sugar?'

'Just milk.' Mild relief washed over her as she spotted an empty table where she could sit with her back to the wall, facing outwards.

Her eyes leapt nervously from one unshaven face to another. None was her adoptive father. None even looked like him. That didn't mean they weren't abusive. Some would have daughters, maybe adopted, uncared for, abused. With her mind more tangled than a bramble in a hedgerow, she surrendered to the urge for a smoke. She began rolling a cigarette of tobacco, no weed this time. It was a fortnight since her last spliff, an encouraging milestone, she told herself. Trembling, uncoordinated fingers spewed tobacco over the table.

'Give it 'ere, luv. I'll do it for ya or you'll end up chuckin' it all over the caff.'

Her head snapped to the left. She stared into the stubbled face of a large man in a grimy shirt with a neck as wide as his head. Her eyes flicked from dirty fingernails to the brown patches of sweat under his arms and she bit her bottom lip so hard she thought it might bleed.

Without thinking, she passed him the pouch and box of Rizlas and ten fingers and thumbs, each the size of a small banana, contorted to deliver a perfectly rolled cigarette.

'Thanks,' she croaked and drew deeply on the cigarette as the man held a steady match to it.

'You all right, luv?'

As nicotine drenched her lungs and began working its magic, she managed to reply, 'Yeah, yes, thanks.'

Revealing intuition beyond his pay grade he reassured her, 'You ain't got no need to be afraid of this lot. Wouldn't 'urt a fly, none of 'em.'

'That's... that's good to know.'

'You 'ad problems wiv blokes then?'

'Sort of.'

'Yeah well, there's too many nasty buggers out there. If it was down to me, I'd stick them fuckin' paedophiles up aginst a wall and shoot 'em.'

Jane squeezed half a smile as she picked a small piece of tobacco from her bottom lip. 'I could do with someone shooting my father.' Why on earth did she tell him that? More bubbling panic.

'Yer old man touch you up, did 'e?'

'And some.'

'Bastard. You still living wiv 'im?'

'No.'

'D'ya tell the law?'

'Can't be bothered. Just glad I'm shot of 'im.'

'Shit 'appens, luv, it 'appens ev'rywhere unless you was born wiv a silver spoon in yer mouf.'

'Yeah, s'pose it does.'

'Lost me mum when I was eight. Me father fucked off, me elder sister wouldn't 'ave me so I was put in a 'ome. Them bastards abused me for years, couldn't begin to tell ya what they done to me. But I knew once I was on me own, I'd 'ave to put it all behind me, forget it and get on wiv me life, otherwise I'd end up in the loony bin.'

Jane relaxed enough to offer a sympathetic smile.

'My motto is,' he continued, 'whatever shit they frows at ya, you just gotta block it. Never let 'em beat you.' His broad, stubby-toothed smile pitched unexpected warmth in Jane's direction.

'Thanks,' she whispered nervously. 'I'm grateful.'

'Fink nuffin' of it, luv.' The big man turned back to his mates and Jane overheard one ask, 'You chattin' 'er up, Phil?'

'Fuck off, Eddie. You're a bleedin' animal, you are.'

For five minutes, Jane endured her discomfort before checking her watch to find it was nearly time for her appointment with Lakmaker. She stubbed the cigarette out in an overflowing ashtray, drained her cup and stood to leave.

'Mind 'ow ya go, luv, won't you?'

'Yeah, I will,' she assured him.

'An' don't let them bastards get to ya,' he called after her as she opened the door.

Now, of all things, having made it to the hospital on time and in the relative peace and security of Lakmaker's consulting room, the doctor is asking her to relive the nightmare of what was going through her mind each time the dirty bastard rammed his filthy dick in her mouth.

The nice man in the café told her to block shit out yet the doctor wants her to dig it all up again. A numbing coldness seeps into her bones, the same feeling that used to overwhelm her as her adoptive father walked ever closer each Thursday evening.

'I don't wanna relive it; I wanna put it behind me. Forget it.'

'Jane, if you bury these memories, you'll never have faced up to them, confronted them.'

'Why confront them, it's like... like scratchin' ol' wounds.'

'To a certain extent perhaps, but it'll also help you come to terms with what happened, accept there is nothing you can do to change the past. It'll make it easier to move on without the past continually returning to haunt you.'

'Maybe I don't wanna move on, not until I've 'ad me revenge anyway.'

'Revenge would solve nothing and would land you in serious trouble.'

Jane turns the doctor's last comment over in her mind. It was fortunate the attack on her father was never reported, although she struggles to believe she would be prosecuted if the truth came out. Perhaps she should confront the enormity of the abuse lest it diminishes with time. Better to bide her time until the moment for revenge presents itself.

'Okay, have it your way, but the thing is, I don't remember thinkin' anything… except for the last time.'

'What were you thinking on that occasion?'

'Going through my plan to kill the filthy bastard. For weeks, I'd practised reaching for that iron bar under the blanket on my bed without him noticing. I rehearsed bending my right knee so the foot was flat on the ground for balance, and the toes of my left foot bent forward ready to push me up as I slammed the bar into his head.'

Lakmaker saw a weak smile cross Jane's face.

'So you *did* plan to murder him?'

'Yeah!' She spits out the one-word answer.

'But you didn't go through with it?'

'Could 'ave if I'd wanted. Could 'ave finished him off while he was lyin' there, but the police would have come after me. Just wanted out of the place.'

'Do you regret not killing him?'

'No, not then.'

'How do you mean?'

'I don't regret not killin' 'im then 'cos it suited.'

'Do you still have thoughts of murdering him?'

'I kill the fuckwit every night, moments before I go to sleep.'

THIRTEEN

From: Robin Farnham
To: Dr Lakmaker
Ref. No: 8

There was a period during my mid-thirties when the gambler inside made its presence felt again. Life had become too comfortable; I was successful and earning good money, but I craved the adrenalin rush of launching my own publishing business.

I discussed the idea with Penny on several occasions but each time she dismissed it out of hand, telling me not to be stupid. 'Why would you want to do that? You've a secure well-paid job where you are.'

Her misgivings highlighted a widening gulf between our mindsets and in our relationship. She had reached a point in her life where change served no purpose other than to create risk and disruption, whereas I was spending more time working and less at home without any good reason other than the one provided the stimulation I lacked from the other. I figured setting up a new business from home would satisfy my need for a fresh challenge and in the process, might possibly restore a normal family life.

In the autumn of 1982, I resigned my senior role in a successful publishing company and the following January set up my own business. I admit it was one hell of a risk, what with two young children and a hefty mortgage, but I was conscious if I didn't take the plunge before turning forty, I probably never would.

Some might argue, and with justification, that it was a selfish move but even now, well into my dotage and with the benefit of hindsight, I would take the same decision again.

Within a matter of weeks, Penny's mental condition seemed to deteriorate. Was it the loss of the fat salary and executive car or the insecurity of self-employment that triggered the decline? Her father remained with the same company throughout his working life so it was possible Penny may well have preferred me to pursue a similar, safer career path.

The troubled mind that led her to attempt suicide almost eight years earlier returned and by the end of the year, her schizophrenia had all but shut everyone out, including the kids and me. Life at home was intolerable.

Most evenings, once the children were in bed or in their rooms doing their homework, the two of us would share supper, taken for the most part in stony silence. If she spoke, it was only to falsely accuse me of having an affair with one of several women outworkers involved in my business.

She rarely left the house, refusing even to drive the children to school. They walked, regardless of the weather, unless I was on hand to take them. Infrequent shopping trips were made at times of the day she was least likely to meet anyone she knew. If she did see anyone, she would cross the road to avoid speaking with them.

I begged her to seek help, reminded her how ECT had cured her illness eight years before. I promised to organise everything, make appointments, take time off to be with her whenever necessary.

Her reaction was always the same. 'There's nothing wrong with me, I'm not ill, I don't need help and I'm not going back to that hospital.'

What was once the happiest of family homes, rich in love and laughter, had become hollowed out, indigent and, for me at least, potent with the dread of what it was doing to our children.

Discontentment is a personal state, often selfish, I'll grant you, yet I'm convinced my overriding concern was for their future rather than my own. That situation changed for the worse early in 1984 when my health began to suffer. A month in hospital with pneumonia and the loss of my spleen convinced me I had no alternative but to leave, as much for my sake as for the kids. Two sick parents was not a great idea.

Early in the afternoon of my discharge from hospital, Penny and I sat side by side in our living room. The transformation in my once-gorgeous wife's appearance stunned me; she'd lost a third of her body weight, her face was pale and drawn, blemished with unsightly spots, and her eyes seemed to stare straight through me, glassy, unseeing.

'Penny, we can't continue living like this. What's happened to you, to my gorgeous, gregarious wife, the woman I fell in love with, the party girl who loved to dance all night? You're a fabulous hostess, a great cook and our friends love you but... but you don't want to see them anymore.'

I was speaking quietly, slowly repeating words I'd rehearsed lying in hospital. How much of what I said was sinking in was impossible to fathom.

'You lock yourself away in this house all day long and won't see anyone. You're worrying the life out of me, and our constant arguing is the wrong environment in which to bring up Giles and Katie. What's changed?'

She answered in her own time. 'Everyone changes as they get older. We're all different and I don't need that stuff anymore.'

'Why not?' I asked. 'You were the one who always insisted on keeping in touch with friends.'

'I'm not like that now. There's nothing wrong with me, I'm not ill; I just want to be at home, away from people looking at me, wanting to know our business. They're watching all the time. I'm safe in this house with our family. We don't need anyone else.'

'For God's sake...' My patience was draining like blood from a punctured artery. 'The way you are now is destroying our family. For the sake of our marriage, for our kids, please see the doctor. He can help you.'

'I'm not talking about it *anymore*.' She turned and stared through the French windows into the grey gloom of the February afternoon.

'Penny, if you don't phone the doctor now, this minute, you leave me no choice. I'm moving out of this house tomorrow – you're forcing me to leave you.'

Her response was delusional, unreal. 'Don't be stupid, you're not leaving, this is our home. You belong here.'

'Then please see the doctor,' I shouted.

'There's nothing wrong with me, don't keep saying that. I don't need a doctor – for God's sake, shut up. I can't take this anymore.'

'If that's the way it is, Penny, you leave me no option. I'll have to tell the kids this evening that we're separating.'

For what was left of the afternoon, my head was scrambled with my fear of the damage I was about to inflict on my kids. Was there any way I'd not thought of that might persuade her to seek treatment? Would leaving have even crossed my mind had she been suffering a physical illness such as cancer? Almost certainly not. Madness challenges all rational thought.

Afternoon dimmed to evening and as supper drew to its close, my hands were trembling as sweat pricked my forehead and white noise filled my ears. What would my leaving do to eleven-year-old Giles, his soft face boyishly handsome, fine blond hair tumbling over his forehead above blue eyes wide with trust? And to Katie, my impossibly gorgeous eight-year-old tiny replica of her once-beautiful mother, a constant reminder of Penny's prematurely faded beauty. What scars would tonight leave?

'Mummy and I need talk to you about something very sad.'

The sound of my voice was barely recognisable, even to me, and I ached for it to be over quickly.

'Mummy and I have been… have… some bad news. You may have sensed that… that there have been a lot of rows and we've not been getting on very well lately. Well… sadly, we've decided we can no longer live happily together in the same house. I'm afraid I have to leave, and from tomorrow, I will be living in another house.'

I vainly hoped my words might have been anticipated, maybe understood, forgiven even. But they were children, loving kids desperate for nothing other than the security and continuity of their parents living with them. For a moment, their faces showed impassive disbelief.

Speaking simple words, I tried to explain how the atmosphere in the house was unhealthy and damaging for us all and how my leaving would put an end to the arguments. 'We both love you so much and always will, but sadly Mummy and I will no longer be here together. You can stay with me at weekends, or as often as you like, and your friends can…'

Giles could take no more; his shocked, accusing eyes leaked tears as he rushed from the room, venting a fractured scream no parent should ever hear from any child, let alone their own. He ran upstairs and I heard him lock himself in the lavatory, yelling at the top of his voice, pleading for what he had just heard not to be true.

Little Katie stared reproachfully at me before turning to her mother, eyes glistening, bulbous with tears. Tiny shoulders heaved as she too left the room and headed towards the stairs, convulsing with each breath.

Penny stared straight through me, her expression an unsettling mix of fear and anger. 'You selfish bastard.'

'I'm sorry,' were the only words I could think to say as I too staggered upstairs to my office and gazed blankly out through the window into February's blackness.

Later, I crept into Katie's room and lay beside her, hoping she may have found relief in sleep. As I slipped an arm underneath her head and held her close, her slow rhythmic sobbing beat against my chest. Neither of us had any words left. How much hate would she store in her heart for me?

Later still, I heard Giles unlock the lavatory door and dart into the sanctuary of his bedroom. The door slammed noisily. Little point in following; there were no words left that might help. As Katie's muffled sobs settled into sleep's steady breathing, I kissed her forehead and returned downstairs to Penny.

She was perched on the edge of the soft-brown sofa we had been so excited about choosing five years earlier. I cast my eyes around our sitting room of bold, brown-patterned carpet, brown furniture and gold, Regency-styled wallpaper that had somehow distorted into outdated 1970s Essex chic. It had been Penny's choice, and only later did it occur to me it was perhaps chosen to suit her state of mind.

Aimlessly, she picked at the loose skin on the back of her hand with her thumb and index finger, eyes trained at the wall, glazed, unblinking. Everything that needed saying had been said.

After a night endured on the sofa bed in my tiny office, I awoke startled out of a dream in which I was in court accused of an unknown crime and friends, work colleagues and family appeared in turn as witnesses for the prosecution. The judge asked each witness in turn if I was a good man, a diligent and honest man. Was I the sort to abandon my children? I could not hear their answers, or if I did, I cannot remember them.

I skipped breakfast and drove an obdurately unresponsive Giles and Katie to school before packing my work stuff and as much clothing and bedding as could reasonably be squeezed into an average-sized family car and for the second time in my life, left home.

MEMO ENDS rf

*

'That was a dramatic change in your circumstances, Robin,' Lakmaker suggests as he walks into the room little more than seconds after Robin finished writing.

Robin gazes into the middle distance and smiles at the sound of the blackbird singing in the beech tree. Why is its song so comforting?

It was all such a long time ago, thirty-six years, half a lifetime, and yet he can picture himself living alone in the wretched flat he rented as vividly as if it were yesterday. It was on the top-floor of a twelve-storey tower block in Surrey, less than 100m from his new offices. The estate agent described it as a desirable penthouse apartment offering comfortable living with outstanding views over the Surrey Hills. In reality, it was little more than a damp, cold, concrete box overlooking a tiny shopping mall in a neglected part of Wallington. A fleeting testament to the arrogance of 1950s architecture that was quietly demolished a few years later to make way for a Sainsbury's supermarket. Progress of a dubious kind.

It came part-furnished, and he gave it a semblance of personality and warmth for Giles' and Katie's sake with pieces of second-hand furniture bought through advertisements posted in local shop windows.

He rarely cooked, happier spending evenings in the steak house on the parade below, where he could continue working while the jovial team of chefs and waiters cared for him.

Dr Lakmaker reminds Robin he is expecting an answer.

He turns to look at the doctor. 'I don't recall feeling depressed about the break-up, if that's what you're asking. My only emotion was a sense of relief I no longer lived inside the bubble of my wife's psychosis. Don't forget, I'd had a year to get used to the idea the marriage was falling apart.'

'What about your children? I'm told they spent most weekends with you?'

'That was no hardship, I was desperate to maintain a close relationship with them. Every Friday, I'd happily collect them from Essex and return them each Sunday evening. Time spent in the car, often well over two hours in rush-hour traffic, was precious. They chatted nonstop about school, their friends, how they were feeling about… my situation and their mother.'

'And how was that?'

'On the surface, Giles seemed pretty much okay, certainly at that stage—'

Lakmaker interrupts Robin's hesitation. 'Are you happy to continue talking about this?'

He nods although he has mixed feelings about reviving emotions from what now seems a different lifetime. 'I think Giles was beginning to understand why I'd found it impossible living with his mother. Katie was different. On Fridays, leaving her mother ripped her apart and on Sundays, she'd sob as she was leaving me. Her parents not living together upset her deeply.'

'When and where did you meet Lucy?'

Again, Robin hesitates. 'Is all this *really* necessary?' he protests.

'Robin, day-to-day monitoring of the speed with which you recall events from your past tells us how effectively the new drug is managing your Alzheimer's.'

Robin is wrestling with the probability that this is just another one of Lakmaker's deceits, convinced this so-called doctor is merely probing for more evidence to incriminate him. But he is also aware the only likelihood of his being permitted a visit from Lucy is by giving him what he wants.

'We met at a party at an acquaintance's flat in October '84, eight months after I'd left Penny. I was in the kitchen pouring myself a glass of wine and heard other guests greet her arrival. I turned to look in the direction of the voices and… and saw this woman standing in the doorway and I was instinctively, almost magnetically, attracted to her.

'She was tiny, little more than five foot tall, dark, almost black hair, high cheekbones, gentle eyes and an easy smile from a sidelong glance that quickly broke into an infectious giggle as she spoke.' Robin pauses to draw breath, instinctively smiling at the memory. 'She was wearing pale-blue dungarees although, I somehow recall, she later insisted they were white.'

'I sense this was a special time for you.'

'Very special. Love at first sight.'

'Really?' Lakmaker's eyes widen as he raises both eyebrows.

'Yeah! Overnight, she transformed me into a stupid crazy-in-love teenager again. It was so sudden, the intensity, the needing to be with her, talk with her, discover her likes and dislikes. Within a matter of days, I knew we'd spend the rest of our lives together.'

'It didn't cross your mind you might have been on the rebound from the breakdown of your marriage?'

The doctor's suggestion strikes Robin as insensitive. He, too, must have fallen in love during his life. Robin turns towards the blonde woman staring out from the photograph on the bookshelf and shakes his head.

'I cannot conceive that you haven't, at one time or another, instinctively fallen in love. That split second you set eyes on someone for the first time and somehow sense a positive energy between the two of you.'

A strained silence hangs in the air for a moment as Robin loses himself in thought. 'You know, a Frenchman once wrote that love doesn't consist of gazing at each other, but in looking outward together in the same direction. I knew in that instant we were two people searching for the same things out of life.'

Lakmaker takes his time writing a note. 'Do you think this might have been a connection you never found with your first wife?'

Robin closes his eyes. 'Very possibly.'

'What was Lucy's situation at the time you met?'

He pauses. 'She'd recently divorced a cheating husband and was living on her own.'

'How did your children react?'

A second pause. 'At first they seemed okay, on the surface anyway.'

'On the surface?'

Robin's breathing becomes erratic, and he knows why. His heartbeat is pounding as he struggles for words. 'Do we... must we carry on with this?'

'Face your demons, Robin, face them head-on.'

Robin is angry. Doctors shouldn't speak this way to their patients. Is he even a doctor?

'It's not relevant.' His body is now as still as stone, his mind focused on slowing his breathing, regulating his heartbeat. Lakmaker realises what his patient is doing and waits.

When he finally speaks, Robin is wide-eyed, and his fists are clenched in his frustration. 'Look, it was a new beginning. I'd hoped to rebuild my family, a fresh start for the kids and me, but I misjudged it. I got some of it wrong and it's best left where it is.'

'I'd like to know what it was you got wrong, Robin.' Suddenly, Lakmaker's face has turned ugly, a gargoyle glaring disapprovingly from on high.

'Lucy and I bought a house together in the summer of '85 and Katie met a girl the same age living a few doors further up the road. The two became inseparable, long Saturdays at the riding stables and frequent sleepovers. Weekends were fun again. It couldn't have worked out better.'

'And?' Lakmaker isn't giving up.

Robin knows the doctor will wait for as long as it takes for an answer. He breathes deeply, hoping for more oxygen to slow his heart rate and ease the tightness in his throat. 'I was wonderfully happy, so happy that even now it makes me emotional. The problem, the awful problem was I couldn't give my kids the comfort and security of a normal family life.'

'Why was that?'

'A whole bunch of reasons. Look, this is ancient bloody history, it's gone, forgotten. I screwed up, okay? Just forget it.'

'But how did you screw up, Robin?'

The old man's breathing accelerates, short breaths, half-controlled at first but growing faster, more irregular. His cheeks burn and blood pulsates through his temples.

He swallows hard. 'I'm not going to talk about it. It's not relevant. None of it has anything to do with whether or not I'm a murderer.'

'I'm not so sure you're right about that!'

All of a sudden, Robin explodes. 'What in God's name do you mean by that?' He stands more quickly than he has this past ten years, outstretched arms whirling frantically above his head like those of a drowning man. His mind turns somersaults as flashes of a migraine aura cloud his peripheral vision.

'Leave me alone. FUCKING LEAVE ME ALONE.' His voice spirals into a scream and from nowhere, the two male nurses dash through the door and pin his arms tightly to his sides, forcing him back into the chair.

A peculiar sensation now begins to consume him. His conscious mind is leaving his body, floating upwards over the chairs and table, above the nurses pinning him down. He looks down on them as if watching a movie. He exists in two places at the same time.

He watches as his body struggles to break free from the nurses, but they restrain him as Lakmaker forces an oxygen mask over his mouth and nose. They pin him in the chair, softly encouraging him to take deep draughts of oxygen.

Lakmaker raises Robin's shirtsleeve and inserts a hypodermic needle into his arm. He feels no sharp prick but hears a voice, distant, as if through cotton wool. It is the doctor's. 'I'm sorry, Robin, I shouldn't have pushed you so hard. This'll calm you. You'll quickly drift off to sleep.'

It isn't quick, it's immediate, and blessedly, as he slips into a dreamless sleep, he senses he is slowly easing back into his own lifeless form.

*

It seems only a matter of seconds before his eyelids open again, although the fog in his brain suggests he's been unconscious for some time. He feels surprisingly refreshed, his muscles loose, relaxed. Lakmaker is opposite, watching warily.

'Something weird happened as the nurses restrained me, Doctor. My brain seemed to separate from my body and float upwards. I hovered above you. I've just had an out-of-body experience.'

Lakmaker leans in closer. 'At what point in our conversation did the separation start?'

'Shortly after I lost my temper and began shouting.'

'Have you ever experienced anything like this before?'

'Not that real. Odd occasions at work when I lost my rag with someone, it seemed I was almost watching the conversation as a spectator.'

'But it only happened at work?'

'Think so, but then I spent most of my adult life working.'

Lakmaker riffles through the pile of papers in front of him before picking one up to read. 'It says here, Robin, that your wife is convinced that throughout your life, work gave you greater satisfaction than your home life. She describes you in old age as a retired but slightly frustrated workaholic. Do you agree with her?'

'Up to a point, yes, but with Lucy, our home and work lives merged, we worked together for over twenty-five years building the business.'

'But the company went through a traumatic period in the early '90s, causing you both a great deal of distress, didn't it?'

'Yeah, it did. Almost destroyed us.' It dawns on Robin where this conversation is heading.

He nods, resigned yet again to do the doctor's bidding. 'That's a lot of writing.'

'Not talking?'

'There's no way I can sit here and talk you through it all. To this day, I'm not sure I believe it. Yeah, writing it, getting it straight inside my head… maybe it'll help one of us anyway.'

FOURTEEN

Six weeks after her first consultation with Lakmaker, Jane returned to the bedsit on Westbourne Terrace to be greeted by her flatmate Julian with the news she'd been dreading. He and his boyfriend had made the decision to set up home together, which left Jane happy for them both but in need of a cheaper place to live.

Through an advertisement in the *Evening Standard*, she found a shared room in a boarding house in Colville Terrace, a short walk from Notting Hill. The rent was just about manageable and included breakfast and dinner five days a week and the location meant she could remain in her job at McDonald's, a short ten-minute ride away on a No. 27 bus.

She was apprehensive about sharing a room with a stranger, but it was safer than sleeping rough. As it turned out, she and Monica Liscombe hit it off straight away. A year older than Jane, fresh-faced, slightly taller and stockier with natural blonde hair cropped around her ears, she was habitually dressed in black jeans and dark T-shirts in sharp contrast to Jane's preference for brighter colours.

The two differed in other ways. Monica was openly friendly, easy to talk with and enthusiastically tactile, whereas Jane was reserved, almost withdrawn and shunned physical contact. They shared a love of weed and Monica introduced her roommate to the joys of cheap white wine on those occasions when collective finances stretched to such a luxury.

Jane was beginning to enjoy the positive therapy of mixing with someone her own age and gender who knew nothing of her past. That is, until the evening when the bitter cold of January and a layer of frost on the inside of the window of their unheated basement bedroom prompted Monica to suggest they huddle together in a single bed and share hot water bottles to keep warm.

Both teenagers were on their backs, side by side, and surprisingly, Jane found close contact with someone other than in anger or lechery a reassuring experience.

'Sometimes, I look at you, Jane, an' all I see is sadness,' Monica commented. 'Are you a sad person?'

'Not as sad as I used to be.'

'You don't talk about yourself much, do you?'

'Not much to talk about.'

'Are your parents still alive?'

'Far as I know.'

'That all you wanna say?'

'Well, you tell me about yours,' Jane replied defensively.

'I grew up in the West Midlands with me mum, dad and older brother. Everything was great 'til I got chucked out of school at sixteen.'

'What d'you do?'

'Stole a car.'

'What for?'

'For fun, I s'pose.'

'Were you caught?'

'Yeah, but my dad's a police inspector so he sorted it out, but he made me leave home and get a job in London.'

'Bit harsh.'

'Yeah, he reckoned it'd be better if I left town, for him an' me.'

'D'you miss your mum and dad?'

'Not really. Better this way.'

'What, without family?'

'Yeah, I can get on with life as I want. What about you?'

'I'm adopted.'

'D'ya see your parents much?'

'Nope.'

'You have a row or something?'

'Don't ever wanna see 'em again.'

'Oh, did you do something bad too?'

'Yeah.'

'Go on then, I told you about me.'

In the anonymity of an unlit room and absence of eye contact, Jane found her roommate's inquisitiveness less intrusive than she might have expected and, over the ensuing twenty minutes, described the horror of her childhood and the attack on her father. Monica remained silent throughout, struck dumb by the awfulness of what she was hearing.

By the time a combination of tiredness and the bottle of Spanish white wine enjoyed earlier pitched them into an easy sleep, a heavy weight had lifted from Jane's shoulders.

The cold spell continues this evening and the roommates are again sharing a bed, side by side in the darkness, both staring at a ceiling they cannot see.

Monica re-opens the previous night's conversation. 'I've been thinkin' all day 'bout what you told me last night, Jane. Your parents should be locked up. You should go to the police, you know.'

'No point. I'll get even with 'im one day.'

'I've also been thinkin' about somethin' else.'

'What's that?' Jane asks, turning to face Monica.

'Well, you've been open with me and, well, I… I feel I should come clean with you. I wasn't totally honest with you last night an' the trouble is… I'm worried.'

'What about?'

'Worried if I tell you the truth, it might mess our friendship.'

'Try me,' her voice sounding concerned.

'I'm lesbian.'

Jane turns back to face the ceiling, content for her flatmate to continue.

Monica recalls how, from an early age, she could never quite fit the image her mother endeavoured to mould her into, and by the time she was in her early teens, she understood why. She was more attracted to girls than boys. She stole the car with a girlfriend from school with whom she was in a relationship, so they could be alone together. They needed to experiment, be sure about how and what they were feeling. When her father questioned her about the theft, she told him the truth and admitted her sexuality. He assured her it made not the slightest difference to the way he felt about her. 'Live whatever life makes you happy, darling, apart from stealing cars.'

Her mother, on the other hand, was appalled. Anything other than a conventional heterosexual relationship defied every law of God and nature. The atmosphere in the house grew strained and her father suggested she left the family home in Halesowen for London and a career at Harrods as a trainee window display designer.

'D'you still see them?' Jane asks.

'I see Dad a couple or three times a year. He comes down to London on his own and we have a meal together, but I never see Mum. She gave up work the day my brother's wife gave birth and devotes her life to her two grandchildren. She can't be bothered with me.'

Jane is quiet again and her stillness worries Monica.

'Please say something, Jane. I'm scared I've messed things up between us, you know, with me being the one who suggested we shared a bed to keep warm.'

'Is that the real reason you suggested it?'

'Don't know.'

'Doesn't matter anyway 'cos I'm probably not normal either.'

'What's normal, for Christ's sake?' Monica asks. 'I'm not attracted to men. The thought of a guy kissing me and the other things they wanna do revolts me but...' and she hesitates, moistening dry lips with her tongue, 'I find you attractive.'

Jane remains on her back, her body board-rigid, a thick blanket tucked tightly under her chin. She stares into the pitch black of the freezing room, her warm breath streaming from her mouth in a fine mist. Monica senses her processing what she's heard.

'I've screwed things between us, haven't I?' she asks, forlornly.

Still nothing.

'Jane, please say something.'

'I don't know. I can't imagine letting any man touch me, let alone doing anythin' else. I know *why* I feel like that, my psychiatrist explained it, but even he can't tell me if I'll ever want any sort of... you know... sexual relationship with anyone, man or woman. I never think about blokes, so I guess we've got that much in common.'

Monica makes a soft whistling noise through her teeth. 'Who the hell gets to decide what's normal? We ought to be allowed to get on an' live our lives as we want to. Could you forget what I've said and just love me as a friend? Maybe even like we're sisters?'

Jane eases back onto her side and moves her face towards Monica's. She softly kisses her friend on the lips.

'Yeah, like sisters is good,' she whispers.

FIFTEEN

'You've made good progress this last twelve months, Jane.'

Dr Lakmaker looks up from checking her medical notes, smiling as he speaks.

'Thanks, I feel a lot better but… but I still need the Valium.'

'I've written to your GP asking her to reduce your dosage over the coming three months. It's important you try and do without the midday tablet from today and in six weeks' time, cut out the one you take first thing in the morning.'

Jane shifts uneasily in the white plastic chair opposite the doctor for this, her last scheduled session, and as he speaks, her fingers nervously twist the strap on her handbag. He has given her the skills she needed to put her life in some semblance of order, shown her ways to face her childhood abuse and taught her how to control anxiety. She is slowly learning to ignore situations she is incapable of doing anything about and to focus exclusively on those she can.

The supplement he prescribed combined with a diet heavy on Big Macs has brought her up to a more normal body weight for her height and age. Her complexion, for years blemished by skin rashes and acne, is rose-pink more than pasty, despite the junk-food diet. For the first time in her short life, she likes what she sees in the mirror.

He has also given her the strength of mind to control the flashbacks. They creep up on her less frequently but when they do, Lakmaker's breathing technique and use of trigger words keep them under control, ease the panic.

'I'll try an' cut down on the pills, I promise.' She doubts she'll keep the promise.

Deliberately, and with a sort of theatrical flourish, Lakmaker takes a folded sheet of paper from his patient's file and holds it at eye level.

'In my hand, Jane, is a letter I think you will find exciting. Three weeks ago, I placed in motion a search of your records, in an attempt to trace your birth mother.'

Jane's eyes widen and she leans forward, her teeth biting into her bottom lip. 'Have you found her?' She extends her right arm towards the doctor in a vain attempt to grab the letter.

He lifts it beyond her reach. 'Yes, I have, Jane, and I also took the liberty of contacting her to find out if she would be happy for you to be given her name and address.'

'Oh God, this is amazin'. Come on, Doc, what she say?'

Lakmaker smiles warmly at the teenager, who by now is bouncing up and down on her chair like a five-year-old tempted with chocolate cake.

'She would love to meet you, Jane.'

'I can't believe it,' she squeals. 'I'm goin' to see my real mum.' With that, she stands high on her toes and hugs the doctor tightly around the neck before stepping back, suddenly uncomfortable with the intimacy of what she has done. He blushes too.

'Thanks, Doctor, thank you so much.'

SIXTEEN

The forty-five-minute rail journey from Paddington to High Wycombe is painstakingly slow and all the while, anxiety is nibbling at Jane's insides.

The quarter-full carriage is doing its best to stifle her barely contained excitement with threadbare seats, discarded newspapers and foetid stench of stale perspiration. She watches as a young mother in a grey tracksuit comforts her crying baby and two railway employees argue loudly over the last slice of a shared pizza. She averts her gaze from the man across the aisle, whose fat fingers and tattooed arms glisten with sweat as his eyes glide up and down her body.

On any other day, the nearness of a large man in soiled work clothes and hands the size of buckets might trigger a panic attack. Today, it will take more than that to dampen the excitement. Forty-eight hours ago, she spoke with her real mother for the first time by telephone and today, they are to meet in person.

The tension reaches breaking point the moment the ivy-clad tree trunks towering up from the embankment pass more slowly as the train snakes its way into its destination. She is first onto the platform and, like a greyhound fresh from the trap, she sprints through the ticket barrier onto the station concourse. With little idea of what her mother looks like other than she'll be dressed in blue, her eyes dance in every direction.

Within moments, she catches sight of a slim, upright woman in her mid-thirties and elegant in a blue two-piece walking briskly in her direction. Breathless with excitement, she calls out, 'Mum, Mum, is that you? Are you really my mum?'

The lady smiles warmly as the heads of passers-by turn in the direction of the young girl's excited voice. 'If you're Jane, then I'm your mother and I can't *begin* to tell you how wonderful it feels to finally meet you. Come, let me hold you.'

For two minutes, Jane clings to her mother as tightly as her younger self would have clutched a favourite teddy bear. When, finally, they draw apart, the older woman grasps both Jane's hands and steps back to take a good look at her daughter. She sees her younger self, the same high cheekbones, similar colour eyes and slightly upturned nose. She is beautiful, and it is clear she has made an effort to look her best for today's meeting. A midnight-blue raincoat open at the front reveals a pretty blue-and-red cotton dress, tight under the bust and cut above the knee.

'Come on, Jane, we can't stand around here all day.'

Mother and daughter link arms as they walk into the spring sunshine and join the queue at the taxi rank.

'Where're we goin'? To your house? Are you married? Do I have brothers and sisters?' Others in the queue listen in quiet fascination.

'Jane, I'm as thrilled and excited about today as you are, I promise you, but let's calm ourselves a little. We're having lunch at one of my favourite restaurants, a place where we can sit and talk on our own for as long as we want.'

'Oh, okay; I have lots to ask you.'

'Then I hope you're a good listener because I've lots to tell you.' Her mother smiles warmly.

In the back of the taxi, an unsettling thought casts a shadow across Jane's elation. 'This restaurant, is it posh?'

'Quite smart. Why?'

'Well… I've only ever eaten at McDonald's and pizza places. I don't know what to do in posh restaurants.' As a child, meals were taken on her lap in front of the television, or alone in her bedroom, mainly using a fork. She had seen films on TV of people in restaurants, tables filled with knives and forks and napkins and different-shaped glasses. Panic was rising.

Her mother rests a reassuring hand over her daughter's. 'You mustn't worry, my love, I'll guide you through the meal. There's no need to be frightened.'

In bright sunshine, the white stucco frontage of Don Antonio's restaurant is in stark contrast to the dull red brick of the solicitor's and estate agent's offices either side. On stepping from the taxi, Jane spots the logo of a familiar pizza restaurant further down the road and wishes they were eating there. At least she would know what to order.

Inside the restaurant, her mother is greeted zealously by a large middle-aged man with greasy black hair, an oily, pockmarked complexion and glistening brow. His voluminous stomach is barely contained inside a black cummerbund worn with a white shirt and black bow tie fighting a losing battle with several chins.

'Buon giorno, la signora Rogers, it'sa good to see you again. Please, your table is ready, follow me.'

Mother and daughter are led through a large open-plan dining room with more white stucco walls littered with framed photographs of smiling, rosy-cheeked diners, arms draped over each other's shoulders. Jane's heart sinks at the sight of pale-green tablecloths set with knives, forks, spoons, and a variety of glasses. Her mother, sensing her apprehension, rests a guiding hand in the small of her daughter's back as they are ushered to a table adjacent to French windows overlooking a small garden and comfortably out of earshot of most other diners. Jane's pulse eases a little on sitting down.

Antonio flamboyantly lifts a neatly folded napkin from the plate in front of her, shakes it open and, to her surprise, leans towards her and lays it across her lap. He does the same for her mother before handing menus to both. 'One for la signora and one for la signorina. Allora, would you like something to drink?'

'What would you like, Jane?'

'Um! Coke, please.'

'Wouldn't you prefer a glass of wine? After all, we are celebrating.'

'Don't think I should, thanks.' She had earlier swallowed two Valium to make certain anxiety would not spoil her day. Wine wasn't a good idea.

'One Coca-Cola and a large glass of Gavi di Gavi, please, Antonio.'

'Va bene, signora.'

Jane watches as the huge man trudges heavily through the restaurant before asking, 'Do you live close by?'

'A mile or so away. We use this restaurant quite regularly.'

'You're married?'

'Yes, my husband's name is William Rogers, our sons are John and Jeremy, they're twelve and ten, and our daughter, Jennifer, is eight.'

'So, you're Jo Rogers?'

'I am.'

'Can I call you Mum?'

'Of course, that's what I am. Now, before we really start talking, we'd better choose. What sort of food do you enjoy?'

'Pizza. That's Italian, isn't it?'

'I'm afraid they don't serve pizza here, but you might perhaps enjoy some fish, maybe a fillet of seabass. Do you like fish?'

'I like fish and chips.' What little confidence Jane possesses is disappearing faster than daylight on a winter's afternoon.

Jo cocks her head to one side and is smiling as she speaks. 'I tell you what, how about we both try the seabass and perhaps there'll be something on the dessert menu that'll take your fancy afterwards.'

The meal is ordered and some twenty minutes later arrives at the table, and by the time plates are cleared, it is doubtful Jane or her mother even notice what they have been eating, such has been the intensity of the conversation.

Dr Lakmaker had forewarned Jo of her daughter's abused childhood, and shortly after the fish is served, she asks if Jane is comfortable talking about that part of her life. The teenager is hesitant, reluctant to resurrect a past she is still fighting to contain, but also eager to spare her mother any feelings of guilt over her adoption.

Slowly, and as dispassionately as Lakmaker had taught her, she describes her first sixteen years in its awful detail. As she finishes, her mother blinks several times and takes a small white handkerchief from her handbag to dry both eyes. She then looks away and with eyes closed, takes three or four slow breaths.

'Mum, you mustn't blame yourself, you weren't to know.' Jane is surprised how easily she refers to someone she has known for little more than an hour as her mother.

She turns back, still fiddling with her handkerchief. 'Perhaps I am being too harsh on myself. My father shares much of the blame; it was him who forced me to put you up for adoption.'

'Why did he do that?' Janes asks.

'Well, Jane, to my shame, I was an eighteen-year-old schoolgirl when I found I was pregnant with you and in those days, unmarried girls were often forced to give their babies up for adoption.' Jane notices her mother's cheeks are bright red.

'Is the man you married my father?'

'No, no, he's not.' She is speaking slowly, picking her words carefully. 'Your father was… he was tragically killed in a car accident a few months after you were born.'

Disappointment clouds Jane's pretty features. 'Oh! Oh no. What… what was his name?'

Her mother takes a moment to reply. 'John… John Warner.'

It is Jane who now dabs her eyes with a handkerchief and her mother reaches across the table and takes her free hand.

'It's a complicated story but my father never forgave him for making me pregnant, banned me from ever seeing him again. I wasn't allowed to even mention his name. He was a hard father, and he could be cruel too.'

'Where's my dad buried?'

Again, she hesitates and her eyes dance around the room. 'Somewhere in Wiltshire, near Swindon, I think. I wasn't allowed to go to the funeral; my father forbade me.' She draws several deeper breaths. 'Anyway, that's all in the past now. What, my dear, have you been up to since you moved to London?'

Jane explains how she slept on and around Paddington station for two weeks before meeting Julian and sharing a bedsit with him. She talks enthusiastically of her therapy with Dr Lakmaker and the extent to which he has helped her come to terms with the abuse and how to control her anxiety. She gives her mother the whole story apart from sharing a room with Monica, which, for a reason she cannot quite rationalise, she is uncomfortable discussing.

'So, you currently share a room in a hostel?'

Jane nods.

'Do you get on with your roommate?'

'Yeah, she's okay.'

'And you're working in McDonald's?'

'Well, it pays the rent.'

'Hmm! Don't you think it might be better long-term if you were to train for something more worthwhile? A career that would pay enough for you to live comfortably?'

'Got no qualifications, it's all I can do.'

'I can help. I'll pay for you to go to college, perhaps pass some GCSEs, learn to type or bookkeeping or something like that.'

'You'd do that for me?'

'It's the very least I can do, Jane.' Her mother pauses for a second and appears to decide what it is she needs to say next.

'There's something I need to tell you, Jane. I'm currently having some personal problems of my own. My husband and I are in the process of divorcing. He's found someone else and is forcing me to sell the house and downsize. The children are still going to live with me and much as I'd love to have you come and join us, we just won't have the room.'

'Oh,' is the only word Jane can manage.

'I'm a junior school headmistress so I'm earning enough to live comfortably, and my ex is helping support the children.'

'That's sad. I feel so sorry for you.'

'There's no need to feel sorry for me; I'll survive, and I'm determined now we've finally met to help you get a better start in life. However…' Jo pauses mid-flow and for a second, seems lost in thought.

'What?' Jane snaps, impatience getting the better of her.

'Well, it's like this, Jane. I don't think it makes sense to complicate my children's lives at a time when they're still coming to terms with their parents splitting up.'

'Don't understand.'

'Well…' Her mother is visibly struggling with her words. 'I… I think it would be… well, better if we waited a little while before you met them.'

'What, you don't want them to know about me?'

'No, it's not that, it's just not the right time.'

'So *when* will be the right time?'

'I'm not entirely sure. Perhaps once all the dust is settled over the divorce.' As she speaks, her face and neck flush cherry red again.

'That's the way it is then, is it? You didn't want me when I was born and you don't really want me now, do you?' Jane's girlish features are washed white.

'Of course I want you, Jane, and I appreciate how tough this must be for you, but please give me a little time to sort it all out. I'll fund you through college, help you find somewhere better to live and we'll meet as often as we can.'

'What… in places like this? Jesus Christ!'

'It's better than us not meeting at all, isn't it?'

Impulsively, Jane stands as her eyes dart nervously around the room. The white walls are closing in and her breathing is shallow.

'Are you all right, Jane, do you need some fresh air?'

'No. I'm not all right as it 'appens. You can't understand, can you? All I want is a proper family, brothers an' sisters, Christmas an' holidays an' stuff like that. Stuff I never 'ad 'cos… 'cos… oh, fuck it. Fuck the whole world.'

She turns sharply on her heels and, only vaguely conscious of diners watching her, marches awkwardly through the restaurant and out into the afternoon sunshine, where she slumps onto the pavement, her back against the restaurant wall. Her mother follows, assuring Antonio everything is all right and they'll return shortly.

*

'And that's how my wonderful first day with my real mother ended,' Jane says, sitting on the end of her bed. 'I lost my temper, grabbed my coat and got a taxi straight back to the station.'

Monica is stretched out on her bed, listening intently as her roommate relates the day's events. Jane clumsily rolls her second spliff since returning to the hostel, takes a first long drag then tucks her chin on her knees and starts to paint her toenails.

'What you gonna do?'

'Bugger all. Pretend it never 'appened. I've lived without a proper mother all m'life. I don't need her *or* my half-brothers and sister.'

'No, you mustn't be like that. She's your mum and she's going through a tough time too. She's offered to help you find somewhere to live and fund you through college, for Christ's sake. That's brilliant, isn't it?'

The spliff is working its magic and Jane turns towards Monica. 'If she pays for a better place, will you come too?'

'Did you tell your mum about us?'

'Nah, no point, none of 'er business.'

'Look, Jane, you don't wanna be stuck working in McDonald's for the rest of your life, do you, so take her money. Maybe once she's sorted her problems out, the two of you will get back together properly and you'll get to meet your brothers and sister. It'll be okay, you'll see. You get to go to college and you an' me get to live somewhere better than this hole.'

SEVENTEEN

From: Robin Farnham
To: Dr Lakmaker
Ref. No: 9

By the beginning of '91, life was pretty good. My seven-year relationship with Lucy was deeper and happier than I ever hoped it could be. Giles was having the time of his life at university and sixteen-year-old Katie appeared, on the surface at least, to have accepted that her father was settled in a long-term relationship with a woman who was not her mother.

Financially, I was stretched. We were mortgaged to the hilt on our house in Surrey and Giles' and Katie's living expenses were setting me back £750 a month.

The business side of life was more comfortable. I was surefooted in what I was doing; twenty-nine years in magazine publishing and eight running my own business afforded a wealth of experience. Years that were nothing if not eventful.

On starting my new publishing business back in '83, I launched a magazine called *Electronic Data Index,* a cutting-edge indexing system for the electronic industry that made money from day one.

Over the next four years, I added three further titles, the largest of which was a joint venture with the UK Vegetarian Association to publish their members' magazine, *Vegetarian Life*.

The magazine had been published in-house for over half a century as a tacky black-and-white newsletter mailed to the 12,000 members. The editorial was poor and the design archaic, with the result it attracted little advertising and had been a sizeable drain on the Association's resources for years.

Most of the staff at the UKVA were pleasant but commercially naïve, although its chief executive, Janice McCarthy, was easy-going and happy to leave me to get on with relaunching *Vegetarian Life* as a modern, newsstand magazine.

The joint venture seemed a godsend, a real opportunity to expand from business-oriented titles into consumer magazine publishing, hoping for richer rewards through a larger circulation and greater advertising revenues. We signed a publishing agreement in January 1989 in which both parties agreed to jointly fund the relaunch and profits were to be divided equally between us. Reluctantly, I had to sell the electronics magazine for a little under £100,000 to fund our share.

We redesigned *Vegetarian Life* as a glossy, four-colour monthly packed with topical news features, lifestyle interviews and vegetarian recipes. By the end of 1990, we were selling over 45,000 copies an issue and advertising revenue was up by more than six hundred per cent.

Early in March of '91, Janice McCarthy resigned as chief executive of the Association and my initial contact with her replacement was not encouraging. From the outset, Trevor Thornbury seemed eager to impress me with his publishing credentials which, from what I could make out, amounted to a brief spell selling advertising on a men's soft-porn magazine.

We met for the first time at my offices in Surrey in April and the day turned out a good deal more eventful than I could have imagined. He arrived around 11am and was offered coffee before being shown to my office. He didn't drink coffee, only herbal tea. Fortunately, we had plenty.

'Pleased to meet you, Trevor.' It was a sallow-cheeked man in his early thirties, of medium height and pasty pallor, who stood before me. The handshake was limp, and the jacket of his grey business suit hung loosely across bony shoulders. He made no attempt to establish eye contact.

'How're you settling into your role at the Association?' I asked.

'The place is a bloody mess,' he bemoaned abruptly. 'Half the buggers are bone idle, and the other half incompetent.'

Not a good start. 'Let's hope you find us more on the ball, then.'

He sipped tea as I ran through circulation figures and advertising revenues and gave him what I thought was an impressive set of budget projections for the coming year.

'No more than I would have expected,' he said. 'Let's face it, the market's booming, over a thousand people a day are switching to a vegetarian diet. With the number of new veggie products being launched, trained bloody monkeys could sell advertising right now.'

His dismissive attitude took me by surprise. 'That's… that's a little disingenuous,' was my instinctive response.

'The best salespeople in the world couldn't increase ad revenue without a substantial increase in copy sales, which is a direct result of us giving readers a damn good editorial product. Everyone's pulled out the stops to make this magazine work.'

'Yeah, well, you would say that.'

Was it his attitude or mine causing the meeting to start off on the wrong foot?

'Come on, Trevor, before we took it over, that rag of a magazine of yours was costing the Association around twenty grand a year and its circulation hardly broke 12,000 an issue. Give us some credit.'

'I don't like the editorial stance, it's weak.' Not once could he bring himself to look me in the eye.

'How do you mean, weak?' I asked, as the lines in my forehead tightened.

'We need more campaigning features, force the British public to acknowledge the amount of cruelty in modern farming and animal slaughter.'

I hadn't seen this coming, and the man's attitude was beginning to worry me. 'Trevor, we're talking to the converted, our readers are already veggies. Why confront them with grainy black-and-white photos of sordid scenes from abattoirs and donkey sanctuaries when they already know about that stuff?'

All of a sudden, he was wagging a long, sinewy index finger uncomfortably close to the end of my nose. 'The Association is first and foremost a campaigning organisation, with the ultimate objective of stamping out the factory farming of animals. They have as much right to life as you and me.

'Meat is murder, we don't kill our friends, is the mantra I intend to adopt as the magazine's editorial policy. It's our magazine, not yours; it belongs to the Association. You just publish it on our behalf.'

Spittle flew in all directions as he was speaking, and I sat mesmerised by his onslaught of wholly unjustified criticism. Slowly and calmly, I explained the reasons why the magazine's relaunch was successful. Sales were increasing by an average 4,000 copies per issue, which to my mind, vindicated an editorial policy focused on vegetarian recipes and celebrity vegetarian lifestyles. Our reader research substantiated this.

Thornbury remained impassive, languidly making notes in scratchy, spidery handwriting on dull, recycled paper the colour of his complexion.

He looked up. 'I need an office to interview each member of the team.' The statement was a fait accompli. He had rendered me powerless in my own business.

Around 4.30 that afternoon, he popped his head around my office door to announce he had a room booked at the Cadogan Hotel in Sloane Street and wanted to continue our meeting over dinner. 'Give me a call on my mobile and let me know where we're eating,' he barked before leaving to find a cab prepared to take him from Surrey to central London.

What a turn-up, him staying at the Cadogan and wasting charitable funds on taxis and five-star luxury.

I booked a table at Veeraswamy's in Regent Street, figuring a top Indian restaurant would offer good vegetarian food, which it did. Thornbury wasn't averse to a decent glass of wine either and there was some discussion over the most suitable wine to accompany hot, spicy food. We went with his choice.

'You need to talk to that editor of yours, remind her who's in charge around here,' he mumbled through a mouth full of poppadum, fragments flying straight at me.

'Trevor, look,' I replied, summoning my best conciliatory tone while desperately searching for a hint of tractability. 'It's clear your and my management styles differ. I agree overall editorial policy should be decided by you and me as publishers but I'm sufficiently old-school to believe an editor should have the final say on day-to-day matters.'

'I don't,' he answered bluntly. There wasn't a scrap of empathy between us.

'Trevor, please, you should trust my judgment a little more. After all, how much relevant publishing experience have you had apart from a short spell selling advertising space?'

'I've had enough to know I don't want airy-fairy young women telling me what does and doesn't go into *our* magazine.'

The hairs on the back of my neck were pricking against the collar of my shirt. '*Vegetarian Life is* a joint effort and to date we've done a bloody good job.'

The conversation paused as a waiter loaded the table with three dishes of spicy vegetarian food and a bowl of rice. A few king prawns in the mix might have whetted my palate and, just possibly, soothed my temper.

'We haven't made a penny of profit yet.'

'What do you mean? Each issue is now in profit.'

'We've not recouped our £100k investment in the launch.'

'Nor have we, but by spring of next year, we both will have, and by then, we'll be looking at over a hundred grand a year clear. You've seen the projections.'

'Yeah, well that's as maybe,' he said as he chewed open-mouthed. 'Fortunately for you and your stroppy editor, I don't have the time to get involved right now; need to get shot of too many time-wasters doing bugger all at HQ. I want fresh blood, my kind of people, talented youngsters prepared to learn and work to my principles.'

This sounded like a very thinly veiled threat, and he wasn't finished. 'We'll meet again in August and thrash out how things will be handled from January onwards.'

I nodded, bored with the conversation, and bored with this shit of a man, who appeared to revel in an ability to be disliked while possessing the charisma of a discarded toenail clipping.

His next question stunned me.

'That's enough business. Where's good to go after we've finished eating?' My thoughts were of catching an early train home to Lucy. Thornbury had other ideas.

I took my time chewing a mouthful of spiced cauliflower, not wishing to spoil the enjoyment. When eventually I answered, it was with another question. 'What had you in mind?'

'Clubs. Used 'em all the time when I was on *Penthouse*.' I stared at him, dumbfounded. The prat spends the whole day slagging off my business and now wants me to go clubbing with him.

'Robin, I like to have some fun when I'm away from home. We'll go to Miranda's. I'm a member there.'

After I settled the restaurant bill, we walked the short distance to Miranda's in Kingley Street where Thornbury immediately ordered a bottle of champagne. There seemed little doubt who would pay for that, as well.

We were hardly settled in our seats before an attractive young woman, slim of body and heavy on facial make-up, eased her scantily covered figure onto the crimson banquette alongside Thornbury. Seconds later, she was groping him with sufficient enthusiasm to suggest she actually found the pasty-face, half-pissed wimp attractive. A second such hostess was declined.

After thirty minutes watching the two of them behave inappropriately while other ladies stood on a small stage and took their clothes off to music, I decided it was time to leave, for me at least. I settled the drinks bill, advised my engrossed dinner guest any additional services were down to him and caught the last train home while wondering if the night porter at the Cadogan might turn a blind eye to Thornbury's tastefully dressed companion.

August came, and with it the promised telephone call from Thornbury and we agreed to meet in the Metropole Hotel at the National Exhibition Centre outside Birmingham. At least there would be no Miranda's afterwards.

'Good morning, Trevor,' I said, gripping his limp, clammy hand. 'Good to see you again.'

He said nothing, merely nodding in the direction of two leather sofas in the far corner of the hotel's ground-floor lounge. It occurred to me that he might prefer sitting on something other than leather. We don't sit on our dead friends, do we?

I suggested coffee but he reminded me he didn't drink coffee. No, that's right, he preferred fruit tea, champagne and ladies in strip joints.

He reached inside the opaque plastic briefcase he carried in his left hand and drew out a sealed white envelope. 'Read this letter before we begin our discussion,' he ordered.

The letter inside was nothing if not straight to the point.

Dear Mr Farnham,

The purpose of this letter is to serve formal notice of termination of the Publishing Agreement between RSG Publishing Ltd and the UK Vegetarian Association dated 1st January 1989 in accordance with the terms and provisions contained therein.

Under the terms of said conditions, the UK Vegetarian Association will resume full publishing responsibilities of its magazine, Vegetarian Life, *with effect from 1st January 1992 and RSG Publishing Ltd will acknowledge receipt of this letter and complete all necessary actions on termination of the contract. These actions include passing to the UK Vegetarian Association all relevant sales records, commissioned articles and page layouts as are required for the smooth transfer of responsibilities.*

Furthermore, on completion of the contract, RSG Publishing shall immediately destroy all confidential information concerning the contract and any other matters relating to the UK Vegetarian Association.

The Association would like to thank you and your staff for the commitment extended on our magazine during this last two and a half years.

Yours sincerely,
Trevor Thornbury
Chief Executive

I read the contents a second time, slowly absorbing the implications. Five members of staff out of twelve worked directly on *Vegetarian Life*. The magazine accounted for over half our turnover and as much as sixty per cent of current profit. My brain was in overdrive.

'You can't do this,' I said, staring into Thornbury's cold, unblinking eyes, which were finally locked on to mine. He was basking in his moment of triumph, relishing the impact the contents of his letter were having.

'This is in breach of our agreement. The only justifiable reason for terminating the contract is if the magazine is not trading profitably within the first three years of the agreement – and it is.'

'Unfortunately for you, it isn't.' His tone was dismissive.

'It is,' I snapped back with conviction. 'The last two issues alone generated £12,500 net profit.'

'It may be in profit on a month-by-month basis,' Thornbury responded icily, 'but as I pointed out during our last meeting, we've yet to see a profit on our total investment since the relaunch. With our initial investment, coupled with the trading losses during the first year, we're still almost £100k down.'

'So am I, but the clause in the agreement relates to the magazine trading profitably on an on-going basis. The term "net profit" doesn't include the return of the initial investment made by both parties to fund the relaunch.' I hoped my voice concealed the panic rising from the pit of my stomach.

'That's your interpretation. Our lawyers assure me the agreement clearly confirms we're free to cancel if we've not seen a profit on our investment by the end of this year and there's no way that'll happen. We're taking our magazine back in-house from the 1ˢᵗ January.' The satisfied smirk told me how much he was enjoying seeing me squirm.

'So you think it ethical to take the magazine back the moment it starts making real profits and deny us the opportunity to recoup our investment?'

'You signed the contract,' was his blunt response.

I needed to control my growing anger. 'Is this the way to treat five people who've put their heart and soul into regenerating *Vegetarian Life* over this past two and a half years? A magazine that was costing you the thick end of twenty grand a year before *we* turned it into profit?'

Thornbury licked his lips before replying, as if savouring the moment. 'You'll just have to make them redundant, won't you? An experienced entrepreneur like you must have handled this sort of situation before.'

The way he enunciated the word 'entrepreneur' as four elongated syllables sliced through me like a scythe. An abundance of self-control was needed to resist the urge to punch the pasty-faced wimp in the face.

'Fuck you, Thornbury,' I yelled. 'I'll fight you all the way through the courts on this one.'

'You'll need deep pockets. We're a charity and we're loaded,' was his parting shot as he walked away.

'Yeah, and I've seen how you spend the charity's funds,' I yelled.

*

As I climbed the stairs to my office after a turgid three-hour drive back from Birmingham, I had decided we had little option other than to fight back.

Apart from the immediate loss of turnover and impact on the jobs and lives of five members of staff, the UKVA also owed us over £75k for mailings, inserts and brochures. Thornbury was certain to concoct a million reasons not to pay.

The loss of fifty per cent share of the profits from *Vegetarian Life* over the next two years and the £100k we'd invested in the magazine's relaunch left me and the business on shaky ground.

At that time, we were publishing four magazines including *Vegetarian Life,* but the other three alone would not generate sufficient profit to keep us solvent.

Our only chance of survival was to launch a new magazine in direct competition to *Vegetarian Life* with an editorial profile identical to the one we had published for the past thirty months. We knew our readers loved it.

EIGHTEEN

From: Robin Farnham
To: Dr Lakmaker
Ref. No: 10

Leading city lawyers Bush Williams were retained to handle the breach of contract dispute with the UKVA and senior partner Roger Potty asked for a week to study the original publishing agreement to determine the strength of our case. For the privilege, he charged me an eye-watering £1,500, roughly equivalent, I guessed at the time, to the cost of the Savile Row suit he was wearing.

Nigel Prince, my bank manager in Woolwich, south-east London, would also be a vital ally. An old-style manager, he had eased into middle age making decisions in front of clients he had known for years and now resented the shift in power sweeping through his industry. Any attempt at a reduction of his authority or interference from Regional Office was pointless. Or had been.

He took a copy of the agreement and promised to get his 'legal boys' to go over it with a fine-tooth comb, 'merely a precaution, dear boy, so we all know where we stand'.

A week later, his team confirmed the UKVA was certainly in breach of contract. The bank was confident, although could not guarantee, we would be successful in suing for the £75,000 worth of outstanding invoices, my £100,000 investment in the relaunch and a figure in the region of £250,000 in respect of the loss of profits over the coming three years.

The lawyers agreed, but warned the verdict hinged on the interpretation the judge might place on the phrase 'net profit'. The UKVA could well seek to define 'net profit' as a surplus created *after* taking into account the total investment made by both parties in funding the relaunch.

'No,' I assured Potty, 'both parties agreed that if after three years the magazine was not *trading* profitably, the UKVA had the right to terminate the agreement and take it back. We are clearly trading profitably.'

'That's as may be, Robin,' Potty replied, 'but sometimes a phrase can be deemed to have two meanings. This might very well be one of those occasions.' The vagueness of his response made me uneasy.

The first issue of our brand-new magazine, *Vegetarian Living*, hit the bookstalls in January ahead of *Vegetarian Life* and early feedback from readers and advertisers was encouraging.

By the summer of 1992, we commanded seventy per cent of the available advertising spend and reported average issue sales in excess of 50,000, twice those achieved by *Vegetarian Life*. And we were in profit.

A third meeting with the lawyers was less satisfactory. Potty reported the UKVA had rebuffed our claim for breach of contract, which was 'only as expected'. They also denied the validity of the outstanding invoices for £75,000 dating back a full year, even though they had not previously disputed them.

The only option open to gain compensation was to take them to the High Court.

Potty pointedly enquired as to my company's financial situation and its ability to survive a possible £75,000 bad debt along with the loss of our £100,000 investment and future profits.

'You need to enter this with your eyes wide open,' he warned. 'Court fees are calculated as a percentage of the sum claimed and our fees, together with the barrister's, will mount up quickly and the opposition will almost certainly apply for costs should they win.'

'Realistically,' I asked, 'what might our costs be?'

'I doubt they'll be less than £100,000, which is what the other side's legal team will ask to be placed on deposit.'

'What do you mean, on deposit?'

'It's standard procedure in these cases for both sides to deposit agreed amounts as security in the event of the other side being awarded costs.'

'So I've got to find £100k cash as a deposit?' I croaked. He nodded grimly.

It took me a moment to digest this bombshell. My business was already uncomfortably close to its £100k overdraft limit and now I'm told we need a further £100k to proceed with the action.

'Level with me, what are our chances?'

'Good to very good but there's never a cast-iron guarantee with these actions. The contract isn't watertight, no contract ever is, but we're confident, Robin… you should win but…'

In that moment, my cousin Robert's words echoed ominously in my ears. *'Time after time the guilty walk free from court and the injured party is the one that suffers.'*

The following day, Nigel Prince juggled me a thirty-minute slot at the bank, amid what he referred to as 'a frightful schedule stuffed with wall-to-wall meetings.'

'How can I help, old boy?' was his usual affable greeting.

'Nigel, I know I'm close to my limit on the £100k overdraft but the business needs a further £100k for a deposit to cover the costs of the High Court action. Any chance you could extend our overdraft until the case is settled?'

Prince reached inside a blue file on his desk and withdrew a sheet headed with the bank's logo.

'Our legal boys agree the contract supports your action, but they also point out nothing is ever one hundred per cent watertight. Your financial exposure if you lost would be enormous, over a quarter of a million.

'And don't forget, Robin, your house has been signed over as security on your overdraft. Do you want to risk everything, and I mean *everything*, on the whim of a judge?'

I felt the blood drain from my face. 'You're not suggesting I throw in the towel, write off our losses and get on with life?'

'Your decision, old boy, but the bottom line is we can't extend your overdraft. If you press on with the court action, you'll have to find the money elsewhere.'

He returned the papers to the blue folder and rammed it shut in a thinly disguised hint and I stood to leave.

'The only option I can suggest,' he added as he escorted me to his office door, 'is sell one of your magazines to raise the funds.'

Later that same day, I telephoned *Vegetarian Living*'s magazine distributor and spoke to Jeremy Owen, the executive handling our account.

'Jeremy, treat this in confidence but I'm looking to sell the magazine.'

'What on earth for?' came his bemused response. 'It's going great guns; we're knocking the opposition for six on copy sales.'

'I know, but we need money to fight the Vegetarian Association. They owe us a fortune and our lawyers reckon our case is strong.'

By the following morning, my inclination was to give up, put the UKVA debacle down to experience and get on with publishing *Vegetarian Living*. By the afternoon, my options were abruptly curtailed on learning through the publishing grapevine that *BBC Good Food* magazine was about to launch a brand-new vegetarian title.

The news was a knockout blow. The market was tough enough with two vegetarian magazines fighting for a share of the meagre advertising spend. We had competed and won hands down against the amateurs at the UKVA, but the financial clout of the BBC would present an altogether different challenge.

Three days later, Jeremy Owen called to report a sniff of interest in buying *Vegetarian Living* from a publisher called IJL Magazines.

I knew of the company. They were a management buyout formed in the wake of the Mirror Group meltdown following Robert Maxwell's death. Dave Lewis, its managing director, came across as an affable sort when we met the following week. I was upfront and explained the impending lawsuit and the planned launch of the new BBC magazine.

He looked through the trading figures for *Vegetarian Living* and the projected profits and his body language suggested there was interest. We arranged for his accountant to undertake due diligence.

Lewis asked what price we were looking for and showed no negative reaction when I ventured £100k.

We met again a fortnight later and he greeted me with a wide grin and firm handshake. 'Good news, Robin, we'd like to buy your magazine and we also want your three key members of staff to come with it.'

I took care not to sound too eager. 'How much are you prepared to pay, Dave?'

'My board has approved a price of £60,000.'

My brain turned the figures over. Sixty thousand was forty below my target but it seemed the best deal I was likely to find. Even so, the gambler's instinct sniffed more.

'I was prepared to drop a little on my one hundred thousand, but I'm not convinced £60,000 is a realistic valuation of *Vegetarian Living*. You'll recoup that in under eighteen months.'

My brain was screaming at me, *Take the fucking money, bite his hand off. You need every penny to sue the UKVA.*

Lewis scratched the side of his nose, more a nervous habit than any need to service an itch, I thought. 'Okay, I'll level with you, the most my board is prepared to pay,

Robin, is seventy-five grand, but only on the condition that the editor, assistant editor and sales manager agree to move with the title.'

It broke my heart losing *Vegetarian Living* although it was a relief three key members of staff kept their jobs. Every magazine I've ever published is a part of me sent into the outside world where it lives forever. Like your kids, each issue grows into a life of its own, yet sustains a tiny part of me inside them.

This was no time for any regret as I was still twenty-five grand short of my target. My last hope rested with the bank agreeing to extend the overdraft to cover the shortfall.

MEMO ENDS rf

NINETEEN

From: Robin Farnham
To: Dr Lakmaker
Ref. No: 11

Nigel Prince was clearly not his usual self when we met two days later. He shook my hand firmly as normal but unusually, avoided making eye contact.

'You've been busy,' he commented, as uneasily, he shuffled bits of paper around his desk before sitting down.

'Sure have,' I answered. 'I've sold *Vegetarian Living* and raised seventy-five grand of the hundred needed to fund the High Court action. I'm hoping you'll cover the shortfall by increasing my overdraft to £125k.'

'Hmm,' he mused. 'Where does that leave your business in terms of revenue streams?'

An unsettling edge to his tone made me anxious. 'Unsure what you mean, Nigel.'

'What's your projected turnover for the next twelve months?'

'Umm… I replied, juggling the figures in my mind. *'Fine Food* should achieve a little over £240k, *Good Cheese* publishes twice yearly at £50k, and *Cash and Carry* will do around £160k. All told and with a fair wind, our turnover should be a little under half a million.'

Nigel made another non-committal throaty noise, his eyes still averting mine. 'It appears *Vegetarian Living* was your largest revenue stream and without it, your turnover will halve. From what I can see, your creditors' schedule suggests you owe close to £85k in rent, PAYE, VAT and print bills. Your business looks to me to be in a pretty precarious state, Robin,' he commented gravely.

I went to speak but he hadn't finished. 'Regional Office has instructed me to advise you that the bank is unable to continue your £100k overdraft facility, let alone sanction any increase to a business with a turnover clearly incapable of servicing it.'

'Do you *agree* with your Regional Office's instructions?'

'That's immaterial, although, in the circumstances, I'm afraid I do.'

'So… so what happens next?' Any composure left in me had drained away.

'Well, the moment we cancel your overdraft, your business is insolvent, which means legally you cannot continue trading. We'll hand the matter over to our Liquidation Department.' His voice was flat, hollowed out.

'What… what, you're closing me down?'

He puffed out his cheeks as he exhaled. 'Unfortunately, Robin, as from today, the matter is out of my hands. There's nothing more I can do for you.'

Here was yet another betrayal, another way out slammed in my face. I couldn't accept it.

'There is.' My voice raised several decibels as my mind worked feverishly for a plan. 'There *is* something you can do. You can give me two weeks before you call in the liquidators.

'If I can't find a way to continue in business, my only means of earning a living will disappear and along with it, my ability to support my son and daughter through university. Nigel, I'm close to losing everything, including my house, and all because of a single, mad, fucking vegetarian!'

A steady hum from the traffic in the road outside was the only sound in the room as I stared straight at Prince, determined not to break his gaze, which was, at least, engaged.

'You owe me these two weeks,' I blurted, perhaps a little too loudly, 'you bloody well know you do!' There was much left unsaid in those final words, but they hit the spot.

'Okay, you've got two weeks but no more and we'll discuss the details across the road in the pub, not here.' Prince's three decades in banking had rendered him supremely adept at preserving a detached objectivity to what was, for me, a matter of survival.

'Do you have a plan, Robin?' he asked offhandedly once we were settled in the pub opposite the bank.

'Yeah, one of sorts. The business doesn't own *Fine Food* or *Good Cheese*. I bought them with a personal cheque back in '87 and can prove it so the liquidator can't touch them. My plan is to set up a new company with just two staff plus myself and hopefully trade my way out of this hole with those two magazines. Clearly, it'll need working capital which I'll take from existing company funds as a return of some of my outstanding director's loan. I'll need a few weeks to set all this up but whatever happens, I'll end up owing the bank an arm and a leg. But… maybe, just maybe—'

'Tell you what I'll do then,' he interrupted, leaning back but looking away, perhaps making sure no one was eavesdropping.

'I'll inform Regional Office you're on holiday for two weeks. Phone me Friday week and advise me that in view of your company's insolvency, you have no alternative other than to enter into voluntary liquidation. That way, you can appoint your own liquidator. You okay with that?'

'Thank you… yes.'

'Our corporate insolvency division in north London will handle the outstanding overdraft from that point. This'll probably be the last time we meet, Robin,' Prince said later as we stood to leave. 'Least I can do is pay for lunch.'

I accepted his offer to pick up the tab for my sandwich of wafer-thin plastic ham wrapped in supermarket white bread and washed down with a single glass of a lacklustre South African Pinot Noir. I hoped the irony was not lost on him and that his spreading waistline owed much to meals in fine restaurants and the odd weekend in country house hotels, some of it paid for by my business.

That same evening at dinner, I struggled to sound confident as I told Lucy of the meeting with Nigel Prince. She looked at me, eyes brimming. 'Be honest with me, Robin, how much trouble are we really in?'

At that moment, my words were hopelessly inadequate in revealing the gravity of our situation. 'It's gonna be tough starting all over again but what option do I have? I need to earn a living and at forty-six, how many companies are on the lookout for a failed middle-aged magazine publisher?'

'No, Robin, I mean the house. Will we lose our house?'

Reaching across the table, I grasped her left hand tightly in both of mine. 'This is my mess, Lucy, and it's down to me to get us out of it. And I will, that's a promise.'

At the time, I had no idea if I would be capable of keeping that promise but I was just not prepared to burden her with problems of my own making. I was incapable of sharing my fears for the future, even with the person whose love meant more to me than anything else.

We cannot choose our children, or those our children choose to marry, or our grandchildren. The only choice we make is our life partner, and many, like Lucy and me, get it wrong first time. Some fail on the second or even their third attempt but the urge to bond with another human being drives most of us to make the right choice in the end.

The extraordinary feeling of betrayal over the loss of Jo had long gone. The acute disappointment of my failed first marriage had troubled me little since meeting Lucy.

I had revealed more of myself to her than to anyone before or since. How much of herself she revealed to me I'll never know.

She too had known hardship; a cheating husband who left her with his unpaid tax bills, forcing her to wait at tables in a local wine bar to supplement her teacher's salary and clear his debts.

That was in the past, something she rarely felt the need to examine, and nor was she overly taxed about the future, apart from normal concerns over family. One of her abiding characteristics was, and still is, that she exists on the premise life is about today, the past is dead and gone and tomorrow is tomorrow's worry.

I couldn't share that luxury. So much rested on my ability to survive tomorrow and next week, and the week after. What threatens our survival is soon of little consequence. Once you're in the shit, what put you there is immaterial; the priority is how you get out of it.

Later, in the darkness of a disturbed sleep, I reached for Lucy's sleeping warmth and swore never again to show a single glimmer of weakness, to the bank, the liquidators or any other bugger who tried to screw me.

MEMO ENDS rf

*

From: Robin Farnham
To: Dr Lakmaker
Ref. No: 12

Shortly after lunch on Friday 16th October 1992, I telephoned Nigel Prince as arranged and confirmed I was placing my business into liquidation. The conversation was brief, lacking any of the good-natured bonhomie that characterised our earlier relationship.

I summoned all the remaining staff into the main office, and it was clear they sensed bad news. My tongue felt like it was wrapped in cotton wool and was sticking to the roof of my mouth as I went to speak.

'I've just this minute put the phone down on a call to Nigel Prince, our bank manager. Despite selling *Vegetarian Living*, the bank has withdrawn our overdraft facility, leaving us without the working capital we need to stay in business.'

I was struggling to meet the glazed, staring eyes of nine anxious faces.

'On top of that – no, actually because of that – we don't have the money to take the UK Vegetarian Association to Court, so we're unlikely to see any of the money they owe us. Whichever way you look at it, this company is insolvent and cannot continue trading.

'A firm of liquidators has been appointed and absolutely nothing can be done now without their authority.'

A doleful female voice from the back asked, 'Does that mean I've got no job?'

'Afraid so,' I answered, thankful her face was shielded from mine and no eye contact was required.

'What about our wages?' asked another.

'That's a decision for the liquidator next week.'

I needed to end this torture, for them and for me.

'We should all go home; there's nothing any of us can do. We'll know more on Monday.'

I was struggling to hold myself together. This monumental fuck-up was my fault. A fuck-up that touched decent people's lives, people with mortgages and children and responsibilities.

'I'm so, so sorry it has ended this way… I really am.' I turned and walked to the sanctuary of my office, shut the door and stared at a blank wall for half an hour.

Maybe Penny, lost in the fog of her schizophrenic mind, saw it all more clearly. Was it madness to resign a secure, well-paid job, bust up a marriage and screw up my kids' lives merely to satisfy a selfish urge to run my own business?

A hundred and more times since that day, I've asked myself if I could have avoided the collapse of my business.

A collapse orchestrated by a charity run by a complete arsehole with access to so much money he could twist every point of law, thwart every attempt to recover what was rightfully mine.

I never found the answer; eventually I stopped looking.

Humiliation was shredding my insides. When shit happens, it tends to be dumped on you from gigantic, overflowing buckets of the stuff.

MEMO ENDS rf

TWENTY

'Wow! That's quite some story, Robin.' A smile lights up Lakmaker's face. 'Now I can understand the pressure you were under during that period.' For the first time since meeting him, Robin senses a hint of genuine sympathy. It is short-lived.

'But how did you find closure – *did* you manage to find closure?'

Robin had worked his balls off, wrung himself emotionally dry writing the story, but still this man wants more.

'Why are you putting me through all this crap? We both know Thornbury died in a hit-and-run accident and the police questioned me about it for two days. But I didn't do it, even though I thought about it on many occasions. What more do you want me to say?'

Lakmaker is not easing up.

'Do you feel up to talking about the months following the liquidation of your business?'

Robin gives vent to a deep sigh.

'I simply remember it as a bloody tough period of my life.'

'How much did you end up owing the bank?'

'Over seventy-five grand. I don't remember the actual figure, it was increasing by the day, interest rates were sky-high at that time. It was a complete nightmare, I couldn't afford to pay the mortgage and house values were falling through the floor.'

'Did you discuss this with the bank?'

'Yeah, of course I did. I visited their Liquidation Department twice and the people there were charming and courteous but only really interested in one thing – their money.'

'But you were never bankrupted?'

'No, at least I was able to stay in business.'

'Did you ever get any of the money back from the vegetarians?'

'Not a penny.' Robin senses an old anger resurfacing. 'The only compensation was that their magazine, *Vegetarian Life*, slid downhill fast, due entirely to Thornbury's incompetence. The Association eventually realised they'd employed a complete prat and fired him.'

'You clearly held him in contempt.'

'Of course I did.'

'And following his murder, being questioned by the police must have been… well, traumatic.'

A dull ache above Robin's eyes works its way around his forehead, settling uncomfortably into both temples.

'No, it wasn't traumatic because I was innocent. How much more of this do you expect me to take? I'm weary. I feel like I haven't slept since… I've no idea when I last had any real sleep. How long have I been here in this godforsaken hospital, anyway?'

Lakmaker stays silent and stares at his patient.

'You don't believe me, do you? You think I murdered Thornbury.'

'Robin, at the time, everything the police had on you was circumstantial, but this new forensic evidence appears more damning so, like you, I want to be certain there's no hidden side to your character.'

Robin squeezes tired eyes and shakes his head from side to side. He too is unsure, and the doctor's words provoke an uneasy disquiet. For most of his adult life, gaps in his memory had troubled him, although he drew comfort from the assumption few, if any of us, recall each detail of every day.

Our lives are littered with trivia. Weeks pass when little of any consequence takes place. For five of his teenage years, he assiduously kept a diary. A dozen lines each evening in pencilled longhand recording the weather, the monotony of school, the tedium of family rows and the joy of loving Jo.

One evening, sitting in bed, poised to put pencil to paper, he reread his writings of the previous week and the tedium of his existence so depressed him, he slammed the diary shut, never to open it again. Better to forget the ordinariness of our lives.

But if days we cannot recall conceal a darker side, how much do we know of who we really are?

He calls to mind a poem by the writer and broadcaster, Clive James, recounting first sight of a portrait of himself he barely recognised.

'And so this other man slowly appears

*Who is not me as I would wish to be,
But is the me that I try not to see.'*

Robin knows he must see himself as he really is before his addled brain steals any last vestige of self-awareness.

*

*From: Robin Farnham
To: Dr Lakmaker
Ref. No: 13*

We live in our house in Caterham until tomorrow. We move out on the last day of August '94. Tonight, I sit alone on the grassy bank leading down from the terrace and swimming pool.

It's not losing the house, or the wine Lucy and I shared over supper fuelling the melancholy; it's the memories this house embraces. We were married while living here. My children grew to adulthood and left home for university during those years. We shared long summer evenings in the company of siblings and friends, eating and drinking and laughing long into balmy nights.

This house had become the bargaining chip in the toughest battle of my life. A battle I lost. I walk inside and open a second bottle. I know this is a bad idea but fuck it, I need the soporific comfort it affords. I take the glass and the bottle back to the terrace, gaze upwards towards a gibbous moon and relive the past weeks and months.

A year ago, the bank ordered me to sell our house. They were short of money, desperate for the £75,000 I owed them. In the wake of Black Friday, houses prices fell through the floor. Or maybe it was Black Monday; there have been many black days of late.

It took a year before a young family showed an interest. That was less than a month ago. They agreed to buy our house on condition we moved out by the end of August. Their children needed to start the new term at the local school. They offered £210,000; exactly £40,000 less than we paid for the house six years earlier.

The bank insisted we accept their paltry offer. Completion took just three weeks, made possible because the purchaser paid in cash. He's a baggage handler at Gatwick Airport.

The gentlemen at the bank behaved impeccably. Well-mannered, polite and respectful as they stripped me. Capitalism has no feelings. 'Nothing personal, "old boy", we're merely doing what Head Office tells us must be done.'

When the bank owns part of your house it grows into a monster; its wants, its needs become paramount. It was all too reminiscent of that desperate passage in Steinbeck's *The Grapes of Wrath*.

'But – you see a bank or a company can't do that, because those creatures don't breathe air, don't eat side-meat. They breathe profits; they eat the interest on money. If they don't get it, they die the way you die without air, without side-meat. It is a sad thing, but it is so. It is just so.'

As I poured the remains of the second bottle into my glass, I could see no chinks of light in the blackness. And then I remembered what it is we're supposed to do to our enemies.

Forgiveness? I don't think so.
MEMO ENDS rf

TWENTY-ONE

Jane twists her body onto her right side away from Tony, who is now facing in the opposite direction and snoring loudly. Barely five minutes ago, they finished making love, although it was no act of passion or need to gratify lustful urges. Not on Jane's part anyway.

The union might better be described as a shared participation in pre-programmed sex for the exclusive purpose of procreation. Today is exactly fourteen days after the last day of her last period. The clinic advised this is the best time for ovulation, the moment Jane's eggs are released from her ovaries.

The saga of the couple's attempts at conception stretches back eighteen months. She and Tony were married almost two years ago, when Jane was thirty-two and at a time when they both shared a yearning to start a family. She daydreamed of life as a wife at home with two children, a boy and a girl, embracing the sort of idyllic family setting she enviously watched in television commercials.

The smell of their intimacy fused with Tony's perspiration revives unwanted anxieties. She reminds herself, as she has a hundred and more times this past two years, sharing a bed with a man would be worthwhile the moment she becomes pregnant.

Her need for a family started eating into her consciousness some six years ago. Her relationship with her mother had faded into a peculiar on/off friendship that failed to arouse the warmth Jane suspected they both craved from each other. They met for lunch three or four times a year and Jane felt better for doing so but was never sure why. Her mother seemed too absorbed in her teaching role and her other three children to find time to fill the emotional void in Jane's life. To this day, she has never been invited to her mother's house nor met her half-siblings.

She was grateful for her mother's financial support. She funded her through college which qualified Jane for the well-paid position of deputy to the financial director of a medium-sized construction company based on a dismal trading estate off the Purley Way in south London.

A college education instilled confidence, taught her how to mix with her peers, speak as they speak, behave as they do, eat confidently in good restaurants.

Her mother subsidised the rent on the comfortable two-bedroom flat in Surrey she and Monica shared until they were both earning enough to secure a mortgage and buy it from the landlord. She never once expressed any desire to visit her daughter's home.

Jane's relationship with Monica was as perfect as she could have wished, and the trauma of her teenage years ought to have precluded any thoughts of male intimacy.

As a sporadic stab of discomfort in the mouth becomes, in time, a raging toothache, her longing for the family she never enjoyed as a child mutated from idle daydream to all-consuming despair. She awoke one morning fresh in the realisation she must face her demons if her pain was ever to be placated.

Oral sex with a man was out of the question, but as long as there was no intimation of violence, she had reached a stage in her life when she thought she might put herself to the test.

She met Tony by accident at an accountancy conference in a west London hotel. He was one of the presenters, who, as delegates were packing to leave, asked if she might fancy an early evening drink. A handsome man, over six feet tall, lean with black, close-cropped hair, a jaw seemingly chiselled from granite and blue eyes that sparkled as he spoke.

An unattached thirty-four-year-old accountant with a decent position in a City firm of stockbrokers, he was sufficiently well-heeled to own a comfortable four-bedroom house no more than a couple of miles from Jane and Monica's flat.

He spoke in a gentle manner and treated her with consideration and as it turned out, conventional sex with a man wasn't as stomach-churning as she imagined or feared, although it soon became clear a man could never appreciate the complexities of the female body in quite the same way as a woman.

The relationship blossomed over a period of three achingly awkward months during which Jane, desperate to allay suspicions her regular absences might arouse in

Monica, signed on for but failed to attend twice-weekly evening classes in advanced bookkeeping. Racked with shame over the deception, the moment Tony proposed, Jane knew she would have to face the most difficult conversation of her life.

During that evening a little under three years ago, two bottles of Sauvignon Blanc were consumed, Monica screamed loudly, and Jane narrowly avoided physically injury.

She confessed her relationship with Tony and Monica admitted suspecting as much, but Jane's admission was no less painful for that.

What prompted Monica's violent eruption was Jane's announcement that she had accepted Tony's offer of marriage. She was soon hyperventilating, managing little more than a strangled squeal of a response.

'Oh, Jane, no, please, no, you can't do this to me.' She then erupted, leapt from the sofa, yelling, 'Bitch, bitch, fucking bitch,' at the top of her voice, slapped Jane's face hard and stomped to the bathroom, locking the door after her.

Jane curled up in a corner of the sofa, her face stinging and her brain wallowing in self-pity over her inability to perceive her life in any kind of perspective. Since leaving her adoptive parents in Bristol, she had struggled with her emotions. She and Monica had lived together and loved each other for more than a decade but Jane's obsession with family was now pitching their relationship into an abyss.

Growing up, she never knew love, leaving her little point of reference as to what constitutes a loving family relationship. Would she know how to love a husband, let alone a child of her own? Had her own childhood rendered that impossible?

She and Monica once promised to love as sisters, but the relationship had blossomed into a closeness beyond anything Jane could have imagined. Now, she seemed intent on destroying the only real happiness she had known and all for the sake of a barely understood fantasy gnawing at her insides.

She once read that fantasies are better locked inside our heads for fear they might mess with reality. Was it so unreasonable to try and make hers real?

Her thoughts drifted back a couple of years to the only other major row she and Monica ever had. Jane was going through a bad patch at work, and on arriving home one evening, instinctively pulled away as Monica moved to kiss her. Months of frustration seemed to rise to the surface as Monica erupted, accusing Jane of being cold, incapable of giving affection.

'Do you actually love me, Jane?' she screamed. 'Are you actually capable of loving anyone?'

The question left Jane speechless, incapable of putting together any sort of answer, and Monica hurled the spoon she had been using to stir a casserole across the kitchen in Jane's direction, grabbed her coat from the stand in the hallway and disappeared out through the front door.

'You know your problem, Jane Foster?' she slurred on her return several hours later. 'There's some sort of weird caution inside you that stops you loving me, or anyone else for that matter.'

At the time, Jane accepted her partner's words were uncomfortably close to the truth, and yet now she was prepared to throw caution to the wind and marry a *man* of all things and one she was struggling to love.

Monica's sobs were now less frequent, and Jane moved cautiously to the bathroom door and softly pleaded with her to come out and talk.

The door opened slowly, and the warring couple trudged warily, one behind the other, back to the sofa. Jane took a handkerchief from her skirt pocket, moistened it with saliva and wiped Monica's puffy eyes and mascara-stained cheeks.

'Monica, I desperately want us to stay close, but can't you understand why I need to try for a family?'

Monica blinked furiously as fresh tears welled. 'No, no, I can't,' she snivelled. 'Are you marryin' 'cos you love this… man or just 'cos of some strange compulsion to have the family you never had as a kid?'

'I don't know,' Jane answered honestly, as she drained the last of her wine and walked to the kitchen. She removed the cork from a second bottle before slumping back on the sofa and refilling both their glasses.

Monica's arms were folded tightly across her chest and as she spoke, her eyes stared upwards to the ceiling. 'D'you honestly think it's right to marry a guy just 'cos you want to have kids?'

'I thought that was one of the main reasons people get married.'

'No, in this country and in most of Western society, I think you'll find women and men marry for love. The family bit comes later.'

Jane fumbled for an answer. 'I… I don't care. I just know if I… if I don't try, I'll feel… sort of cheated.'

Monica turned to face Jane, her features knotted in anguish. 'I don't know how to live without you, Jane, please don't leave. *I'm* your family. *We're* a family, aren't we?' The shrillness of her voice echoed around the room.

Jane took a mouthful of wine before answering. 'Monica, I've agreed to marry Tony and I must go through with it, even though I'm petrified I'm gonna lose you.'

'Then change your bloody mind, tell him about us. Tell him you've been in a gay relationship for more than ten years, an' you made a big fucking mistake, an' you don't love him 'cos you love me.' Her despair was making her breathless.

'I can't.'

'You know you can, and you know it's me you love,' she screamed. 'Stop being a stupid bitch and be happy with what we've got. This home, our life here, is the best bloody thing that ever happened to you and is ever likely to happen.'

'Please don't make it more difficult for me, Monica.'

'Difficult, difficult? You bet your sweet fucking life I'll make it difficult and I'm starting right now. Pack your bags first thing in the morning and go live with your darling fiancé. The man you're not really sure you love but everything'll turn out a bed of fucking roses as soon as you breed your two-point-five screaming brats.'

Monica lifted herself from the sofa and stood in front of Jane, her face a worrying mix of despair and anger.

'It'll be a bundle of fun stuck at home all day ramming food into their mouths and wiping shit from their bums while lover boy is out shagging his secretary or someone else's wife because you're too knackered to let him shag you when he gets home. And when he finally decides to trade you in for a younger, prettier, sexier model, which, as sure as eggs is eggs he'll do, don't come back here blubbing your eyes out.'

Without realising it, Jane's fingernails dug deeply into the palms of her hands, and it hurt. 'Please, Monica, no, it mustn't be like that. I… I don't want to lose you.'

'And that's the shame of it. You don't want to lose me because I know you love me but you're incapable of saying it out loud. What's worse is I also know you don't love him, but you'll still go ahead and marry him. You can't have it both ways. You can't break my heart and expect me to behave as if nothing's happened.'

Monica was shaking her head from side to side in a frenzy. 'I'm going to bed. Sleep in the spare room. I'll be gone before you in the morning, so you'll have plenty of time to pack.'

'Monica, please, angel, please can't we talk this through?'

'Don't angel me. I'm done talking. Goodnight and goodbye.'

She stomped off to what, until that moment, had been the bedroom they had shared for more than a decade. The door slammed and Jane heard the rumble of furniture as a chest of drawers was dragged across the floor to block the door. Throughout most of an unsettled night, Monica's muffled sobs pricked Jane's sleepless hours.

Tony, of course, was overjoyed to find her on his doorstep the following evening and listened sympathetically to her account of the previous evening's high drama.

'I figured you were in a gay relationship. I don't have a problem with it. Invite Monica to the wedding, she can even join us on our honeymoon, could be fun.' The smile that cracked the chiselled jaw was more a smirk.

Monica refused to take Jane's calls and the wedding invitation was returned unopened. Jane's mother came alone and Tony's parents, along with a bunch of uncomfortably rowdy work colleagues and teammates from his football club, were also in attendance.

Few if any fond memories remain from the day. She struggled to connect with his parents and reached the conclusion they thought Tony could and should have married better. Her own mother's face was cast in alabaster for most of the day, relieved only by the thinnest of smiles as she wished the couple every happiness.

Jane wrote to Monica, agreeing that she should continue living in the flat as long as she paid the mortgage, but if she were ever to sell, they should split the proceeds. She also confirmed she had no objection to her letting the spare room to help with the mortgage. No reply was forthcoming.

Now, two years on and lying beside her wheezing, snorting husband, Jane acknowledges it is now unlikely she will ever conceive. The loveless sex has become, well, loveless, and the arrival of her period each month an unwanted pressure in a marriage already straining every fibre of her being. She is certain Tony is shagging his PA, an over-confident, long-legged thirty-something on the prowl for another woman's husband, and the marriage is turning out exactly as Monica predicted, only without the kids.

In the moments before sleep consumes her messed-up mind, she decides that, if tonight's sex proves another wasted effort, she'll call it a day and abandon thoughts of having children.

TWENTY-TWO

Two weeks later, Jane's morning journey to work, normally a tolerable twenty-minute drive, has already punished her with ninety minutes of bumper-to-bumper torment. This week, unlike most in her life, will etch itself indelibly into her memory.

It started badly two days ago with the arrival of her period, and she broke the news to a strangely disengaged Tony over the breakfast table. 'You don't seem very disappointed,' she remarked, as her husband spooned porridge into his mouth, soggy oats dribbling from his chin onto the tablecloth.

'We'd both reached the conclusion it wasn't going to happen, hadn't we?' His words, plump with porridge, sounded thin on feeling.

'Well, yes, but… but in the early stages, we were both keen to have kids, weren't we? Aren't you even a little bit disappointed?'

He looked straight at his wife, his eyes unblinking. 'Look, Jane, let's not beat around the bush, shall we?' he answered matter-of-factly. 'You were in a gay relationship for ten years before you met me, and I sensed even before our wedding you were worried you might be making a mistake.'

'So why did you go through with the marriage?'

'I thought it might be fun,' he said, wiping porridge from his lips with the back of his hand.

'What, you thought there might be a chance of a threesome?' She spat the words straight at him.

He gulped another spoonful, ignoring Jane's question. 'What's more to the point is I'm also certain you've twigged I'm sleeping with my PA, so quite frankly, I don't see any sense in prolonging the agony.' He stirred a spoonful of sugar into his coffee and again looked straight into her eyes. 'Let's just call it a day, shall we?'

Two days later, what still stunned Jane was how such a brutally short conversation could end a marriage, albeit one built on such shaky foundations. Tony admitted he'd been having an affair with his PA since before he met Jane and there was only the briefest of breaks during the first few weeks of their marriage.

Jane, for her part, confessed to marrying Tony primarily to satisfy her need for a family, which engendered little hostility, merely the perfectly reasonable enquiry as to why she had to marry him to get pregnant.

She knew only too well why marriage was important. Her mother's disapproval of giving birth to a child out of wedlock would have threatened an already shaky relationship. The unanswered question was why Jane still conceded to her mother's blinkered morality.

That same evening, Jane drove to the flat she once shared with Monica. For twenty minutes she remained in the car, struggling to control her anxiety over the reception she was likely to receive from the woman she had hurt so badly. Not a single word, birthday or Christmas card had been exchanged since the night of the split. Jane was wrestling with a panic attack triggered by the very real fear Monica might have found a new lover in the two years since.

For the first time in years, she was using Dr Lakmaker's technique for anxiety control. Condensation misted the inside of her windscreen as she focused on the milky blur of a church steeple in the middle distance, half-lit by street lighting. Breathing in through her nose and exhaling slowly through pursed lips, she silently mouthed the mantra that had served as a crutch since her late teens.

Butterflies teased her insides as she rang the bell under the all-too-familiar front porch and moments later, a wary Monica peered out through a half-opened door into the gloom. No words were spoken; none were needed as the sadness in Jane's eyes told the story and the warmth of the silent hug washed away the two years of bad blood.

A bottle of Sauvignon Blanc later, the couple joyously shared the bed Jane had so brutally deserted two years before, and the following evening, three carloads of clothing and personal items refilled her still empty wardrobe and drawers of a shared dressing table.

Shunting along the Purley Way at a snail's pace, the shrill blast of Jane's mobile snaps her back to the moment. It's her mother. Surely Tony hasn't called her and spilled the beans on their broken marriage. He isn't that much of a bastard, is he?

'Hello, Mum, how are you?'

'Hello, is that you, Jane?'

'Yes, Mum, it's me.'

'Oh, oh, good. Sorry to call you like this but… but I must talk with you urgently. Can you take tomorrow off?'

'Why, what's the problem? Can't we talk over the phone?' Jane is reluctant to ask for a day off at such short notice.

'It's, umm… it's a delicate matter and I have to speak with you in person.'

Jane sighs loudly. 'All right, I guess I could book a day's holiday. The usual place?'

'No, no, come to my house.'

Fourteen years of sterile conversations over drab food in the same dull Italian restaurant and, finally, she is invited to her mother's home.

'I thought you didn't want me involved… you know, with your family. What's changed?' Jane asks, perhaps a little too offhandedly.

'I'll tell you tomorrow. Get here as early as you can, Jane.'

Her mother gives brief instructions on how to find her house before the line goes dead. The thought Tony might have called her mother and spilled the beans about her relationship with Monica stirs uneasy concerns.

That same evening, her relief at being back with Monica is blighted by her anxiety over what tomorrow's meeting might throw up.

'I don't believe for a moment your mum is about to disown you 'cos you're gay. Bloody hell, she suffered with a violent father just like you did; he forced her to put you up for adoption. She couldn't be that insensitive.'

Monica is perched on their bed in her customary position, knees tucked under chin, hands clasped around shins and an open book resting on the duvet. She is dressed in a thin, white cotton dressing gown, the sleeves stretching loosely over her hands. Jane turns from the dressing table mirror where she is busy cleaning make-up from her face.

'Well, we're not that close these days but it will still upset me if she cuts me out of her life.'

'Look, silly, she wouldn't ask you to her home if all she was going to do was chuck you out. She'd have told you over the phone. Maybe she wants you to meet your brothers and sister. That'd be good, wouldn't it?'

'Yeah, maybe,' Jane comments ruefully as she turns back to the mirror and lifts a cotton wool pad to her eyelids. 'It makes no sense for Tony to phone her; he didn't seem any more bothered about the end of our marriage than I was.'

'Well, he's got his darling PA to look after him now. You selling the house?'

'Doubt it.'

'You're entitled to half.'

Monica turns her attention back to her book and reads while Jane silently finishes moisturising.

'No, I'm not pushing for half the house, it's his and he paid the mortgage.'

'Yeah, but you must have helped pay the rates an' for food an' things.'

'I did but… well, I just want a quick divorce and he says he'll pay for it and then we're both free to get on with our lives.' Jane finishes cleaning her face and twists round to face Monica. She envies her lover's close-cropped naturally blonde hair, neatly trimmed around her ears and into the nape of her neck, sculpting her head like a young Audrey Hepburn. In the moment, she realises how much she missed her during her two years with Tony.

'You do love me, Monica, don't you?'

A little bewildered by the question, she looks up from her book. 'Of course I do.'

Jane sits in silence.

'Why the hell ask me that now? I bloody well took you back, didn't I?'

'It's just, well… I guess… I'm still confused about what the hell I do or don't feel.' She leans forward on the padded stool in front of the dressing table and rubs her calf muscles, not to ease discomfort in her legs but to avoid holding eye contact.

'What, you're not sure if you love me?' Monica asks, her eyes narrowing as her lips stretch tightly over white teeth, an expression that as Jane looks up, revives memories of that awful evening two years ago.

'No… no. I mean, yes. I need you but I lived for sixteen years on my own without feeling any emotions other than fear and hate. I found you and Dr Lakmaker and Tony, who let's face it, in spite of everything, is a decent sort of bloke and—'

'Apart from shagging his secretary behind your back,' Monica interrupts, her mouth twisting in distaste.

'I know but he was quite loving towards me in the early days, and I never felt threatened by him. Yet I walked out on him feeling bugger nothing. I don't miss him, no sense of loss and yet, somewhere deep down, I thought I sort of loved him.'

'If ya don't miss him, ya didn't love him,' Monica commented matter-of-factly.

'S'pose not.'

'Did you miss me while you were with him?'

'That's my problem, I don't know what I miss, what I want, or what I don't want.' Jane stands and moves to sit on the end of the bed close to Monica's feet, self-consciously stroking the soft, hairless skin on her ankles. Tony's hairy body repulsed her; too many reminders.

Monica smiles warmly. 'What about your mum? You said you don't know what you'd do if she rejected you because of our relationship. You must love her.'

'Yeah, I should feel something for her, shouldn't I, but I'm not sure I'd even miss her if I never saw her again. I'm a bloody mess.'

'Jane, for most people it's normal to give and take love easily. Your response to affection was completely fucked by your father.'

'Yeah, he's got a lot to answer for.'

TWENTY-THREE

The navy-blue Golf draws to a halt outside the modern semi-detached red-brick house on the edge of a 1980s-built estate in a tiny village four miles outside High Wycombe. Jane recognises her mother's car in the narrow drive leading to a semi-detached mock-Georgian house with white multi-paned bow window frames and matching front door. A net curtain ripples in a downstairs window as she walks up the drive.

As the door half-opens, Jane is stunned. Her mother's sallow cheeks sink deep below jutting cheekbones and the few locks of hair still clinging to her pink, flaking scalp are snow-white and wispy fine. She looks at her daughter through narrow, watery eyes buried in pools of grey and offers the thinnest of smiles.

'Mum, what's the matter, you look dreadful. Are you not well?' Jane leans towards her mother, her lips brushing dry, papery skin on her cheek.

'Come in, darling,' she urges as she hurries her into the hall. 'I've just brewed a pot of tea. Would you like a cup?'

'Thank you, yes, that would be lovely.'

Jane follows her mother along a narrow hallway into a small, square sitting room at the rear of the house.

'I'll get the tea.'

'Can I help?'

'No, no, you stay here for a moment.'

Jane settles in an upright chair facing French windows looking out onto a neat, rectangular garden, mainly laid to lawn but peppered either side with shrubs, many in bloom. If she only knew the name of one or two plants, it might brace the fragile connection between her and her mother.

The room is gloomy, despite bright sunshine streaming in; walls a listless shade of magnolia, beige carpet half hidden by a threadbare brown rug, dated, dark wooden furniture and armchairs covered in tufted upholstery, each a shade of dreary.

Jane notices three silver-framed photographs on a small writing bureau to her right. Group shots of youngsters, two boys and a girl at different phases of childhood. Her half-brothers and sister. She lifts a frame and studies faces, eager for signs of a family resemblance between herself and them.

They look happy, contented, well cared for.

Her mother struggles in with a loaded tray, arms shaking as she almost drops it on a small table in the middle of the room. Holding the teapot unsteadily, she manages to pour two cups as Jane cuts slices from what she thinks might be a slightly stale Victoria sponge.

She bites into the cake, remembering to keep her mouth closed as she chews, swallowing before taking a sip of strong tea. 'Mum, you don't look well, what's wrong?' Jane's hands are shaking too and remnants of the dry sponge break in her fingers and crumbs fall to the carpet.

'Oh, I'm sorry, Mum, I—'

'Don't worry about that now, Jane.' Her mother's shoulders heave as, seemingly with great effort, she takes one shallow breath after another.

'There's no easy way of telling you, my love, but I was given the worst possible news last week. I've been receiving treatment for bowel cancer for six months and—'

'Oh, Mum,' she says with a sigh. 'Why on earth didn't you tell me before?'

'I didn't want to worry you, but I've now been told the cancer has spread.'

'How bad is it? Can they operate?'

'I'm at stage four and it's too late. Scans found cancer in my liver and lungs and the doctors think it might have spread elsewhere. My chances of surviving a year are pretty slim.'

Jane leans towards her with both hands outstretched but in the moment of movement, the impulse weakens. The spontaneous warmth of the extended hug shared the afternoon of their first meeting was never repeated. Greetings and farewells became shorter, less tactile; a brief touching of cheeks, a ritual perhaps endured so as not to hurt the other's feelings.

She clasps her mother's right hand in both of hers and strokes shiny, translucent skin sagging from fleshless bones. 'I don't know what to say, Mum, it's so awful. Are they certain there's nothing they can do?'

Her mother shakes her head. 'No, Jane, there's no magic pill to cure me, I'm afraid.'

'Have you umm… told… my… your other children?'

She sighs. 'Yes, I have. Unfortunately, they live such a long way away now. John, my eldest, moved to work in Scotland after graduating at Manchester. I don't really see much of him. I believe he lives quite close to his father.' Her voice trails to silence.

'And the other two?'

'Oh, umm… well, Jeremy is on a two-year IT training programme in Brisbane in Australia. He's met a young lady over there, Australian, I think, and it seems he might settle there. Jenny is still at uni in Cardiff studying politics and philosophy so I'm on my own now.' The wan smile is more succinct than her words.

'And you never met…?'

'No, no, I couldn't bring myself to even think about another relationship. I still feel badly let down by my ex-husband but in truth, Jane, the only man I ever really loved was your father.'

'And he's dead.'

Her mother's eyes squeeze shut as she sits motionless, apparently lost in thought.

'What can I do to help, Mum?'

Her eyes open. 'Nothing really. No one can and anyway, you've responsibilities to your husband.'

'We're separated, Mum, as of three days ago.'

'Oh no, Jane, that's so wretched for you.'

'No, it's not, Mum. If you want to know the truth…' Jane cuts herself short in mid-sentence, aware of what she might be about to reveal.

'Yes, Jane, I would love to know the truth as I'm not entirely sure either of us has ever been completely honest with each other.'

Jane turns from her mother's gaze and stares out through the French windows. The red flowers closest to the window are crocosmia, she knows that now. She remembers once asking the gardener her husband employed a day a week what they were. She could never find the time nor inclination to understand gardening; at no time was it part of her life experience.

The back garden at her adoptive parents' house was a grassless junk yard of old motorcycles, half-mended engines, rusting wheels and the like. A long-repressed memory flashes into her mind of watching her father one warm summer afternoon as he repaired an old Norton motorcycle. She must have been about ten at the time and knew it was a Norton as the name was embossed on the side.

She remembers watching as he fixed a greasy-black metal component onto the engine with a gentleness she envied. She asked what it did on the motorbike.

He glared at her through cold, half-closed eyes before turning his attention back to tightening the nut securing the component. As he finished, and without looking up, he told her to 'get back in the kitchen and do the washing up.'

Her real mother's voice drifts back into her consciousness.

'Jane, Jane, are you listening to me? What's the matter?'

'Sorry, Mum, I was miles away. What were we saying?'

'Honesty, Jane. I was talking about us being honest with each other.'

Jane is deeper into this conversation than she wants to be.

'Mum, I don't wanna talk about the break-up of my marriage right now, it's still too raw. What's more important is you and how you're going to manage this illness. Can't Jenny take time out of university to... to be with you, to care for you?'

'No, she mustn't. Her education is more important than caring for me. If she gives up now, it could affect the rest of her life.'

'So... assuming you can't stay here in this house on your own, what are you goin' to do?'

'I thought I might search for one of those specialist cancer-based hospices, although I think they're quite expensive, even those run by charities.'

'You could sell this house. That would buy you the best treatment.'

'The thought crossed my mind, but I'd hoped the house would go towards helping my children with deposits on houses of their own. It's so expensive for young people nowadays.'

For a moment Jane wonders if she might be included as one of her mother's children. Her thoughts are quickly dashed.

'Now you've separated from your husband, surely there's nothing to prevent you from coming to live here to look after me?'

TWENTY-FOUR

From: Robin Farnham
To: Dr Lakmaker
Ref. No: 14

What was left of my publishing business was just about making enough for Lucy and me to risk taking a lease on a small apartment in Weybridge in Surrey in August 1994. We were surviving, although the business was fragile, and the slightest challenge could see it crumble.

One evening, a few weeks after the move, Lucy was away for a few days visiting her elderly parents and I was relishing the solitude. There was so much to think through.

My thoughts were interrupted by the ring of the landline and as I lifted the receiver, a vaguely familiar voice asked, 'Hello, would it be possible to speak with Robin Farnham?'

'Speaking.'

'My name's Robert Partridge. I'm wondering if you might happen to be a long-lost cousin of mine?'

That was one big shock and the sound of his voice brought so many happy memories flooding back.

'My godfathers, talk about a blast from the past. How the hell are you, Robert?'

'I'm really good, couldn't be better in fact,' he replied. 'I'm recently retired, doing a lot of fishing, playing a bit of golf, badly, and spending time tracing what few relatives I still have. I traced your name from the electoral roll and thought there was an outside chance you might be the cousin who shared those evenings with me back in the '60s. Still playing poker?'

That's odd, I thought, *we only moved into this flat a few weeks back and had yet to register our new address.*

'Not a single hand since that bloody awful night I was stitched up. Where're you living?'

'In Suffolk. I recently bought a flat in Ipswich.'

'We should meet up,' I suggested, with guarded enthusiasm.

'That's the reason I called. I'm driving down to Surrey for a police pension meeting tomorrow afternoon and hoped we might catch up, perhaps grab an early bite to eat.'

'Sure. I'm around after six. I'll book us a table at the local Italian. It's not bad.'

I was relieved Lucy was away; it was not her sort of evening, reminiscing with a long-lost relative. There would be a lot of catching up.

He arrived dead on time, and I could see middle age was resting easy on him. Close-cropped hair heavily streaked grey, but still broad-shouldered and rock-solid of build. Not, as I later discovered, from hours in the gym but regular running and care in what he ate and drank.

For the first half hour, we talked of nothing other than the old days, drinking in illicit clubs, evenings dog racing and long nights at the poker table. I told him of my regret in not heeding his warnings over my relationship with Penny.

He brushed my words aside, explaining his only marriage lasted little more than two years. Like me, work took precedence.

He had spent ten years working undercover, embedded in London's narcotics scene, tracking down obscenely wealthy drug barons. He grew increasingly animated describing how he would work his way into an illicit cartel, live as one of them while painstakingly amassing sufficient evidence to bring them to justice.

He claimed it gave him an exhilaration close to that which he enjoyed at the poker table. I said nothing but thought how similar in character we were and how much we had both missed by not staying in touch.

When he was finally transferred back to regular police work, he struggled with the raft of new regulations that were generating mountains of paperwork, leaving bugger-all time for crime detection.

'I bent the rules to bang up real villains, Robin. I made sure they got what they deserved regardless of what it took. Nowadays, everything must be done by the book. Pain-in-the-arse reports for every minor incident to prevent half-bent lawyers swinging not-guilty verdicts citing obscure breaches of police procedure. It really pisses me off.'

'You always were one for natural justice,' I commented. 'D'you remember that night in Westbourne Terrace when you helped that squaddie who'd been robbed by a prostitute and her cronies?'

'Yeah,' he answered with a rueful smile. 'My less refined methods are frowned on these days but in my time, I banged up a good many nasty bastards. Anyway,' he said, leaning back in his chair and stretching out his long legs, 'I stomached the desk job for a couple of years, then woke one morning and realised I'd had enough. So I took early retirement.'

- Meeting him again relaxed me, just as it had all those years ago.

We talked family stuff: who had died, when and from what. He hadn't seen either of his brothers in over thirty years and appeared to have no urge to re-establish contact. So why seek me out, a mere cousin he hadn't been in touch with since the '60s?

Before long, he had drawn me into explaining my situation. No point in lying so he got the full story, leading up to me losing the business and our house.

'Bloody hell, Robin, you must think that creep Thornbury got his just deserts, then,' Robert said, his steely eyes now strangely cold.

'What do you mean?' I asked, confused at the sudden turn. 'What's happened to him?'

'You must have read the press reports of the hit and run in Suffolk.'

'No.'

'Yeah, he was killed in what the police are convinced was no accident.'

Was this a dream? Is Thornbury dead? Is that what he's telling me? Has what I longed for with every part of my being become reality?

'Give me a moment to take this in, Robert,' I mumbled.

'The evidence suggests someone wanted that man dead.'

'I wanted him dead,' I blurted, without a thought as to any implication my words might convey, and in that instant, it dawned on me why my long-lost cousin had searched me out.

'You suspect me, don't you?' I asked with a growing anxiety. 'Is that why you're here? You said you were retired.'

He hesitated for a split second. 'I'm... I'm sorry for the deception, Robin, but yes, I am *sort* of working. The Chief Super in charge of the investigation is an old buddy of mine from Paddington Green. We were chatting over a pint the other evening and he explained their inquiries had thrown up the name Robin Farnham as someone who might have a reason for wanting Thornbury dead. I mentioned I had a cousin of that name and he asked if I'd have an off-the-record chat with you.'

'Jesus Christ,' was my instinctive response.

'It's a little irregular, I know, but I figured if you had nothing to do with it, it would save police time and give us a chance to meet up again.' He finished his words with a smile that fooled no one, least of all me.

My first instinct had been right. His line about the electoral register was a ploy, a lie.

'So are you officially questioning me?' My hands clenched tightly around my knees; were they shaking? Be careful. Be wary. But Christ Almighty, I hadn't done anything.

'Look, Robin, I'm still a copper at heart but after hearing what Thornbury did to you and the impact it's had on your life, I understand how you must have felt, still feel, about him.'

'No, you don't!' I snapped angrily. 'You've no idea how I feel or can possibly understand how much Lucy and I lost. That man was a total arsehole with a giant ego and I'm glad he's dead.'

'But it was murder, Robin. No one has the right to take another person's life.'

'I know that,' I answered forcefully, 'and fortunately, most people, and that includes me, are instinctively opposed to killing another human being.'

'Okay, Robin, let's get this out of the way. Where were you on the night of the 22nd September, 1994? Shouldn't be difficult, it's only a couple of weeks back.' As he spoke, he took a notebook and pencil from the inside pocket of his jacket.

Jesus Christ, he's serious. He's asking me for an alibi. I didn't need to think long. 'I was in the Midlands at the Novotel Hotel in Coventry, just off the M6 motorway visiting a trade exhibition at the NEC.'

'Can you substantiate that?'

'Yes, I can,' I snapped.

'Go on.'

'I left here early for Coventry, checked into the hotel around 10.45am and drove to the Chilled Food Exhibition at the NEC for meetings with clients.'

'What time did you leave the exhibition?'

'I guess I went back to the hotel sometime around 5.30pm and worked in my room before going down to the bar.' I hesitated for a moment, scratching at vague memories. 'I think I ordered a pizza and a bottle of wine and chatted with clients from the show who were staying at the hotel. It must have been after midnight before I went to bed.'

'Bit late, wasn't it?'

'Don't sleep too well these days.' My words were deliberately clipped.

Robert read back over his feverishly taken notes. 'One thing isn't clear, Robin. Why go straight to the hotel so early in the morning? Most don't allow check-in until after 3pm.'

'I check in early even if the room isn't ready; it guarantees me a quiet room. That Novotel overlooks the motorway and rooms facing the road are noisy.'

'The clients you had meetings with, can you provide me with their names and telephone numbers?'

How surreal was this? He was actually 'interviewing' me in connection with a murder.

My breath whistled through my teeth. 'Yes.'

I moved to the Georgian writing bureau bought at auction years earlier, at a time we could afford such luxuries. I pulled my diary from my briefcase and returned to the sofa.

I read the names of clients met at the exhibition, along with telephone numbers and the time of each appointment, along with those I spoke with later that evening in the bar.

As he finished writing he looked up at me, his eyes cold, steely. They put the fear of God in me. 'Are you familiar with the location of the hit and run?'

Is he searching, probing for a weakness in my alibi? Alibi? Why do I need an alibi? I have nothing to hide.

'No, where was it?'

'Long Melford in Suffolk.'

'I know it vaguely. Lucy's mother and stepfather live in Sudbury and on a couple of occasions we've taken them for a meal in a pub on the main street.'

'Can you remember which one?'

'I think it's called the Swan but wouldn't swear to it. Her mother made the booking.'

'What car do you drive, Robin?'

Really, is this real life? 'A Rover 2000.'

'What colour?'

'White. Why?'

'I'm not at liberty to reveal the evidence the Ipswich squad has collected on this… murder.'

He allowed this last word to hang in the silence and it stung me. Murder! How on earth had a dinner reunion with a cousin I'd not seen in three decades embroiled me in a murder investigation? As if there wasn't enough crap going on in my life.

If he used that word to frighten me, it worked. I eased my anxiety a little by telling myself most people would react this way. Murder? Not me, mate.

'What's the registration of your Rover?'

I told him and he noted it.

'Robin, you were a pretty good poker player. I've seen you bluff all the way on a pair of threes, so I hope your alibi is solid.'

'You think I murdered Thornbury, don't you?'

He nodded slowly as he spoke. 'You're the only person in the frame with a genuine motive. Your rage over the injustice of what he did to you makes for credible provocation, but I'm not convinced you've sufficient cold blood running through your veins to brutally kill in that manner.

'Most murders are committed on impulse, the result of an argument or in the fog of an uncontrollable rage or too much booze. With no advanced planning, most killers have no opportunity to contemplate the impact of their crime before it happens.

'A well-planned murder, on the other hand, gives the culprit time to rationalise the enormity of his crime… and the consequences.' Robert paused for a split second, a little too dramatically, I thought.

'Whoever killed Thornbury must first have come to terms with the implications of taking a human life and the possibility of being caught and spending the rest of his life behind bars.'

My cheeks flushed up badly. He must have noticed, although he would know such reactions are commonplace when someone is under suspicion for murder. And a murder I was capable of committing with not an ounce of regret; might even have enjoyed doing it. That part was easy to accept but the thought of spending a lifetime in prison; that was different.

Robert hadn't finished.

'As a detective, I have to ask myself if you're the kind of person prepared to put his wife and family through the pain and shame of his arrest and trial. Personal lives opened up on the pages of every tabloid newspaper, everything exposed for public scrutiny. Are you that type of person, one capable of putting your family through that sort of pain?'

'Once a copper, always a bloody copper. Isn't that what they say, Robert? What happens next?'

He smiled thinly. Had he been trying to break me, force a confession? 'The Ipswich team will check what you've told me but rest assured, they'll find who did it. It takes real genius to commit the perfect murder.'

He let that hang in the space between us too.

My mind was in meltdown. Was he implying I might be a genius and get away with it? Or was it a warning I wouldn't? Vague images flashed around the periphery of my vision; was that a collision between a car and a man? Was that me driving the car?

Thornbury's death made me feel good, but it wasn't me who had killed him. I needed Robert out of my flat. This flat which was not my home because Thornbury stole mine from me.

'It's time you were on your way, Robert,' I announced bluntly. 'It's a long drive back to Ipswich and for some reason, my appetite's disappeared.' My voice was flat, empty. The cumulative impact of his interrogation and my disappointment that the reunion turned out to be anything but social had drained me.

As we walked to the front door, I saw a sadness in his eyes.

'We had some good times together, Robin, you an' me. We were close back then, similar people, and I'd hoped…' His voice drifted into silence as he fought to find words he realised would not come, or he could not say.

A sense of loss hit me too. Robert was no longer my cousin; he was a stranger, a retired detective in search of evidence to charge me with murder.

Yet, he was right. I should have stayed his friend. At the age of eighteen I needed someone badly and he was there for me. Now it seemed he was implying I should have been there for him, too.

I wanted to balance his words by thanking him for his past generosity of spirit in sharing a life philosophy that accepts society's imperfections but never gives up the fight against injustice.

My words wouldn't come either and there was little hope we might opt for a wordless hug, even though there was no possibility we would ever meet again.

Just before the door closed, he laughed emptily as he called back, 'You'd better cancel that restaurant booking, you old bugger.'

MEMO ENDS rf

TWENTY-FIVE

From: Robin Farnham
To: Dr Lakmaker
Ref. No: 15

The police arrived as dawn was breaking three days after my cousin's visit. A psychological ploy, I guess. As it happened, they didn't catch me sleeping, undressed, unshaven or in need of a shower. The combination of missing Lucy, a bottomless pit of business worries and the rumble of Boeing 747s approaching London's Heathrow Airport made certain I was up and fully dressed. To this day, I wonder if they thought I was waiting for them.

The plainclothes detective and two uniformed officers were polite and respectful, much like bankers as they steal your home. The detective announced in formal tones they had reason to believe I might be able to assist them with their inquiries into a fatal hit-and-run incident that took place on 22nd September last. He made it clear I wasn't under arrest, merely 'helping with their inquiries', and asked me to accompany them to Ipswich police station for questioning. They also asked if I possessed trainers, shorts, tracksuit bottoms and T-shirts, all of which I did, and they dropped them into clear plastic bags which were sealed and placed in the boot of their car.

They then demanded the keys to my car, explaining they needed it for examination and that a low-loader would arrive shortly to transport it to Ipswich. 'If you bend it, you mend it,' I commented meekly, only half joking.

We enjoyed the most peaceful of journeys on that crisp autumn morning, bright sunshine burning gold, brown and yellow onto leaves clinging to the trees for dear life. They'll lose the battle, as they do every year.

The plainclothes detective sat alongside me in the back of the car and throughout the three-and-a-half-hour journey to Ipswich, no one spoke. It didn't matter; I was comfortable in my solitude.

Thinking back over my thirty-six hours in police custody, the experience has assumed a surreal, almost dreamlike quality, although at the time, it was alarming. Somehow, I found the resilience to stay in touch with reality, convinced they would never find any evidence to charge me because I was innocent. I was apprehensive, of course; you hear things about miscarriages of justice, don't you?

But what if it *had* been me driving that car? The thought of revenge had often crossed my mind and that man deserved to die. Did I kill him, and my subconscious had parked the memory of doing it somewhere beyond my recall?

No, if it had been me who had murdered Thornbury, I would be triumphant, relieved, and slowly shedding the distress he caused.

At the Ipswich police station, a fresh-faced young constable, still physically awkward with both his years and his uniform, led me to a dark-green, soulless and airless interview room, where he suggested I sit at a black metal table opposite two empty chairs. I was left alone for a full ten minutes. All part of the softening-up process, I presumed.

On the end of table against the wall was what appeared to be a recording device, an imposing darkened pane of glass to my right had to be an observation window and set high in the far right-hand corner was a closed-circuit TV camera. Someone was watching me.

The door flew open and a stocky, middle-aged man walked in followed by a large woman in her late thirties. Neither was in uniform and both clutched buff folders fat with papers under their arms. The man introduced himself as Detective Chief Superintendent Davidson and the woman beside him as Detective Sergeant Susan Malloy.

He wore the experience of his years and was probably the officer from Paddington Green who first mentioned my name to Robert. A look of world-weariness was etched into his lined and jowly features, and he hadn't kept himself in as good a shape as his former colleague, carrying too much around his middle.

He leaned in towards the recording device and announced, in a voice dulled by routine, the date, time and names of those present in the room.

He then cautioned me. 'Robin Giles Farnham, you have been brought to Ipswich police station for questioning as we have reason to believe you may be able to help us with our inquiries into the death of Trevor James Thornbury who we believe was the victim of a deliberate hit-and-run killing in Long Melford shortly after 8pm on the 22nd of September last.'

He further informed me that I was not under arrest and had the right to a legal representative present during questioning. I was not obliged to say anything, but anything I did say might be used in evidence or something along those lines. We've all heard it a thousand times on television and in movies.

Both officers filled the seats opposite me before Davidson continued, 'Mr Farnham, you have agreed to be questioned without the presence of a legal representative, is that correct?'

I nodded.

'Would you please verbally confirm you're happy to be questioned without the presence of a legal representative?'

'I confirm I do not require a lawyer to be present. I've had enough of lawyers to last me a lifetime.'

'Mr Farnham, what is your occupation?'

'I'm the owner and managing director of a small magazine publishing company based in Surrey.'

'Mr Farnham, did you know the deceased, Trevor James Thornbury?'

'I did.'

'In what capacity did you know the deceased?'

'I knew him as the chief executive of the UK Vegetarian Association. I first met him in April 1991, shortly after his appointment. My company published a magazine called *Vegetarian Life* on contract for the UKVA.'

'Is it correct, Mr Farnham, that the same Mr Thornbury cancelled your company's contract to publish the *Vegetarian Life* magazine in January 1992?'

'He did.'

'And did you consider that the cancellation was in breach of the agreement between yourself and the Vegetarian Association?'

'Yes.'

It was evidently clear the Suffolk Police knew everything about me, including my selling a magazine in a vain attempt to raise funds to pay for the High Court action, the details of the company's bank overdraft, the liquidation, and the loss of my house. They even knew about my current start-up company, too.

DCS Davidson painstakingly talked me through the saga, from time to time asking me to confirm certain facts were correct.

'Following the liquidation of your original business in October 1992 and the subsequent forced sale of your house in August of this year, how would you describe your feelings towards Trevor Thornbury?'

'I hated the man with a passion and an intensity I've never previously experienced. I wished him dead at the time, and now I know he is dead, a great weight has lifted from my shoulders.'

'Can you explain in more detail why his death lifted a great weight from you?'

'After what Thornbury did to my business, his continued existence weighed me down and would continue crushing me for as long as he lived. Now he's dead, that burden is easing and if it was murder, I would happily shake the hand of the person who killed him. Clearly, someone else also hated Trevor Thornbury.'

It was difficult to discern if my honesty shocked the two officers or not, as neither reacted.

'Mr Farnham, can you confirm your whereabouts on the evening of the 22nd September last?' DS Malloy asked, her eyes blinking as her voice droned. Like Davidson, she too had a weight problem, which she either didn't acknowledge or did nothing about. You'd expect greater self-discipline from police officers, but...

I deliberately rolled my eyes as I answered. 'You already know where I was, Detective, all the details were given to my cousin, ex-Detective Chief Superintendent Robert Partridge. I'm certain he must have been acting on your instructions when he visited me a few days ago and by now, you'll have checked everything I told him.'

'That's as may be, Mr Farnham, but we still need you to answer all our questions during this interview.' I drew an exaggerated breath, more for dramatic effect than any need for oxygen, sighed on breathing out and proceeded to tell my story again, from leaving the flat in Weybridge at 7am to going to bed in the hotel around 12.30am.

While I was speaking, both my interrogators referred to notes inside the folders on the table.

'Thank you, Mr Farnham,' they said in unison as I finished.

Malloy's eyes widened as she looked at Davidson, who nodded at her, before she asked, 'Both Peter Clark of H. Webster and Co and John Lawson of Clifton Cheese confirm you visited their stands during the afternoon of the 22nd September, but both are convinced you arrived earlier than the scheduled meeting times. Care to comment on that?'

'Detective Sergeant Malloy, working on a stand at a trade exhibition can be manic. You're in a bubble, immersed in conversations with dozens of different clients and real time ceases to exist. It's hardly surprising they can't confirm the exact time they saw me.'

'Is it possible you arrived early for these visits?'

'No.'

'If, as you maintain, time ceases to exist inside these exhibition halls, perhaps you too were not entirely sure of the times you met these people.'

'These appointments were arranged by me, so it was my duty to arrive at the specified times.'

'Then might it be possible you deliberately arrived early for both meetings?'

'Why would I want to do that?' I asked, genuinely puzzled at the suggestion.

The detectives shuffled themselves on their chairs and again exchanged glances. The woman officer shrugged her broad shoulders expansively, so Davidson answered my question.

'Because, Mr Farnham, it would give you sufficient time to drive to Long Melford, murder Trevor Thornbury and be back at your hotel in time to eat a meal in the hotel bar. None of the guests you claim you spoke with in the bar that evening was certain of the exact time you arrived.'

Before I had the chance to answer, DS Malloy tapped her index finger impatiently on a typewritten sheet of paper on the table in front of her. 'You explained to ex-Detective Chief Superintendent Partridge that there was a period of several hours during the evening when you were alone in your room. What exactly were you working on that took so long?'

The exact details of what I was doing that evening were hazy even though it was only a couple of weeks back. 'I'm almost certain I spent the evening passing pages for the next issue of my magazine, *Fine Food*.'

'Almost certain? Come on, Mr Farnham, it wasn't that long ago, surely you can remember what it was that you claim occupied you for an entire evening?'

'Yes, that's it. I must have been passing pages as the issue closed for press the following evening. It's not always easy for me to be specific as I work late most evenings.'

'And yet you recall the *exact* time you went down to the bar for your meal.'

'No, I don't! I just know it was late.'

Both detectives sat dumb and accusing, clearly waiting for me to carry on. Why not oblige them?

'Okay! It must have been close to 11pm because I vaguely remember phoning the bar to check if any hot food was still available.

'Oh yes, and I called my wife. If you've checked as much as you say, you'll have gone through my mobile phone records. Next time I'm scheduled to be questioned about a murder I'll take better care to note what time I eat!'

'No need to be impolite, Mr Farnham, we're merely trying to eliminate you from suspicion in this case.'

'There'd be no need for me to be *impolite,* as you so delicately put it, if you'd stop asking questions you already know the answers to.'

'Yes, we've checked your mobile telephone provider and you called home at exactly 10.52. Your mobile handset was tracked as not moving from your hotel room all evening. Still, it's little late to have dinner, isn't it?'

'That's the way it is when you have the balls to run your own business.'

The challenge, the implied insult, flew over their heads but perhaps they'd heard it all before. No one likes to be in this situation. Both detectives riffled through sheets of paper before Davidson seemed to set off on a fresh approach.

'Robin, having listened to your story, it's clear Thornbury was an unpleasant man; he treated you appallingly and we have every sympathy for the way you must have felt.' *Ah, here it comes*, I thought, *the softly, softly, we're on your side, approach.*

'In fact, I'd go so far as to say,' he continued, 'I might have reacted in much the same way. Revenge would taste very sweet after what he did to you.'

I was unsure what he wanted me to say, so stayed dumb.

'You planned it all very carefully, didn't you, Robin, as indeed I would have done. In fact, I'd go so far as to say it was brilliantly executed. You worked out your every move, right down to the last minute. I'm impressed, but also a little confused about the gaps in your alibi for that evening. Several hours when, as you are telling us, you were working in your hotel room, but no one saw you.

'You see, I believe those hours gave you just enough time to make the return journey to Long Melford, didn't they, Robin? Time enough to run Thornbury down. To kill him. No one would blame you for doing it. For wanting to pay him back for what he did. After all, it was because of him your business went to the wall. It was because of him you lost your home, wasn't it?'

His voice softened almost to a whisper. 'I understand how you feel after what he did. To you, your wife and your children.'

He wasn't getting to me. 'Mr Davidson, thinking isn't proving. I freely admit on most days, I imagined what it would be like to kill Thornbury. I've admitted on a hundred or more occasions that if I saw him standing in the middle of the road while driving, the brake would be the last pedal I'd hit.

'He was an egocentric, self-centred excuse for a human being who ruined my business, threw good people out of jobs, destroyed a profitable magazine and lost me my house. He deserved to die and I'm glad he's dead.'

I was moving into another gear; into a mode I used occasionally throughout my working life and think of as a 'controlled loss of temper'. It may look as though I'm out of control. In reality, I know exactly what I'm saying.

'And he wasn't the only bastard in this saga!'

My voice was climbing the decibel scale.

'British civil justice is as much the villain. Controlled by the pompous privileged few, exclusively reserved for the wealthy. If someone buggers you up in business, the only recourse to secure compensation is through the courts and only if you have a big pot of money. If you're broke, as I was, you'll stay broke because the lawyers and the courts don't wanna know you.

'The vegetarian charity Thornbury worked for is obscenely rich. Old ladies die leaving the association their life savings because they're soft on badgers, cows, chickens and donkeys. That's not in itself a bad thing but the Charity Commission is understaffed, too toothless to monitor the way charities waste their money, including paying their senior executives big fat salaries.

'Thornbury was a nasty piece of work who enjoyed the company of high-class hookers in West End clubs. He was granted unsupervised access to the most expensive legal advice from top City lawyers who made bloody sure I couldn't afford to bring the case to court.'

'Mr Farnham,' the woman officer butted in as I drew breath, 'we're discussing the crime of murder and don't have the time to listen to your views on a failed breach of contract action.'

'I don't give a damn what you do or don't want to hear. The fact is I wouldn't be sitting here if the courts were more accessible to ordinary people like me.'

At this point, I was going for broke. I stood and faced them both from the corner of the room.

'There's no judicial system protecting the weak from the strong, the poor from the rich. Instead, it builds a bloody great wall between them. If you have no money you end up sucked dry, a victim of the selfish arrogance of those with power and wealth. That's why I've got "views", as you so patronisingly put it.'

I sensed frustration in DCS Davidson's voice as he stood no more than a foot away from me and pointedly stared into my eyes.

'Robin, please, sit down. We're investigating the deliberate killing of a human being and that's a serious business, no matter what you thought of him.'

He resettled his more than ample backside on the chair as I returned to mine. Still using my first name. What was he hoping to achieve by that?

'What does interest me, Robin, is your claim that, and I quote, "I wouldn't be sitting here if the courts were more accessible to ordinary people like me". It seems you're stating as fact that Thornbury's death is a direct result of your inability to pursue your case for breach of contract.'

'No! You're saying that. I'm saying that if access to the courts had been available to me, we would have won and got back the money owed, plus damages for breach of contract, which would have kept me in business.'

I graced him with my best smile but wasn't quite finished.

'Do you know what, Chief Superintendent, I don't give a flying fuck who killed that man. I know exactly where I was that night, and there are good people who'll vouch for me, and you'll find it impossible to prove otherwise.'

A long pause ensued before the next question. Perhaps a deliberate ploy to increase tension.

'Robin, let's move on, shall we? Can you explain what you were doing in Lavenham on the evening of the 22nd September last?'

'What the fu…? I've just told you where I was that evening, and it was nowhere near Lavenham. Are you not listening to me?'

Further silence and shuffling of papers. *Another tactic*, I thought.

'Could you explain then, Robin, how it is your white Rover 2000 was seen in a car park in the town of Lavenham, which is only a short distance from Long Melford?'

'No, I can't, because I know my car was in the car park at the Novotel in Coventry. All bloody evening!' I banged the table hard with my fist. 'There're hundreds, if not thousands of white Rover 2000s in this country. Someone got it wrong.' As I spoke, I squeezed my eyes shut, bemused at the man's stupidity. In the back of my mind, though, I recalled reading somewhere we instinctively close our eyes when we're lying. But I wasn't lying.

'A local resident visited Lavenham police station to report the fact that he had accidentally scraped the front offside wing of a white Rover as he was leaving the car park in the town's main square that evening.'

This is a trap. Bugger, my car does have a small scratch on the front wing, a very small scratch. Had it happened before the 22nd? Not sure. He's bluffing. Isn't he?

'Come off it, Chief Superintendent, no one is that honest anymore; they'd have left a note with their telephone number on the windscreen rather than waste police time.' I added one further comment in an attempt to clinch my argument. 'Anyway, it's doubtful the local nick was even open at that time of night.'

Both pairs of eyes went down and stayed down. Point to me, maybe.

'What was the registration number of this Rover?' I asked, calmly.

He ignored my question. He was not ready to reveal his hand yet, so it was time for me to be helpful.

'You'll find a small scratch on the offside front wing of my car, but it happened while I was parked in the station car park in Weybridge sometime last August.'

'Don't worry, Mr Farnham, we're going over your car in microscopic detail. If you were in the vicinity of Long Melford that evening, we'll find the evidence.'

Malloy butted in. 'Are you a runner, Mr Farnham?'

So, they avoided revealing the strength – or weakness – of the evidence on the scratch and were now heading in a different direction. 'I run most days, first thing in the morning. Keeps me fit and I enjoy it.'

'What about during the evenings? Did you, for instance, go for a run on the evening of the 22nd September last?'

'Do you know what, I'm almost certain I did. I'd left home early that morning and hadn't had time for my normal run. Thinking back, I'm sure I left the hotel and ran for about forty-five minutes at some point during the evening.'

'So you *weren't* in your room all evening working, as you previously stated?'

'No, I went for a run. It slipped my mind because it's such a regular part of my daily life. I run every single day of the week.'

'Why didn't you take your mobile with you?'

'Didn't want to be disturbed while running, needed to clear my head.'

'You take your running gear with you on business trips?'

'Always. I also ran the next morning before breakfast.'

An uneasy silence filled the room, deliberately letting me think over my situation, perhaps. Finally, Davidson spoke. 'You were seen entering the hotel lobby of the Novotel in your running gear at around 10.45pm. Rather late for a run, isn't it?'

'No,' I shouted in frustration, banging my fist a second time. 'Look, I'd been working for hours so a run just before eating was the perfect way to wind down.'

'It was raining heavily that evening in Coventry, wasn't it?' asked Malloy.

'Can't remember.'

'We don't think you're being very honest with us, Mr Farnham,' she said. Her eyes glanced up at Davidson. He nodded and she, well, maybe you'd say she went for the kill.

'We think that during the afternoon of the 22nd September, you returned from the NEC to the Novotel, possibly mid-afternoon, and changed into your running gear before driving to Lavenham.

'On arrival, you parked in the main square and took a taxi to pick up a stolen Volkswagen Golf motor vehicle which we believe you had parked at Sudbury station the previous day. You drove the Golf to Long Melford where you cold-bloodedly murdered Trevor Thornbury. Immediately afterwards, you drove the Golf into a field close to Lavenham and set fire to it, ran back to your Rover in Lavenham, drove to the Novotel in Coventry and entered the hotel reception dressed in a manner suggesting you were returning from your evening run.'

She paused dramatically. 'That's how you murdered Trevor Thornbury, wasn't it, Mr Farnham?'

'That's a good story, you really ought to take up writing murder mysteries. I almost wish I were clever enough to have done it that way. But it wasn't me and you don't have a shred of evidence to substantiate any of it. My Rover wasn't in Lavenham that evening and I didn't drive a Golf to Long Melford. I've never owned a Golf or even driven one.

'And as I told you barely a minute ago, I returned to the hotel late because I had been out running for at least three-quarters of an hour. Mr Davidson, I would really like to go home now. I've told you everything; there is nothing further I can add.'

'Mr Farnham, we're forensically testing your running shoes, your tracksuit and your Rover car as we speak. You can't think you'd get away with crashing that car in the maize field without some microscopic residues from the car and the soil in the field ending up on your clothing and transferring to the inside of your car, do you?'

'Test away. You'll find nothing.' I shrugged my shoulders expansively.

Sucking her teeth noisily, Malloy theatrically pulled an A4 colour photograph out of a file and, with a flourish, laid it on the table in front of me. 'Take a *good* look at this, Mr Farnham.'

The body was twisted, flattened, bloody, grotesque. The head crushed so badly it was difficult to imagine what the face had looked like in life.

The photograph drew me in like a magnet. It had to be Thornbury as I was desperate for it to be him. Deep inside me was a longing to know he really was dead and had suffered in the process of dying.

'Not very nice, but if that's him, don't expect me to feel any sympathy.'

'What about his wife and two children?'

Two children? That was cheap. If his bloodied image couldn't evoke sympathy, maybe the thought of fatherless children might.

'What about my wife and children and what he did to them!' I reached forward and slammed the photograph over as dramatically as she had produced it.

'Look. I barely knew this man. He visited my office once, for a day. We went for supper that evening in London and, at his insistence, moved on to a strip club. I left after he started getting too involved with one of the hostesses.

'We met for a second time on the morning he presented me with the letter confirming the Association's intention to withdraw from the publishing contract.

'As to where he lived, if he was married or had children, I didn't know and didn't care and don't care now. Why would I?'

'You cared enough to want him dead.' The woman spoke slowly, her voice chilling, but I recognised it as mere technique. There was nothing else she could use to frighten me. She appeared to enjoy the cruel side of her work a little too much. Her problem and I wasn't prepared to let it be mine.

It was hard to do but I smiled sweetly and let out a long, noisy sigh of frustration. 'We've already discussed this, several times. How much longer are you going to ask the same bloody questions over and over again?'

'You're not under arrest, Mr Farnham, you're helping us with our inquiries. We can hold you for questioning for up to twenty-four hours if we want to but as this investigation involves a murder, we could apply to hold you for a further twenty-four hours if necessary. Technically, you could leave here in the morning, but it would be helpful if you remain of your own free will until we finish questioning you.'

- In the end, they held me for around thirty-six hours and strangely, the experience recharged me wonderfully. By that time, I had acquired a firmer resilience to pretty much anything the world cared to throw at me. Thornbury was dead, a comforting thought that came close to compensating for the bank stealing my home, and the certain knowledge I wasn't responsible for his death gave me the upper hand during the police interrogation. My mental state while in custody, assuming that was what it was, seemed surreal, almost as if I was on a higher plane than those around me. The police thought they determined the pace of the interview but in reality, it was me. I disproved each of their wild theories, eliminated each improbable deduction by asserting what I knew to be the absolute truth.

Thinking over the day's events while stretched out on the firm mattress in a cell furnished with a cracked handbasin and stained lavatory pan relaxed me. I was comfortable enough to enjoy a surprisingly good night's sleep although the meagre supper of bought-in fish and chips was less satisfactory.

It was late afternoon on the second day before they finally released me, although it was on the understanding they might need to question me again as their inquiries progressed.

As they escorted me from that oppressive interview room, I remember turning back and deliberately staring into the eyes of both coppers.

'I'm not guilty of Thornbury's murder. I'm pleased he's dead and under the circumstances I really hope I don't hear from either of you ever again.'

MEMO ENDS rf

TWENTY-SIX

'Did you tell your wife you were questioned by the police on suspicion of murder?'

Robin blinks tired, scratchy eyes as he looks up at Lakmaker, who has just this minute walked into the consulting room.

'No, I didn't and as far as I'm aware, she never found out. A fluke of good fortune somehow prevented my name from leaking to the press, so there was no need for me to tell her. The police drove me back to Surrey that evening and returned my car once they'd completed their forensic examination. I fibbed to Lucy it had been in for a major service.'

'Why didn't you tell her?'

'Not sure. Maybe I felt she'd been through enough.'

'You never heard from the police again, did you?' Dr Lakmaker's question is clearly rhetorical, merely checking facts from notes in front of him. Robin doesn't answer.

'And your cousin, you never re-established contact with him either?' Lakmaker is writing as he speaks.

'No.'

'You weren't moved in any way to renew the friendship.'

'It was too late. We were different people with different outlooks by that time and anyway, he was convinced I'd killed Thornbury.'

'Yes, yes, he was, as is Detective Chief Superintendent Davidson. The case was recently reopened, and I have here a copy of the latest report.'

Robin senses an edge in Lakmaker's voice.

'A blue Golf was logged by a parking attendant overnight at Sudbury station the night before the murder, although the registration did not tally with that on the burnt-out wreck, which the police eventually discovered had been stolen near Croydon several weeks earlier.

'None of the witnesses you had meetings with at the exhibition or those you spoke to in the bar could be certain what time they met up with you and forensics found nothing on the Golf. It was totally gutted by the fire and what few footprints there were on the edge of the field were from the boots of firemen extinguishing the fire.

'There was no trace of soil or any other residue on your trainers or clothing linking you to the scene. They checked waste bins at the hotel where you stayed and at the exhibition centre for any discarded clothing but reached the conclusion that if any had been dumped at either location, they would have been moved to landfill. Extensive searches at two local sites revealed nothing.

'It also appears they lied during your interrogation as the report states they fully checked out Thornbury's wife, and it appeared it was a happy marriage but with no children.'

'Happy apart from his fondness for night-club hostesses,' Robin adds dryly.

Lakmaker continues, 'And there wasn't a single witness at Long Melford able to provide details of the car or the driver and the report closed by stating, and I quote, "During the first day of questioning Farnham ranted on about British justice, barristers, small businesses forced into liquidation and everything else he clearly holds strong views on. At one stage, we thought we were dealing with a mental case".'

A broad smile lights up Robin's face.

'But the police were not trying to trick you. An elderly man did visit the local police station the morning after the murder to report he had scraped a white Rover 2000 in Lavenham Square car park on the evening of Thornbury's murder, although the registration on the car he damaged was not yours.'

'I told them it wasn't me.'

'At the time, police forensic experts were unable to match the paintwork on your white Rover to the paint residue on the old man's car. However, recent advances in forensic science have now made it possible to establish beyond all reasonable doubt it *was* your car parked in Lavenham that evening.'

'That can't be true. No way was I there. I'd remember. I'd know if I killed Thornbury.'

Lakmaker cocks his head slightly to one side and squints through narrowed eyes in an uncharacteristic way. 'In your memo, you made no mention of the interrogation on your second day in police custody.'

'It was such a long time ago. I couldn't remember the details, but I presume they asked pretty much the same questions as on the first day.'

'They didn't.'

'They didn't what?'

'They opened a new line of enquiry on the second day. It appears your cousin's suspicions were aroused by the possibility you might be capable of murder, and he called for the files relating to the investigation into the death of a Brigadier Simon Robson.'

Robin swallows hard and his voice is barely audible. 'I have no memory of being asked about any other man's death.'

'I doubt the police report on your questioning is false, and it clearly states here that you were told about this second murder, and you confirmed your connection to the victim. You were unable to substantiate your whereabouts on the night Robson was robbed and killed and the police were forced to close the investigation due to insufficient evidence.'

Robin lifts his face to the ceiling; he cannot for the life of him recall any such conversation. He is exhausted and confused; what little strength he still clings on to is fading fast.

'You remember nothing about that line of questioning?'

'No, no, I don't, and I can't understand why.'

Lakmaker nods slowly as he lifts a sheet filled with handwritten notes from Robin's file and reads. A few minutes pass before he looks back at his patient.

'Following your wife's attempted suicide back in 1975, the symptoms you presented at the time led your psychiatrist to diagnose a mild nervous breakdown triggered by the uncertainty of your family situation. I now believe it possible you may have been suffering a more complex form of inner conflict.

'Let us assume for a moment you *were* violent towards Penny during the days leading up to her suicide attempt...'

Robin leans forward and moves to interrupt but Lakmaker checks him by raising an open palm.

'Supposing you *were* violent towards her, it could be described as an act out of character with your normal self, the self you see as a pacifist, a gentle man who cared for his wife and children.'

Robin nods.

'For any psychiatrist, accurate diagnosis of a psychiatric illness is an inexact science. A collection of presented symptoms can deceive us into assuming we're dealing with one condition when it's conceivable we should be looking for something completely different.

'I've allowed two of my colleagues to read my notes and listen to the recordings of our discussions. They've also read your memos, including the one in which you admit to attacking Penny and causing the car crash that killed Jo's lover.'

Again, Robin moves to interrupt but Lakmaker continues, 'Like me, Robin, they accept your explanation that you have no memory of writing that particular memo.'

'So you know who wrote it, then?'

'Yes, Robin, we know it was *you* who wrote it but please allow me to finish before asking more questions. We believe you might be suffering from a psychological condition known as Dissociative Identity Disorder or DID.

'This is a condition in which the most common symptoms include out-of-body experiences and the manifestation of two or more distinct identities or personalities within a single body. Sufferers generally experience periods of amnesia that cannot be explained away as everyday forgetfulness.'

The tight ball of hot pain in the pit of Robin's stomach compels him to lean forward and wrap both arms across his tummy. He sits staring dumbly at Lakmaker.

'Having talked things over with my colleagues, we agree your symptoms indicate the possible existence of two distinct or split identities, each of which appears capable of controlling your physical behaviour.

'These separate identities are known as "alters" and one will often differ from the other in gender or even race. They may even speak with different accents, exhibit different postures and mannerisms. During the period each alter reveals him or herself, it controls the body and its actions. It is a common characteristic for one alter to be unaware of the existence of the other although the second alter is generally conscious of both personalities.'

Robin's face is a mix of confusion and blind panic. 'Doctor, you're scaring the shit out of me. You can't seriously be suggesting there's a second person, a completely different personality, living inside my body? One who commits murder without me knowing?'

'I am, Robin, and we believe you may have lived most of your life unaware of his or her existence, as it's clear you're the primary personality in control for the majority of the time. If our diagnosis is correct, I need to meet your alter as soon as possible.'

'This can't be real; it cannot be happening to me.' Slowly, he lifts himself from the chair and wraps the palms of both hands over his face, shaking his head furiously. A fire is raging inside him, and he is desperate to escape the horror of the here and now and return to happier times when life was normal.

'What could have caused this, Doctor? Am I mad?'

Lakmaker stands, walks to his desk and taps on the computer keyboard. A minute passes before he speaks.

'Well, it states here that the principal reason why people develop DID is not entirely understood, but there is evidence to support severe and prolonged trauma during childhood, particularly physical and sexual abuse as the cause.'

'I wasn't abused as a child so I can't possibly be suffering this DID thing.' Robin's plea falls on deaf ears as Lakmaker continues.

'This was once a rare disorder, but it has more recently grown more common and controversial. Many doctors believe that because DID patients appear to be highly suggestible, their symptoms are at least partly iatrogenic – in other words, prompted by their therapist's probing. Brain imaging studies, however, have corroborated identity transitions.'

Robin responds immediately. 'So that's the answer; your telling me about the bruising on Penny's body, and the police suspecting me of murder, *prompted* me to admit beating her and killing Jo's lover.'

'That is conceivable, Robin, although we do need to eliminate the possibility you have an alter.'

'Under what circumstances would it… might this personality thing reveal itself?'

'You recall when you became angry during an earlier discussion?'

Robin nods, his tongue moistening his parched lips.

'You described leaving your body and watching from above as we sedated you. I think your alter may have been in the process of taking over and we interrupted the transformation by giving you the sedative.'

Robin settles back in his chair and reaches for a glass of water. Is he a wife beater, a murderer? Did he kill two, possibly three people, maybe more, but has no memory of committing these acts?

He had always been conscious of the divide between how he saw himself and how others viewed him. He never understood why he was so often perceived as cold, unsympathetic, lacking emotion. Inside his head, he was none of these things yet in the eyes of others, he knew that was how they saw him. In his later years, he drew comfort from assuming that none of us is ever the person we think ourselves to be.

Which begs the question, why did anyone think it made sense to keep him alive? What purpose is it now serving, other than to clear up a few unsolved murders? It can't change history. Those people are dead and if he had done the job properly, his suicide would have sent him off to join them.

Lakmaker looks up from the computer screen and speaks slowly, choosing each word carefully.

'Robin, I'm going to open a fresh avenue of questioning which you may find uncomfortably intrusive. Please answer as honestly as you're able. I would like to know the extent of your grief over the death of your father in 1984.'

The sudden change in the conversation confuses Robin. 'What in God's name can that have to do with whether or not there is another person living inside me?'

'Robin, please trust me and answer my question.'

The old man rises again unsteadily and walks to the middle of the room. He felt grief in the wake of his mother's death but later thought it more likely regret that he had never adequately repaid her generosity of spirit. But had he grieved over his father's death?

'I… I last saw him in a hospice, less than a week before he died. I hadn't seen him for at least a month, maybe longer.'

He squeezes his eyes shut, and in the blackness, retrieves the image that met his arrival. The June sunshine filtering through windows thick with dust accentuated the ashen gauntness on the faces of the nearly dead, gaping mouths drawing shallow breaths, wide eyes weary from the pain of living.

'Cancer had diminished my sixty-seven-year-old father's stocky six-foot frame to a skeleton of barely moving bones wrapped in wilting skin. Five-and-a-half-foot of me lifted him from his bed onto a trolley and wheeled him to the smoking room where we could be alone while he enjoyed a cigarette. If he was aware this might be the last time we'd see each other, he didn't acknowledge it.

'I'd hoped we might reminisce about my childhood, share memories of Mum or my siblings, maybe even his hopes for his grandchildren. His only concern was that the England cricket team was taking a beating by the West Indies. And he asked if I had any whisky on me.'

Robin opens his eyes and looks at the doctor. 'There was no final bonding. I don't even recall shaking his hand as we parted.'

Robin pauses for a minute, reliving a moment. 'D'you know what, Doctor, the only time I ever kissed that man was as he lay in his coffin and...' He draws breath and then slowly exhales. 'And I think I see it now as a deliberate gesture, one last futile attempt at breaking down a barrier that had existed between us since my early teens.

'As my lips brushed his cold, waxen forehead, the only word that came to mind was "goodbye". Nothing meaningful or relevant, no expression of forgiveness that might bridge the gulf that kept us apart all those years. No,' he answers, slowly shaking his head. 'I felt no grief.'

The doctor gives Robin time to come to terms with what he has shared. When, finally, he speaks, his voice is composed, his words measured.

'Grief is often confused with regret. We, the still living, regret our failure to do enough for those we've lost. Do you think it possible it was regret you felt? Regret for not having tried more to help your father speak about those things?'

Robin's cheeks and neck burn crimson. 'For Christ's sake, what is it with you? I see only too well the direction you're heading with this conversation and I'm not about to oblige you. It's all in the past, it's done, so just let it rest, shall we?'

Lakmaker is taken aback by Robin's outburst. 'I need you to trust me in what I'm about to—'

'Trust? Why the bloody hell should I trust *you*?' Robin turns and strides the length of the room and back with an energy not enjoyed in years. 'All you do is mess with my head. You kept me alive when I wanted a peaceful death, you've locked me up in this bloody awful place, refused to let me see my wife, forced me to write stuff I'd happily buried years ago and then try and convince me I'm some sort of serial killer.'

With his palms flat on an arm of Lakmaker's chair, he leans in towards him, his face inches from the doctor's.

'And now you concoct some cock-and-bull story about a weird alien inside my body that made me commit murder. What d'you take me for? You're a fraud, a liar, and a conman. This personality, this alter thing you're banging on about, is you, isn't it? You're not real, you're the Jekyll inside my head screwing me up and I've had all I'm prepared to take.'

Robin turns from the doctor, his arms flailing feverishly around his head as a burning rage starts to spread through him like wildfire across dry scrub.

Blood coursing his veins pounds the inside of his skull, and a familiar sensation clouds his sight. Zig-zag flashes of white light fill the periphery of his vision as hollow fragments of emptiness, like missing pieces from an unfinished jigsaw, carve gaping holes in what he sees. It is a migraine aura.

And now he is drifting upwards, floating as the gaping holes grow wider and the wildfire more stifling. Squinting through a migraine mist, he sees himself standing opposite the doctor. He watches as his mouth moves and he hears himself speak, only it is not his voice. It's deeper, harder-edged. He is at once mesmerised and horrified as his body moves menacingly closer to the doctor and, summoning every ounce of fading consciousness, he screams out, 'No, no, stop. Don't hurt him.'

His other self, the stranger below, turns to look upwards but at that moment, one of them drifts into the darkness.

TWENTY-SEVEN

'Hello, Doc, good to meet you. I've been looking forward to joining one of your cosy little chats.' Robin extends his right arm and grips the doctor's hand as if it was the first time the two had met.

His posture is now more upright, his shoulders broader, arms extending potently, assertively in a vaguely intimidating manner. His previously droopy, old-man eyelids sag less, grey-blue eyes glint in the sunlight spilling into the room.

The doctor takes a moment to compose himself before he speaks. 'It's good to finally meet you, too. Please, please take a seat. Are you also Robin or do you have a different name?'

'To the outside world, I'm Robin, but I've always referred to myself as Krait; not that I need a name.'

He sits bolt upright in Robin's chair facing the doctor; the tone and expression in his voice suggests a new confidence, an arrogant brashness, even. 'Isn't Krait a type of snake?' the doctor asks.

'Yeah, it is. Tell me, what's this fancy psychological phenomenon you think Robin's got?'

Even bathed in autumn sunlight, the atmosphere in the room is different, colder, heavier, more constricted. Professionally, Lakmaker is treading untrodden territory, unsure of his footing.

'I believe you're an alternative personality sharing the same body as… as Robin. Is that right?'

Krait shows no surprise. 'Yep, I guess that's about the size of it. What d'you call it?'

'Dissociative identity disorder.'

'Nah, you've got that bit wrong, Doc; he's not suffering any psychological disorder, he's as sane as you and me. I joined him when he was nineteen, the weekend he drove to Shaftesbury to stay with his parents, the weekend I killed Jo's boyfriend.'

Lakmaker blinks, his eyes then widen; Krait's blunt confession surprises him. After scribbling a quick note, he asks, 'So your arrival was linked to the bracelet?'

'You got it, Doc, and what a miserable sod he turned out to be. I thought I'd been lumbered with a right loser. Had to do something quick to cheer him up so I got rid of the new boyfriend. Trouble was, he never found out the bugger was dead, so there was no reason for him to get back in touch with her. As it turned out, it wouldn't have made any difference, anyway.'

'How do you mean?'

'You'll find out soon enough.'

Lakmaker is riveted to his chair, scarcely daring to breathe. 'So, you have no way of communicating with Robin?'

'Nah, he's oblivious of everything I do. Weirdly though, I'm conscious of every moment of his life, which by and large is quite normal, apart from an inability to get tough with those who bugger him about. I do his dirty work.' Krait's jerky arm movements seem aggressive.

'You enjoy violence?'

Krait leans forward as if he is about to share a confidence. 'I wouldn't say I enjoy violence. It's the planning and successful execution of a killing that gives me real pleasure. Revenge is a profound indulgence, Doc, and as the saying goes, best taken cold. An obligation discharged the moment he who caused the pain pays the price.

'Retribution is as old as time; history is a litany of vengeance visited by one tribe, race, religion or nation on another. Whether it's ethnic purging, annexation or reprisals in war or uprisings, humans relish administering what they perceive as natural justice to maintain control. Kings did it; presidents, dictators, religious fanatics and politicians continue to do it. Vengeance killing is all part of the natural order of things.'

'That's an appalling perspective, Krait. History is certainly littered with man's inhumanity to man, but the human race is slowly learning more peaceful ways to co-exist.'

Krait shakes his head. 'No, Doc, mankind's instincts are controlled by his genes, not by acquired attitudes. I was put on this planet to square circles, deal with those who evade the justice they deserve.'

'But you couldn't possibly justify murdering Jo's boyfriend. His death wasn't retribution.'

'To be honest, I don't think I actually meant to kill him but maybe his luck just ran out. Collateral damage, isn't that what the politicians call it?'

'And what about the violence towards Robin's first wife, Penny? That was cowardly and at a time she was clearly depressed.'

'Ah, well, there's the thing, Doc, I'm not sure which of us is the guilty party there. I don't remember hitting her but nor does Robin; maybe neither of us wants to remember.'

'Are you saying Robin abused his wife?'

'I don't know, Doc. Like you all, he has a good and a bad side although, unusually, he possesses no inclination towards violence, let alone murder. That's where he and I differ. I get the job done and Robin suffers no conscience.'

The roles are reversing; Krait is assuming control of the consultation. The doctor tries to draw the discussion back onto his terms.

'Tell me about your background. Are you the same age as Robin?'

'I'm not human, Doc, I don't age. I'm a gene.'

'What do you mean, you're a gene?'

'You must know what genes are, Doc. They're the purist form of basic human instinct, underpinning all behaviour. Look, it'll be impossible for you to get your head around what I am until you understand how I operate during the periods I take control of Robin's body.'

'Knowing that would certainly be… helpful.'

Krait sucks his teeth. 'Like my friend, writing's better than talking.'

'You won't disappear when… when Robin's anger subsides?'

'No, I won't disappear, not until it serves no purpose hanging around and anyway, these days I can take control pretty much anytime I want to, what with his illness.'

'And when you disappear, in what kind of state do you exist? Are you sleeping or... or what?'

'I live alongside his brain. I sleep when he sleeps, feel hunger when he needs to eat and am aware when he feels pain. Thankfully, I don't experience any of his other human emotions. To love, feel empathy or be troubled by anger or anxiety are sensations I don't suffer. In truth, I have no concept whatsoever of what it must be like to be human. Though, there was one...' Krait's voice fades into silence.

'One what, Krait?'

'Not important, Doc, not now anyway.'

Lakmaker's body is ramrod-stiff; he is uncomfortably outside his comfort zone.

'I think perhaps... I... I'd better leave you to it,' he stammers as he stands and moves towards the door.

TWENTY-EIGHT

Jane has barely moved from the uncomfortably upright chair close to her mother's bedside for more than three hours. The room in the Mellows Care Home, eight miles from High Wycombe, is eerily peaceful, apart from the distant hum of traffic from the M40 motorway drowning out the soft sighs of her mother's breathing.

A further three months of chemotherapy granted her another year of life, a year neither Jane nor her mother expected to enjoy. A year during which Jane resigned from the job she adored and moved into her mother's house. She and Monica were parted again, only this time there was at least the compensation of Friday and Saturday nights together in a local pub.

Two months ago, the cancer polluting her mother's lungs made her dependent on oxygen and unable to do anything much for herself, leaving little option other than a move into a care home. She rarely left her bed now, taking what food she could manage through a straw in the privacy of her room. Life's departure lounge.

Jane looks kindly on the diminished form propped at a forty-five-degree angle on three plumped-up pillows, her face now little more than dry skin sunk deep into grey hollows beneath bulging cheekbones. She lifts a damp flannel from a bowl on the bedside table and lays it across her mother's liver-spotted brow. Slowly, the head turns and her eyelids half open for a couple of seconds before drooping as she falls back into sleep.

Jane's fury over her three half-siblings' unwillingness to share the vigil at their mother's bedside has been eating at her insides this past twenty-four hours. Not once during all the months of care was Jane permitted to meet them. On the odd occasion they managed to visit, either at home or in the hospice, it was firmly suggested that Jane take herself off for the day.

So many times, she has asked her mother why she was not allowed to meet her half-siblings, and on each occasion, the reply was the same. 'Not now, Jane, please, just leave things as they are for the time being.' Later, as the cancer spread, her mother used her frailty to sidestep the issue.

Yesterday, the nurse checking her mother's condition every half-hour told Jane all three had been informed their mother was close to the end, but each explained there were circumstances preventing them from being at her bedside.

For a good hour, Jane mulled this over. Had there been some major family split to which she wasn't privy or was it because of her? Had her three half-siblings decided they were not prepared to spend their mother's last hours sitting alongside her bastard daughter? If this was how normal families behaved, her own disturbed upbringing hardly seemed out of the ordinary.

'Did you tell them I would stay with her?' Jane asked the nurse.

'No, we didn't. I shouldn't really tell you this, but your mother told us we must never mention you to her other children. We don't understand why but those are her orders.'

Finally, it was confirmed. Her mother had blocked three of her children from knowing of the existence of the fourth. A familiar cold numbness ripples through her body. She has rarely felt this anxious in more than a decade.

Later that same evening, as her mother drifts into deeper sleep, Jane bids goodnight to the nursing staff and drives to meet Monica at the nearby pub where she has a double room booked. Over supper in the cosy, low-ceilinged dining room, Jane updates her partner on the latest developments.

Monica reaches across the small square table and takes both Jane's hands in hers. 'It's so sad she won't let you meet your half-siblings after all you've done for the woman. It must make it difficult for you to love her.'

'I'm sure I love her after a fashion, despite everything. She must have a reason for keeping me away from them.'

'Yeah, more likely still carrying the guilt of getting pregnant and giving you up for adoption. People were like that in those days. She'll take her shame to the grave.'

'I guess the other three will show up for the funeral,' Jane comments wryly before taking a comforting mouthful of wine.

'For the reading of the will more like, and how d'ya think they'll take the arrival of another sister on the scene when it comes to divvying up her estate?'

'I doubt there'll be anything in the will for me. She gave me more than enough supporting me through college.'

'If you're not mentioned in the will, they'll never know that you're part of the family.'

'Which is probably what Mum wants. She's never made our relationship easy.'

'How d'ya mean?'

'Well, no matter how much affection I tried to give, I don't think I've ever got through to her, rarely felt close. She's never revealed a thing about herself, how she feels about me or her other children or even feelings she may have over the break-up of her marriage. I know no more about her now than I learnt the day we first met.'

'What the hell did you talk about during all those hours you spent with her?'

'She was *sort* of interested in my life but only up to a point, and each time I started asking about hers, she'd pick up a newspaper or switch on the television.'

'Come off it, Jane, you weren't altogether honest about yourself either. You weren't prepared to tell her about us.'

Jane lowers her eyes and stares down at her hands now resting on the crisp white tablecloth, her index finger idly herding spilled breadcrumbs into a tiny pile.

'You're probably right, but how much do we ever know about each other? What actually goes on inside our heads?'

'I think I read your mind pretty well and I'm honest with you about everything I'm thinking.'

'What, all the time? Every single thought?'

'Don't you think we're honest with each other?' Monica leans back in her chair and folds her arms across her chest. Jane is biting her bottom lip.

'Jane, are you hiding something from me?'

'No, of course I'm not,' she replies, blood rushing to her cheeks.

'You are, I can tell.'

'Please, Monica, don't get cross with me. I'm in a state at the minute. I *do* need to talk to you about something, but it'll have to wait… until Mum has… has gone. Be patient with me, please.'

'You're worrying me now.'

'Let's just go upstairs to bed. I'm dog-tired and need to be back at the home first thing in the morning.'

As good as her word, Jane is up and out before seven, grateful Monica didn't stir while she was dressing. As she is about to close the door, she looks back at her lover, eyes closed, firm straight nose, flushed cheeks and cropped blonde hair spiking in all directions.

TWENTY-NINE

It is shortly after 10.30 that morning when her mother's eyes open. Slowly, her head turns towards Jane. The nurse had just this minute left the room after bringing Jane a cup of coffee and checking her mother's pulse.

'Hello, Mum.' Jane smiles warmly. Her mother struggles to raise her right hand to her face to wrench the oxygen mask from over her mouth.

'Jane, it is just you here, isn't it?' Her voice is thin, each barely audible word squeezed out through dry, cracked lips and on shallow breaths.

'Yes, Mum, the others will be here later,' she lies. Only a little white one, she tells herself as she dabs her mother's peeling lips with a damp flannel.

'They won't.' Her mother heaves another breath. 'Listen.' She swallows and again draws breath, as deep as her poisoned lungs permit. 'I've written you a letter, it's… it's in the left-hand side drawer in the bureau at home.' The dying woman pauses, longer this time, and Jane sees she is fading.

'Find it before the others… get to it. There's something you must know…'

'Know about what, Mum? Please don't…'

What little strength she had summoned is drained and the dying woman slips into what will surely be her final, dreamless sleep. Within the hour, her breathing grows weaker and quieter, until Jane moves close to her mother's lips and hears no sound, feels no warm breath on her cheek. She searches for a pulse she is certain is no longer there and squeezes her limp hands, sobbing quietly as she silently thanks her mother for what she has been and what she has given her. Now is no time for recrimination.

Later that afternoon, once the tearful formalities are done, she leaves the home for the final time and drives her tired but serviceable navy-blue Golf straight to her mother's house.

On unlocking the front door, she races upstairs to the bedroom she has used this past year and fills two battered suitcases with her belongings. After heaving them downstairs one by one, she walks to the sitting room at the rear of the house and opens the bureau. In a narrow drawer on the left-hand side are four white envelopes, each addressed in her mother's shaky, dying-person's handwriting to her four children.

Jane places hers in her shoulder bag, closes the bureau and returns to the hallway. As she opens the front door, a car pulls up behind hers in the road and a woman in her early twenties steps onto the pavement. Jane recognises the face from the photographs in her mother's sitting room. Her half-sister walks to the front door and positions herself in the doorway, clearly attempting to block Jane's exit.

'May I ask what you're doing in my mother's house?' The tone is far from friendly.

Jane's brain moves as quick-fire. 'You must be Jennifer, Jo's youngest.'

'Yes, I am, but that still doesn't—'

'I've been your mother's live-in carer this past year, perhaps she mentioned me. This is my stuff, which I thought I should move now that she's… oh, you do know, don't you?'

'Yes, yes, I was called earlier by the home. They didn't tell me about you, though.'

'No, no, they wouldn't. I've been with your mother for most of her time at the home and was with her when she died. You can ask the staff there if you don't believe me. They told me you lived too far away to get here in time to be with her at the—'

'Yeah, well, that's my business, not yours. Now she's dead, I'll have her front-door key back, assuming you've collected all your things and not helped yourself to anything of Mum's.'

'No, I haven't.' Jane hopes her wide-eyed expression conceals her shock at the young woman's insensitivity.

'I'm not sure I trust you. The papers are full of stories of carers ripping off old people, stealing their money and stuff. How do I know you've not been inside taking whatever you fancy? I've a good mind to call the police.'

'Call the police if you want but you'll wait forever for them to turn up. I've stolen nothing and you're welcome to search these suitcases if you don't believe me.'

'Yeah, well, if me or my brothers find anything's missing, we'll be on to you.'

'There's nothing missing, I promise you. Your mother told me there is a letter for each of you in the bureau in the sitting room and if you have nothing more to say to me, I'll be off. My name is Jane Foster, and my telephone number is on the board in your mum's kitchen. I'd be grateful if you'd call to let me know when and where the funeral will be.'

As she drives away, Jane is in no mood for any sort of conversation, not even with Monica. Driving for an hour and with little idea in which direction she is heading, she finally arrives by accident, or maybe subconscious design, at Hughenden Manor, a few miles north of High Wycombe. She had driven her mother to the National Trust former country-pile of Benjamin Disraeli a week before she made her final journey to the care home. It had been their last day out together.

She parks at the far end of a large bare earth and grass car park and ambles slowly through the manicured gardens in the direction of a less formal area where, hidden among trees and high hedges, she finds the bench she and her mother shared that day.

The place has taken on a different air, tranquil in the absence of human voices, serenity tinged with regret. That afternoon, Jane had ached for her mother to finally offer a measure of closure on her reasons for keeping her apart from her half-siblings and why they, in turn, were so insensitive towards their dying mother. No such enlightenment was given and now, it seems it never will. All Jane has is a letter.

Trembling fingers ease open the flap on the envelope. Inside, are two sheets of unlined pale-blue writing paper filled with her mother's handwriting. It takes some deciphering, but Jane's eyes widen with each sentence.

Three time she reads each of the four sides. Three times, it leaves her quietly sobbing.

My darling Jane,

I must firstly thank you for being the child I never had but always wanted. You have shown me more love in a painfully short time than my other three children have since the day their father and I separated.

I'm aware you sacrificed so much to look after me this last fifteen months, including living apart from the lady you clearly love and are happy living with. Yes, my love, I guessed some time ago about your relationship and wanted nothing more than to meet dear Monica but I'm afraid I carried too much guilt.

Each time I think of the pain your adoption caused during your first sixteen years, it rips my heart in two. You must believe me when I tell you my heart had already been torn apart at the age of eighteen when my father ordered me to end my relationship with the only man I ever loved. As you know, I also grew up with a violent father, and knew only too well what he was capable of doing to me, if I disobeyed him.

To my shame, I have not been as honest with you as you had a right to expect, which I think you probably suspected. At the age of sixteen, I fell hopelessly in love with a young man called Robin Farnham who attended the local grammar school. For two years, we were inseparable. I loved him and he loved me, and we were both convinced we would spend the rest of our lives together. My father had different ideas, and in September of 1964, he forbade me ever to see him again.

You see, my dear, he decided Robin was not good enough for me. He saw him as the ne'er-do-well son of an idle alcoholic from the local council estate. I knew differently. We loved each other in a way that now, some thirty years later, still leaves me breathless.

It broke my heart having to finish with him and, at my father's insistence, take up with John Warner, his best man's son. He too was a gentle man, but I could never love him. Then, unfortunately, John died in that car accident the year you were born.

That, my dear, is only part of a story I failed to share with you. I met William while at college and when, three years later, we were married, it was more in hope of finding comfort and security than with any certainty I loved him. Sadly, the relationship was fractured from the start.

We can never fake love; it will always reveal itself as a sham. I yearned for Robin, but so long as my father was alive, even as an adult I could never bring myself to disobey his orders. Stupid, I know, and you, my darling, might call me weak, particularly in the light of your astounding bravery in dealing with your abusive father.

After my father died in 1981, some nine months before you and I finally met, I traced Robin to his home in Essex, only to discover he was married with two children. It would have been wrong of me to intrude on his life.

William found Robin's details in my diary and an awful row ensued, during which he admitted he was having an affair with the woman he later married.

When a relationship crumbles, vindictiveness so often replaces love and, cruelly, he lied to our children. He told them he was divorcing me because he'd discovered I was in a relationship with an old boyfriend. Sadly, they believed him, despite my attempts to explain the truth, but to this day, they blame me for the break-up of our family.

I know I should be angry with them, but somehow, I'm incapable of seeing them as anything other than the children I nurtured from birth. In hindsight, I failed them badly. My years of teaching other people's children at school taught me everything I needed to know, apart from how to love my own.

And that, my darling, is such a weak excuse for the way I have favoured them above you. I wasn't allowed to nurture you from birth, to forge the unbreakable bond between a mother and her child. Unfortunately, from my children's point of view, that bond is a fragile one and not one they reciprocated.

I feel so guilty over my refusal to allow you to meet them or for them to even know of your existence. As such, even in death, I cannot allow them to know of my shame in giving birth to you as an unmarried teenager and offering you for adoption to a family who treated you so badly.

I hope and pray your generation is the last to suffer the shackles of Victorian morality. You, my darling, seem wonderfully untainted by the outdated moral code my husband and I cursed upon our children. You must be free of any association with them, free to live your life as you wish. Were my three children ever to find out about your sexuality, they would treat you as unspeakably as they have me. You are a far better person than any of them ever will be.

All of which means I am unable to include you in my will and acknowledge the love and care you have shown me. That doesn't make me a good mother, or a nice human being, and I will take my shame to the grave. However, I am aware you borrowed heavily to pay for my end-of-life care and am so grateful for the kindness you have shown me. In order for you to clear the debt you must have incurred, and hopefully have something left as compensation for my weak character, you must contact my solicitors, Messrs. Lambert and Drew of North Street, High Wycombe, who are holding something for you.

My darling Jane, there is one last confession I must make although I'm certain this will bring joy to your heart. John Warner, the young man who died in the car accident, was not your father. I found I was expecting you two months after my father forced me to break with Robin. John could not have been your father as I refused to make love with him. I was still in love with Robin.

The police questioned me after John's accident and asked if I knew of anyone who might have held a grudge against him. They suspected it might not have been an accident and that a brick or stone may have been deliberately thrown at his windscreen. I lied, even though I knew Robin was deeply upset over the way I finished with him.

I have no idea if he had anything to do with John's death, although I doubt it. He often spoke of his strong pacifist principles, and I struggle to believe there was a violent bone in his body.

You are a level-headed, wonderfully natured young lady of whom I am fiercely proud, and confident you will use this new-found knowledge wisely. If you decide to seek out your father, which, of course, you are at liberty to do, please be careful you don't risk upsetting the balance of his family.

Once all the dust has settled, I hope you will find it in your heart to forgive me for the hurt and the lies. I implore you to hold on to the love you have with Monica but, if possible, hold a little in your heart for your mother as well.

With all my love.

Jane's heart is pounding; she can barely breathe. Her father is alive.

She reaches into the bottom of her large bag for the tin and disposable cigarette lighter there for emergencies. With fingers shaking, she fills the white paper with the mix of tobacco and weed and rolls a thin spliff.

Drawing deeply, she inhales the blue-grey, aromatic smoke and for five minutes stares with unseeing eyes at her mother's letter. Finally, she carefully re-folds it before placing it back inside the envelope.

It is ten minutes before closing time when she finally makes it back to the pub where she and Monica are staying. The landlord snarls a blank refusal to make her a sandwich at that time of the evening, but it matters little; Jane has no appetite.

'Your girlfriend's already gone up,' he growls, his ugly, unshaven face leering at Jane, raising hairs on the back of her neck. What is it about men's attitude towards gay women? It's 1999, for fuck's sake.

Monica is sitting up in bed reading and assumes from Jane's expression that the inevitable has happened.

'I'm so sorry, love. Did she wake at all?'

'Only for a moment.' She pauses, as a bizarre thought flashes through her mind. 'Do you know, I almost believe she woke at that particular moment quite deliberately. She was hardly able to speak but managed to tell me she'd written me a letter and left it in the writing bureau at her home. It's as if she timed it to make certain there was no way I could read the letter while she was still alive.

'She was only conscious for a few seconds before drifting back into a deep sleep and she stopped breathing shortly afterwards. The doctors must have pumped her full of morphine or something. Not a bad way to go, I guess.'

Monica notices Jane's dark-blue eyeliner has smudged a trail down both cheeks and beckons her to sit on the bed.

'You collected the letter from her house?'

'Yeah, and all my belongings. I also met my half-sister.'

'Really?'

'She arrived at the house as I was leaving.'

'What, that soon after her mother had died but she never went to see her… at the end?'

Jane nods slowly.

'Cow. Did she know who you were? What she say?'

'I told her I was her mother's carer. Better that way than... well, you know.'

'And the letter, what did that say?'

'It explained why she kept me apart from her other children and a whole load of other things to do with... please, Monica, I don't want to talk about it now. It's too raw and... well, painful.'

'You poor love, you've been through so much. I hope that bloody woman told you how much she appreciated what you did for her.' Monica is still hurting a little from Jane's decision to live with her mother a matter of days after she had returned to their flat following the break-up of her marriage.

'She loved me, Monica, she really did, in spite of all the shit with her other children.' She dabs her cheeks with the tiny, embroidered handkerchief her mother had given her last Christmas.

Monica rests an arm on her partner's shoulders and kisses her cheek. 'I'm just so happy to have you back. I love you too, you know.'

'I know you do but I'm afraid I have an admission to make and know you're going to be angry with me.' Monica looks at Jane, her face rigid as she waits for her to continue.

'I borrowed money to pay for Mum's stay in the home.'

'Why, she owned a bloody house, she could have raised money against that.'

'She wouldn't. She wanted to leave the money to... to her children.'

'Scheming bitch. She made you give up your job to look after her, took you away from me, pressured you into paying for her care and the house goes to three kids who didn't have the decency to show up before she died.'

Jane closes her eyes and shakes her head. She has no words.

'What an absolute cow.'

'I couldn't leave her, Monica, not like that. It wasn't her fault they didn't come to see her at the end.'

'No, it was theirs and they don't deserve to inherit a penny until you've been repaid. How much have you borrowed?'

Jane barely manages a whisper. 'Almost ten grand.'

'Jesus Christ, Jane, ten thousand quid? How the hell are we ever going pay that back? How much interest are you paying?'

'Please, Monica, please don't be cross, not now. I know it was stupid, but I had no choice. I want you to read Mum's letter. It tells so much about her and me... and... and my real father.'

She takes the envelope from her bag and passes it to Monica, who snatches it, lays it flat on the bed and reads for the time it takes Jane to walk to the dark wooden wardrobe in the corner of the tiny room and undress for bed.

'My God, Jane, this is incredible... almost... it's unbelievable.'

Monica looks up from the letter and blinks as she speaks.

'Wow! I'm so sorry. I shouldn't have lost my rag with you like that.'

'Don't worry.' Jane's face breaks into a smile for the first time that day. 'I think I might have a real daddy.'

'That's so good *and* your mum left you something she says will repay the loan and with money to spare.'

'We'll go to the solicitors in the morning, collect whatever is there for me and go home. That'll be good too, won't it?'

THIRTY

From: Krait
To: Dr Lakmaker
Ref. No: 16

Okay, Doc, you deserve to hear the full story, particularly as you were smart enough to figure out that I exist.

Back in '64, Robin was a little happier after meeting his cousin in London, although he was still pining for Jo and struggled to build relationships with other women. As he told you, he took to gambling and was reasonably good at it until those cheating bastards ripped him off. The Brigadier had to pay.

I took over for a couple of days and found an old iron bar on a patch of waste ground south of Hammersmith Bridge. I bought a pair of Marigold gloves, a cheap black raincoat a size too large and a black trilby and avoided touching any of them without wearing gloves.

It was so much easier in those days. Closed-circuit TV surveillance was in its infancy and a lot fewer people were wandering the streets of London in the early hours.

The only real risk was the journey up to the West End on the Underground. The bar was tucked up inside a sleeve of my coat and was virtually imperceptible to anyone who might look at me. Stop and search was still a thing of the future; these days I'd need to take more care.

It was important to keep an eye out for coppers patrolling the streets. There were many more back then and like buses, they tended to arrive in pairs. A convenient shop doorway almost opposite the gambling club shielded me from the street lighting and rain. It was a good hour before that pompous stuck-up bugger finally emerged onto the pavement and marched off briskly in search of a cab to take him home.

I followed at a distance until he was halfway along a deserted street and closed in to about twenty yards or so before sprinting up behind him. I hit him with all my strength and luckily, blood spurting from his skull sprayed away from me as he stumbled forward. I then hit him a second time on the back of his head to make sure he didn't retaliate.

His skull cracked noisily as he hit the pavement like a sack of coal and rolled into the gutter. Blood streamed from the wound, its blackness dissolving in the torrent of rainwater flowing into a nearby drain. Blank, unseeing eyes confirmed he was dead, which was a shame. I wanted Robin's face to be the last thing he ever saw. God, it felt good. He would never cheat again.

The tight bugger wasn't carrying as much money as he took from Robin, but it was enough. Natural justice, I thought.

I dropped the iron bar in the Thames off the North Bank at Temple and walked a mile along the Embankment before managing to hail a cab home to Hammersmith. I kept my hat pulled forward over my face and left the cab on the north side of the river before walking south over the bridge and back to Robin's flat.

The following night, I dumped the raincoat and trilby in a waste bin close to Robin's old hostel in Colville Terrace. A local rough sleeper rummaged through it most nights and would be glad of the warmth on offer.

I hid the Brigadier's money in Robin's bedroom, in a drawer he rarely looked inside. Over a period of months, I gradually added notes to those already in his wallet and am certain he never noticed the extra cash.

I was completely thrown when the police brought the Brigadier's murder up during the second day of questioning over Thornbury's death. Fortunately, Robin had started to lose his rag with that woman copper which gave me the opportunity to step in.

The police had no evidence linking Robin with the murder, apart from the Brigadier cheating him at poker, but it would have worried him if he'd known they suspected him of a second killing.

He filled you in on the Penny saga so there's little more to add there. She was great in the beginning; I liked her, she encouraged the miserable sod to be more outgoing, almost turned him into a party animal. Almost.

During the years she was in remission from her schizophrenia their married life was normal, although she knew exactly how to get under his skin. Looking back, I'm convinced there were times she deliberately made him angry, just to wind him up.

That's when I would appear. She knew there were two sides to us, two different personalities. Not the details, of course, just the change in personality. Women notice these differences and it was possible she preferred me. Tougher but more fun.

The one you want to know about of course is the fuckwit Thornbury and, exactly as the police suspected, it was me at the wheel of the dark-blue Golf on that damp night in Suffolk.

It was around February '94 that the seed of an idea began to germinate. The advantage of being two separate personalities is I watch carefully as things happen and enjoy the luxury of time to plan my strategy.

It started the afternoon Robin was driving home after spending the afternoon with Lucy, who was recovering in hospital following her hip operation. His mobile phone rang, and he answered on hands-free. I hope you understand, Doc, I need to refer to him in this way, as it is him and not me that I'm writing about at this stage of the story.

'Hi, Robin, it's Will.'

He recognised the broad south-London accent straight away. Will Maynard, a cheese wholesaler.

'Hi, Will, how's it going?'

'Pretty good. How's Lucy?'

'She's doing well, thank you for asking. I've been with her all afternoon.'

'So you're on your own this evening?'

'Yes, why?'

'Let's have a bite to eat at Swiss Mountain.'

Robin hesitated for a moment. He really didn't need a boozy night, with Will or anyone else. Yet, he felt genuinely lifted that he had taken the trouble to call and invite him out.

'Umm, okay, but I'll drive, as I need to get away at a sensible time. Got a busy day tomorrow.'

'Great. Can you pick me up?'

'7.30?'

'Cool.'

He liked Will. In fact, we both liked Will. He was a cheese wholesaler who sailed a little close to the wind. My sort of bloke.

He sold mainly to sandwich bars, cafés, restaurants and delicatessens, the owners of which regularly read Robin's magazines. Will would occasionally pay his advertising invoices in folding stuff, irregular but useful. Frankly there was always a bit of a thrill doing something slightly underhand. Not Robin's style, of course, but we all have our moments.

Robin sounded his car's horn as he pulled up outside Will's large, boldly decorated Ponderosa-style bungalow in a quiet, tree-lined village off the A22 in Surrey.

In an instant, he heard Will's voice shouting 'Goodnight' to an unseen wife as he swaggered down the drive. He was a boxer in his younger days but even in his early sixties, only an idiot or a drunk would pick a fight with him.

He was what you might call a snappy dresser. Crisp white shirt finished with a heavy silk tie and diamond-studded gold tiepin and a midnight-blue mohair suit tailored to fit the contours of his body, a style more fashionable in the '60s than the '90s. Rather too many oversized gold rings, too, and a chunky bracelet that looked as though it weighed what I do. Definitely a Del Boy, a good guy but capable of doing some damage if required.

Robin pointed the car north towards Croydon.

'Nice wheels,' Will commented as he ran his fingers along the riddled walnut dashboard. At that time, Robin was driving a Jaguar.

'You've seen it before.'

'Yeah, I know. Well-made, these Jags. What size engine is it?'

'4.2. Drinks petrol. I could do with getting shot of it. Interested?'

'Nah, too rich for my customers. They'd think I was rippin' 'em off,' he commented with a laugh.

'Shame, 'cos I owe more to the finance company than it's worth.'

'D'ya wannit nicked?'

'Nicked?'

I told you Will was a bit 'wide', but this startled us both. Almost everything Robin had done to get into and out of the Thornbury mess had been legal. It never occurred to him to look for solutions amongst London's shadier characters.

'Yeah,' Will replied. 'I'll introduce you to my mate John, he'll be there tonight. He nicks cars to order. He'll nick yours, doctor it so it's untraceable, flog it on and give you the difference between the amount you need to clear the HP and what the insurance company pays you. Clean as you like.'

Just like that? Problem solved so simply? Clearly, we hadn't met the right people. Or perhaps we had but never made enough use of them.

'Tempting,' he stuttered, 'but I'm not sure it's a route I want to—'

'Don't be a big girl! You should 'ave a chat wiv 'im. You've nuffink to lose, 'ave ya, boy?'

Will and Robin were ushered into a large dining room at the rear of Swiss Mountain. An overload of dark beams and heavy wooden louvres fashioned a claustrophobic, almost womb-like atmosphere. Whoever designed the place had never seen the inside of a real Swiss chalet.

The place bustled with an eclectic selection of the local underworld. Everywhere Robin looked he saw real-life clichés of gangsters. Camel-coloured overcoats draped over the shoulders of dark, double-breasted, striped suits, trousers hanging in razor-sharp pleats to meet black, patent-leather winkle-picker shoes.

We were shown to a table by a window and immediately joined by two other south-London characters; one was Will's mate John. A large man in every sense of the word, he broke the norm by taking off his overcoat and jacket and hanging them on a stand.

His fitted white shirt traced his body outline like a second skin and his torso reshaped its capacious volume as he sat, a resting giant, bulbous elbows on the table. His neck was the same width and diameter as his head and one ear lobe flashed a diamond. Apart from the fact that he wasn't green, he brought to mind the Incredible Hulk.

Robin felt intimidated and was way outside his comfort zone but there was no escape. Will was determined to help.

'John boy, Robin 'ere needs to get shot of 'is wheels; 4.2 Jag, free-years-old. Werf less than what 'e owes on it.'

John didn't waste a second. 'Got the motor wiv ya?' he asked. Robin nodded weakly.

'Where's it parked?'

Robin swallowed hard, frantically searching for a way to side-track the conversation before finding himself in too deep. The skin beneath his left eye began to twitch. He lifted a hand to his face, hoping to disguise what John might interpret as fear.

'It's not that urgent, John,' he told him, extravagantly waving with his right hand. 'But, well, I might possibly need your help over the next week or so. Any way I can get in touch with you?'

John glanced at Will and raised both eyebrows. 'Is 'e kosher?'

'Yeah, yeah, 'e's a good boy. You got no worries wiv 'im.'

'Gimme a serviette,' he said. On it he wrote his mobile number, using a ballpoint he'd snatched from the apron pocket of a passing waitress before gently patting her backside. ''Ere ya go. Sorry, mate, what d'ya say your name is?'

'It's Robin, Robin Farnham. I'll… I'll give you a call in a couple of weeks when I'm ready. By the way, do you supply cars as well?'

'Pretty well any marque you want, mate, wiv plates to fit year, model and colour.' The pride John took in the quality of the service he could offer was palpable.

'No chance of being traced.' He winked and nodded sagely.

The food at the Swiss Mountain was close to inedible and the conversation flew straight over both our heads although I enjoyed it more than Robin. I worked out most characters in the club ran businesses on the fringe of, or just outside, the law.

Robin was in unfamiliar territory, and it took a while for him to understand that theirs wasn't idle chatter but an alternative way of life. A profitable one too, assuming the chat around the table was to be believed. It was also clear that if one of them was stupid enough to muscle in on another's territory, retribution would be swift and unpleasant. They were talking my language and even Robin was learning fast.

An idea was slowly growing, a very nasty idea but one I knew would be relished in this room.

Fantasy into reality is something we both understood. More than once Robin defied doubters and made possible what looked impossible. Together, we might do it again.

Robin knew someone who had muscled in on his territory, someone who deserved swift and unpleasant retribution.

MEMO ENDS Krait

*

From: Krait
To: Dr Lakmaker
Ref. No: 17

It had taken eight months. Serve revenge cold. I was frozen.

Here's what happened.

The tipping point was that final evening in Robin's house in Caterham, the night he drank too much wine as he fumed over what Thornbury had done to him.

The anger fermenting inside Robin made it easy for me to take over pretty much whenever it suited. One Sunday afternoon in March of '94, Robin squandered a couple of fruitless hours trying to juggle the company's cash flow, so I took control the moment I realised the answer was not too far away. I called big John.

The Jag had to go, and the man was as good as his word. It disappeared from a car park the following day. The insurance company took their time reimbursing the car's book value and John paid the difference in cash so I could settle the outstanding debt to the finance company. Job done. To this day, Robin is convinced the car was genuinely nicked and the finance company forgot to chase him for the difference.

John asked if I needed something to replace it, but Robin bought a one-year-old Rover 2000 at a realistic price from a less shady dealer.

'I might need a car for one of my staff though,' I lied. 'A Golf or something similar. It doesn't need to be top of the range or anything. How much warning d'you need?'

'Gimme a couple o' weeks. What colour?'

'Prefer black or blue but it must have dark windows.'

'Give us a bell when you're ready.'

You see, Doc, I'd remembered one or two snippets of information about Thornbury that Robin had forgotten; personal details that came to light the evening the two of them shared that dinner in London, before Thornbury's attention switched to the hooker in Miranda's. He wasn't easy to engage with and Robin struggled to find any common interest.

'Do you play cricket?' he had asked. At the time, Robin played most weekends in summer.

'No,' he answered bluntly.

'Do you run?' Robin ran for thirty minutes most mornings.

'No.'

'Play any sport?'

'Not sure you'd class dominoes as a sport, but I play every Thursday evening with some mates in my local pub.'

Robin suppressed an urge to scoff. Dominoes? Yeah, right.

'Where's that?'

'The Crown in Long Melford. I live right opposite. Rarely miss a Thursday.'

'Okay.' Robin feigned interest in what was clearly a humdrum existence. Humdrum enough for him to need the services of hostesses in West End clubs.

'Do you eat in the pub?'

'Nah! I leave around eight. Don't eat pub food, it's not real vegetarian. My wife makes a meal for the two of us around half-eight.'

'You got kids?'

'Nope, only been married a couple of years.' Thornbury clammed up after that and Robin sensed an implied reluctance to expand further on his personal life.

At the time, it was a conversation of little consequence that Robin pushed to the back of his mind and forgot. Only I didn't. Two years later, a broken business and a lost home gave it an appealing relevance.

I knew where the poisonous toad lived and where he wasted part of his Thursday evenings. And at what time he would be vulnerable.

Lucy's mother and stepfather lived in Sudbury, a mere handful of miles from Long Melford. Twice a year, at times when work permitted, she and Robin would stay with them for a couple of days. On their next trip early in July, I took over from Robin one evening and excused myself on the pretext of checking a possible venue for a client meeting. An amusing pretext, now I think back. I drove to Long Melford and parked close to the Crown Inn.

At 8.10pm precisely, Thornbury stepped out from the pub, checked left and right for traffic, and crossed over to a row of old terraced houses. He unlocked the front door of the middle one and disappeared inside. Gotcha!

The mere sight of the man raised hackles, but I needed to temper my enthusiasm with measured planning. I needed to be as cool as the nineteen-year-old Robin learned to be at the poker table, maybe not as reckless.

A familiar sense of anticipation filled my senses. Killing can be sexy. For me anyway. The odd thing is, Doc, all the time I was planning the act of retribution, Robin was half thinking he might do it himself but as ever, his conscience got the better of him.

I suffer no such qualms and a plan was taking shape. First, I needed a car.

Big John was waiting.

How could I get rid of the car afterwards?

Burn it.

If I burnt it, how would I get back home? What sort of alibi could I create if the police should question Robin?

On the morning of Wednesday 21st September, dressed in new blue workman's overalls and white trainers and carrying a brand-new brown canvas bag, I made my way by train to South Croydon station. I walked around the side of the station into a narrow street some two hundred yards away, to find John standing proudly beside a dark-blue Golf GTI Mark 3, complete with menacingly darkened windows. It looked like a Dinky toy alongside his gigantic frame.

He walked me around the car, pointing out its impeccable bodywork, even lifting the bonnet to show off an engine in pristine condition. I wasn't remotely interested; all I needed was a fast car, one capable of killing.

'You're certain it's untraceable, John.'

'On my boy Adam's life, Robin. There ain' a mark on 'er what could lead to where it come from. Dead kosher.' Kosher wasn't perhaps the most appropriate word to describe the transaction.

Discreetly, I counted sixty-five crisp five-pound notes and he swaggered off. I was full of admiration for the amiable Hulk, comfortably straddling both sides of the law. My sort of bloke.

I took a pair of disposable gloves and a dark-blue baseball cap from the bag, stretched the gloves over my hands and pulled the cap forward as far as possible over my head to cover my face.

The last item in the brown bag was a pair of dummy registration plates I had made two days earlier by attaching Letraset dry transfer lettering to white polystyrene foam boards. Two double-sided sticky pads on the reverse of each board secured them over the car's front and rear number plates.

The growing intrusion of closed-circuit television cameras on highways and in filling stations made it imperative I covered my tracks.

I drove north through the Dartford Tunnel to Colchester, topped up the Golf's tank and bought and filled two plastic petrol cans. I paid in cash.

Two hours forty-five minutes later, I eased the Golf into an empty bay at the far end of Sudbury station car park, removed the false number plates and secreted them under the driver's seat before locking the car. I bought a forty-eight-hour parking ticket from the machine outside the station building and displayed it on the dashboard.

John had been right; it was a good car, fun to drive.

I boarded a train to Liverpool Street, took the Underground to Waterloo and a train to Weybridge before finally taking a taxi home. Throughout the journey, I kept my head down and the baseball cap pulled low over my face. No one would remember a workman in blue overalls carrying a bag of tools.

Now here's the clever part, Doc. All this preparation was planned around the date of a food exhibition at the NEC in Birmingham which I knew Robin would need to attend. He had already organised a full day of meetings at the show and had booked a hotel room overnight. The perfect cover should the police ever track him down for questioning.

Early the following morning, I packed an overnight case with a change of clothing, including a brand-new tracksuit and pair of trainers. Inside the anonymous brown canvas bag was a box of Swan Vesta matches, another set of false number plates and a second new tracksuit and pair of trainers.

I then allowed Robin to do the driving and by 10.45am he arrived at the Coventry Novotel, checked in early as he usually does and collected the room key.

He drove to the NEC and caught the shuttle bus from the satellite car park to the Chilled Food Exhibition, where he registered at the front desk and pinned his badge to the lapel of his suit jacket. Proof he was at the show.

Early that same afternoon, I took control, turned up early for Robin's last two meetings and then headed back to the hotel. After parking the car, I took the lift to the room and changed into tracksuit and trainers.

The Novotel is always busy during major exhibitions, and I banked on no one noticing the shortish, fair-haired man in running gear crossing the lobby for a late-afternoon run. I was also grateful modern technology means you no longer leave or collect room keys from a receptionist who might possibly remember you.

Once onto the M6 east, I pulled into the first service station, parked up behind a large lorry and attached false number plates to the Rover.

I calculated the 117-mile drive from the Novotel to Lavenham should take a little under three hours. My mind was so focused on what I was about to do, it probably took half that time.

The adrenaline pumping through me was identical to the sensation Robin had enjoyed all those years before at the poker table. We shared so much. British law favours the rich and powerful. Time to reset the Scales of Injustice.

On arriving at Bury St Edmunds, I took the ring road south and picked up the A134 and inside twenty minutes, drove into Lavenham's Market Place square. The time was 7.15pm so any parking charges had finished.

I took the canvas bag from the boot, locked the car, and walked the length of the High Street to a public telephone kiosk on the corner of a side street. Fortunately, it hadn't been vandalised and I called a local taxi company whose business card I found pasted to the window. The driver picked me up outside the Swan Hotel.

A quarter of an hour later, the taxi dropped me in Sudbury High Street. In that part of the world, wearing a tracksuit and trainers while carrying a canvas bag made me invisible.

I jogged the short distance to the station car park and collected the Golf. My first priority was to find somewhere to dispose of it, after dealing with Thornbury. About a mile and a half outside Lavenham, I spotted a six-sided, breezeblock-constructed building, vaguely reminiscent of a Second World War bunker.

It was virtually hidden some twenty metres off the road on the edge of a field of tall maize, leaves browning in the autumn sunshine and fit for harvest. Perfect. The rundown state of the isolated building suggested it hadn't been used for years and the only sound heard was the twittering of swallows congregating on a power cable above the field beyond. They too were preparing for a dangerous journey.

Best of all, the ground was baked concrete-hard by the sun and was thick with matted couch grass. No chance of leaving footprints.

I drove through Long Melford, past the Crown pub, almost to the end of the High Street. I turned into a narrow side road and reversed out onto the main street, facing the direction from which I had just driven and parked up on the left-hand side close to the kerb, some sixty metres from the pub.

Slate grey clouds cloaked the early autumn evening and a fine drizzle seemed to hang like a sea fret in the cool air, giving the place an eerie feel. Appropriate, I thought. From the depths of Robin's brain, I recalled this was England's longest straight High Street. Two and a half miles of what was once a Roman road.

The Romans suffered no prick of conscience over the odd murder when taming the barbarians of Europe and the Middle East. Robin would suffer no conscience either. He doesn't kill people. I do it for him.

Nothing will go wrong.

MEMO ENDS Krait

THIRTY-ONE

From: Krait
To: Dr Lakmaker
Ref. No: 18

A couple of early-evening drinkers left the Crown and trudged slowly up the hill towards the housing estate on the edge of town. Apart from that, it had the feel of a ghost town.

Soon it was 8pm. My gloved hands were rock-steady calm. At this stage, Robin would be trembling, tormented by his conscience and the fear of the consequences of what was about to take place. He would chicken out, drive away.

There was no chance of me leaving; we both hated the man but unlike Robin, the thought of killing him excited me.

No one knows I exist.

Robin is so lucky to have me.

Ten achingly slow minutes ticked by before a figure appeared at the door of the Crown and I immediately recognised the lean pale face and loose-fitting suit.

I fired up the engine, engaged first gear and gently pulled away from the kerb until he was clearly in my sights. I shifted into second and rammed the accelerator to the floor. My target offered no more than a fleeting glance left and right, lowered his face from the drizzle and stepped into the road.

The adrenalin surge was exhilarating, more satisfying even than slamming that iron bar into the Brigadier's skull.

Thornbury looked my way as he realised the danger and broke into a trot. He didn't stand a chance. I swerved deeper into the oncoming side of the road and the direct hit propelled his legs forward and upwards like a dancing marionette, slamming his body onto the bonnet and his skull into the base of the windscreen. For a split second, his terror-filled eyes looked straight into mine.

Did he recognise me? I do hope the smile on my face was the last thing he ever saw.

I hit the brake pedal hard, and his skinny limp body catapulted forward onto the road in front of me. I slammed the car into first gear and floored the accelerator towards my escape, but a part of Thornbury's loose-fitting clothing must have snagged on the underside of the car as it passed over him, dragging him some fifty metres down the road.

I stopped again, reversed to release the dead weight and, on moving forward, swerved slightly to the left to ensure both nearside wheels passed directly over Thornbury's head. Job done.

The Golf was well out of town before the first busybodies were out of their houses to see what had disturbed the grey tranquillity of their September evening.

Within five minutes, I eased the car off the lane into the towering maize crop. It smashed through the plants and into the wall of the building. In a second, I was out of the car, stripped to my underpants and threw the tracksuit and trainers into the car. I grabbed the two full containers from the boot and emptied petrol over the seats.

A single Swan Vesta match ignited the fumes instantly and the wave of intense heat forced me to step back. I tossed the plastic gloves and matches into the flames and tiptoed barefoot twenty metres back onto the narrow lane still carrying the canvas bag.

I put on the second tracksuit and trainers before lobbing the empty bag into the mounting inferno and set off at a steady jog towards Lavenham.

Ten minutes later, I was back in the Rover, and it was a little after 10.45pm that I turned into the Novotel car park. I removed the false number plates and dumped them in the boot before running up to my room where I changed into my day clothes.

I briefly called Lucy before ordering something to eat in the bar downstairs. When it's me and not Robin talking she often tells me, 'You sound different, darling. You okay?' Funny how women always know.

We both slept well that night, better in fact than for almost two years. The following day, I briefly took charge again and dumped the trainers and tracksuit worn on the drive back from Lavenham, along with the false number plates, into three giant waste bins on the perimeter of a car park at the exhibition centre.

That was it: the last pieces of evidence that could possibly connect me to the events of the previous evening were discarded and assuming the coppers ever worked out where to search, the evidence would be buried deep in a landfill long before they turned up.

Trevor Thornbury was killed in revenge for what he did to Robin, Lucy, their two children and Robin's employees. His death was infinitely more justifiable than countless casualties in a myriad of pointless wars somewhere in the world that same day. The only difference, Doc, is the type of war.

MEMO ENDS Krait

THIRTY-TWO

Jane moves her face to within inches of the car's rear-view mirror and pouts both lips in that exaggerated fashion women often do when adjusting their make-up. She reaches inside a large handbag on the passenger seat for her lipstick and carefully traces its crimson tip over both lips. She needs to look her best for the interview.

Her thirty-five-year-old face stares back, her mother's high cheekbones unlined, her complexion clear. She thinks of her mother often, perhaps more so since she died than when she was alive. What is denied is often what we yearn for most.

She had arrived outside the tiny cottage with twenty minutes to spare. Better early than late, she has set her heart on getting this job.

Idly, she opens the monthly bank statement that landed on the door mat as she was leaving early this morning. Old anxieties over money vanished the day she and Monica collected the box left for her by her mother at the solicitors.

The ring was unusual, dramatic even. A small, solid-gold serpent biting its tail and crowned with what looked to be an impressively large diamond. She thought it ugly, almost vulgar, something she would never wear.

The eyes of the valuer at the plush Bond Street auction house widened as he examined it. He asked for proof of ownership in the form of the solicitor's letter confirming the bequest was legitimate. Jane also showed him a copy of her mother's grandfather's will in which the ring was described as an heirloom that had been in the family since the middle of the nineteenth century.

The £60,450 raised at auction after commission and costs was sufficient to feature in two quality dailies on account of the ring's probable, but unproven, connection with Queen Victoria.

Her half-sister never called with the date of the funeral, but the care home kept Jane informed. She slipped into the church at the last minute, settled at the back and left quietly before she was noticed at the end of the service. She spotted the daughter she met at her mother's house and a son, both hunched forward in the front pew. Jane presumed the son in Australia hadn't bothered to make the trip.

Once the funeral was out of the way, she set about tracing her father, which presented little difficulty on account of his company's high-profile food awards, exhibitions and magazines. She discovered he had moved his home and business to Dorset five years before.

The proceeds of the sale of the ring cleared all Jane's debts and as a treat for herself and Monica, she arranged a week of luxury in a smart West Country spa hotel before setting about finding a new job.

On their way down to Cornwall, the couple broke their journey with an overnight stay at a pub in north Dorset, close to where Jane's father's business was now based. Idly scanning the local freesheet at breakfast the following morning, her heart missed several beats on spotting a recruitment advertisement for the role of finance manager/director designate in the very same company. It had to be fate.

That evening, over supper at the swish five-star country house hotel close to Falmouth, she announced her intention to apply for the post. Monica's face was a confused mix of disbelief and concern.

'Do you think working for your father is a good idea?'

'I wouldn't tell him… well, not straight away.'

'You can't do that.'

'Why not? I'm a bloody good accounts person, the job description fits me perfectly and it'll give me the opportunity to get to know him before deciding if he needs to know who I am.'

'Christ, isn't that a bit dangerous? Your mother thought he might have had something to do with her boyfriend's death.'

'I don't believe that for a moment. What worries me more is he has a wife and family, and his son works in the business too. After all the hassle I had with my mother's family, I don't want similar problems with his.'

'But what about us?'

'How d'ya mean?'

'You can't commute to Dorset from Surrey.'

'Thought about that on the journey down and it all hinges on whether you're made redundant from Harrods. If you are, we could let our flat, rent an olde-worlde cottage in the wilds of Dorset and you can look for a new job down here.'

'What, as a window dresser? In Dorset? You're kidding me, aren't you?'

A strained silence followed until Jane casually added, 'It may never happen, sweetie, and if it does, let's worry about it at the time.' She raised her wine glass. 'Here's to a fun week.' Monica's misgivings were clear from the weak smile offered as she lifted her glass.

September was as warm as a child's kiss and the hotel's secluded beach the perfect antidote to the muddled emotions of the previous fifteen months. On the couple's return to Surrey, Jane had posted her CV and letter of application to her father's business and is now no more than ten minutes from the interview.

Free of money worries, she has embraced a fresh optimism and flushed her remaining Valium tablets down the lavatory. The occasional spliff is now purely recreational.

The tension in her tummy is excited anticipation rather than nervous anxiety. The reference from the company she was forced to leave on account of her mother's illness had boosted her confidence. It confirmed her as 'exceptional in her role, diligent, professional and competent,' words she never dreamt might appear in the same sentence as her name all those years ago when working in McDonald's.

She checks her watch, locks the car, and smooths her post-box red jacket over a tight black skirt, cut a little higher above the knee than usual. She wants this job as much for the professional kudos it will give as for any longing to be close to her father. A new millennium, a new start and the next chapter in her life.

The pretty white-fronted cottage is set back from the narrow main street beyond its own car park. Jane enters a small lobby door which opens into a rectangular open-plan office and three women look up from computer screens as she walks in.

One is young, maybe little more than twenty, casually dressed in cheap tight denim jeans and skimpy yellow top and is borderline anorexic. The second is older, maybe early forties with jet-black hair and a figure tightly corralled inside a black jacket and skirt. The oldest of the three is shorter, petite and pretty in a patterned dusky blue dress. Jane figures her to be in her late forties.

'Hello, you must be Jane,' the oldest of the three says affably. 'Please take a seat for a moment and I'll let Robin know you're here. Can I get you a tea or coffee?'

'A glass of water would be fine, thank you,' Jane replies, conscious she still pronounces the odd word with a trace of a Bristolian burr. Before her days at college, Jane's mother would pull her up on her extended 'A' or harsh 'R', and also correct her grammar, although these days, people seem to nurture rather than suppress regional accents.

The lady disappears into a kitchen area at the back of the office and returns with a glass of water before lifting the telephone on her desk. 'Robin, Jane Foster is here.' She nods and replaces the handset. 'Please follow me but do be careful, the stairs are steep and quite narrow.'

At the top, the lady turns to the right and moves to one side, allowing Jane to pass through a narrow doorway. The room is tiny and might once have been a single bedroom complete with tiled Victorian fireplace, a wardrobe cupboard built into the eves and a sash window overlooking the car park to the front of the building.

A middle-aged man rises from his chair and shakes her

hand firmly before beckoning her to sit in the only visitor's chair adjacent to his desk. His eyes move from her face down her body.

'Hello, Jane, I'm Robin Farnham. It's good to meet you.'

She studies him too, appreciating it near impossible to spot facial similarities in oneself and another person. He is shortish, maybe 5ft 6in, stocky with brown hair streaked grey and blue-grey eyes. She notices his plump fingers and examines her hands resting on her knees.

He takes her CV from a buff folder and reads; she uses the moment to glance around the room for family photographs. There are none. Long-buried anxieties stir as butterflies flick the walls of her tummy. She wills herself to stay in control.

It comes as a relief when Robin breaks the silence. 'Well, Jane, it's clear from your CV that you have the experience we need for this role and your previous employer writes about you in glowing terms, but what baffles me is why you're prepared to move from Surrey to Dorset to join our little business.'

She had anticipated this might be one of the first questions and has prepared well. 'As I explained in my CV, I was forced to leave my previous position to nurse my sick mother, who died earlier this year. Now it's all over, I feel the need for a complete change of lifestyle. My partner and I stayed locally on our way down to Cornwall for a holiday and fell in love with the area. That's when I saw your ad.'

Robin nods slowly, casting his eyes back to the CV and, with a cheeky grin, asks, 'I'm not sure these days if potential employers are permitted to ask such questions but I will anyway. Are you and your partner married?'

She hesitates for a moment. 'No, I'm divorced but we've been together for… several years.'

'So how does your partner feel about a possible move? Presumably he has work commitments close to where you live.'

Jane looks directly into her father's eyes. 'My partner is a woman, which also means, of course, there's no danger of me getting pregnant.' She gives her father the cheekiest of smiles.

Another hesitation, this time by Robin, who flushes but quickly collects himself and returns the smile. 'Which, of course, might have been the next question I'm not allowed to ask. Does your partner have a job in the south-east?'

'She was recently made redundant with a decent pay-out and we both fancy the change.'

'I need this position filled quickly; how soon could you move?'

'We plan to let our flat and rent a house down here while we decide exactly where to settle.'

Jane feels her heartbeat pulsating beneath the tight skin above her ears. Thankfully, her hair masks the anxiety, and she breathes deeply, slowly counting backwards from three hundred, another one of Dr Lakmaker's calming exercises. She is grateful for a brief interlude as Robin busies himself annotating her CV.

'Okay, so let me tell you a little about our business and what your role would involve.' Robin takes time explaining that he is in the process of rebuilding a business he was forced to liquidate in 1992 and how he and his wife had also relocated from the south-east to north Dorset, close to where he grew up. The company's turnover is growing, and he needs someone capable of handling the finances, from basic bookkeeping to credit control, and with an increasing responsibility for budgetary and cost control.

He paints an exciting picture of growing consumer interest in fine food and drink and how his business is poised, with its food-related magazines, awards, training programmes and exhibitions to help small food producers and independent retailers compete against large supermarkets. It seems he is on a mission.

He then switches the conversation back to Jane, needing to know more about her experience with various software packages and the degree of autonomy she was given in her previous position. She lists the accounting systems with which she is familiar and speaks confidently on her ability to operate efficiently without supervision.

Robin smiles warmly. 'Does what you've heard about our business sound an attractive enough proposition to convince you and your partner to move west?'

Jane nods. 'It does, and while some of the cost control and budgeting might stretch me at first, I'm pretty sure I'll get my head around it quickly enough.'

'You've not asked about salary.'

'Your ad mentioned it would be competitive, although I don't expect it'll compete with rates in the south-east.'

'What were you earning at your last company?'

'£23,500 per annum.'

'That's a little more than I had in mind but if that's your current market value, it's what we'll have to pay you, but for that kind of money, I'll be looking for real commitment and hard graft too.' He smiles warmly. 'How soon can you start?'

*

'Wow! Just like that, he offered you the job on the spot and matched your salary. Jesus, either he's desperate or you came across as a bit special.' Monica is busy dishing up supper in their small kitchen as Jane sets the table in the lounge-dining room of their flat.

'Listen you, I've got skills and I like what he told me about the business. I want this job.'

'And it makes *no* difference he just *happens* to be your dad?'

'Of course it does, and you know that. I told him I'd confirm a start date as soon as I'd talked it over with you.'

'Seems to me you've pretty much made up your mind, then.'

Jane looks across the room at Monica and smiles. 'Let's do it, sweetie. You've banked a decent redundancy, I'll be earning good money and… well, it's a great opportunity for a new beginning, For us both.'

THIRTY-THREE

Swathed in darkness and comforted by the soft rhythm of Monica's breathing, Jane is still finding it impossible to rationalise the events of her day. A day that started as so many others but ended leaving her mind in turmoil.

The past two years have been all she and Monica hoped for since moving to the West Country. The flat in Surrey was let on a long lease to a secure tenant paying more than the rent on the idyllic cottage they found in the biscuit-tin beauty of a tiny village little more than five minutes from Jane's office.

Monica found a position in an upmarket ladies' dress shop in Sherborne, a fifteen-minute drive from home. Her window-dressing skills attracted her to the flamboyant fashion-obsessed shop owner and the two quickly formed a comfortable, if slightly bizarre, working partnership.

Jane's career thrived and with each successive month, Robin entrusted her with ever more responsibility. The role was challenging and rewarding, both intellectually and financially. Robin's wife, Lucy, worked full-time in the business; she was the eldest of the three women Jane met the day of her interview. She also met Robin's son, Giles, who is also involved in the business, along with his young wife. She had yet to meet Robin's daughter.

Until today, the right moment to admit who she was had never arisen. Her mother's caution over the fragile balance binding families loomed large in her mind and the last thing she wanted was to jeopardise her job or Robin's family. At the company's Christmas party last year, emboldened by a little too much wine, she had asked her father for a dance. He appeared reluctant and, as the music started, she understood why; he was no John Travolta.

He held her in a conventional dance hold and gently, if a little clumsily, moved her around the floor as they chatted. Was this the right time? Maybe, but in the moment of speaking, a fragment of common sense cut through the fog of alcohol. Instead, she told him how much she enjoyed working for the business and he commented that he was happy she had settled in so well. Her relationship with her father was comfortable. He liked her, of that she was certain, and she him.

Today, it all changed.

The crisis was sparked by a telephone call a week ago when Lucy put an irate client straight through to Robin. 'He didn't sound a happy bunny,' she commented on replacing the receiver.

Jane had thought no more about the call until today, shortly after she arrived in the office around 9am. She was hardly through the front door before Robin was at the top of the stairs shouting for her to come to his office.

'What the bloody hell's going on, Jane?' he yelled, the moment she stepped inside the room. 'Close the door,' he ordered. She had not seen him like this before and it frightened her. Instinctively, she gripped both arms of the chair on sitting down.

She blinked nervously as she ran her tongue over dry lips.

'What's the problem, Robin?'

'This is the bloody problem.' He handed her a cheque, which she took and read.

'Oh my God, this has been... it looks like Janice has tippexed out our company name as the payee and written in hers.'

Janice Cooper was a young, brash administrative assistant who'd been with the company a matter of months. Unknown to Robin, Jane had on occasions asked her to take the paying-in book and cheques to the bank, a few hundred yards down the High Street.

'Did I give you permission to allow her to do the banking?' Robin shouted. 'Did I?'

'No, but... it took pressure off me to get on with—'

'That's part of *your* job, Jane. Paying in the money is your responsibility and I've now got a client who you've been chasing for payment telling me he paid us weeks ago and here's the proof. That little bitch Janice changed the name of the payee and pocketed our money.' With that, he lifted the telephone receiver and prodded in a three-digit number.

'Where's Janice?'

Jane could just about hear that it was Lucy's voice on the other end.

'What? When? Oh, for fuck's sake.' The handset hit the cradle and bounced back out. 'She's done a runner. Grabbed her coat and run out the door. Chances are more cheques will have gone missing.'

'I'm sorry, Robin, I didn't think it—'

'No, you didn't think, did you? But that's what I pay you to do, Jane, to bloody think. Get back downstairs, check the aged debtors for any regular advertisers behind in their payments, phone them all and ask if they've paid. Report back to me this evening. Now get out.'

Tears were falling in torrents as she walked down the stairs and Lucy sat her down before making her a strong espresso. She placed a comforting hand on Jane's shoulder. 'He sometime gets like this. He has a short fuse, but it'll blow over in no time, I promise you.'

Early that evening, after everyone else including Lucy had left, Jane trudged wearily upstairs, clutching a list suggesting that £12,578 had been fraudulently stolen from the business. As he gestured for her to sit down, his face suggested his anger had barely softened.

He read her report and, without a word, lifted the telephone handset and dialled a number. 'Is that Gillingham Police?' he asked. He reported the details of the crime along with Janice's home address before closing the conversation. 'So you'll follow it up, and send an officer round in the morning? Thank you.'

He replaced the receiver a little less violently this time. A hopeful sign?

'As for you, Jane, you've let me down badly and right now, I'm in two minds whether or not to—'

'No, no, please, Robin,' she interrupted. 'I couldn't take it if you fired me. I'm sorry, I really am, and I promise I'll make it up to you but—'

'Jane, if you'd gone bust as badly as I did in '92, you'd know every penny is vital, but almost as important as the money is the ability to trust those I'm working with. I trusted you with banking our cheques; it was your responsibility. Lucy handled it before you arrived, but the moment I thought I could trust you; I gave you the task.'

She was crumbling into pieces, tears falling like rain from a leaking gutter. Her hands were shaking violently as she struggled to hold a handkerchief to her eyes. She leaned forward, her head low in her lap, her body trembling.

Robin's face stayed rigid, unsmiling, the silence filling the room heavy with anger. He looked at Jane, not an ounce of sympathy in his expression. She looked up, hesitant, her eye make-up smeared like ink trails on fresh blotting paper. Here was a new Robin, one who frightened her in a horribly familiar way. Old anxieties returned and she started counting backwards from three hundred, breathing out on each soundlessly mouthed number.

She then took a deep breath and spoke slowly and carefully.

'Robin, there's something I need to tell you. Something I have been wanting to tell you since the day I started working here. Something that's going to come as a big shock to you.'

'What now?' The harshness in the man's voice ricocheted around the tiny office as Jane's attention was suddenly drawn to his eyes. They seemed to glaze over, and he stared into the middle distance.

'Robin, are you all right?'

A full minute of hesitation ensued before he answered. 'What is it you need to tell me, Jane?'

THE SNAKE THAT BITES ITS TAIL

The voice was deeper, less angry. Jane swallowed before speaking the words she had rehearsed a thousand times these past two years.

'I wasn't going to tell you, well, not right now anyway, but… but please don't fire me… I don't know what I'd do if I could never see you again because… well, you see, Robin, you're my father.'

THIRTY-FOUR

'Is this you, Robin, or Krait?'

'It's still me, Doc. I figured you'd want to chat after reading my memos.'

Lakmaker shifts forward in his armchair, leans in closer to the table between them. 'I've read what you've written with interest and would like to understand a little better how it is you can commit cold-blooded murder, yet suffer no remorse, no sense of guilt.'

Krait's eyes narrow and the corners of his mouth rise in a half-smile.

'Instinct, Doc, it's as instinctive and as natural to me as breathing is to you or Robin. I'm the purest form of a gene almost every living creature on the planet is born with.'

Lakmaker's eyebrows rise. 'What gene would that be?'

'The aggression gene, the gene that drives mankind's urge to control his fellow beings, to colonise, dominate, suppress. It courses through every bloodline and is passed from generation to generation.'

'And you're the purest form of this gene?'

Krait nods. 'Uncorrupted, pure.'

'A single gene?'

'Yep!'

'So how can you function as an individual if you're a single gene?'

'I occupy an area inside Robin's frontal lobes, the part controlling behaviour.'

'Why Robin?'

'He was selected as my host because, unusually, he doesn't have this aggression gene.'

'Selected by whom?'

'Haven't the foggiest, Doc, although I doubt it was by any of the gods dreamt up by mankind. What I do know is, as the purest form of the gene I can only exist inside someone who is instinctively non-aggressive. Clearly two similar genes in a single body might conflict. Cause some form of internal war.'

Another smile breaks across Krait's face as he alone appreciates the irony of his joke.

'Virtually all nations of the world maintain armies, soldiers trained to go to war; to defend and conquer. The aggressive urge drives the armies of Europe, Russia, China and the USA to poke their noses into other nations' affairs. It's all part of Churchill's "dark, lamentable catalogue of human crime"; nations behaving as mankind has behaved throughout its history.'

Lakmaker is writing furiously and Krait pauses, dutifully waiting for him to finish. The doctor looks up. 'It's not the armies deciding to go to war, it's politicians.'

'True, but wars couldn't be fought without the aggressive genes of foot soldiers.'

Lakmaker's eyes narrow in confusion. 'Let me get this right. You're driven by an urge to kill yet you seem to be against war. Isn't that a contradiction?'

'As the purest form of the gene living inside a pacifist, my motivation is only to kill when provoked by injustice. Living in tandem with someone who is fundamentally non-violent creates the perfect balance. The Brigadier and Thornbury deserved to die; their deaths were justified.'

Lakmaker's expression suggests he doesn't agree.

'So you justify the killing of another human being because you object to his behaviour, his ethics?'

'Mankind only *ever* kills because of a difference in ethics! Civil wars have torn Africa and the Middle East apart for generations and amount to little more than one aggressive bunch of thugs disagreeing with another over religion, land ownership or who has the right to govern a nation, while they syphon the proceeds from its natural resources into Swiss bank accounts.

'Aggression coupled with an instinctive urge to control destroys human decency. Ordinary men become monsters who rape, pillage and slaughter in the same indiscriminate way your ancestors have for millennia.'

'I don't see the logic, Krait. You justify your right to murder as a form of vengeance, then you blame the gene for the worst excesses of human greed.'

'I am the purest form of the gene; my instincts are controlled. In most humans, aggression is a constituent part of a personality which, unfortunately, they rarely possess the ability to restrain.'

Lakmaker appears flustered. 'No, you're wrong, Krait. Most human beings are naturally gentle; their greatest desire is to live their lives in peace, to care for and nurture their families. They hold no instinctive urge to dominate or kill.'

'The gene is an instinct, in the same way it's instinctive for a baby to suckle its mother's breast or to cry when hungry. Watch kids play and you'll see the aggressive gene underpinning their games. It's natural for them to fight, to control and take other kids' toys. As they develop, most learn to harness this instinct, but some don't. Even in those who manage their aggression, it needs little encouragement to expose itself, particularly in the male of the species, or the female if her young are threatened or food is scarce.

'For thousands of years, kings, queens, world leaders, and so-called freedom fighters have manipulated the aggressive gene in whole populations in support of their aims.'

Lakmaker stares at his patient; his face is rigid. 'Raising armies in times of war, marshalling support for a revolution or protection is an unpleasant but generally accepted characteristic in mankind, I'll grant you. But no civilised society could ever sanction revenge murder by an individual.'

'You just don't get it, do you, Doc? Civilisations sanction murder every day of the week. Only they sterilise it, sanctify it inside cosy "rules of warfare". Governments order soldiers to war to kill enemy soldiers who they've never met and with whom they have no quarrel. When they kill efficiently, they're awarded medals but if one of them kills at the wrong moment, in the wrong way or in circumstances infringing their ludicrous rules, he's banged up on a murder charge. Sheer bloody lunacy. My philosophy is much more honest; if a man deserves to die, then die he must.'

Lakmaker walks across the room to the bookcase and takes a few moments searching for a particular volume. Having found it, he opens it at a page on which the top right-hand corner is turned down and reads aloud.

'Krait, I'd like you to consider for a moment what the German philosopher Immanuel Kant had to say about the subject.

'Killing, because it annihilates the possibility of the other person to meet its own goals, is a way of treating someone as a means to an end rather than as an end in themselves. Humans are rational beings and as such deserve to be respected, and to have the pursuit of their own ends respected.'

'The old boy got it wrong, Doc. Genes are sequences of nucleotides forming part of a chromosome that determines the characteristics of every living thing. How could I respect Thornbury's pursuit of his own ends when it resulted in the catastrophic failure of Robin's business? Thornbury refused to respect Robin's pursuits! I'm programmed to react to that situation in one very specific way.'

Krait is in full flow and the doctor seems happy for him to have the floor. 'What you need to understand, Doc, is that aggression, and killing, is as instinctive in humans as it is throughout most sectors of the animal kingdom. It excites, it's dangerous, edgy and offers similar highs to sex, alcohol and drugs. It also deprives humanity of any free will.'

'So, this gene is a curse on mankind which we're unable to change? Is that what you believe?'

'Can you change your instinct to breathe, to bleed when you're cut, to grieve when a loved one dies? No. You were a doctor, you know such things.'

Lakmaker's eyes widen, and he snaps the book he is holding shut as he speaks. 'The medical profession has an armoury of drugs capable of controlling most forms of violent and antisocial behaviour.'

'Yeah, you have, but you only prescribe them to those you deem mad or demented. They should be given to murderers, paedophiles, despots and warmongers.'

'You're not seriously proposing a world in which we're all routinely drugged to suppress undesirable instincts?'

'You tell me, Doc. Is the aggressive instinct better suppressed or encouraged? Would it not lead to a calmer, more peaceful existence if drugs eliminated murder, extinguished brutal dictatorships and neutralised religious fanaticism?'

Krait walks over to join the doctor beside the bookcase. He idly runs an index finger down the spine of a wide volume bound in red leather, cracked like a spider's web with age.

Lakmaker is surprised by the vibrancy in his patient's step; he seems to have shed the weariness of his seventy-four years.

Krait lifts the book from the shelf, and it falls open at a spread divided by a metal bookmark. He reads for a few seconds before looking up. 'Are you familiar with the German philosopher Friedrich Nietzsche?'

Lakmaker nods. 'Some of his writings.'

Krait reads, '*Eternal return or eternal recurrence is one of the most famous and intriguing ideas in the philosophy of Nietzsche. What, if some day or night a demon were to steal into your consciousness and say to you: "This life as you now live it and have lived it, you will have to live once more and innumerable times more; and there will be nothing new in it, but every pain and every joy and every thought and sigh and everything unutterably small or great in your life will have to return to you, all in the same succession and sequence".*

'You've seen Robin's bracelet, you explained that the snake swallowing its own tail is a symbol of eternity. Nietzsche suggested the universe and all existence and energy within it recur an infinite number of times.'

Lakmaker squeezes his eyes shut and exhales through taut lips. 'I believe Nietzsche revoked this concept in later life. Even you cannot seriously suggest our lives are pre-programmed?'

Krait's grin spreads the full width of his face. 'We've seen evidence of this in Indian philosophy, the Pythagoreans and the Stoics. Christianity sort of put paid to it but the evidence is all around for us to see.

'The periodicity of day and night, of sun and lunar phases and seasons of the year. Even the programmed appearance of comets suggest time itself is part of that periodicity. The circularity of time supports the existence of eternal return.'

'Circularity of time?'

'Time as a complete periodic circle, never beginning, never ending. The past, present and future exist forever and together as a single entity. Ask yourself why this book I'm holding contains a metal marker that opened at the exact page I wanted to quote from. Has this conversation taken place countless times before?'

Lakmaker's brow furrows and he shakes his head. 'Krait, I can't take any of what you're saying seriously. According to the Venerable Bede, *"This life of man appears for a little while, but of what is to follow or what went before we know nothing at all".'*

Krait eyes narrow. 'You know that isn't the case, Doc. You and I share common circumstance; we're both familiar with what is to follow.'

Weariness has drained the blood from the doctor's face. 'I noticed you referred to me a few moments ago as "having been" part of the medical profession. You used the past tense.'

Krait nods.

'You know who I am?'

'You're the psychiatrist who treated Robin for his anxiety back in the '70s.'

'He doesn't remember me.'

'He recognises your face but has no idea where or when he previously met you. Bit disappointing, isn't it, Doc? You gave the guy a brand-new life philosophy, taught him how to handle his anxieties and yet he doesn't have the decency to remember you.'

'Perhaps his condition clouded his memory. You don't appear to be affected by his Alzheimer's.'

'Nope, we share two separate states of consciousness. I understood why he wanted to end his life but was uneasy how a premature death might affect me. It's important he finishes his days here at Barton Hall.'

'Why?'

'If he'd died at home or in A&E at Yeovil Hospital, it would have been… well, inconvenient. I watched him steal his daughter's barbiturates and flushed half of them down the lavatory, so he'd survive long enough to be transferred here. You see, Doc, the only way I can be certain of continuity after he's gone is if he died here.'

'So, you… your life, your existence, whatever you call it, continues after Robin—'

'Eternal return, Doc,' Krait interrupted. 'Time is cyclical, no beginning, no end, no free will.' Krait grins broadly at Lakmaker who still has the look of a confused man.

'There's one other thing I need to know, Krait. Are there… were there… other murders?'

'It doesn't matter, Doc. No one gives a shit.'

Lakmaker's voice rises several decibels as the palms of his hands slap the curved arms of his chair. 'Krait, I give a shit, and there are millions like me who give a shit. What happened with Jane?'

'Ahh! The lovely Jane. Is that you or the police wanting to know?'

'You know the police are irrelevant. Jane was a patient of mine during her late teens. She suffered traumatic stress resulting from abuse by her adoptive father. I'm aware she worked for Robin, but I believe there was a major row at some point.'

Krait's features soften. 'I'm very fond of Jane and, well… she was a revelation. She brought me closer than I've ever been to understanding human emotions, although it was for the best that I never let Robin know the truth. It could have screwed him and his family, although, with hindsight, they may have been strong enough to handle it.'

THIRTY-FIVE

From: Krait
To: Dr Lakmaker
Ref. No: 19

It would never have crossed Robin's mind to mention Jane to you; he has no idea of her true role in his life even though she has been a part of it now for over twenty years.

They met in early 2000, at a time when his resurrected business had grown sufficiently for him to need the services of a full-time bookkeeper.

He interviewed four candidates; Jane Foster was the fourth and most qualified and he immediately appointed her on a three-month trial. An attractive lady in her mid-thirties, she fitted in well and her work was competent enough for Robin to offer her a permanent role.

He enjoyed working with her, admired her enthusiasm, she rarely clock-watched and was trustworthy. She was open with colleagues about her relationship with her partner, Monica, and they in turn respected her privacy.

Over a period of two years, Jane took on board more responsibility for the financial control and management of the business and Robin rewarded her well. Unfortunately, that all changed the morning he took a telephone call from an irate client who complained he was being chased by Jane for payment of two overdue invoices, both of which had been paid weeks before and the cheque had been cleared by his bank.

Robin checked through the paying-in slips but found no record of the payment. He asked the client to obtain the cheque from his bank and three days later, he called back.

'Does the name Janice Cooper mean anything to you?'

'It does, why?' Robin replied.

'Your company name has been substituted with her name as payee.'

Grappling with embarrassment over what he had just heard, Robin asked for the cheque to be sent first-class post and marked for his personal attention.

It arrived the following morning and what mystified him was how such an amateur attempt at fraud had managed to fool staff at the bank. The name of his company had been crudely masked with white correction fluid and Janice's name handwritten over the top. He even recognised her handwriting.

His voice echoed through the building as he screamed for Jane to come upstairs to his office, and I could feel his anger growing. If someone needed dealing with, I was better equipped to handle it.

As Jane sat down, he pushed the fraudulent cheque in front of her. She quickly realised what Janice had done and admitted she had delegated the banking to her.

'Did I give you permission to allow her to do the banking?' he shouted. 'Did I?'

'No, but… it took pressure off me to get on with—'

'It's your job, Jane,' he snapped. 'Money is your responsibility, and I've got a top client here who you've been chasing for payment and he's telling me he paid weeks ago and here's the proof. That little bitch Janice changed the name of the payee and banked our money.' Without waiting for any sort of answer, he grabbed the telephone and prodded a three-digit number.

'Where's Janice? What? When? Oh, for God's sake.' The handset hit the cradle with a bang and bounced back out. 'She's done a runner. Grabbed her coat and run out.'

'I'm sorry, Robin, I didn't think it—'

'No, you didn't bloody think, did you, Jane, and that's exactly what I pay you to do, think.' He was hardly drawing breath as he spoke. 'Get back downstairs, check every regular advertiser who appears behind in their payment, phone each and ask if they've paid. Report to me this evening what you've found. Now get out.'

I was in two minds whether to take over at that point but thought Robin might calm a little as the day went on. I was wrong.

Early that evening, after everyone else, including Lucy, had left, I heard Jane trudge slowly upstairs. I think she also sensed that Robin's anger had barely softened.

He read her report, suggesting that a total of £12,578 had been stolen from the business, lifted the receiver and banged in a number. 'Is that Gillingham Police?' he barked. He reported the details of the crime and gave them Janice's home address before closing the conversation with,

'So you'll follow it up, and send an officer round in the morning? Thank you.'

He threw the receiver back down, a little less violently this time. A hopeful sign, I thought. I was wrong.

'As for you, Jane, you've let me down badly, and right now, I'm in two minds whether or not to—'

'No, please, Robin,' she interjected. 'I couldn't handle it if you fired me. I'm sorry, I really am, and I promise I'll make it up to you but—'

'Jane, if you'd gone bust as badly as I did in '92, you'd know every penny is vital. But almost as important as the money is the ability to trust those you're working with. I trusted you with banking our cheques; it's your responsibility. Lucy handled it until you arrived, but the moment I thought I could trust you I gave you the job.'

She was crumbling into bits, floods of tears and hands shaking like a frightened puppy as she struggled to hold a handkerchief to her eyes. She leaned forward, her head low in her lap, body trembling.

Robin's jaw set rigid, his gaze at her seemed to be cutting her in two. I'd rarely seen him this angry; maybe the deep-rooted fear of his business crumbling a second time was controlling his emotions.

Jane raised her head slowly and I could see her make-up ravaged by her tears. I sensed she was seeing a new Robin and, as I learned later, his aggression scared her in a horribly familiar way.

'Robin, I need to tell you something.'

'What is it now?' The unforgiving voice echoed around the tiny office and instinct told me now was the moment to take control. Thank heaven I did.

Jane noticed his eyes glaze over as I began to take charge.

'Robin, are you all right?'

He sat motionless until the transformation was complete. 'What is it you want to tell me, Jane?' I asked.

Her voice was soft, almost a whisper. 'I hadn't planned to tell you this, well, not right now and not in this way but… but Robin, please don't fire me… it'll destroy me if I can never see you again. You see, Robin, you're my father.'

Her teeth bit down hard on her lower lip as a few remaining tears tracked down both cheeks. I looked into her eyes, daring her to look away. She was pretty. Cheekbones set high on the widest part of her face, clear skin sinking below her bones in a classically beautiful line. Chestnut dark-brown eyes held mine in a strangely familiar way.

'I know, Jane,' I replied quietly, 'I know.'

I heard her sharp intake of breath, and she took a moment to compose herself. 'You know? How long have you known?'

'I've known since the day of your interview.'

'How did you find out?'

'Your mother told me.'

'What? When?' Her wide-eyed expression was one of utter disbelief.

'In 1982. Your mother and I met by accident in a London hotel.'

'But… I… I don't understand. She told me she never saw you again, didn't want to cause problems with your family. Why did she lie to me? Why didn't she tell me she'd seen you, even in her final letter?'

'She wouldn't have wanted you to know, Jane.' I was

injecting as much human compassion into my voice as a single gene can muster.

'But... but she told me everything else important in her life. About her father making her finish with you, finding out she was pregnant and being forced to put me up for adoption.'

I don't mind admitting, Doc, I was out of my depth, and it was dawning on me that I probably knew more about her mother than perhaps she did. Not a good time to feed her more lies.

'Jane, I'm ashamed to say that your mother and I had a... had a brief affair in the early spring of 1982.'

'Oh my God! I can't believe what I'm hearing. Does anyone ever tell the truth? Are *you* even telling me the truth?'

I may as well admit it, Doc, Jane's vulnerability put me in a place I'd never been before. She closed her eyes and was breathing slowly and deeply. Her face was the colour of freshly fallen snow and I thought she might be about to pass out on me. I needed to draw breath too.

'Yes, I am, Jane, and complicated though this situation is, the occasion calls for a celebration of sorts; a glass or two of wine might calm both our nerves. Red or white?'

'Um... white if that's okay. I need something, that's for sure.'

I walked downstairs to the kitchen and grabbed a bottle of Pouilly Fumé from the fridge, along with two large glasses, removed the cork and took my time walking back upstairs. I half-filled the glasses before reaching inside Robin's jacket, hanging from a hook on the door, and retrieving his wallet. I had remembered an old photograph.

'You might like to see this,' I said as I handed her the dog-eared black-and-white image.

She blinked several times as she studied the two teenagers, hand in hand, perched high on a farm gate. It was a while before she looked up, precious minutes buying me the relief of time to think.

I was out of my comfort zone; this was more Robin's territory. But then again, was it? This woman could toss a gigantic spanner into his life. He would happily gamble everything on sentimentality. That's the kind of dumb-ass thing he does. I'm Krait, he's Robin, but in that moment, I was closer to him than I'd ever been.

'The two of you look very much in love. I'm so glad I found you, Robin, but what I can't get my head around was why Mum didn't tell me all this in her final letter.'

'Because, Jane, in the same way she hurt Ro… she hurt me, all those years ago, I hurt her as much the second time we met.'

'How?' she asked, before draining her glass a little too quickly.

'Go easy on that, we've both got to drive.'

'Sorry, but it's making me feel a little less stressed. May I have another one, please? I can always get Monica to come and pick me up.'

I poured us both a second glass. I only deal with bad people, card cheats, dishonest businessmen, people who deserve everything they've got coming. I needed to think as Robin but remain as Krait.

'As I said, it was in the early spring of '82, March, I think, at a time my first marriage had started its terminal decline. I'd booked into the Hilton in west London, next door to the

Olympia exhibition hall where I was working at a five-day trade show. On top of my marital problems, I'd had a shit day at the show; one of my biggest clients had told me he wasn't renewing his contract.

'On checking in at the hotel, they hadn't given me a quiet room on the side of the building, like I'd asked, and when I demanded to be moved, they told me the hotel was fully booked. I lost my temper completely, swore loudly and stormed off to the bar, where I ordered a glass of wine and sat at an empty table.

'I became aware of this lady at the next table peering at the name badge on my jacket. "You don't recognise me, do you Robin?" she asked. She was right.

'I studied her face, the high cheekbones, the brown eyes and the way her head tilted to one side as she smiled. Then it hit me who she was.'

Jane leaned in towards me; both her hands grabbed mine tightly. 'That must have been such a shock, for you and her.'

'It was.'

At that moment, Doc, I was treading quicksand. I don't do emotion, it's not part of my armoury, and I was struggling to imagine how Robin might have reacted on meeting the woman he'd loved but who'd caused him so much grief.

'Are you comfortable talking about it, Robin?'

'Yeah… I'm okay, it… it's just…'

'Was it painful, meeting her after all those years?' she asked warmly.

'Yes, it was. I was older, and hopefully a little wiser but it didn't quite work like…'

My voice drifted into silence almost of its own free will.

'What happened?' she asked, eagerly.

In for a penny, I thought. 'Seeing her again left me speechless but I relaxed after she explained how her father had forced her to end our relationship and her problems after discovering she was pregnant.

'We shared a bottle of wine, and then a second over dinner. We talked over old times like a couple of pensioners in a care home and… then, well…' Again my voice drifted away.

'Then what, Robin?'

'Jane, I'm not proud of what happened but, well, she was attending a three-day headteachers' conference at the hotel and… well… I'd lost my rag at reception and told them to stuff the room I'd booked so I had nowhere to sleep and, well… one thing led to another. We ended up spending the next three nights together.'

'Oh.' She drew breath and there was the faintest of whistles as she slowly exhaled. 'And this was at a time you were both married.' The look of dismay told me more than her words.

'Yeah, that's right, and what made it ten times worse was how desperate she was to leave her husband and at the time, I was on the point of leaving my wife.'

'Then why didn't you end up together?'

'Jane, that photograph in your hand is a moment frozen in time; the place, the day and the two people in it will never change. In real life, change is constant and that gate and that field and those two people could never be the same the following week, let alone years later. Your mum and I had matured into different people, our outlooks and ambitions were poles apart and unfortunately, she couldn't accept that.

She thought we could just pick up where we left off but for me, that was impossible.'

'But why, if you loved her, why couldn't you have—'

'That was the problem, Jane,' I interrupted. 'I didn't love her; in fact, I didn't even like her. The extraordinary love I had for her when we were teenagers was for the Jo she was then, the one in the photograph, not the person she'd become at thirty-six. She was no longer the young woman locked inside my head, the one who broke my heart.

'We'd both moved on, and her willingness to leave her husband and children worried the life out of me. She hardly seemed to give it a second thought and this was all happening at a time when I was struggling to find answers to my own family problems.'

'But she loved you, Robin. To the end of her days, she loved you. Her husband found your details in her diary and accused her of having an affair, which it now turns out was true.' I could see Jane was close to tears again.

'I'm sorry, I didn't know that.' I squeezed my eyes shut as I shook my head. 'That's awful.' I was getting good at human emotion.

'It led to the breakdown of their marriage,' Jane added forlornly.

'Jane, her marriage was in a mess before she met me.'

'I'm so glad now I'm never having kids. At least I can't be guilty of fucking up *their* lives. So she told you about me during those… those three days?'

I nodded, desperately seeking a way to change the subject. 'She did, Jane, and maybe I should have come looking for you, but I had enough problems of my own.

What's more important is how we handle the situation we find ourselves in now.'

I needed to get back to the matter in hand and take stock of what the arrival of another daughter might do to the balance of Robin's family. Could Lucy handle a second stepdaughter, the result of a long-forgotten teenage romance? What would Giles' and Katie's reaction be to the sudden appearance of an older stepsister?

'How do you mean?'

'Have you given any thought to how the rest of my family might react to your arrival on the scene?'

She looked down at the dog-eared photograph resting on her lap. She stared at it for a minute, clearly thinking through the options.

'The thing is, Robin, neither of you were ever really my parents, were you? You didn't play any sort of role in bringing me up and neither did Mum, although she was helpful to me, what with paying for my college education and helping with the rent on the flat. I'll always be grateful to her for that, but she was never really a mum.

'You've given me the best job I could ever hope for and the chance of a life in the countryside with the person I love. But you've never been my dad, either.'

She smiled warmly. 'You have a happy life, with Giles, Lucy, Katie and your grandchildren. You're my biological father but I'm not part of your family. I realise now I never can be. Working for you is the next best thing. I see you regularly, I'm close to you without disturbing the balance in your family, but… but if I was never able to see you again, it would break my heart.'

I leaned back, tilted the chair, and stared at the ceiling.

Searching for divine intervention, perhaps. It was needed.

'So have you given any thought to how our relationship might continue?' I asked, buying a few more seconds.

'I've thought of little else since I began working here. I know it would be wrong to disrupt your life. The last thing I want is to risk disturbing the... the harmony in your family.'

I was thinking through my options. Robin had no memory of the brief affair I had with Jo, so Jane would always be a constant reminder of the sadness he lived through more than half a century ago.

Jane interrupted my thoughts. 'Robin, may I keep this photograph of you and Mum, please?'

'Of course,' I answered. Robin was unlikely to notice it was missing; he hadn't given it a second thought in years. In that moment, an idea fell into place.

'Listen, Jane, what I'm about to suggest will sound strange, bizarre even, but you'll have to trust me when I say it's the only safe option open to us both.

'The simple truth is I'm not prepared to risk any possibility of disruption to my family or the business. That said, you are part of this business, you work well with Lucy and Giles. All being well, Giles will take over as MD on my retirement but if he found out he was working alongside an older sister, that holds the potential to create a working relationship fraught with danger.'

Her top teeth bit down on her bottom lip; I could see she feared the worst. The echoing emptiness of the room unnerved me too, but I had to go through with my plan.

'I'm your biological father and must face up to my responsibilities. I'm happy for you to continue working here for as long as you wish, assuming your commitment to the business remains as high as it has been up until now. However, you will need to get your head around one hell of a condition.'

I drew a deep breath, hoping the next two sentences might not sound as bizarre as they clearly were. 'Jane, no one, and I mean absolutely no one, must know who you are, and you must only ever speak to me as my daughter, as and when I bring the subject up first. On all other occasions, our relationship must continue exactly as it has for the past two years.'

Her expression was of utter disbelief. 'So, you're saying no one apart from you and me must ever know you're my father?'

I nodded grimly.

'And I may only talk to you as my father when you bring up the subject?' She spoke each word slowly, enunciating each syllable individually while shaking her head.

'That's right, Jane. That's the way it has to be if you want to remain as part of my life and this business.'

'But… but why?'

MEMO ENDS Krait

THIRTY-SIX

'The man's bonkers, a bloody nut case.' It is late in the evening by the time Jane finishes relating the events of her day. Monica is sitting up on the bed, knees under her chin, arms locked around them, a position she has held from the start of the conversation.

'Why in God's name can't you speak to him as your father unless he brings the matter up first? It's crazy, it defies all logic.'

Jane is perched on the stool in front of the dressing table and can see from Monica's reflection how she too is struggling to understand the day's bizarre turn. 'He suffers a rare psychological condition.'

'He needs treatment of some sort, that's for certain,' Monica adds.

'He's had years of treatment; it's incurable.'

Monica throws her head back like a spooked horse. 'That's bollocks, Jane, he's lying through his teeth. He's the same as your mum, full of guilt 'cos you're the illegitimate child of a teenage romance and worse still is his shame over his affair with her when they were both married to other people. He's petrified what his kids will think if they were ever to find out.'

'No, Monica, he's been diagnosed with a condition called Path…' She looks down at her diary lying open on the dressing table. 'It's called Pathological Demand Avoidance. It's a type of autism that affects the way he relates to people. He can only handle relationships on his terms and needs to keep parts of his life secret 'cos he's afraid those close to him might abandon him. It can make him really angry, like I saw today.'

'Hogwash! Jane, you don't need this sort of shit in your life, you've been through enough already. Tell him to poke his job and his autism and we'll move back to Surrey and civilisation.'

Jane's eyes flash. 'It's okay for you to talk like that, you've got family. I need a father. You're not close to yours but he's still there if you ever need him.'

'Sounds like yours is psychotic. I bet you didn't ask him if he killed your mother's boyfriend, did you?'

'No, I didn't, and I don't intend to.' Monica senses anger building in Jane's voice.

'If you want to go back to Surrey, you go, but you're on your own. I'm staying put. I love my job, I love the business and I'm happy to go along with my dad's rules, no matter how weird they seem.'

'You don't really want me to leave, do you?' Monica asks, the tone of her voice sounding her concern over Jane's suggestion.

'No, no, you know I don't, but I don't want to live with you prattling on about my dad all the time. He is what he is and that's all there is to it. For Christ's sake, he has no problem with you and me. You get invited to all the company dos and there's no discrimination in the business 'cos I'm a woman or gay.'

Monica swings her legs over the side of the bed and moves briskly over to Jane before cupping her face in both hands. 'I'm sorry, Jane, I really am. It just seems so... so far-fetched. But you're right. We must all live our lives as we want and if that's the way your dad wants it, so be it.' With an exaggerated shrug of her shoulders, she smiles before kissing her partner on the lips.

'I don't want to go back to Surrey either.'

THIRTY-SEVEN

What remains of the daylight is casting a cheerless gloom across the consulting room as Lakmaker walks to his desk and switches on a reading lamp. Krait is staring intently at the laptop and the doctor senses the visceral presence of Robin's alter.

'Contrary to everything you claim, your last memo suggests you are capable of some human emotion, Krait. Maybe there's hope for mankind after all.'

Krait looks up from the screen and rubs his eyes. 'I wouldn't bank on it, Doc.'

'You could easily have got rid of Jane, removed her completely from Robin's life, eliminated any risk of her upsetting the family balance.'

'You still don't get it, do you? I had no reason to murder her. I don't kill indiscriminately, in the way humanity does. I made the right decision and they bonded well. Robin trusted her and grew to love her almost as a daughter without ever realising it. In the fullness of time, Jane would talk to him as she would a father and shortly before he retired, he appointed her financial director of the business.'

'Tell me, Krait, how did you know about Pathological Demand Avoidance? It's not a well-known psychological condition.'

'You wrote a paper on it in the late '80s which was reported in *The Times*. Robin read it and interestingly, it crossed his mind he might be suffering from it.'

'Hmm! Not sure I'd have diagnosed it in him.'

'You don't know him as well as I do, Doc. Maybe you should reread your own research. Now I think it's time—'

Lakmaker stops him mid-flow. 'You killed Jane's adoptive father, didn't you?'

'He had it coming.' Krait's face breaks into a contented grin. 'I finished the job Jane started, smashed his skull while he was working in his back garden. He wouldn't have known who I was, so seconds before the first blow, I told him, "This is for Jane." She wanted him dead, even gave me her old address in Bristol. The police interviewed her, and she handled it well. Told them of the abuse, how she attacked him the day she left home and admitted she was pleased he had died violently. Her alibi was rock solid; she'd been working all day alongside Robin's son. They get on well, almost… almost like brother and sister.'

'So she knows you killed her adoptive father?'

'Maybe, maybe not. I got the feeling she didn't really want to know. There was an occasion a few months after his death when we were talking as father and daughter at the office, and she asked if I had anything to do with his death, and with that of her mother's boyfriend.'

'What was your answer?'

'It's impossible for me to lie, Doc, so I asked why she might think I could have been responsible. She looked at me in a confused sort of way and said she now realised she was living alongside a father with two entirely different personalities.'

Lakmaker leans in close, pen hovering over his notebook.

'She told me that I was the colder personality, described me as austere, claimed I treated her almost as if she wasn't my daughter. Whereas Robin, who never knew or acknowledged that he was her father, treated her more like a daughter, although never in a touchy-feely sort of way.'

'Perceptive of her. What was your reaction?'

'I explained it was probably a characteristic linked to my autism and quickly changed the subject by telling her how proud I was of the way she had embraced our unusual arrangement. I asked if she was happy with the way her life had panned out.'

Lakmaker looked up from writing. 'And?'

A rare smile crossed Krait's face. 'She spoke of the three people who had taught her how to love life. One was you, Doc, another was Monica and the third was me, her father. She credits the three of us with having given her more happiness than she had any right to expect.'

'I hope you gave her a hug.'

Krait nodded. 'Guess I'm not all bad then?'

Lakmaker leans back into his chair and closes his notebook. 'The jury's still out on that one. I understand you've changed Robin's will to include her.'

'Yep, and it's all legal and above board. Robin's solicitor is my solicitor. I sign with his signature. Who told you, anyway?'

'Doesn't matter. So you're okay with the family learning the truth about Jane, after Robin's death?'

'Yep, little danger of bad feeling. Just the opposite, I believe they'll welcome her into the family after losing Robin.'

'One final question. Do you think I should tell Robin I'm the psychiatrist who treated him all those years ago?'

'Your decision, but if you do, he's certain to twig what's going on and panic.'

'That's a risk, although he'll find out soon enough.'

'He's an old man, go easy on him. You're too eager to scratch the scars from the unpleasant episodes in his life with little regard to the pain it causes him. You dig too deeply. It's not worth it.'

Lakmaker's right index finger taps on his notebook.

'That's my profession, Krait. It's too late for me to change.'

'A profession is acquired, it's not genetic. You could have changed if you'd set your mind to it, accept there isn't a smart psychological explanation for everything.'

Ignoring the implication of the advice, the doctor says, 'There's one last thing I need to know.'

Krait looks away, bored now with his endless stream of questions. 'Doc, you've had enough out of me, I need to go, got stuff to organise.'

Lakmaker does his ignoring thing. 'Robin is still sensitive about the family relationships between his wife, Lucy, and his children. Was there a rift, a falling-out?'

'Everyone dies with secrets. Some chapters deserve to remain private. Better to leave things unsaid, even until the end. Less painful.'

'Compassion from a personality with so many unpleasant characteristics?'

'I'm not a personality, I'm a gene. I don't have characteristics. I may be unpleasant by your standards, but I'm programmed to behave in one way. It's not my fault; genes can't change. Now,' Krait smiles coldly, 'it's time for me to leave as I think you and Robin are scheduled for one last conversation. Goodbye, Doc, it's been a pleasure.'

Without waiting for a response, Krait's brow furrows and his eyes squeeze shut. In a matter of seconds, the muscles in his face relax, droop a little and his mouth becomes less taut, more turned down at the corners in a regular old-person sort of way.

'Hello, Robin.'

THIRTY-EIGHT

A pink mist seeps through Robin's flickering eyelids as he struggles to drag the world back into focus. Gradually, his vision clears and he reconnects with what he thinks might be reality.

Lakmaker is in the chair opposite, peering at him intently.

'You met my alter?' The question is rhetorical.

The doctor nods and stares at Robin, using that infuriating technique of his to force patients to talk.

'And... well, what's he like, for Christ's sake?' Robin opens his palms flat on the arms of the chair and drums with impatience.

'He's... different, very different. He's called Krait and in almost every way, he's your complete opposite.'

'He killed Jo's lover, didn't he?'

The doctor nods gravely.

'And the Brigadier and that fuckwit Thornbury?'

More nods.

'For pity's sake, no.' He allows himself a long, doleful

groan. 'I'm nuts, a madman, a psychopath.' He wraps his face in the palms of both hands and fights back his old-man tears as he curls into a tight foetal ball.

'Nuts is not a word I'd use, about you or any other patient, and you're certainly not a psychopath, Robin. For most of your adult life, there have been days, sometimes weeks when your every action was controlled by an alternative personality.'

Robin is unable to look the doctor in the face, as if by not seeing him, his words might not be real. He lowers his chin almost to his knees which he encircles with his arms.

The doctor continues, 'Krait can take control of your every physical and mental capability during periods when you experience intense anger. He planned and executed the murders. You're in no way responsible.'

Robin looks up, his features distorted in anguish, and slumps back into a sitting position. 'So that's the way it is, then. At the end of my life, I find out that a monster lives inside me.'

'Perversely, I don't think he's a monster. He knows what he is and gives every indication of being clinically sane. He's a complex character but I wouldn't classify him as a monster.'

'For Christ's sake,' Robin yells, 'he cold-bloodedly killed three people, maybe more for all we know. How is it possible for my body to be controlled by a… by something so alien to the kind of person I am?'

With that, he groans as he lifts himself from his chair and walks to the window, where he places his hands on the sill and rests his temple against the cool glass.

The thickening darkness outside matches his mood. Racked with a guilt that is not his, he has little appetite to learn more. Yet each time the doctor speaks, he is somehow drawn to his words, as if it were an overheard conversation between strangers close to him on a park bench.

'Krait is not a person. He claims to be the purest form of the gene that is the cause of man's instinctive aggressiveness towards his fellow men, the motivation for our urge to control and subjugate.'

Robin lifts his head from the cool glass. 'But why inside me? Why choose me?'

'Because you were born without the aggressive gene. You're a pacifist, the perfect host. Human emotions such as love, compassion and empathy sit easily within the human psyche and remain largely under control. Anger, on the other hand, easily bursts the boundaries of our control, freeing the aggressive gene to do as it will with the world. Krait's personality is not psychopathic; he doesn't kill for pleasure or amusement or even gain. He achieves gratification from planning and killing those he considers deserve retribution.'

'Killing Jo's boyfriend wasn't retribution; he didn't deserve that.'

'He admitted that was a misjudgement, but with the Brigadier and Thornbury, he sensed your desperation for revenge and in his mitigation, I've not heard you express any regret over either death.'

'Do you think I subconsciously willed him into committing those murders?'

'No, I'm saying Krait is aware at all times of what you are thinking.'

'What? Can he hear this conversation now? Does he know exactly what goes on in my life all the time?'

'I believe he does.'

'So, when the police charge me with these murders, will you testify for or against me?'

'You're not a murderer.'

Robin finds little comfort in the doctor's words. 'That's as maybe but I'll be found guilty on the grounds of insanity and locked up in Broadmoor for whatever time is left to me.'

Lakmaker smiles, almost kindly. 'It'll never come to that.'

Robin moves from the window to the door.

'Jesus bloody Christ, Lakmaker, what have you done to me? You kept me alive when I wanted to die, forced me to write about my life, resurrected stuff I'd happily buried years ago, convinced me I'm a wife beater and a murderer and now you tell me I'm not the killer, it's some psychopathic monster living inside me. I've had my fill and I'd be grateful if you'd have the decency to allow me to go home to spend what's left of my life with my family.'

Robin lifts his jacket from the hook on the door, but Lakmaker seems not to have heard. 'Have you read any of the writings of the German philosopher Nietzsche?'

'What?' Robin yells in frustration. 'Are you not listening? What part of "I'm going home" do you not understand?'

'Krait gave me his interpretation of Nietzsche's concept of eternal return.'

'I'm still not listening.'

'How often have you thought an incident, a few words heard or spoken or even a vision glimpsed fleetingly is in some way familiar and has perhaps happened before?'

Robin is halfway to putting on his jacket.

'Krait suggests our lives are repeated over and over again, although I struggle to accept that particular concept. Yet, in his defence, what other explanation, apart from some form of reincarnation, could explain your ability to strip down that machine gun and reassemble it as a teenager in the Cadet Force? Is it possible a veil between this life, your life and a past life split for a moment in time and the memory spilled over?'

Robin turns back to face his tormentor and stares at him through tired eyes. He is weary of life, of Lakmaker and all he has accused him of doing. He'd often thought his life was enriched by the unpredictability of his seventy-four years, but do we relish the 'privilege of ordinary heartbreaks'? Would our lives prove less stressful, more pleasurable if the journey was pre-arranged, pre-planned by hands unseen and we merely characters as if in a play?

He then realises he no longer gives a shit.

'I'm leaving,' he answers tartly.

Still deaf to the old man's words, Lakmaker continues, 'You know, Robin, some scientists believe the mind, our consciousness, is not generated by the brain but is quite separate. It uses the brain as a conduit, a slave even, but exists without it and thus lives independently forever, knowing past, present and perhaps even the future.'

'Death is death, the end. Goodnight, nurse.' Robin turns the handle on the door.

'Robin, you remember Jane Foster?'

'Of course I do, she's our financial director.'

'You worked closely together for years. You have a lot of time for her, don't you?'

'I've no idea what this has got to do with what's going on here but yes, as it happens, I'm very fond of her and we're close. Only last week she came to see me at home, and it was lovely seeing her again.'

'Robin, Jane Foster is your daughter by Jo, your first girlfriend.'

Some moments in a lifetime are never to be forgotten. The telephone call telling you a loved one has died, the moment your first child enters the world or the instant you fall in love for the first and maybe the last time. Each millisecond is like a eulogy on a gravestone, indelibly etched into our psyche in the most intimate detail.

Robin's hand slips from the door handle and, reluctantly, he shuffles back to his armchair. When, finally, he manages to speak, his voice is frail and the confusion of old age palpable.

'But... but why didn't Jo contact me when she found she was pregnant? She knew I'd have been happy to marry her.'

'Her father forced her to end the relationship. You weren't good enough for her. He made her take up with his best man's son. She was forbidden ever to speak about the pregnancy, and he made her give the baby up for adoption.'

'The new boyfriend must have been the father.' Robin's eyes close as he is speaking, dreading what he will hear next.

'Just before her death, some twenty years ago, Jo explained in a letter to Jane that you were the father, as she had refused any sexual relationship with the new boyfriend.'

Robin is past caring, although weirdly, the need to know more burns his insides.

'Who told you this? Was it Jane?'

'No, Krait did.'

'He's lying.'

'I don't think he is.'

'How come he knows but I don't?'

'There was an occasion some years back when you lost your temper with Jane over something she'd done wrong at work. You were on the point of firing her when Krait took control and she told him. Naturally, she thought she was speaking with you.'

'But that's impossible; she'd have mentioned it to me since.'

'Krait was concerned over the impact a second daughter might have on your family, how Lucy, your son and daughter might react. He told Jane he suffered a rare psychological condition that made it imperative she only speak to you as her father when *he* brought the subject up first.'

Robin's mind drifts back to odd occasions when he thought Jane's behaviour had been a little too familiar. At the time, he put it down to normal workplace friendliness, but now those moments assumed a deeper relevance They danced closely together at office Christmas parties, she and her partner regularly joined him and Lucy for supper at home and on leaving, Jane would hug him a little too affectionately. He recalled instances of her asking his advice over non-work-related issues and afterwards thanking him for his 'fatherly' advice.

He needs to see her, to tell Lucy, Giles and Katie who she is. He must explain why he has refused to accept her into his family, make her realise that until now, she has not met her real father.

'Doctor, I must see Jane, there's so much I need to say to her before I... before it's too late.'

'Krait altered your will to include her. Your family will

find out she is your daughter after your death. It's better that way.'

'No, no, it's not better that way. She must be free to love me as her real father.' Robin pauses and seems to compose himself. 'And... and I need to be free to love her as my daughter.'

Lakmaker seems unmoved. 'The decision Krait took was the right one. Your family didn't need the additional complication at a time when they were still coming to terms with other pressures.'

'And what pressures might those be?'

'Perfectly normal tensions affecting the balance of a family business involving a son, daughter, stepmother and daughter-in-law.'

'You know nothing about the balance of my family, and I'll thank you to keep your nose right out of it. I'm going home.' For a second time, Robin struggles to raise his backside from the chair.

'You're still wearing that *ouroboros* bracelet, aren't you?'

With an old man's grunt, he straightens his back.

'You recall the Greek Meander symbol signifies infinite and eternal life and the snake eating its tail, the ouroboros, was interpreted by Greek scholars as an emblem of introspection and eternal return?'

'I'm going,' Robin snaps, his patience wasted. He turns towards the door.

'Krait arrived along with the bracelet. He has remained with you for as long as you wore the bracelet.'

'What? So if I take this... this bloody bracelet off, do I get rid of him?'

'You might but think first what might happen if you do.'

'I don't care. If this thing made me into a killer, I want rid of it.' He claws at the bracelet, desperately scrabbling to unfasten the clasp. The fingernail on his index finger scratches in vain at the gold clip. Nothing gives, apart from a nail, which splits.

Lakmaker's calm psychiatrist tone persists. 'Robin, how long have you been a patient here at Barton Hall?'

Robin looks up from scratching at the bracelet clasp. 'I've no idea; couple of weeks, I guess. Too bloody long, that much I do know.'

'Our first meeting was three hours ago. It's the evening of the day following your attempted suicide.'

Robin's mind flips and swoons as he slumps back into the chair. With an unnatural gasp he is leaving his body again, wriggling out like a damp butterfly from a chrysalis. Before he is totally free, he manages to twist and look back and sees himself, a limp, feeble old man. He cannot allow old age to diminish him; he must stop his murderous alter taking back control.

With the breathtaking swoop of a roller coaster, he slides back into his body, a feeling like being swathed in satin, although he has no idea how he recognises what that feels like.

'Give me a break, *I beg you*,' he pleads. 'This is torment. Show me some mercy, please. I must have slept in that bed next door for at least ten nights, maybe more. It would take me weeks to write all that stuff about my life, for us to have all those discussions together. You even disappeared for a couple of days to a conference.'

'Wonders of the human brain, Robin.'

His mind is spiralling. 'Focus, Farnham, focus,' he cries out loud as he struggles to his feet again. He will not sit here and listen to this man's nonsense any longer.

'I'm discharging myself, Lakmaker,' he shouts. 'I'm sane, back in control. I'm the one calling the shots now, not you.'

Lakmaker reacts quickly. 'Okay, Robin, if you're certain that's what you want, I'll call Lucy to come and fetch you.'

Home. Lucy. Oh God, how much is he looking forward to this? The doctor leaves the room and Robin is moved to take one last look through the window into the garden. The last dregs of autumn light have vanished into the darkness and the blackbird no longer sings from the beech tree. The end of the day, but which day? The day after his attempted suicide? It can't be.

As he turns from the window, he glances down at Lakmaker's diary open on his desk. The date at the top of the page is 21st October 2020, the day following his suicide attempt.

He is breathing but no oxygen is reaching his lungs. His head spins and as he lurches forward clumsily against the desk, the door swings open and in walks Lakmaker.

'Your wife will be here in ten minutes.'

Robin sees his lips move, but cannot hear what he is saying, and he slumps into the chair behind the desk, a feeling of profound hopelessness engulfing him.

'Tell me this diary isn't right, Doctor. Today can't possibly be the day after I tried to kill myself.'

Lakmaker gives a resigned shrug and exhales noisily. 'Robin, please come and sit with me one last time.' He pats the side of the armchair and reluctantly, the old man moves, while silently asking himself if he'll ever be free of this man's clutches.

'On a number of occasions, you've asked me about myself and before you leave, I should explain who I am.'

Lakmaker is articulating slowly and clearly as Robin lowers himself into his chair, consumed by the fear of learning something yet more disturbing.

'What do you mean, *who you are*? Don't tell me you're a copper; not after all this.'

'Robin, you recall the psychiatrist who counselled you at Lewisham Hospital in the 1970s following your first wife's attempted suicide?'

'Yes. I told you about him.'

'How much do you remember of him?'

'How d'you mean?'

'What did he look like?' He pauses a moment, giving Robin time to think. 'Can you recall anything about his appearance?'

'What is this, some kind of sick party game?'

'Please, Robin, picture him.' There's an unnerving edge to the doctor's voice.

'I don't know, it was so long ago. He was quite tall, I think, dark hair, smart dresser. Bit like you, I guess.'

'Do you remember his name?'

'No,' he growled.

'It was Lakmaker.'

'What, he had the same name as you?'

'I am the psychiatrist you saw in 1975.'

'You can't be, he was much older than me. He'd be ancient by now.'

'Unlike you, Robin, I didn't live to a good age. I died when I was fifty-four.'

'What… what the hell does that mean?' Robin croaks, before he swallows hard. 'What are you, some sort of ghost? That photograph, the one of your wife and children, they are…?'

'That was taken over forty years ago. My wife is nearly ninety, a great-grandmother even.'

Robin stares at the doctor, who now seems to have aged four decades in a matter of seconds. 'But… you can still see her?'

'Yes, I can.' His voice is barely audible.

The consulting room walls are closing in; the atmosphere is heavier than an August evening ahead of a breaking storm.

Lakmaker sits glassy-eyed; he looks close to tears. Then Robin is struck by one of those moments of clear insight. This is not about the doctor, who he was or what he is now. It's about him.

He is lost in the depths of one of those terrifying nightmares from which there seems no escape. He must force himself to wake up, get out of bed and put the kettle on to make Lucy her morning cup of tea. He'll then see that nothing has changed, in the real world.

He needs to be lucid again, take back control. This dreadful disease will not destroy him. The new drug they're giving him *is* working; they should start rolling it out to all Alzheimer's sufferers.

Lakmaker's voice is now little more than a whisper. 'Before you leave, Robin, I'd like to tell you the other reason I'm here with you.'

More secrets? More truths? What next? All he wants is for the doctor to be nice, tell him something of comfort, allow the nightmare to end so he can awake to normality.

'I taught you to focus only on that which you could change.'

'Yes, and I thank you for that, but now, just get off my case and let me wake up to reality.'

'But you used it as an excuse for not changing the other weaknesses in your personality. You avoided facing up to your inability to share yourself with those you love.'

'So what? Maybe we're all islands, alone inside our heads. How much of yourself did you share with your wife, Lakmaker?'

Robin is determined to take back control. He fights to be old Robin, BA Robin, before Alzheimer's.

'This is not about me, Robin, it's about you. The buttoned-up you. The Robin who denied access to those closest to him. Never shared what he was really thinking, the emotions he truly felt.'

'What are you, my conscience materialised?'

'That's one way of looking at it.' He nods forlornly. The man's spirit seems to have deserted him; he looks spent.

'Lakmaker, I don't give a shit. I just want to see and touch and smell the world outside these four walls. To prove to myself that you're lying, and that I really do exist.'

'Do you think your refusal to change cursed your son? Did you blight *him* with your inability to share his emotions with his wife and children?'

'How the hell does anyone know what goes on inside other people's minds?'

Even as he speaks, he doubts himself. Did he afflict Giles with his own insular, buttoned-up inadequacies?

'Have you asked him, Robin?' The sudden rasping aggression in the doctor's voice slices Robin like a scalpel.

'No, no, you can't be right. I didn't fuck him up like my father fucked me up. I was better than that. Much better.'

'Are you certain, Robin?'

The old man draws a slow, deep breath, lifts himself from the chair and straightens his back as he composes himself. 'Yes, I *am* certain. Krait got it right, not you. It seems to me we're a cocktail of thirty thousand genes, each one of us so tightly programmed it determines exactly what we are and what we do. I *cannot* change, nor can my son, nor could my father. I don't think any of us have any real free will; we are what we are.'

Lakmaker shakes his head. 'That's too simplistic, Robin. We can all change if we want to.'

'I'm not listening to you; you're a fraud and you've messed with my head for too long. Goodnight and goodbye.'

With one last glance back at his tormentor, Robin leaves the consulting room, slamming the door behind him. Lakmaker has sapped his resolve, nothing seems real, he sees no certainty. Leaning back against the corridor wall, his skin is ice-cold, as if he's been trapped in a glacier for a million years.

Willpower alone forces him to walk in the direction of the main entrance, where Lucy should be waiting, but as he approaches the reception area, he is stopped in his tracks. Three uniformed police officers stand at the front desk, their backs towards him as they talk with the nurses.

He shrinks back against the wall beyond the sightline. He knew it, Lakmaker is no doctor. He's a copper, tricking him into confessing to three murders. Murders he didn't commit. Krait's the guilty one. He needs to confront Lakmaker.

Staying close to the wall, he shuffles back to the consulting room but on storming in, he finds it empty. The window is closed, the blinds drawn.

The doctor's jacket no longer hangs from the hook on the door. The photographs have gone, as have the computer and the laptop.

Robin crosses to the desk and the doctor's diary has also disappeared. Only the buff-coloured folder remains, along with the gold Caran d'Ache fountain pen. He lifts the pen and as he rolls it in his palm, the feeling it generates is all too familiar. It *is* the same pen gifted to him anonymously the day he married Lucy. He never discovered who placed it among the other gifts at the reception lunch.

The pen disappeared the day he was diagnosed with Alzheimer's. Perhaps it was Lakmaker who gave it to him in the first place and subsequently took it back when he knew Robin would come to this place, so that it would never actually be lost, so it would always be a link between the two of them.

Such a fanciful but curiously reassuring thought is just what he needs. He tucks the pen inside his jacket pocket. As he relishes this rare moment of companionship, his eyes drift back to the folder on the desk. Three words are typed on a white label attached to the cover.

Robin Giles Farnham.

Underneath, handwritten in ink, is one further word.

Deceased.

He is consumed by a blind terror and bolts back out into the corridor.

'I can't be dead. No, not yet,' he screams, as he falls back against the wall, overcome by deep, hollow, gulping sobs that fight every breath he struggles to take. Weakening, he sinks to the floor and hears himself howl as he howled that summer morning in '62, the day he learned he had failed his examinations.

This time, his father doesn't tell him to shut up, stop blubbing, be a man. Instead, he wraps his arms around trembling shoulders, assures him he understands his pain and it is a good thing to cry. He promises everything will be fine and he'll always be there for him.

The moment Robin turns to say something, he isn't there. He never was. Robin is alone and he loathes the solitude.

It is several minutes before he can struggle to his feet, chest heaving, right hand clutching the skin on the front of his neck as he strives to control his breathing.

'Robin, let's get the hell out of here.' A voice breaks the silence, but he sees no one. 'Look, there's a fire escape sign on the wall over there.'

Robin glances at the wall opposite. Sure enough, a 'Fire Exit' sign points in the opposite direction to where the police are waiting at reception.

The disembodied voice speaks again, orders him to follow the sign. It is not his voice. 'Who's that?' Robin asks as he looks around.

'Robin, it's me, Krait. Come on, move. We've got to escape; the police are waiting to arrest you.'

'I know, I've seen them.'

Robin's right hand instinctively reaches to his left wrist to unfasten the bracelet. The clasp stays firm.

'I won't leave you, Robin, not here, not yet.'

He walks as quickly as seventy-four-year-old legs allow, anxious his escape route might be alarmed. Lakmaker warned him about the security. On reaching the fire exit, he tentatively pushes the locking bar down and forces the door open. No sirens, no bells. He breathes a sigh of relief.

A blanket of searing white light floods the open area close to the side of the building. He needs to move clear and stumbles as he crosses a gravel path into the darkness shrouding a lawn and tall hedge.

His heart is threatening to burst through his chest. Not a good time to have a heart attack, he thinks, as he breathes slowly and deeply.

'Look in your jacket pocket, Robin.' It's Krait's voice again.

Instinctively, he does as he's told and is surprised to feel the comforting solidity of his mobile phone. That wasn't there earlier. 'How did you know it was there?' Robin is conscious he is now talking to himself.

'I saw Lakmaker put it there.' The voice is outside his head, but instinctively he knows it comes from inside.

'You killed three people. You made me into a murderer. Why?'

'We don't have time to discuss that now, Robin. Let's just get moving.'

'You ruined my reputation, stopped me knowing Jane is my daughter. Why do that?'

'She'd have messed up your family. I did it for you; it was for the best. Now get going.'

Robin presses the power button and the phone fires into life. He navigates to contacts and taps 'call' to Lucy's mobile.

No service. Bugger, emergency calls only. Too dangerous to alert the police. He's unsure what to do.

'Use the torch on the mobile and head around to the front. We can check if the cops are still there.' Krait's voice compels him to move.

Sure enough, a police car is parked close to the hospital entrance, although Robin sees no activity, suggesting his disappearance has been noticed.

A car engine fires up somewhere in the darkness and headlights swirl across in front of the entrance as he hears the unmistakable crunch of tyres over gravel. Wait. That's Lucy driving home without him. It certainly sounds like her car. There's been a horrible mistake and he moves in the direction of the lights, waving desperately, but the car doesn't stop.

'She can't have seen me.'

'Never mind that now, we need to get out of the hospital grounds. I know the direction from there.' Krait's voice echoes in his ears.

Guided by the torch, Robin moves towards what he thinks might be the main entrance.

'Keep going, you're doing okay.'

'Shut up. You've buggered my life up too much already, Krait.' He makes his way unsteadily along the grassy edge of the drive. His torch illuminates two wide gold-painted metal gates in front of him.

'Go through the gates, Robin, that's it. Turn left.'

'Shut the fuck up, will you?'

His own instinct and cunning are all that will save him now, not Krait's.

'Krait, Lakmaker wrote on my file that I was dead. Am I dead, Krait? Tell me the truth, please.'

'Do you feel dead? You're moving, you're thinking. Now keep walking down this lane.'

The narrow country road is blacker than a disused coal mine and he is thankful the beam from his mobile is lighting the way. His laboured breath shoots into the night air like steam from a boiling kettle; it seems unusually cold for September. That first cup of tea by the fireside will be nectar. Better still, a glass of burgundy.

Several minutes on and his every limb is screaming at him. He stumbles to a halt.

'Why have you stopped? Keep moving.' Krait's urging voice boxes Robin's ears like a Victorian schoolmaster.

'Shut up and get the hell out of my head. Old men like me shouldn't be walking along country lanes after dark. Leave me alone.'

'You've no choice. You're not walking a bloody dog; you're running from a murder charge.'

'Yeah, murders you committed, Krait. You killed them, not me.'

'You wanted them dead. You just didn't have the guts to do it. I could never have killed them if you hadn't wished it, thought about it, wanted it to happen. I acted out what you were thinking.'

'I'm not violent, it's not in my character, my genes are not your genes. You're not me and I'm not you.'

'Are you sure about that, Robin? We've lived together for over half a century and maybe I'm you as much as you're me.'

'No, Krait. You're all bad.'

Robin shakes his head furiously. The wrinkles on his forehead deepen over unkempt eyebrows; he doesn't need a mirror to tell him he looks a haggard old wreck.

'Jesus Christ, this is what demented old people do, isn't it? I've seen them at bus stops and in shop doorways, arguing loudly with voices only they hear. I've become the person I would cross the road to avoid.'

'Robin, everyone has more than one personality. To the outside world they appear as a single identity, but from time to time a different temperament takes over, behaves in a way others describe as out of character.

'I'm independent from you yet I am you. I bleed when you bleed, I share your worries, your compassion, your grief. I thought about killing Jane, you know. Eliminate all risk she might cause problems with your family, but I knew you wouldn't want her to die, so I killed her adoptive father instead.'

'You what? For Christ's sake, what the hell is going on inside my head? Is this the Alzheimer's or is it your bloody *eternal return*? Does every step I take mark something that'll happen over and over again for the rest of time?'

Krait doesn't answer.

'Are you still there?'

'I'm here, Robin.'

'Is what's happening predestined?'

'Quick, Robin, into the hedge, there's a car coming.'

Robin backs into a thicket, coaxing aching limbs through a thorny hedgerow on a bank.

'There's a road below. That's the one we need to be on. You can't see it but trust me, it's there, Robin, it's the road leading home.'

Needle-sharp thorns attack his jacket and trousers, digging into him as he crouches low between the bushes at the top of the bank. Breathlessly, he peers into the darkness and watches the car pass by; it is not the police.

He waits for the sound of the engine to fade before straightening but the pain in his legs is excruciating. They refuse to carry his weight and instinctively, he leans forward to steady himself on the sloping ground.

He overcompensates and his left foot slips on damp soil. As he falls forward, his head slams into the side of a fallen tree trunk and he slides down the steep embankment. He bounces off another tree stump before his fall is broken sharply on hitting the cold tarmac of a road.

'Jesus, that hurt!'

His left shoulder burns as if he's been stabbed with a red-hot poker.

'Get up, you're on the right road now. Don't be such a bloody wimp.'

'Shut up, Krait. I know what I'm doing.'

'Oh yeah, talking to voices in your head?'

Robin hauls himself up, swaying, wishing the thorn and nettle punctures on his face and hands would stop stinging.

The mobile phone was knocked from his hand as he fell, and he almost topples over as he bends forward to retrieve it. Stooping with pain, he directs the beam left and right and sees he is on a steep hill. That's a good sign; it probably is the right road. His instincts are still working. Or maybe they're Krait's.

He spots a signpost in the bank on the opposite side, which he can't read.

'Cross the road, you'll see it better.'

'Fuck off, Krait.'

He stumbles in the direction of the sign. Halfway across something slips silently from his left wrist. He directs the wavering beam onto the tarmac and sees the bracelet. The clasp has broken.

A disturbing thought crosses his mind. 'Is the circle of the *ouroboros* broken, Krait?'

His teeth bite hard over his bottom lip and his eyes refuse to focus. 'Are you still there, Krait? What does it mean if the circle is broken?'

No answer.

'Krait, where are you?'

Still no answer and the solitude he relished all his life now frightens him.

As he stoops painfully to retrieve the bracelet, the night silence is shattered by the roar of a petrol engine at speed. He looks up as the glare of headlights switched to full beam emerge from around the bend to his left.

The car heads straight for him and the anguished squeal of brakes is the last sound he hears as his consciousness furls into the mist.

THIRTY-NINE

Lucy Farnham arrived at her husband's bedside early on the morning following his attempted suicide. The doctors explained that they had attempted to absorb the drugs and alcohol in his stomach, using activated charcoal, but feared the treatment had been too late and the damage to his essential organs was irreversible.

Typically, there wasn't a spare bed at Yeovil Hospital so in the early hours of the morning, Robin was transferred to Barton Hall.

Hour after hour she watched and listened. Not right now, please, she prayed, and yet she wanted relief for him. Was that a cruel thought?

Even the calming drugs they injected failed to provide the serenity she hoped for him. Robin doesn't deserve to be agitated on what might be his last day, yet it was clear something was going on; some sort of inner turmoil was making him continuously mumble and rail.

A nurse arrives and checks whatever fluid they are feeding him through a drip is at the correct level. She smiles at the little old lady. No words need to pass between them.

For hours more he is still, except for his head, which moves slowly from side to side, occasionally suggesting he is growing ever more agitated. She thinks he might be trying to resolve, hoping perhaps to atone, or understand, maybe to forgive.

She then wonders if each event, every happening or occasion in our lives, exists for ever, or does it die along with those who were present at the time? Is it then forgotten, or will it exist until the end of time as a specific moment, existing alongside every other moment that has ever happened and ever will happen?

Against all evidence, she longs for a sign that he is remembering their wonderful moments, the extraordinary love they shared, love bonded by their struggles and how they had worked as an inseparable team to triumph over all that had been hurled at them.

She recalled the way he would smile on hearing a familiar song and even latterly, when his mind seemed in torment, he had never forgotten how to listen to the favourites stored on his mobile. Now there is no music in his ears, and she thinks this wrong, he is missing an important element of comfort.

She gently cups the headphones securely over his ears and presses start on an album she's certain he must have listened to a thousand times. He rips them off, shaking his head in apparent frustration, screwing up his eyes as though needing to concentrate on something else.

Nothing he mumbles makes sense until suddenly he yells a single word.

'Lakmaker!'

Lucy calls for the nurse, who arrives quickly and listens as he repeats the word again and again. She shakes her head. She has no idea either. Yet she senses something only her long experience can teach. She reaches for Lucy's hand and holds it warmly.

'Perhaps he's transitioning, getting himself ready to let go.'

Lucy gasps, uncertain how she should react, but instinctively she knows Robin would want her to be calm and undemonstrative, happy for the release he had chosen from his awful deterioration. She tries again to place the headphones over his ears, and this time he lies still as she selects what she knows is the track he would want to hear… to make him comfortable at the close.

Then, as night begins to fall, his breathing slows. She prepares herself for a long wait, but soon notices ever-lengthening pauses between each breath.

When it is finally over, when Robin is released in body as well as in mind, she gently lifts the headphones from around his ears and pauses his favourite track on the mobile. She stares at her husband for many minutes, knowing she must never forget this image. In death, Robin's face is softening; she sees tranquillity and peace.

Robin's widow thanks whatever God there might be that he has finally resolved his internal struggles and has left this earth with pride in all that he and *she* achieved.

It is unusually cold outside; autumn has come early. No wonder her arthritic fingers struggle to grip the steering wheel and turn the ignition key. Well, she thinks, she might do something about this now that there is only her. She checks herself, startled she can think so selfishly. Or perhaps it isn't selfish now she has no one else to worry about.

She's had so many sad and isolated months to get used to this idea. Months when Robin was alive but had already begun his journey into darkness. She wonders why there is so little help or understanding for the real victims of dementia. Those who are shut out and suffer daily as the patient slowly numbs. Those who sit alone in torment as they suffer the long, drawn-out pain of watching and waiting. That dreadful no-man's-land is worse for them, she thinks, as she tries her best to ignore the tears stinging her eyes.

Her car swings in a wide arc around the hospital car park, its headlights piercing the dark shadows of the gardens. Once out through the gold entrance gates, she turns left and drives the short distance down the hill to Semley Hollow, where she turns right towards Shaftesbury onto the A350 and home.

On unlocking the front door, she instinctively checks for post. Among the usual bills and charity letters is a sturdy manila envelope sealed with clear tape but with no stamp attached. Who would have delivered something this size by hand?

Her twisted fingers struggle to work scissors along the top of the large envelope before lifting out a thick bundle of typewritten sheets. Thinking it then empty, she is surprised to feel something solid at the bottom and upends the envelope.

A gold fountain pen tumbles out, a pen just like the one Robin was so upset at losing a year or so back, convinced it had been stolen from his jacket pocket. A jet-black iPhone follows, and a yellow handwritten post-it note attached to the screen states only 'RF case recordings'.

She fills the kettle to brew herself a pot of tea and while waiting for it to boil she stands transfixed by the top sheet of the papers. It is a memo from Robin to a Dr Lakmaker at Barton Hall.

Lakmaker? Wasn't that the word he called out? And a doctor?

She'd never heard mention of a Dr Lakmaker.

She hurriedly flicks through a selection of the papers. All seem to be numbered memos addressed to this Dr Lakmaker, all apparently written by Robin. She senses these papers might resolve the mysteries of that deep, dark part of Robin she knew he could never share, even with her.

As she goes to pour boiling water into the teapot, the thought occurs that Robin would never drink tea at this time of the evening.

She finds what she hopes is a decent bottle of red wine on the bottom shelf of the rack under the stairs. She recalls Robin buying a case from this particular chateau at auction, several years ago, and how much they had enjoyed sharing it. He had been keeping this last bottle for a special occasion.

Having extracted the cork, unsteady hands tilt the bottle as she carefully pours the wine through Robin's metal filter into his favourite decanter. He would have approved. She fills a glass and collects the numbered memos together before settling into her favourite chair in the sitting room, the one next to his.

Before lifting the glass to her lips, she raises it in a silent toast to her husband's empty chair and begins to read.